> "I've got a hunch...
> that all this effort will
> amount to nothing."

...Kuuro, are you okay?

CUNEIGH THE WANDERER

A homunculus that accompanies Kuuro. Possessing wings, she flies about like a songbird.

KUURO THE CAUTIOUS

A leprechaun that was formerly a part of Obsidian Eyes, the most notorious spy guild in the land. He possesses an irregular sensory perception known as clairvoyance, but his gift is slowly fading.

Ultimate clairvoyance. That was all in the past.

It was withering away to the point that he needed to leave all observations outside his immediate focus in the hands of this small homunculus.

Nevertheless, though he could no longer be certain about this vague threatening premonition, he had no choice but to trust it.

"Amazing! So many swords!
Ha-ha-ha-ha!"

MESTELEXIL THE BOX OF DESPERATE KNOWLEDGE

A miracle child created by self-proclaimed Demon King Kiyazuna the Axle. With a body capable of limitless regeneration, Mestelexil overcomes his cause of death each time he revives.

"I'll chop up your whole body...until you hand over the enchanted sword."

TOROA THE AWFUL

A blood-drenched god of death straight out of a horror story, who appears before anyone in possession of an enchanted sword. Rumor has it that he was killed at the hands of Alus the Star Runner. However...

I will protect Aureatia from anything and everything.

ROSCLAY THE ABSOLUTE

Aureatia's strongest champion, excelling both in traditional swordsmanship and Word Arts. Serves as the Second General among Aureatia's Twenty-Nine Officials.

The greatest royal tournament to date, put together for the purpose of determining a hero.

If the outcome of this event would change the very course of history, one could expect the duels to be anything but simple.

ISHURA

II

The Particle Storm in the Realm of Slaughter

Keiso

ILLUSTRATION BY

Kureta

YEN
ON
New York

Keiso

ILLUSTRATION BY

Kureta

ISHURA Vol. 2 SAKKAI MIJIN ARASHI
©Keiso 2020
First published in Japan in 2020 by KADOKAWA CORPORATION, Tokyo.
English translation rights arranged with KADOKAWA CORPORATION, Tokyo, through TUTTLE-MORI AGENCY, INC., Tokyo.

English translation © 2022 by Yen Press, LLC

Yen On
150 West 30th Street, 19th Floor
New York, NY 10001

Visit us at yenpress.com
facebook.com/yenpress
twitter.com/yenpress
yenpress.tumblr.com
instagram.com/yenpress

First Yen On Edition: August 2022
Edited by Yen On Editorial: Payton Campbell
Designed by Yen Press Design: Andy Swist

Yen On is an imprint of Yen Press, LLC.
The Yen On name and logo are trademarks of Yen Press, LLC.

The publisher is not responsible for websites (or their content) that are not owned by the publisher.

Library of Congress Cataloging-in-Publication Data
Names: Keiso (Manga author), author. | Kureta, illustrator. | Musto, David, translator.
Title: Ishura / Keiso ; illustration by Kureta ; translation by David Musto.
Other titles: Ishura. English
Description: First Yen On edition. | New York : Yen On, 2022.
Identifiers: LCCN 2021062849 | ISBN 9781975337865
  (v. 1 ; trade paperback) | ISBN 9781975337889
  (v. 2 ; trade paperback) | ISBN 9781975337902
  (v. 3 ; trade paperback) | ISBN 9781975337926
  (v. 4 ; trade paperback)
Subjects: LCGFT: Fantasy fiction. | Light novels.
Classification: LCC PL872.5.E57 I7413 2022 | DDC 895.63/6—dc23/
eng/20220121
LC record available at https://lccn.loc.gov/2021062849

ISBNs: 978-1-9753-3788-9 (trade paperback)
       978-1-9753-3789-6 (ebook)

10 9 8 7 6 5 4 3 2 1

LSC-C

Printed in the United States of America

The identity of the one who defeated The True Demon King—the ultimate threat who gripped the world in terror—is shrouded in mystery. Little and less is known about this hero.
The terror of the True Demon King abruptly came to an end.

Nevertheless, the champions born from the era of the Demon King still remain in this world.

Now, with the enemy of all life brought low,
these champions, wielding enough power to transform the world,
have begun to do as they please,
their untamed wills threatening a new era of war and strife.

To Aureatia, now the sole kingdom unifying the minian races,
the existence of these champions has become a threat.
No longer champions, they were now demons bringing ruin to all—
the shura.

To ensure peace in the new era,
it was necessary to eliminate any threat to the world's future,
and designate the "True Hero" to guide and protect the hopes of the people.

Thus, the Twenty-Nine Officials, the governing administrators of Aureatia,
have gathered these shura and their miraculous abilities from across the land, regardless of race,
and organized an imperial competition to crown the True Hero once and for all.

POWER RELATIONSHIPS

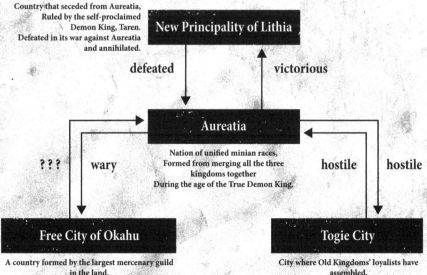

Country that seceded from Aureatia,
Ruled by the self-proclaimed Demon King, Taren.
Defeated in its war against Aureatia and annihilated.

New Principality of Lithia

defeated — victorious

Aureatia

Nation of unified minian races,
Formed from merging all the three kingdoms together
During the age of the True Demon King.

??? — wary — hostile — hostile

Free City of Okahu

A country formed by the largest mercenary guild in the land.
A group of elite soldiers that deploys a military force on par with any nation state,
Completely independent of any outside authority.

Togie City

City where Old Kingdoms' loyalists have assembled,
To try and restore the kingdoms to how they were.

GLOSSARY

❖ Word Arts

① Phenomenon that conveys the intentions of a speaker's words to the listener, regardless of the speaker's race or language.
② Or the generic term for arts that utilize this phenomenon to distort natural phenomena via "requests" to a certain target.
Something much like what would be called magic. Force, Thermal, Craft, and Life arts compose the four core groups, but there are some who can use arts outside of these four groups. While necessary to be familiarized with the target in order to utilize these arts, powerful Word Arts users are able to offset this requirement.

❖ Force Arts

Arts that inflict directed power and speed, what is known as momentum, on a target.

❖ Craft Arts

Arts that change a target's shape.

❖ Thermal Arts

Arts that inflict undirected energy, such as heat, electrical current, and light, on a target.

❖ Life Arts

Arts that change a target's nature.

❖ Visitors

Those who possess abilities that deviate greatly from all common knowledge, and thus were transported to this world from another one known as "the Beyond." Visitors are unable to use Word Arts.

❖ Enchanted Sword • Magic Items

Swords and tools that possess potent abilities. Similar to visitors, due to their mighty power, there are some objects that were transported here from another world.

❖ Aureatia Twenty-Nine Officials

The highest functionaries that govern Aureatia. Ministers are civil servants, while Generals are military officers.
There is no hierarchy-based seniority or rank among the Twenty-Nine Officials.

❖ Self-Proclaimed Demon King

A generic term for "demonic monarch" not related to the One True King among the three Kingdoms. There are some cases where even those who do not proclaim themselves as a monarch, but who wield great power to threaten Aureatia, are acknowledged as self-proclaimed demon kings by Aureatia and targeted for subjugation.

❖ Sixways Exhibition

A tournament to determine the "True Hero." The person who wins each one-on-one match and advances all the way through to the end will be named the True Hero. Backing from a member of the Twenty-Nine Officials is required to enter the competition.

CONTENTS

---◆◆---

⚜ *THIRD VERSE:* **EYE OF THE STORM** ⚜

⚜ *FOURTH VERSE:* **THE REALM OF SLAUGHTER,** ⚜
PARTICLE STORM

ISHURA

Keiso

ILLUSTRATION BY Kureta

Third Verse:

EYE
OF THE
STORM

The sun reigned over a cloudless sky, allowing the changing colors of the flora to appear ever more vibrant.

Along the outskirts of the Sine Riverstead, on a hillock overlooking the lowlands and bountiful pastures, there stood a tract called the Needle Forest, the origin of the name being plain enough even for young Miroya to understand.

From a distance, it looked as though countless iron needles were protruding from the hill, creating an environment too desolate for even a single tree to grow.

A determined climb up the hill revealed the true identities of the needles. Every one of them was a thick iron pillar, the same as those seen every year during the Offering Festival.

Miroya kicked the heel poking out from the sea of iron.

"C'mon, wake up! It's past noon already!"

Just the sole of the foot Miroya kicked was nearly three times as tall as he was.

"Quit your barking... Ugh, not you again, stupid brat..."

"You're a lazy good-for-nothing! All you do is lie around all day!"

For a long, long time, there had only ever been a single inhabitant living atop the barren, iron-covered hill. A gigant. His name was known to everyone in the village—Mele, the Horizon's Roar.

"Hnnnggh... Up we go."

Grabbing one of the nearby pillars, the gigant languidly sat himself upright. The iron pole that took twenty adults to carry every year warped horizontally—like a clothes-drying pole—with a grating metal squeal.

He was a huge man. Too huge.

He was clad in simple clothing, woven from trees and vegetation through the use of Craft Arts. His head, even when sitting cross-legged, was so high that Miroya needed to crane his neck all the way back to be able to see his face.

Miroya had heard from the village chief that even among the ancient gigants, Mele was special.

Just as it was with minia, there were tall gigants that towered above other members of their race, and Mele's height was, in Central Kingdom metrics, between twenty and thirty meters tall.

"Well then, get into another fight with your pops, did ya?"

"That's not it! Your bow! You have one, right?!"

"Oh, that thing? Where did I put it...?"

"How could you even lose something that big?! Look, it's lying right over there!"

His voice frantic, Miroya easily located the item in question. Of course, anyone who lived outside the Sine Riverstead would never have recognized it as a bow.

The black, impossibly large weapon had been crafted from some unknown material. It looked almost like part of the landscape as it lay out on the ground, amid the gaps in the stalwart pillars.

"Pook said that just being able to move that thing's bowstring even a little bit would automatically make you the strongest person in the village. Is that true?"

"C'mon, give me a break. A brat like you becoming the

strongest in the village doesn't mean a damn thing, anyway. I'd still be a thousand times stronger."

"Like I care about how strong *you* are, Mele! Pook made fun of me and said there was no way I could do it, so I'm gonna find out for myself!"

"What a pain..."

The gigant sluggishly lay back before plucking the massive bow from the earth with his fingers. It dragged along the grass and soil, loudly grinding down into the hill's surface.

Miroya sighed, exasperated. In his eyes, Mele was even more of a lazy slob than his older sister. Could someone like him *really* be the village's guardian deity?

"Hey, try not to get pinned underneath this thing and die on me, got it? Not that I'd expect much else from a puny weakling."

"Oh, shut up."

With a biting reply, Miroya tried pushing at the taut metal bowstring.

The string was almost as long as the gigant was tall, yet still Miroya devoted his entire body weight to moving it, but it did not budge—it was a firm iron rod, not unlike the pillars standing tall around him.

He started to wonder if there was some truth to the legend of a wild boar appearing in the Needle Forest and dying after colliding with the black bow. Even in that story, the bow hadn't moved a single inch off the ground.

"Argh, hnnnggh, c'mooooon...! *Haaa*."

"Bwah-ha-ha-ha! Just give it up. You're too young to be throwing your back out."

"W-well, I've lifted up a whole water barrel by myself before, okay?! But there's no one who can move *that* thing!"

"Of course, there is. You're talking to 'im."

"Ugh, you know what I meant."

Mele turned over on the barren soil once more, his interest waning.

Miroya had never once seen the gigant move with any sense of urgency.

"Oh yeah, that reminds me. A few decades ago, some idiots from the village all got together and tried to prove their strength by lifting up another *something* of mine. And I'm not talking about my bowstring."

"What 'something'?"

"C'mon, isn't it obvious? My manhood."

"Huh?!"

Miroya instinctively looked at the gigant's crotch. The area under his grass skirt was indeed fully visible.

"Um…h-how many people did it take?!"

"Five guys didn't cut it. So, they decided if they were gonna seriously attempt to pull it off, they'd need at least six. All six of 'em were considered some of the strongest men in the village."

"Why were there even six adults stupid enough to do something like that anyway?!"

"Try asking your pops or granddad about it. Men stay stupid no matter how old they get. Truth is, I couldn't really tell if they actually managed to lift it up or not…"

"What…? Hold on, you can't just cut the story off there!"

How in the world could he not know if they managed to do it or not?

Mele scratched his stomach, looking a bit uncomfortable.

"I'm not lying. I really couldn't say for sure. Having six people touch me down there…you know…I sorta got this ticklish feeling, and… I mean, if you really wanna split hairs over it, they technically *did* get it into the air…"

"...Are you serious?!"

"*Bwah-ha-ha-ha-ha-ha!* They got a real shock, too! Started asking me, 'Wait, do you swing that way?!'"

Mele's conversations were always filled with these nostalgic accounts of utterly baffling episodes with the villagers.

One example was the time the village kids discovered the dangerous pastime of competing to see who could be blown the farthest away by Mele's sneeze.

In another story, when the village chief's father was young, Mele had let him ride on his shoulders to peek into the woman's bath, but Mele was so conspicuous that the village chief's father ended up getting punished.

Yet another was when his singing during a certain woman's wedding ceremony was so awful, it was banned forever, with the provision still existing in the town's records.

From small children to the village's elders... Everyone living in Sine Riverstead had memories with the long-lived gigant. Miroya himself would likely remember the bow—so firmly stuck in the ground one would think it had put down roots—for the rest of his life.

"Still though, Mele, for how giant your body is, you don't fight at all. Can you even use this bow?"

"Don't you worry about that. Hell, it'd be best to never need to fire it at all. Didn't anyone teach you that?"

"Whaaat? If it was really better to never fire a bow, then bows and arrows wouldn't exist in the first place! You've never actually fired your bow, have you?"

"Got a smart-ass comeback for everything, don't ya, kid?"

In truth, it was just as Miroya said.

Mele's herculean strength and his remarkably large frame were the talk of the village.

However, among these conversations, there wasn't a single story about Mele courageously wielding said strength to fight and expel his enemies.

Mele was a champion of the village, without question, but a champion of unknown valor and heroism.

"Hey, I'm just worried about you, that's all. Aureatia even has that Rosclay guy, right? There's even Toroa the Awful, too; he shows up in all the scary stories! I don't think there's any way you could ever beat them!"

"Now you're really talking nonsense! I keep telling ya, I'm the strongest there is. If I went all out, no one could hold a candle to me. You'd be quaking in your boots, no doubt about it."

"Whaaat?! All you do is laze around! I bet Rosclay is waaay stronger than you!"

Hearing that their guardian deity would be going to the royal games in Aureatia excited Miroya a great deal.

Was the biggest presence of Sine Riverstead, present from time immemorial, really the strongest being in the lands?

However, the other candidates like him—for example, the Second General of Aureatia, Rosclay the Absolute—had prestige and fame that wasn't confined to a single village. The Second General was a great champion, beloved and looked up to by minian children everywhere. Miroya was no exception.

"You're supposed to tell me I'm gonna win, even if you don't mean it. What an ungrateful kid… Aureatia's reward is no joke, trust me. I could rebuild Kutoy's house that got struck by lighting and even replace the old waterwheel out west."

"Oh yeah, that waterwheel is pretty run-down, isn't it?"

"It's been in use ever since your grandfather was a young boy, even after several repairs. What else is there…? Oh, right, right, the expenses for Poani's childbirth. It'll be her third to date. I can buy Mizemura some Aureatia machinery to help cultivate his fields, too."

"Who cares about that weird old fart Mizemura...?"

"Bah-ha-ha-ha-ha-ha! Since I'm gonna win it all anyway, I bet we'll get even more money! What's the point in being stingy with the other villagers, right?"

"...I was right. There's no way anyone who says stuff like that is gonna win!"

Mele was always laughing with optimism.

Whether it was someone's troubles with school or farming, or the tragedies of the world at large, compared to his massive body, they all seemed so small.

That was probably why the people of the village, even without any pressing reason in particular, would come to visit the Needle Forest.

Miroya tried to move Mele's bowstring one last time. It didn't budge an inch.

"*Argh*, this sucks...! Listen, you better not break this bow or anything! By the time you lose and come back here, I'm gonna pick this bow straight up off the ground."

"Cheeky little brat, aren't ya? C'mon now, time for you to head back home."

Suddenly, Mele got up. He seemed to be looking far into the wild blue yonder.

Though to Miroya eye's, all he could see was the ordinary, empty blue sky.

"There's a storm coming."

"Wait, really? It's still clear out, though."

"Yep, a bad one. The clouds say it all."

"Riiight... Okay then, see you tomorrow."

Miroya quickly scampered down the hill as he made his way home.

Mele and his towering frame had no roof to shield him from the wind and rain. Nor did he need one.

The Needle Forest, overlooking the Sine Riverstead, had been his home for a long, long time.

"Let's see… Should be sometime tonight…"

There was no one else who could see the shape of the clouds as they drifted along the very edge of the horizon.

Mele took up his black bow.

This year, once again, the Sine Riverstead's day of ruin was approaching.

◆

It came not with a hiss, but a crackling roar.

The rain sounded almost like an earthquake, with the dark, raging sky appearing as though it was trying to drown the whole land at once. The storm winds from the neighboring mountains began blowing whole trees into the air. A number of them crashed into Mele's skin with significant force, but he felt no pain at all.

The hulking gigant stood on both legs in the middle of the moonless storm.

Two fearsome eyes glinted, emerging from the colossal shadow, thrusting up to the heavens.

Coupled with the terrifying torrential rain raging, anyone unfamiliar with Mele who saw the scene for themselves would think they were witnessing ruin incarnate.

"…Looks like it'll be here soon."

Mele's groan wasn't directed at anyone in particular.

He pulled up one of the deeply embedded pillars of the Needle Forest, still standing upright despite the roaring winds.

They were presented to him only twice a year.

High-quality iron ore, mined from the region, was dissolved, and every year the individual with the greatest Craft Arts skills shaped it into beautifully straight pillars. Then, they were smithed to prevent rust. The pillars were Sine Riverstead's greatest craftworks—the heart and soul of the entire village poured into each one.

They were Mele's treasures.

Mele was always looking down over his one and only spiritual home.

The lights of the people's homes as they went about their lives trembled in the apocalyptic downpour.

A peaceful village, blessed with bountiful waters, mining resources, and soil able to support crops and animals.

Two hundred and fifty years ago, in the time when all he knew was solitude, the village hadn't existed.

"……"

He closed his eyes and concentrated.

The moment the flow of the river, rampaging like a dragon, changed—

In the middle of this torrential onslaught, battering all his senses at once, it was the one moment he absolutely couldn't let pass him by.

The low, continuous roar from the river…pitched the slightest bit higher.

Mele opened his eyes. Together, at the exact same moment he had his premonition, the gigantic main river, flowing to the ocean, rushed backward from the sea into a small river that shot off from the main stream. The river that passed right through the center of the village.

Sine Riverstead was a village blessed with bounteous water and nutrient-rich soil. However, this also meant that among its long history, it was a region constantly threatened with this kind of river flood.

Once a year, torrential rains on a terrifying scale passed through this region, and each time the flooding was beyond control, with the village everyone had built destined to sink deep under water.

This was the day of Sine Riverstead's destruction.

As ever, Mele the Horizon's Roar wasted no time.

He simply pulled back the black bow that no one but him could draw or even lift.

The "arrow" he nocked was one of Needle Forest's iron pillars, presented to him by the villagers.

Within the deluge that was barreling upstream against the river's flow, three different currents became one.

One current was diverted by a large boulder on a sandbar, boring into the left bank. Another was an uninterrupted breakneck current. Finally, there was a slow but powerful current coming up from the seaward side of the river behind the village.

Even from this distance he could tell. Even on a night like this, where the view of Sine Riverstead was drowned out by the black clouds and torrential storm, facing off against a raging deluge, constantly shifting its shape, to Mele's eyes alone, everything was clear.

Would the soil bed, weakened by the rain, hold out? Had it been dug out deep enough? Were any of next year's cultivated fields in the path of the rapids? Were any of the places where Miroya and the other children liked to play in peril?

The moment before he took his shot, all of these thoughts passed through Mele's head in an instant.

It was only a single hunch—honed from years and years of experience—that showed him the path to salvation.

"There."

He fired his arrow.

The air split open with a loud crack—louder than roiling thunder. It was the sound of the heavens themselves being torn asunder.

The arrow's trajectory looked like little more than a streak of light.

It thrust into the ground.

Sine Riverstead's soil split open down to bedrock deep in the bowels of the land.

The arrow, perfectly hitting its mark, penetrated further into the soil, and its direct trajectory leveled the terrain.

The impact sent a torrent of dust and debris shooting into the sky, nearly darkening it.

Saying the impact was *like* an earthquake didn't do it justice. The shot from Mele's bow was cataclysmic in its own right.

Even from so far away, a single shot aimed at the very edge of the horizon.

"...There we go."

Mele, for the first time that night, was able to smile with satisfaction.

The deluge veered away from the village populace and poured into the low-level and arid wasteland on the town outskirts.

The one arrow he fired was so perfect, there was no need to notch another.

"All right...! Time for bed!"

The day of Sine Riverstead's destruction had come another year.

However, once again, Sine Riverstead was not destroyed. It had been the same last year. The year before that, as well. Two hundred and fifty years ago, there had been no village here. Once a year, a disastrous flood beset this land. Only twice a year, these iron pillars were presented to Mele. Now these pillars sprouted up from the top of the barren hill, numerous enough for it to become known as the Needle Forest.

Mele the Horizon's Roar was a champion of unknown valor and heroism. Among the legends told by the villagers, there wasn't a single story about Mele courageously wielding his strength to battle and drive off his enemies.

◆

Stars were twinkling high in the night sky, dotting the infinite cosmos.

To the children, this night sky must have been unbelievably beautiful and so very, very sad.

The starlight framed the cart in shadow, climbing up the hill.

Many children called out incessantly as they continued to desperately pull the cart along.

"You see it, right? Look...the same iron pillars as always. We brought you to the Needle Forest! Ilieh!"

"Ilieh, hey! You better not be sleeping back there!"

"We're here together, okay? You're not in pain are you...?! Ilieh!"

"...Yeah... I'm okay..."

Sitting inside the carriage was a young girl, wrapped up in a yellow blanket.

The pallor on her face was severe enough to see even beneath the moonlight, and she blinked in a fevered haze.

At the time, hers was a disease with no cure.

One of the boys jumped out in front and rushed off toward the middle of the Needle Forest. He raised his voice and called out a familiar name.

"Meleeee! Ilieh's here! She said she wanted to see you!"

The gigant was almost always lounging around on his back, but that was the one night when he wasn't sleeping like a log. He joylessly sat with his back to the children.

"Give it a rest, will ya...? Who the hell's that supposed to be? You brats all look the same to me."

Mele grumpily spat back without turning around.

He had almost never called the child—exceptionally small, even for a minia—by her name.

Part of it might have been because he was scared to develop any attachment to the all-too-feeble creature.

"Get off your high horse, you jerk! This is really gonna be the last time, got it?! You've been close with her ever since she was born, haven't you?!"

"......"

The gigant rubbed his face with a large hand, seemingly big enough to hold three full-grown adults.

In stark contrast to his everyday optimistic laugh, he spoke with a tremor in his voice.

"...Is it really time?"

The time for goodbyes always came, without fail. It came when someone set off on a journey, free of regrets, just as it came at times like these—always too soon.

"Damned minia… Your kind is too weak…too feeble by half."

At long last, the cart caught up to the boy. Adults, appearing to be the young girl's parents, gripped her delicate and fragile hand. The children whom Mele saw day in and day out were each calling out the girl's name.

Ilieh. She didn't even have a second name. Ilieh of Sine Riverstead. She was born into this world, and she would leave it without achieving anything at all.

"…Mele…you're awake… I'm glad……"

"…Just a coincidence, that's all. I was so bored I was counting the hairs in my beard."

"Oh, were you…? Um, Mele, listen… I always had…so much fun…"

"Is that right? Well, I'm happy to hear that. You enjoyed your life to the fullest, didn't ya, Ilieh…?"

It was around this time that the eyes of all the children in the area began welling up with tears, one pair after another.

Even the troublemakers, often fond of putting on a brave front, lost their composure.

Ilieh had been a precious friend to all.

Mele wasn't going to be swayed by these weaklings' tears, however. He was the strongest gigant of all, and the village's guardian deity besides.

He decided that he wanted to show her something big and impressive.

Wrapping both of his massive hands around the cart, Mele forced his trademark smile to his lips.

"All right. Well, if you're gonna kick the bucket today anyway, I'll grant any request you have. What'll it be, missy?"

"…Th-then, one more time…Mele. The stars…like you did before…"

"Oh sure, sure! You sat right up here on my shoulder and got a good look at 'em, didn't ya?"

"I...love...this village. The stars are...so pretty..."

"Bah-ha-ha-ha-ha! What, these tiny things? When the time comes, I'll decorate your grave with as many of 'em as you want!"

With his massive hands, big enough to hold three full-grown adults, the gigant carefully cradled the small, blanketed girl.

She was still here. She was still breathing, still warm, still full of life.

He remembered the day she was born. The sky had been just as clear as it was this night, with the stars dotting the heavens.

In an instant, her time had flown by.

Mele the Horizon's Roar had been born strong.

Minia... Their lives are so painfully short...

"Anyone else wanna look at the stars with me and Ilieh?"

"I do!"

"Me too...!"

"Ilieh! I'm coming, too!"

"C'mon, me too, me too!"

"Hop on, all of ya! No matter how close the stars seem, don't go trying to grab 'em!"

Mele held the precious little lives in both hands and lifted them high into the sky.

As he raised them higher and higher, even he got a good look at the glittering stars.

It was an exceptionally beautiful, and exceptionally sad night.

Higher still, so that she could get a better glimpse of the stars she loved so much. Higher than ever.

A memory from the distant past.

◆

"…Hey, Dad."

It was the night following the deluge.

Away from the fireplace, the air was a bit chilly—the final remnants of the storm.

Finished with dinner, Miroya was brushing his teeth as he posed a question to his father, who was brushing his own teeth beside him.

"There was someone that went off to Aureatia from Sine Riverstead, right?"

"Oh, you talking about Misuna? Do you want to go to Aureatia, too, Miroya?"

"Nah, that's not it really, it's just… I wonder why Mele's heading off to those royal games."

"Hm? Where's this coming from?"

"…Well, it's a pretty long trip from out here to Aureatia, for one…"

"And you don't think he needs to go that far to earn money for the village, is that it?"

The serene and spindly father had the complete opposite personality and build from Miroya, who took more after his mother. Nevertheless, he was always able to see through and understand what exactly his son was thinking.

"To tell you the truth, the royal games stuff was something we all decided in part for Mele's sake, too."

"…For Mele's sake?"

"That's right."

The father thoroughly wiped down his face with a cloth and put on his normal pair of homely glasses. Since they had been exposed to the heat from the lamp, they were slightly fogged over.

"Mele's, well… He's never been outside Sine Riverstead before."

"Whoa, no way! Really?!"

"Yup, that's right. He's always been up on that hill, sleeping... eating what the village brings him, shooting down wyverns for meat... It's always been that way, even back when my great grandfather was a boy."

"Doesn't he ever want to travel?"

"I'm sure he does. Normally, gigants live nomadic lifestyles. If they stay in one place, they more than likely run out of food... Not that that part really matters much to Mele."

It was the first time Miroya had given any consideration to what life must be like for Mele.

Up on that barren, weather-worn hill for two hundred and fifty years. No changes in scenery, and without meeting any other of his gigant brethren. Although he was the guardian deity of Sine Riverstead, he couldn't live together with the minia in the village. Both sides knew the difference in scale between minia and gigant was far too vast in every conceivable way.

Despite having eyes that could see farther than anyone else, he had never once visited the landscapes he beheld.

"This year's storm is over. That's why we want him to travel, just for a little while. With our survival assured for another year... we thought it would be nice if he could make some memories outside of this village."

"But he's gonna be fighting in the royal games. Even Rosclay will be there. Isn't that scary?"

"Hmm.... I think that might be a bit difficult for you to understand right now, Miroya."

The father folded his arms, vaguely pondering and frowning.

The chirping sounds of the birds could be heard coming in from the nighttime still beyond the window.

"Mele, well...he's strong."

"I mean, sure, but even still."

"...He's strong. Far stronger than you think he is, Miroya."

Mele the Horizon's Roar was a champion of unknown valor and heroism.

Strangely, despite that, there was no one in the village who doubted he was the strongest in the world.

"Must have been about eight years ago now. Did you know the Demon King Army had spread out very close to where we are now?"

"What...? No way..."

"It's the truth. Honestly, I was terrified, and as a baby, you would cry nonstop every day. The whole area was crawling with soldiers of the Demon King's army...but if we didn't flee, we would've all been forcibly conscripted into the Demon King's army at some point, too. The situation was so bleak that there were some families that...seriously considered ending it all."

"......"

Among the children, fond of telling stories about dragons, ogres, or even monsters like Toroa the Awful, the True Demon King was one figure that none of them ever joked about.

Everyone understood it to be a topic far too serious for their games.

"But that didn't happen. Everything else fell to the Army, but our Sine Riverstead alone remained safe... I remember it all. Almost every day, Mele would stand up on that hill, and look out over the Demon King Army. He had that black bow in his hands. He didn't fire any arrows... But the grim look he always had on his face was like nothing I had ever seen before."

"It's all thanks to Mele...that the Demon King Army never came here...?"

"Incredible, isn't it? Mele beat the True Demon King. It's the honest truth."

Maybe this was the sole anecdote describing Mele's heroics.

Miroya got the feeling he knew the reason why the adults never mentioned it. Imminent destruction, and rampant, shapeless despair. The day the smile disappeared from Mele's face.

Anything and everything completely different from the way the village was now... It was an event that everyone wanted to remember as nothing more than a bad dream.

Sine Riverstead was peaceful.

The residents of this small village continued to live on the lands of their ancestors, never forced to relocate to Aureatia, or have their bountiful resources devastated by the True Demon King.

Much like a select few of the other remote, unexplored regions scattered across the world, this was one of the minority of places that had been able to preserve its form through the age of the Demon King.

"Mele's a warrior. He's been strong forever...probably from even before he came to this village."

"...Even without anyone to fight?"

"Mele's always been strong on his own. It must be lonely. If he did fight, he'd be stronger than anyone else... Still, though, he continues to protect this village, without ever showing off his strength to anyone..."

Miroya didn't know about what sort of conversation occurred between the adults of the village and Mele when he said he was going to join the games.

...However, if this was all true, if Mele had truly been a warrior the entire time...

He must have been so sad. So lonely.

Though the villagers brought him food, offered him arrows, and shared memories with him, this one part of him must have never felt satisfied.

The era of the True Demon King's tyranny itself gave birth to the various champions across the land. Thus, in this village, its safeguard of peace and tranquility unyielding, that meant not a single individual as strong as Mele ever appeared among them.

"...Dad. You think Mele can beat Rosclay?"

"Sure he can."

"But I've never even seen Mele fire an arrow before."

"Hm? You sure? I'm pretty confident you have."

The father cocked his head, puzzled, before opening the window that looked out on the hill.

The Needle Forest that overlooked the village was clearly visible from every house in the village.

"When you were seven, you said you saw a shooting star, didn't you?"

"Yeah... I can't remember it all that well, though. What about it?"

"Look. You can see it really clearly tonight, right?"

"......!"

Miroya instantly leaned out the window with excitement.

A shooting star. The clearly visible star was racing across the night sky.

However, the star was *climbing* up to the heavens.

Scores of burning lines raced across the sky from the direction of the hill. Rows and rows of them.

On a normal night, they might have been overlooked.

A pale light, too faint to be seen if not for the clear skies following the storm.

"...The lights from the burning earthen Craft Arts arrows. Far off into the sky there. Fast enough to scorch the earth below. Only Mele is capable of such a feat, and he does it every night."

"Mele…!"

Miroya simply hadn't noticed, but these shooting stars had been sparkling every night.

The huge gigant, always lazing around and laughing at everything…shooting his arrows night after night, right here in this village.

"Hey, Dad… Dad!"

Miroya stared so intently at the light he nearly fell out the window.

Mele was a big liar. He shot his arrows after all.

Not only that, but he could pull off amazing stuff like this, too.

Now, Miroya could believe.

He wanted to believe that the biggest presence in the Sine Riverstead for as long as anyone could remember was truly the strongest person in all the land.

"…You think Mele can beat Rosclay?!"

◆

Stars were twinkling high in the clear sky. They stretched out across the wide-open skies.

…A beautiful sky, the storm long gone.

"Ahhh, dammit… Damn near had it, too."

Looking up at the star twinkling in the sky, small enough to pass through the eye of a needle, Mele clicked his tongue quietly.

Nocking an arrow he pulled from the ground, drawing his bowstring, and then, aiming up high into the sky…he sent his arrow flowing toward the small speck in the heavens. He continued until he had exhausted all his strength and could enter a deep sleep.

He was sure that his aim was still just a little bit off.

He was sure that his arrow was still falling just a bit short.

Still, today was better than yesterday. That was why he knew he'd hit it eventually.

"Just watch."

Dragons don't devote themselves to training. The same was true for gigants and elves, who possessed equally long lifespans.

It is believed that, among the races of the world, it is only those ones with a limited lifespan who are able to hone their skills and pour such fervent efforts into their endeavors.

However, if the long-lived races were able to devote the entirety of lives to the pursuit of a single skill...

The gigant cupped the star-filled night sky above him in both his hands.

He was never without his confident grin.

On nights when the stars shined bright and clear, this was what he would do.

"These should do nicely for her grave."

He possessed the apex of visual acuity, able to see past the edge of the horizon with his extraordinarily massive body.

He boasted near-godly accuracy, capable of changing the flow of raging rapids with a single shot.

He fired his bow with destructive force, each arrow impossible to block or evade—a single shot capable of leveling large swathes of terrain.

His astral arrows were launched from a place far from the realm of terrestrial comprehension.

Archer. Gigant.

Mele, the Horizon's Roar.

Ever since her youth, one girl thought the mountain glow visible from the desert was rather mysterious. According to what adults had told her, it was the light from a city known as Itaaki, and people totally different from them lived there.

Ani was a child who asked many questions.

"Just how different are we from them? Do they have lizard faces like the zumeu?"

"No, no, that's not it. Those highlands folks' faces aren't that different from our own. But their god's different."

"Their god?"

"You know how long, long ago the scary True Demon King showed up, right? Back then, all the people in the highlands city died. But our people managed to survive. The Particle Storm protected us."

"The Particle Storm is a god? Not part of the weather?"

"It's both. The god's power appears in our world in the form of the weather phenomenon known as the Particle Storm. A god solely for us people of the desert. The Particle Storm's come through the Yamaga Barrens many times over the ages, but it's always spared our village, right? See, that's because he's protecting us."

Outside of Ani's village, apparently everyone worshipped a god called the Word-Maker. But, since that god didn't protect anything from the True Demon King, the Particle Storm must have been the stronger of the two.

One day, when she went to draw the afternoon water, she saw the Particle Storm pass through the gap between the village and the oasis.

The desert sky was completely covered, and despite being noon, it was as though the whole world had been plunged into darkness.

A thunderous sound, the likes of which she had never heard before, rang in her ears and rattled around her head until it finally passed through. The sound had absolutely terrified the young Ani.

Chena had accompanied her to the oasis, but since she had finished drawing her water sooner, she had been completely erased on the road back to the village, without even a single finger of hers left behind.

Just as its name suggested, the Particle Storm shredded anything and everything it engulfed into tiny particles. The tremendous amount of sand swirled together into a tempest, and like a file chiseling away at a stone, scraped away at the bodies of any living thing until there was nothing left behind.

Even in the Yamaga Barrens there were a great many living creatures. Cats, mice, and lizards could be seen scampering around, and woodpeckers nested in cactus holes. The amusing movements of the white spiders were a particular favorite of hers.

Nevertheless, with the Particle Storm's passing, it all disappeared entirely.

"…Mom. Aren't you scared of the Particle Storm getting you?"

"Not at all, silly. My older brother, our neighbor Litta, they all went to the land beyond the storm."

"The land beyond the storm?"

"Everything disappears after the Particle Storm passes through, right? Yamaga is too arid and dry to comfortably sustain life...so he made a country to save us all. Everyone embraced by the storm is living together in peace there."

"Then, we should all just let the Particle Storm bring us over there."

"We can't do that."

"Why not? If things aren't scary or painful over there, then we should all just go."

"The Particle Storm gets very angry when children try to go over to the other side. Instead of sending them to the land beyond, it brings them to a bad and scary place in hell. Everyone has to wait for the day when he comes to welcome you."

"......Mom? He never welcomed you?"

"......"

"Did Chena go to hell?"

The villagers always needed to make sure the Particle Storm was never angered.

No matter how hard things got, the rule was to endure it together, and continue to perform their daily duties.

This was also why Ani crossed the desert to draw water. Whenever she encountered a sandstorm, she grew hopelessly scared that it was the angered Particle Storm instead. She heard that the Particle Storm's anger grew even more intense during the years someone left the village.

Thus, everyone worked the same way, day in and day out.

Ani never once complained.

There were many other adults who did jobs far more difficult than hers.

Coughing violently from the sand, she carried her bucket filled with water.

She made the round-trip repeatedly. Even if her shoes got worn down by the hot sand, there were times when no one would fix them for her.

The corpses of children, dead from disease, were wrapped in furs and carried to the barrow where the Particle Storm was enshrined.

Now and again, Ani would look at the lights of Itaaki on the mountaintop.

The adults pitied the people there who lived without the protection of the Particle Storm.

She watched the small and large moons travel over and over again across the beautiful night sky of the Yamaga Barrens.

Just how long had she repeated her routine, day in, and day out? Ani was now twelve years old.

That day, the oasis was different from normal. A carriage was stopped there.

"Who's that?"

"Oh, well, well, well!"

A zumeu woman saw Ani and smiled. Both her dress and her carriage were of higher quality than anything Ani had seen before.

"This is perfect timing! Are you from the Yamaga village?"

"Yeah. I'm Ani."

"Eh-heh-heh! Why hello there, Miss Ani."

The zumeu were a minian race with the faces and scaly skin of lizards, and they primarily lived in dry and arid regions, such as deserts. They were not a race to be feared. The merchants who came selling salt to the village were all zumeu as well. So if anything, Ani was more accustomed to seeing them than other minia from outside the village.

"Are you a traveling merchant?"

"No, not at all! It pains me to say, the only things I could possibly put up for sale are laughter and flattery! I am but a humble zumeu harlequin. Do you enjoy string craft?"

"...Harlequin?"

"Unfamiliar with harlequins, are we? Well now, let's see here. I know I have a picture somewhere around here that should clear things up."

The zumeu woman searched the inside of her overcoat—her protection from the harsh sunlight—and made an exaggerated display of bewilderment when her search came up empty.

"Did you lose it?"

"Oh, no, perish the thought, I found it just now... Ta-dah!"

Finally, the zumeu woman took out a single sheet of hemp paper, but it was soon caught by the wind and slipped cleanly out from her hands.

"Oopsie."

Staggering along, she followed the paper as it danced in the air. Just as she was about to grab it, at the very last minute the paper would again escape her grip.

Greatly surprised, the zumeu continued to comically chase the airborne scrap of paper around and around. Without any spoken Word Arts, the piece of paper began flapping up and down like a bird's wings.

"Oh, knock it off now! Stop, right this instant! A-aaaah?!"

The paper seemed to be teasing the harlequin as it tossed her about, and she grew dizzy following it around, eventually collapsing onto the sand.

The double-folded bird became a simple piece of paper once more, and gently fluttered down over her reptilian face.

It was the first time in Ani's life she had ever seen such a strange and amusing spectacle.

"Pfft, hee-hee-hee."

"Did you enjoy my performance?"

Folding up the paper into a small square and putting it back in her overcoat, the zumeu took an extravagant bow.

"Is that paper alive or something?"

"That *is* the question, isn't it? I need to open it up and check again for myself... Oh my! It's good as new!"

The paper was hopping in the palm of her hand like a bug, but when she handed it over, Ani could tell it was nothing more than a simple piece of hemp paper. There was an illustration of a flower drawn on it, the kind little children enjoyed.

"*Ah-hyah-hyah*! Well it seems it's taken quite a liking to you, Miss Ani. Well then, it's yours!"

"Are you sure I can have it?"

"Why, of course. In exchange, would you be so kind to point me toward your village? I could search for it with my own two feet, but I'm so very worried I'll get myself lost. I fear I'll end up walking myself in circles, you see."

"You can follow this road. Where the ground color's different. The kids on water-drawing duty stamped the sand down... What do you want with our village? Is this carriage for your harlequin job?"

"Oh, heavens no! I must accompany this exalted individual. This responsibility is far, far more important than my harlequin trade."

"......"

Ani looked at the lovely white carriage, parked in the shade of a tree. In complete contrast to the cheerful and sociable zumeu in front of her, the carriage was quiet. At a glance, there didn't seem to be anyone inside.

Ani cut in front of the carriage and went to draw the water.

"Even with your foot injured, you came out here to draw water?"

"Huh?"

Her legs instinctively stopped when she heard the clear and gentle voice speak to her.

The zumeu came running over.

"Oh, my humblest apologies! How could I fail to notice your injuries, Miss Ani? Did you cut a tendon in your foot? It happened about four days ago, yes?"

She made an exaggerated display of worrying over Ani, but it seemed more like the zumeu was responding to the person inside the carriage. This zumeu probably noticed Ani's foot injury from the very beginning.

"I'm fine."

Ani answered the zumeu. The cut was causing her constant pain, but to her, there was no longer any point in worrying about it.

"The Particle Storm is coming for me tomorrow. We don't have any Life Arts users who can heal my foot. I waited for the day he would come, rather than seeking him out myself."

"Ah-hyah-hyah! Is that how the Particle Storm is spoken of in your village, Ani? Well, well, that's quite—"

"Let us dress her wound for her. Some things are best kept secret."

"Why, yes, most certainly."

The harlequin seemed as if she was about to make some kind of comedic remark, but the voice from inside the carriage cut her off. The zumeu swiftly produced thread and bandages, and wrapped Ani's wound to try and ease her pain.

"Now then! That should make things a bit easier."

"Why...?"

Ani was a child with a lot of questions.

"Why are you being so nice to me?"

"Well, I wonder. Maybe because in the world beyond the

desert, such a thing is normal. Why, I could very well be a nefarious scumbag, you know."

People from beyond the desert weren't as hardworking as the desert residents, and they weren't protected by the Particle Storm at all.

Ani had been told they she shouldn't get involved with them, as they were foolish and driven by greed.

"...Nuh-uh. I'm glad I met you both before I left."

She headed toward the oasis, dragging her foot along.

Ani had been told that since the Particle Storm was coming to take her away anyway, there was no need to tend to the wound on her foot.

Even she herself had thought it all meaningless, and yet...

"Miss Harlequin."

"Ah-hyah! What is it?"

"Can you show that fun stuff to everyone in the village too someday?"

The voice from inside the carriage answered.

"Yes. I promise."

"Ah-hyah-hyah! But of course!"

The zumeu twirled the bandages she had used for Ani's foot in a large swirling vortex, until finally, it changed into a multicolored cloud of confetti. To Ani, who had lived her whole life in the drab desert, the winds were filled with color, like nothing she had ever seen.

"Take care now, Miss Ani!"

Perhaps this event was what spurred her on.

Before the Particle Storm could come to take her away, Ani decided she would go and see the barrow in the night.

It was always the adult's job to carry the children to the barrow, but its distance from the village and its whereabouts were things the village children inadvertently learned themselves.

In the morning it'll come for me.

The sand at her feet grew damper as she got closer, and the terrain gave way to a rock surface covered in soil.

She was heading there by herself, illuminated only by the light of the two moons, unable to properly use one of her legs. Nevertheless, she felt like she had to make sure of something. Having always lived her life in accordance with what adults told her, it was the first time Ani had decided to do something herself.

There was a world outside the Yamaga Barrens. One unknown to Ani, just like the harlequin and her companion had been.

The Particle Storm protected the village from the terrors beyond the desert.

It extinguished living creatures with its fearsome rage.

Which story was true? Were they both, in a way?

...That's the barrow.

The moons were hidden behind the clouds, and the landscape was pitch-black, but there was no doubting that this colossal boulder in the center of the windless hollow was the barrow the adults had said enshrined the Particle Storm.

"Particle Storm..."

She was frightened. Even if she died here at this barrow, waiting for her on the other side was the land beyond the desert.

There was a brittle noise.

It was the dry sound of something snapping underfoot.

Her shoes had been tailored for her big day the next morning.

The moons came out from the clouds and shined their light on her barrow destination.

"What?"

She was covered in a viscous black substance.

Even beneath the purple moonlight, she noticed that the color was one she had seen before.

"No, no…"

Blood. Congealed from accumulating layer after layer.

The things Ani had stepped on were almost like pebbles, yet curiously, they were all gathered around the bloody surface.

Thin, white, yet oddly rounded fragments.

"No… it can't be."

Then, she looked out at the scenery stretching out behind the barrow.

There before her was the land beyond the storm.

The mummified, crumbling corpses of children—decayed down to the bone—had been simply cast aside and piled on top of one another. There were no indicators that the bodies had been scavenged by wild animals. Their deaths served no purpose at all.

"Aaaaah!"

The dead children had been carried here by the adults and offered to the Particle Storm, as were the still-living children who made it here.

But… But if the child to be offered was still alive…what would the adults do in that case?

There were traces of blood in the barrow. Bone splinters. For years… So many people… Splattered across the ground… Over and over again…

There was another snapping sound at her feet.

"N-no."

She had stepped on a skull fragment. In Ani's village, most children born didn't make it to adulthood. This was their fate.

I'm not scared, silly. My older brother, our neighbor Litta, they all went to the country beyond the storm.

At that moment, what truly terrified Ani wasn't the knowledge that she was going to die.

It was the fact the adults had known the truth the entire time— the mean adults, the nice adults, the village chief, the elders, and even her own family. For generations they had lied to the children without so much as a twitch in their placid expressions.

The one thing she believed in, and diligently worked to protect, had been a lie.

A lonely breeze blew by.

"Help…"

The tears on her cheeks immediately dried up in the wind. Within the Particle Storm's barrow, where even bone splinters remained undisturbed in their final resting place among the still air…a breeze blew.

"I-I…I'm sorry! I'm sorry!"

Despite being mistaken about everything, despite everything she had been told being pure insanity, this raging wind alone was unmistakable.

The fine sand, the bone splinters, traveled on the wind and coiled around Ani.

The particles scraped the inside of her lungs and windpipe. Even the blood spilling from her mouth dissipated in a fine mist against the thunderous squall.

Ani was the one at fault.

She had sprained her leg and couldn't carry out her duties.

She had listened to the words of the harlequin and her companion.

She had stumbled too close to the truth.

She had questioned the Particle Storm.

"...*Hngaugh*, f-for...forgive..."

It was a pain worse than death.

Her blood, her tears, her screams, and her regret had all vanished without a trace.

The wind died down, and another fragile life had been snuffed out in its entirety.

Not a single trace had been left behind.

In order to survive, theft was a necessity.

Like a large majority of the minian races, Kuuro the Cautious had been able to live out his youth without stealing. While he certainly hadn't been rich, the sounds and colors of the world were far more brilliant and vibrant than they were now.

The terror of the True Demon King had swept through, and he knew those days were eternally gone.

Everything given to him in his young days was now only obtainable by forcibly snatching them with his own power. The day's food. A safe refuge. Even his very lifeblood itself.

This was why he was currently fleeing through the outskirts of Togie City.

His plan to make contact with Aureatia had been compromised. His pursuers were likely the muscle of loyalists of the former monarchies that used the city as a base of operations.

The three kingdoms that governed this world fell to the menace of the True Demon King and had united to form a new nation called Aureatia. The Old Kingdoms' loyalists who sought to restore the nations of the past had a deep-rooted hostility toward Aureatia.

Figures there'd be a lot of minia in this district. I'm gonna stand out a bit.

The characteristic boyish facial features and physique of the leprechauns should be a dead giveaway to the ones pursuing Kuuro the Cautious. Keeping his hands stuffed into the pockets of his dark brown coat, he remained vigilant about the crowds coming and going behind him, without once looking back.

"They just crossed over the bridge. There's thirteen of them coming."

A young girl's voiced whispered to him from somewhere. Only Kuuro's ears could pick up the buzzing and her soft whisper.

She's wrong. I'm hearing fourteen people's footsteps.

Once he knew his enemies were near the bridge, Kuuro the Cautious was then able to accurately grasp the precise number of pursuers. He could do this simply by focusing all his senses in the bridge's direction.

He was in a market at noontime, with several hundred people of different physiques and gaits coming and going. Kuuro chose to flee in this direction in an attempt to lose his pursuers in the hustle and bustle.

This covert artifice was one of the skills he had cultivated before beginning his detective activities within the city.

Five of them are trying to move without making a sound. These ones are in front of the rest of the soldiers and slipping through the crowd. The fourteen soldiers are decoys to grab my attention and get a reaction out of me. These five others are the ones actually tasked with capturing me.

He concentrated his senses on one of the soldiers shuffling into the crowd.

Kuuro cast his eyes downward as he walked, never dropping his pace and taking care not to move too quickly. He masked his presence by blending into the crowd. However, his aim wasn't to give his enemies the slip. He quietly withdrew one of his hands from his coat pocket.

Pierce the windpipe. Sixth cervical vertebra.

With a metallic *clink*, a small vibration ran up his arm. The sound came from operating the small fold-out crossbow hidden inside his coat sleeve. The delicate arrow, constructed from a kraken's feelers, flew without a sound, encountering almost no air resistance at all.

"Hrngk!"

Kuuro was the only one cognizant of the soldiers' dying gasps. That was why he fired at the windpipe. It was to prevent them from getting a word out and alerting the others.

It was impossible to evade his techniques. His projectile moments ago had passed through the gaps in the underarms of two pedestrians traveling through the area. He hadn't even been facing his enemy, who had been fatally wounded with only the slightest movements of Kuuro's fingers.

There are rare instances when, among the massive number of people born among the minian races, individuals are born with visual and aural acuity far beyond others of their race.

Conversely, there are those individuals who, due to their talent and self-discipline, gain an intuition that exceeds the potential of their five senses.

There are also stories about even more exceptional senses, such as sensing heat or magnetic forces, or synesthesia.

Kuuro the Cautious, too, experienced such supernatural senses. *All of them, all at once.*

Clairvoyance.

The name had been given to this remarkable gift, solely possessed by one individual, Kuuro the Cautious.

"One of them, he's turned his head this way," the young girl's voice cautioned.

Unlike radzio communication, he was only able to listen to the faraway voice with his extraordinary sense of hearing, but as long as Kuuro was the only one able to hear it, that was more than enough.

The man to the northwest. His breaths have become shorter. He's discovered me... I'll take advantage of that hat.

During the single moment when his pursuer's line of sight became obstructed by a passerby's hat, Kuuro shot him from over his shoulder.

The bolt opened a small hole in the hat, penetrating the target's eye socket and lodging itself in their brain. Once again, the soldier collapsed to the ground without even a groan. Kuuro didn't turn back to admire his work; however, he clearly perceived everything up until the final moment. He wouldn't feel safe otherwise.

Kuuro's eyes, which reflected the beauty of the world in his younger days, were now fixed solely on the deaths of his enemies.

"Kuuro."

The young girl's voice was very close now—she had cut through the crowded marketplace.

"The soldiers on the bridge spotted you, I think. We should probably run."

"Then you shouldn't be making any conspicuous movements, Cuneigh."

She looked like a little bird, small enough to fit in the palm of his hand. From afar, most people would mistake her for exactly that.

However, this creature with the wings of a bird was even tinier than the leprechaun. Her body wasn't naturally born into this world, even with its varied and abnormal beastfolk.

"If the Old Kingdoms' folks find out about you, that's gonna cause me a lot of trouble later on."

"*Tee-hee.*"

In Kuuro's hand, the young girl chuckled with embarrassment.

"Kuuro. Hey, Kuuro, are you worried about me?"

"…I'm worried about everything. Everything that puts my life at risk."

Kuuro continued shooting his crossbow without looking behind him. One soldier had their diaphragm shot clean through and squatted down where they stood. They then served as an obstacle, disrupting the steps of the rest of the formation. Just as Kuuro planned.

He killed them in cold blood. Nevertheless, he killed only the bare minimum to serve his goals.

"Cuneigh. They're not going to ambush us at the meeting point, are they?"

"Nope. I looked! It's okay, Kuuro."

"…I wonder."

Lowering his small frame, he raced off in an instant. He moved like a shadow, without brushing against the clothes of the pedestrians walking around. Moving across the plaza, he would sometimes pass through the street stalls as he moved on. Cuneigh curled herself up inside his coat.

Her second name was Cuneigh the Wanderer.

While she appeared to be a young girl, save for her tiny size, she was not a normal living creature.

She was a homunculus—an artificial race, similar to constructs, formed using a living minian body as a base. In contrast to skeletons and revenants, it was said that the simulacrum itself possessed latent knowledge from its base body. Additionally, by splicing together and modifying developmental-stage cells, it was even possible to create individuals like Cuneigh, who had both arms replaced with wings.

In part due to the advanced arts required, not many were created, and their individual lifespan was short. The average person didn't even know they existed. Moreover, Cuneigh had clearly been a failed creation, completely unfurnished with any of her base body's latent intelligence.

"We lost them, right?"

"Not sure about that."

Kuuro looked back behind him one more time. Despite taking perfect precautions, he was far from relieved.

In the past, he had fought against an intensely powerful foe. Facing off against this many Old Kingdom troops, he probably could have fought them face to face and won. However, he knew plenty of examples where that sort of presupposition could lead straight to death.

If he took the common rank and file lightly, he would die. No matter how unlikely the chances were, all battle was conducted with the possibility of death.

"They're chasing us knowing full well who I am. Don't you think they've sent along someone even stronger than I am?"

"...There isn't anyone stronger than you, though."

"There is among them, though. Each and every one of them is trying to kill me."

Kuuro the Cautious's exceptional gift was called clairvoyance. In the extreme chaos that was the era of the True Demon King, he had used this ability in service of a spy guild, racking up legendary achievements one after another as a champion of the shadows.

All of that was in the past.

"Cuneigh. Don't leave the cover of my coat."

"Okay."

They arrived at the designated meet-up spot. Looking through each and every one of the carriages coming in and out of the marketplace with his supernatural visual acuity, Kuuro was able to spot the one with a rather small green seal engraved on the door.

With light movements only possible for leprechauns, completely masking his body weight, he slipped into the moving passenger carriage.

"I am Kuuro the Cautious. Are you the messenger from Aureatia?"

He announced this as he climbed inside the carriage. Inside was the lone passenger, a woman with an air of grace and elegance, with her chestnut hair tied up behind her.

"Yes. I am Aureatia's Seventeenth Minister, Elea the Red Tag. You have my gratitude for responding to our proposal."

An unseen threat filled Kuuro with a sense of foreboding.

...*What was that?*

It wasn't related to the woman in front of him.

"Seventeenth Minister... We're in enemy territory. I didn't expect one of Aureatia's Twenty-Nine Officials to come all the way here."

The supreme bureaucrats, twenty-nine in total, who ran the assembly in Aureatia, the largest minian city in the world. Elea the Red Tag was a young woman of intelligence, exercising control over their espionage operations.

"Well, infiltrating into the middle of enemy territory like this is the job of spy units such as myself. Besides...Aureatia believes you're valuable enough to send one of the Twenty-Nine to meet you. The keenest sights among all of the Obsidian Eyes spy guild, Kuuro the Cautious."

"...I'm no more than a simple private eye now. More pressingly,

I'm being followed. I tried to shake off my pursuers as much as possible, but there's no guarantee that they haven't blocked off the carriages."

"Now, now."

Kuuro observed her demure reaction. He wished he could pinpoint the exact location of the threat.

To him, even her alluring smile and enchanting features were nothing more than a single layer of skin composing the surface of her minian face. There was an unnatural tremble in her muscles. Changes in the intervals of her blinking, and her demeanor.

The Old Kingdoms' loyalists in Togie City got wind of his plan to make contact with a messenger from Aureatia...

Or perhaps, Kuuro thought, Aureatia's side had *deliberately* leaked the information themselves.

Ever since he departed Obsidian Eyes, he had been working as a street investigator, unbeholden to any other power, which meant as soon as this current plan was found out, he lost any other path of egress, except to go with Aureatia.

Of course, Kuuro also considered that a more desirable outcome. Supposing that was indeed true, it meant that currently, Aureatia had no plans of disposing of him.

Being used wasn't the true threat.

He felt that the true form of this threat originated elsewhere.

"I want to leave Togie City immediately. Are you ready?"

"But of course. My business here concluded the moment I picked you up. It doesn't seem we'll be able to avoid the checkpoints along the roads... Our only choice is to slip through the marshlands."

"It rained just a couple days ago. There's a chance we'll get stuck in the mire."

"While this may be shaped exactly like the standard large

merchant carriage, I'm using a horse skilled at off-road travel, and the frame's been hollowed out to reduce its weight. A shallow swamp won't be enough to slow us down."

"...The same style used by Obsidian Eyes, then?"

"Indeed."

Formerly known as the largest spy guild, Obsidian Eyes acted behind the scenes during the war-torn age of the true Demon King and conducted any and all forms of espionage activity. Kuuro had heard that with the end of the era, many members resigned, with select personnel and technologies being onboarded for Aureatia's spy force. Exactly as he was being onboarded right that moment.

"Are you fine with leaving that homunculus girl back in the city? I heard that she always accompanied you."

"......So, you knew about her, too, hm?"

He sighed. Togie City had resisted Aureatia's control even before becoming occupied by the Old Kingdoms' loyalists, so he had taken solace in the fact that he had been able to hide her from Aureatia's eyes.

"You can come on out, Cuneigh."

The songbird of a young girl crawled out from inside his coat and looked up at Elea with wide eyes.

"H-Hello."

"Cuneigh the Wanderer. I'd like to bring her with me if possible. You have the authority to make that happen, right?"

Although they admitted a small number of beastfolk and monstrous races as part of the labor force, Aureatia was a nation of minian races. Given the ethical problems involved in their creation, much like with constructs, there was a high probability that he wouldn't be granted asylum with a homunculus accompanying him.

On the other hand, if they demanded he hand Cuneigh over to

them for research purposes, he wouldn't be able to refuse. Kuuro was being hunted by the Old Kingdoms' loyalists and could no longer continue his detective work in Togie City as before. He had long been cut off from any other escape routes.

"How unusual. Homunculi themselves are rare enough...but I've never heard of any examples of one purposely being given wings. Why exactly was she constructed that way?"

"I don't know. I wasn't the one who built Cuneigh, and I haven't the faintest clue what thoughts were going through the crazy self-proclaimed Demon King Icareh's head. Maybe it was an attempt to revive the ancient harpies or something."

He heard that much like forests had elves, the mountains had dwarves, and the deserts had zumeu, there once used to be a minian race that claimed the skies as their domain. However, as the wyverns thrived, the harpies went extinct, and as a result, the minian race who achieved the greatest success were the ones who lived *between* these different domains—the Minia themselves.

"A simple constructed pet. She poses no danger like with the construct races. Up to you whether to believe me or not."

"I don't mind. If that's all there is, then we'll let you in under my personal discretion."

"Really?!"

"...Sorry about this. She may not look it, but she's a necessary part of my work."

It wasn't that Cuneigh possessed some outstanding power outside of her wings and small size. She didn't happen to be gifted with any intelligence. From Kuuro's perspective, her spycraft techniques were terribly indiscreet. Nevertheless, she had utilitarian value—at the very least, to help ensure Kuuro's survival.

"That's great, isn't it, Kuuro? We're together again."

"Employment extended. What do you want for compensation? Aureatia should have just about anything you could ask for."

"Huh? That's okay. I don't need anything."

"...Nothing more important than payment. Especially when talking about employment. Spend the time before we arrive thinking on it."

Disregarding Kuuro and Cuneigh's back-and-forth, Elea was looking out the peephole behind the carriage.

"...Are those the pursuers you mentioned?"

Although the carriage was just about to clear the city, the Old Kingdoms' soldiers pursuing Kuuro had finally made their way through the crowds of people. Deftly mixed in with the merchant carriages, they were unable to identify the Aureatia vehicle.

"That's them. About a year ago, those Old Kingdom bastards started making inroads in the upper echelons of Togie City. Even since Gilnes the Ruined Castle joined their faction, more and more soldiers join the cause... Judging by how their numbers are increasing, they're at the stage where they're gathering troops from other cities. They're preparing for come what may with Aureatia."

"We're quite aware. Their existence has been an even deeper-rooted problem than the New Principality."

During the age of the True Demon King, this world was brought to the brink of ruin, and all but a single member of the royal family perished.

The True Northern Kingdom. The Central Kingdom. The United Western Kingdom. The three kingdoms that once existed were all brought together under the name of the young queen to form Aureatia. However, a section of the Central Kingdom's power, which served the biggest foundation for Aureatia, were still trying to restore the Central Kingdom they all believed in.

"I want some clarity on what's going to happen now. Is my job going to be cleaning up these Old Kingdoms' loyalists?"

"All I can say is that it depends on the war situation. For example, do you know the current state of affairs with the Free City of Okahu?"

It was the name of the city ruled by the self-proclaimed demon king Morio. If Obsidian Eyes was the largest spy guild in the land, then the Free City of Okahu was the country founded by the largest mercenary guild in the land. They were known for being a group of elite soldiers who deployed their military might, rivaling that of an established nation state, unbeholden to any outside authority.

"Those warmongers, then? I heard they lend quite a number of soldiers to the New Principality."

"Presently, those two powers are the ones we need to keep an eye on, broadly speaking. If the current situation on the Free City front goes south, know that I could ask you to head over there, too."

"I want to settle on hard terms for my contract. Putting the Old Kingdoms' guys aside, I don't really want to make an enemy of the Free State."

"Ha-ha-ha. Naturally, you're right that the Old Kingdoms' loyalists are a high priority. Now, regarding Obsidian Eyes, then—"

"Wait. There are soldiers outside. Best to stay quiet."

They were no more than your garden variety soldier, of course.

However, Kuuro trusted in the foreboding premonition he had gotten when he first boarded the carriage. For him and him alone, his illogical gut instincts were more accurate than his logical train of thought. He possessed senses surpassing known knowledge and wisdom.

The carriage was just about to pass the soldiers meandering near the gate. They weren't stopped for an inspection.

"…A little too worried, don't you think?"

Elea spoke up a little while after they had passed through the city gate.

"You and your clairvoyance are the only things capable of picking up a conversation through a carriage's frame."

"Not so sure about that. Sorry, but I was born cautious."

"The Old Kingdoms in their current state shouldn't be able to set up a full travel blockade. Even after gathering all these soldiers here, they haven't placed the city under martial law. They don't have enough sway to do that. They're nothing compared to what the New Principality was like under Taren the Punished's command."

Kuuro could tell that Elea the Red Tag had some thoughts of her own regarding the New Principality's downfall. Nevertheless, he knew it wasn't something he should pry into too deeply.

The carriage continued down on the road with Togie City at their backs. The city was surrounded by woodlands, but on their right-hand side a wide marsh dominated the scenery. Deviating from the road, they continued on into the middle of the swampy mire.

"…Still, Seventeenth Minister. You're still one of the Twenty-Nine Officials at the end of the day. What were you planning to do if those guys on our heels did catch up to us? My skills aren't capable of taking a couple hundred opponents on at once."

"Would you believe me if I simply said that I prepared to make sure that didn't happen?"

"And those measures would be enough to beat back two hundred soldiers?"

"……"

"Then, what about out our safe passage through the swamp? You know the reason why there are no roads or checkpoints along this area, don't you? It's wurm territory. If we're unlucky, this whole carriage will get swallowed up in one bite."

Even now, he had a bolt loaded into the crossbow hidden up his sleeve. However.

"Does the person in the cargo bed have something to do with it?"

"Ha-ha, the stories of that legendary clairvoyance were true, weren't they?"

An elegant smile appeared on Elea's face.

It was impossible to mobilize a large bodyguard force when not infiltrating an enemy city. However, the total weight limits this carriage structure could handle left room for one additional person, even when factoring in Kuuro's added weight.

Additionally, this carriage had *already come through* this stretch of marsh on the first half of the trip.

The splashing sound of the carriage wheels brushing the swamp echoed.

...Deep, even breathing. Shifted their weight. The sound of something hitting the floor... A shoulder, not a foot. Sleep.

A bodyguard of one of Aureatia's Twenty-Nine Officials, sleeping in enemy territory?

They're sleeping.

There was no longer any question in his mind—there was no other path available to Kuuro than yielding to Aureatia.

Supposing that right now, he fatally shot Elea the Red Tag. With Kuuro the Cautious's skills, he could do it in the space of a single breath, without even making a sound. He could most likely end the life of the driver, who was undoubtedly also a spy, without them realizing anything that was going on. Despite that, he was certain he couldn't react faster than the *sleeping* person in the cargo bed.

From the moment he snuck into this carriage, Kuuro had felt a foreboding premonition.

"Kuuro?"

At Cuneigh's words, Kuuro shifted his senses elsewhere. There was another threat from outside the carriage closing in.

"I know... A wurm's headed our way, Seventeenth Minister. Things are playing out exactly as I feared."

Looking outside the carriage, a torso, thicker than a thousand tree trunks put together and seemingly infinite in length, split through the surface before winding itself back into the ground.

It possessed neither wings nor limbs. Its evolution, progressing in the exact opposite direction of the wyvern, allowed for larger dragonkin to spend their lives underground. Its skull, which it used to dig into the hard-packed earth, was as dense as a dragon's scales. Similar to the principles that governed a dragon's breath, it could maintain Force Arts by vibrating its cranium.

Moving through the ground at will, as though swimming, and ravenously hunting for prey—these were the wurms. Only about one in twenty sightings happened so close to populated areas. Without question, this was a spot of bad luck.

"...Can you take watch over the backside of the carriage, Cuneigh?"

Kuuro muttered. He was tirelessly checking the mechanisms of his crossbow to prevent any kind of malfunction.

The bolt he loaded into the crossbow was not one used for assassinations, but a wooden-shafted bolt for sniping. Sitting in his head, Cuneigh worriedly looked up at him.

"What are you going to do?"

"When it opens its mouth, I might be able to shoot the nerve ganglion deep inside its throat. Even if I can't kill it, I think I'll still inflict enough pain to stop it in its tracks for a short while. The inside of a wurm's mouth is pretty tough, too, but... Either way, I'll just have to do what I can."

The wurm's silhouette drew close. Their enemy had clearly become aware of the carriage.

"No, Kuuro the Cautious."

Elea murmured.

"That won't be necessary."

There was an explosive rupturing sound.

The sound of a foot stepping forward. The recoil from the person in the cargo bed jumping into the air sent the back part of the carriage sinking deep into the ground.

It was a man wearing red clothes, unlike anything Kuuro had ever seen before. A dull practice sword was slung atop his shoulders.

The man clearly shouted out just two simple words.

"Killin' time!"

He sped through the swamp like a stone skipping across a lake. The wurm turned its colossal head toward him. There was a splash. He instantly pinpointed the locations of the wurm's lightning-fast fangs and dodged them with a leap. The wholly unfamiliar figure in red clothes made a half-spin in midair. Mid-spin, the man's shoulder collided with the wurm's scales. The blade dangling behind him wasn't keeping up with the man's own dexterous movements. However, this was all on purpose. He was building up strength like a wound spring.

The blade, which had been poised the whole time it was slung behind his back, released that pent-up energy from extremely close range.

The silver flash arced in a semicircle.

Before its body hit the ground, the wurm's scales were cut through to the flesh beneath. The wound was a fourth of the way down its body from the base of its head.

"...There's the heart."

Kuuro shuddered. Even with most of the wurm's body underground, unable to see its entire form, he was sure. The beating sound of the wurm's heartbeat was irregular. He could tell, even from this distance.

He couldn't believe the feat was something the minian, or any person of this world, could possibly try to match.

That blade length... At that distance, the slash that came right as their bodies came together should've barely been in range. Even then, it was enough to injure the relatively tiny right atrium. Not only that, but...

The swordsman landed on the ground and once again hoisted his blade over his shoulder.

The wurm stopped moving, and there was a pause—a single beat.

Its heart, with its extremely small yet fatal injury, burst open under the colossal body's blood pressure, and rivers of red gushing laterally like a crimson waterfall stained the marsh.

"Boooring. It was nowhere near the challenge I thought it'd be, c'mon."

Kuuro could hear his frustrated muttering, not directed at anyone in particular.

I can tell. That was this guy's first time killing a wurm. Like my clairvoyance, he was able to locate his heart from the outside...and instantly pieced together a plan to slice it open.

"Soujirou the Willow-Sword. That's his name."

Elea mumbled next to Kuuro.

"Aureatia requires fighting strength. Strength like *yours and his.*"

These people...

The New Principality of Lithia was no more. The official story given was that it happened in a great conflagration caused by their wyverns going out of control.

Old Kingdoms' loyalists. The Free City of Okahu. In this age, where many threats had been destroyed by the True Demon King, there now remained only a few rivals to threaten Aureatia.

The royal games...

What was Aureatia's purpose behind consolidating these abnormal and irregular abilities?

In the Queen's name, a great tournament to determine a single Hero was about to begin.

They needed to host the tournament without interference.

They're intending with this next phase to clean up all of their opposition.

◆

Several days later in Aureatia, a figure in a dark brown coat traversed through the amber lamplight.

He was noticeably shorter than the other minian people around him, and the being he embraced in his arms was even smaller than that.

The bustling streets, far more bright and cheerful than those in Togie City, were filled with numerous conversations, bustling footsteps, and shadows perfect for an ambush. These were the only things Kuuro the Cautious picked out from the scene of the busy avenues.

"You enjoy the Aureatian play?"

"...Kuuro, you slept the whole time."

"Hey, I was awake. I can't react to a surprise attack if I let myself fall asleep completely."

"Are plays not fun for you? What about singing? Food?"

"What's any of that got to do with me? You're the one who said you wanted to see a play."

Kuuro employed the small homunculus girl. Given that she was unable to show herself in front of other people, giving her a monetary reward was meaningless, and Kuuro tried to give her whatever she asked for as much as possible. Including a request to see a play together.

"It's just, you only ever eat food that's cheaper than mine, and you never smile, so I thought about what might make you happy..."

"Being alive makes me happy."

Kuuro had no pride left. He had left Obsidian Eyes and kept a low profile in Togie City to make sure no one knew he was there, and now that Aureatia had discovered him, he obeyed them. There was a chance that if he was told to sell Cuneigh to them, he would go right ahead and do so.

Death was terrifying. It was the end of everything.

He remembered the scenery he had seen with his immensely powerful clairvoyance.

"...I know. No matter how much fun you have, no matter how lavishly you live, death comes for all, and swiftly at that. I've...always lived my life on the razor's edge. That's just how it's always been."

He had no ties to Cuneigh outside of their employment arrangement. There was no past relationship, nor did he remember ever doing her a favor to be repaid. After he broke away from Obsidian Eyes, he had encountered her by coincidence. But now, Kuuro couldn't help but depend on Cuneigh.

Everything he gave her was not because he cherished her. It was solely out of fear of betrayal.

"There's no longer any clairvoyance in me."

Assassinating important figures. Massacre as a diversionary tactic. Incinerating villages where the Demon King's Army had spread.

He could still recall all the scenes he had witnessed with his all-sensing and wide-reaching clairvoyance.

Being ordered around by an organization, urged on by the terror of the True Demon King—he was fed up with it all.

Living in constant fear of death and stealing to survive had worn Kuuro's spirit down.

He didn't want to see people die. He didn't want to hear their screams. And so it was. From around the time he passed age twenty-one, Kuuro had slowly been losing his clairvoyant perception.

He couldn't tell whether or not there was an ambush ahead.

He hadn't sensed the movements when the wurm was closing in.

Though he possessed senses far keener than the average person, the world Kuuro saw now was no longer the same rich and robust world he had felt in the past. He had lost the delicacy that could once individually identify grains of gravel, and he could only follow movements outside of his line of sight by concentrating all his focus on them.

Continuing onward, he had arrived at a large bridge outside of town. A world for him and him alone. By now, these were the only sorts of places that would bring Kuuro the Cautious any comfort.

Kuuro placed his hands on the railing and stared at the city lights.

"...Cuneigh."

Cuneigh was not unhappy. The lifespan of a homunculus was particularly short, with even the most generous estimate giving her only five years to live. If she died, what would happen to Kuuro?

To him, Cuneigh's was an existence he should have loathed most of all, and also the one most necessary to him.

"I've got a hunch. A hunch that everything will be for naught."

Ultimate clairvoyance. That was all in the past.

It was withering away to the point that he needed to leave all observations outside his immediate focus in the hands of this small homunculus.

Nevertheless, though he could no longer be certain about this vague threatening premonition, he had no choice but to trust it.

"Something awful is about to happen."

There were thirty-eight days left until the disaster's arrival.

Mercantile complexes that clustered several storefronts together were growing in popularity. The building's interior, covered by a wide ceiling, was illuminated by the warm glow of the lamps now that the sun had set—just in time for the opening of the late-night businesses.

"In our world these are colloquially referred to as 'muskets.'"

Situated in one corner of the marketplace, a very young boy lined up small firearms before the leading figures of the Commerce Guild.

He was a peculiar boy.

Outwardly, he looked to be around thirteen years old, but his hair was an ashen gray dusted with white. He wore a suit and tie, as if playing pretend grown-up, yet the look suited him, oddly enough.

"To be precise, the term *musket* was the name given to them when they were developed nine years ago. As of six years ago, they had already been improved with added spiral grooves carved inside the barrel to rotate the bullet, but guns built with this structure are called 'rifles' in the Beyond. Given that the name *musket* has been well-established, this is nothing but useless trivia. However, I believe if you take a look at the newest models' performance, you'll quickly understand for yourself."

The attendant standing next to the boy was just as short as, if not shorter than, him. While they did almost appear to be a leprechaun, their whole body was cloaked in a robe, their true form unclear.

The attendant brandished the musket and pulled the trigger. The gunshot rang out, and the distant wooden target board fell to the ground.

"...As you can see, even someone with a childlike physique can fire it. With enough target practice, from firepower, to reload speed and shooting range.... I believe you'll see this serve as an effective means of attack, superior to someone of the same build wielding a bow. Up until now I've limited my dealings to a select clientele, but going forward, I would like to expand our market to those of you gathered here."

"Hmmm. We wouldn't need to rely on black market goods from Aureatia merchants anymore."

"No point in using firearms unless you have a bunch of them, after all. If we could get these new models sold to us wholesale on top of our existing deals, well, we couldn't ask for anything better."

"I heard this from a wyvern-hunting friend of mine, but they said that Alus the Star Runner, the one that got Toroa the Awful, uses firearms as well. We can promote 'em by saying you can win against an enchanted sword if you use 'em right."

"That's an intriguing idea. Rosclay, Aureatia's strongest, uses a sword, right?"

"Are you suggesting that with a gun, even those Old Kingdoms' folks could win against Rosclay the Absolute? That's gonna sound like a load of nonsense no matter how you try to explain it. Give it up."

Handling a weapon loaded with live ammunition while

standing in front of the masters of the guild—it was a testament to the rapport the boy had built up with them over a long period of time.

"…What's the main business opportunity, then?"

One among them, a fattened merchant, raised his hand.

"If we don't have any leads on a market, no matter how cheaply we can buy these weapons, we wouldn't be able to sell them to anybody. Right now those Old Kingdoms' folks seem to be all worked up, but I, at the very least, don't think they really plan on starting a large war. The way I see it, the Old Kingdoms' soldiers aren't as skilled as the New Principality's were. Hell, even *they're* smart enough not to waste everything by gambling on a losing battle just because they've got numbers on their side."

"Thank you for that comment. You bring up an excellent point."

The boy nodded. The question was exactly what he had been expecting.

"Of course, I think there is a business opportunity here. In truth, ever since General Gilnes arrived in Togie City, the population of the Old Kingdoms has been booming. However, taking into account the time and money spent training such a large number of soldiers, there's no mistaking that the Old Kingdoms' soldiers are lacking in conventional tactical strategy and advanced coordination. You're absolutely right."

His speech was smooth and fluent. The boy had a grasp of the internal conditions among the Old Kingdoms' loyalists. They were also important trading partners of his.

"However, muskets are, without a doubt, exactly what such an army needs. Wieldable even with a childlike physique, and easier to train with than any other weapon. Additionally, completely unlike bows, whose effective range is decided by the user's muscular strength and technique, a gun's power is determined entirely by the performance of the weapon."

Together with a light click, the young attendant pulled the breechblock and ejected the spent shell casing. This was known as "bolt action."

"The Old Kingdoms' loyalists already have strength in numbers. If they collected the newest models, they could gain the upper hand. I believe that to them, this could prove to be a factor that pushes them toward war with Aureatia."

"Heh, I see," the fat merchant muttered with a hand to his chin.

"So, you're suggesting we sell them to the Old Kingdoms under that pretense then?"

"Once again, that's exactly right. This same logic would apply to Aureatia's side as well. If Aureatia deployed the same new model of firearms, at the very least, they would lose their dominant position on the front lines. In other words, you employ these new models, and you have both powers preparing themselves for war. Both of these occurrences are would-be business opportunities, and I believe both are not without their uncertainties. Regardless of whether or not war actually breaks out, I'd like you all to take this golden opportunity to *sell at a profit while you can*. That is precisely why this time, I've made the decision to expand my sales to intermediaries, such as yourselves."

Underneath the lamplight, the guild dignitaries stirred, exchanging opinions in hushed voices.

"The Old Kingdoms *are* a rather large market."

"Still, Aureatia's army already has plenty of archers, and given that they already have quite the collection of guns, they won't go out of their way to spend time on training with the latest models. If they were going to do it, they'd probably introduce them into one of their commando units first."

"Well, I wouldn't be sure about that. Their current combat strength may be enough for the Old Kingdoms, but there's a chance they could introduce the newer models as a precaution against Okahu. There's always a chance they decide to replace all their guns at once, isn't there?"

The boy looked from face to face. In addition to the new-model muskets laid out on the floor, he had already prepared to move a stock of ten thousand additional units. He was confident his negotiations would be successful.

"When all is said and done, we are only selling weapons wholesale. As far as which power should serve as your market, I entrust you all with that decision. What I can say for certain is that there is not much time to delay if you want to turn a profit from this opportunity. The situation is sure to change in a big way, so..."

"...I'll take six hundred units."

"Well, someone's raring to go, aren't they? Why, I'll take two hundred, myself."

"Spare us the snide comments. Just watch us sell a thousand of these things."

"Thank you very much. I look forward to doing business in the future as well."

Leaving the remaining negotiations to his attendant, the gray-haired boy left the scene. The remaining deals would all close favorably without him saying a word.

Up until nine years ago, the weapons known as "guns" hadn't existed in this world. However, with the chaotic era of the True Demon King now over, these new weapons were experiencing an explosive growth in popularity.

◆

...I'd like to employ other elements to blow hostilities wide open, aside from the new gun models. One more push should do it.

The boy left the warmth of the lamplights and walked out to the dry riverbed. The nights of the Sikma Spinning Ward were plenty bright, but they were still nothing compared to the luminance of the world he once knew.

I need some more new developments. There is still room for progress to be made... This world has possibilities.

Any profits earned from his firearm deals were nothing more than a single part of preparation for his goal. What he aimed for was a much more long-term prosperity for many more people.

"Yo."

A voice came from the darkness of the dry riverbed and in walked a man with a large build.

He was dressed in dingy clothes, wholly different from the wealthy merchants' moments prior. With an intimidating machete attached to his hip, he was cloaked in a threatening aura. One look made it clear he was some sort of bandit.

The young boy opposite him wasn't even accompanied by a bodyguard. He appeared to be nothing more than a petite child.

He turned his gaze to the bandit and smiled.

"...You're right on time, Erijite."

"Whatcha mean? This is a deal with the *master*, after all. Didja think about what I said?"

"It shouldn't be a problem at all."

The boy sat on the ground, thick with weeds. Exactly as when he had been meeting with the merchants, he didn't ingratiate himself with the man. In contrast to the age suggested by his outward appearance, he left an impression of wisdom and maturity.

"However, this is all assuming that your band of thieves is able to get it done under the conditions I've set. In the last dispute, two people died, which I believe makes exactly four deaths total. Do you think you can do it?"

"Yeah, we'll steal Toroa the Awful's enchanted swords. If you've finished preparing the connections on your end, then we're ready to move whenever. We want to get recommendations to join the Old Kingdoms' folks. No matter how many enchanted swords we can get our hands on, we're still nothing but common outlaws."

"Understood. I'll work things over with the Old Kingdoms."

"...We're counting on you. You're just about the only one who understands guys like us."

It was believed that Toroa the Awful was dead.

The world was entering an age where even champions could die. In such a case, the truly powerful needed to have a means to ensure their continued survival. Weapons. Connections. Strategies.

"Erijite. Here."

The boy tossed a small item to the large man. It was a proto-type he had kept secret during the earlier business negotiations.

"...What's this?"

"We've recently developed it. It's a low-caliber gun. Once the chaos of war dies down, then it'll come time to carry firearms for self-defense, you see. I'm sure with your skills, you'll be able to use it well."

"Heh, a bit careless, don't you think? Should you really be handing a weapon to an outlaw like me?"

"...That doesn't concern me. Equality, on the other hand..."

The young boy smiled.

"Soon, we will enter an age where everyone is equal."

A majority of the manufacturing industry in this world consisted of domestic handicrafts that relied on skilled artisans. Artisans with expert Craft Arts could construct even the most complex of mechanical goods. However, the highly advanced manufacturing techniques needed to produce guns in large quantities and under the same specifications were still unknown.

There was no one who had successfully discovered where in the world the Gray-Haired Child's production facilities were or how he was manufacturing his goods.

Others spread rumors that he was importing his goods directly from the Beyond.

He was a visitor, after all.

...If Erijite is successful, then there will be a large number of enchanted sword wielders joining up with the Old Kingdoms. Once that happens, I should have created enough of a catalyst to spark the fires of war.

What truly lay at the end of all this *was not a war.*

It was ruin itself, spreading death far and wide, and leaving nothing but devastation in its wake. No one—not Aureatia, nor the Old Kingdoms' loyalists, nor even the Gray-Haired Child— knew of the encroaching calamity. It was on a scale exceeding any and all estimations.

On second thought, there's one more move to make.

Guns. Enchanted swords.

By granting the Old Kingdoms' loyalists the final piece, they would open hostilities with Aureatia.

But his true objective lay beyond even that.

There were twenty-six days left until the disaster's arrival.

CHAPTER 5 — The Great Bank City of Lithia

There used to be a large metropolitan city called the New Principality of Lithia.

With an enormous wyvern air force at her back, the independent nation established by Taren the Punished was annihilated in a single night as a result of their war with Aureatia. Officially, its ruin had come at the hands of a massive conflagration.

The sections that suffered damage in the conflict were still slowly being restored under Aureatia, but the wyvern soldiers' spires, now with no one to make use of them, were left behind as a peculiar part of the town's scenery.

Although the New Principality army Taren commanded was disbanded, she had still left a large impact, and to Aureatia, Lithia continued to be a dissident element they couldn't ignore.

"And that's why you were sent out here to monitor us; is that it, Kuuro?"

An ogre looked down over the city from a room in one of the spires. He was a former soldier of the New Principality who went by the name Zizma the Miasma.

The difference in build between him and Kuuro the Cautious, sitting down close to the door, was even more stark than between an adult and child.

"No, of course not. I don't plan on spending a long time here.

I was just the best person to come talk to you—given our old friendship."

Zizma the Miasma had another career in his past. There was a time when he worked as an intelligence agent with the spy guild Obsidian Eyes, just like Kuuro.

"What I want to know is where the New Principality army wandered off to. I've heard after the great fire, a not-insignificant number of soldiers drifted over to the Old Kingdoms. I wanted to hear all the details."

"Pfft, ha-ha."

The ogre scoffed.

"The clairvoyant Kuuro, coming out and *asking* for info? Almost like a detective. Nothing like how we used to...how Obsidian Eyes used to do things."

"I *am* a detective," Kuuro replied, irritated.

With his former talents, he could've known everything there was to know while sitting in the spire. Now things were different. He had to ask for information directly.

"Those Aureatia guys, well...they think someone's vouching for those guys. There were some in the New Principality from the beginning who had ties with the Old Kingdoms' side of things, so goods and soldiers were flowing between the two."

"There're some real idiots out there. Even if they're both against Aureatia, the Old Kingdoms are rigid in their dedication to the royal monarchy, and the New Principality was all about anti-minian rhetoric—basically the exact opposites of each other... Though some of them still went over there, huh? A bunch of ideologically inconsistent fools that don't give a damn as long as they get to war against the Aureatia they hate so much."

"...There isn't anyone out there that can wage war with logic. Anyone would try to take back something stolen from them.

There's gotta be some of them that think they deserve some sort of reward for New Principality's sacrifice."

"What about us? We put our lives on the line to fight, and were we ever rewarded with anything?"

"......"

"Lana the Moon Tempest died. She was in a miserable rotting heap on the outskirts of the city. I buried her, but I later heard that she had been an Aureatia collaborator. What was Obsidian Eyes, anyway? What happened to all those ideals we touted? Were we just simpletons? Useless without war? Killing for the sake of killing?"

During the age of the True Demon King, as the largest spy guild, they were roped into wars in every region, continuously fighting without any regard for the powers they were affiliated with. This wasn't only the case for the ogre, Zizma. Both Lana and Kuuro were people unable to live in the bright open world. They were soldiers of the shadows who thrived during times of war.

Equality among all classes of people, regardless of appearance or race. They believed that during war, where all life is stolen equality, they instead might be able to make this ideal a reality.

"For the monstrous races, eating people is a way of life. There's nothing I can do about that. The minian races expelled the goblins from this world, and now they're trying to do the same to us ogres. I...at the very least, I fought for a world where I could live a proper life. Guess that was a meaningless fight in the end."

"...We lost. You lost, and I lost, too. In every fight, there is a winner and loser. If you're thinking of taking it all out on me, you picked the wrong guy."

"You hate fighting, then, Kuuro?"

Zizma pulled out his weapon. A deeply curved, sickle-like blade.

"I thought that you and Lana were both comrades. But in the end, *you people* are still minian races in the end. You're exactly right. The New Principality lost, and you people won. Whether the Old Kingdoms wins or Aureatia wins, it's all the same to me now."

"...I'm sick and tired of this."

Kuuro lowered his eyes. He had determined the intelligence agent who had connections to the Old Kingdoms' loyalist. Nevertheless, putting down Zizma here wasn't going to solve a damn thing.

"Too late for that now. The weight of the lives you stole is enough to drag you to the pits of hell."

Zizma's slash didn't come. Kuuro clicked his heels. Though the color in the air didn't change, he sensed that the transmission of sound had sped up, ever so slightly. This was because the composition of gases in the air had changed.

"...Poison, then? You've changed up the mixture from what you used before."

"You're slow on the uptake, Kuuro."

Zizma himself was also engulfed in the gaseous poison. Even if he exposed himself to the same gas, the effective doses of poison for an ogre and a leprechaun were vastly different. With his opponent first to have the poison flowing through his veins, he then relied on his ogreish vitality to force them into a fight and kill them—such was Zizma's modus operandi.

"That clairvoyance talent of yours faded away, huh?"

The sickle blade glinted. The ogre, with his long arms and legs, was in range to kill Kuuro instantly. Now, engulfed in poison, he was blocked off from the basic breathing necessary to move to the counterattack.

Zizma stepped forward. Kuuro could see everything.

"Say that again."

A bolt pierced Zizma's eyeball.

It happened in an instant.

Kuuro's hand was already finished with its follow-through.

"One more time, go ahead."

"...Hngh, augh..."

"My clairvoyance has what now?"

Even when confronting a hardened master of combat face-to-face, he could deliver a surprise attack. Perceiving every single iota of the opponent's behavior, he recognized the exact moment when the ogre would be unable to react. This was clairvoyance.

"Hrng... Keh-heh-heh... Don't be so mad. That was just a joke, Kuuro."

Zizma chuckled in self-deprecation, his eye having been fatally pierced through.

With his back against the wall, he slid down to sit on the floor.

"...Winning against you...? I w-would've never even dreamed of it..."

"...What are the Old Kingdoms planning?"

He couldn't step inside the room filled with poison gas. Kuuro kept his crossbow trained on Zizma as he questioned him.

"I've intercepted communications from the frontier. Am I the only one worried about this? I've got a bad feeling... A feeling that all our efforts will amount to nothing."

"I couldn't tell you one way or another. They don't tell me anything..."

The ogre murmured vacantly. The age had come where even former Obsidian Eyes comrades fought against one another.

"No one trusts any of us monstrous races."

"......"

Zizma's labored breaths and weakened heartbeats both came to a stop. All five of Kuuro's senses perceived the truth of his passing.

There was nothing else for them to discuss. From the very beginning, this was how things were fated to end.

Clenching his jaw, he turned away from Zizma.

I'm fed up.

He longed for a life in which his hands weren't constantly stained with blood.

...Who am I to even say that?

More than anything else, he was scared. If people knew he truly had lost his clairvoyance, death would find him soon enough. His usefulness to Aureatia...and his ability to survive on the battlefield were both owed to his clairvoyance.

He could only live through killing and inciting fear. With his clairvoyance, he should have had a whole host of possibilities before him, but this was the only way he ever used it.

Zizma, who had killed in order to eat minians, was a considerably finer person than he.

◆

"Kuuro!"

Exiting the spire, Cuneigh fluttered up and dived inside Kuuro's coat.

It had been necessary to have her keep watch over the entrance. While he was engaged with a master hand from Obsidian Eyes, in his current state, he couldn't keep his focus on constant lookout for other intruders.

People hired with money would eventually turn the knife on you. Even longtime comrades wound up killing each other sooner or later.

Silly little Cuneigh was the only companion he could trust.

"No one came by at all! Hey. You got to talk with your old friend, right?"

"Yeah. He was one of those friends I never quite saw eye-to-eye with, though."

He could feel the quick pulse in Cuneigh's hands—a reminder of her fragile lifespan.

If Kuuro was in her position, he would probably be terrified of being squeezed to a pulp within her grasp. She should've feared that she would one day outlive her usefulness and end up betrayed.

"I need to reward you for being a good lookout. What would you like?"

"Hmm, I want to eat hawthorn berries. Is that okay?"

"Is that really all you want?"

Kuuro chuckled dryly. If it kept her from betraying him, he wouldn't begrudge her asking for jewels or paintings, and yet she only ever requested the simplest rewards.

He was a man capable of killing his former comrades. Kuuro's true nature was one of brutality and mercilessness, but perhaps Cuneigh's childishness was what allowed her to keep placing her trust in someone like him.

"I envy you..."

"Hm?"

"Never mind. It's not important."

There were eleven days left until the disaster's arrival.

"D-dammit, what... What the hell's with all this...?"

Surveying the miserable state of the army base, Bihat the Outstanding Tool groaned. It was the supply base on the outskirts of Togie City. Even for a high-ranking Old Kingdoms' officer like himself, who had engaged in a number of military operations in the past, he had never seen such an instance of a rearguard camp being hit with such a destructive raid.

"Over half the soldiers stationed here confirmed dead. Enormous damages to resource storehouses... All of it was true? Th-this is a helluva lot worse...than what the report said, right?"

Bihat timidly walked through the ocean of blood. In truth, it was in a dire state.

The foul odors mixing together made his back tremble. The corpses of soldiers with more than half their bodies missing littered the ground. The lack of a sharply cut cross section suggested the impact from a high-speed blow was the cause of death.

Examining one corpse's cross section, he questioned his assistant.

"...This here. Is this what happens when an ogre punches you? Are there any records of a gang of them being let through a checkpoint?"

"According to the report...the enemy was airborne. That would mean it was a direct attack from the sky, but..."

"Don't be ridiculous. You think a flying enemy could do *this* to someone? What was it then, a dragon? Impossible."

"What about Alus the Star Runner, who joined up with Aureatia? Or worst-case scenario, Second General Rosclay... Rosclay the Absolute might have carried out the attack directly... I mean, they say he managed to slay a dragon all by himself."

Holding back his urge to vomit, Bihat pointed out the corpses stuck to the roof.

"Mnghh... I think I'm gonna be sick. There's nothing efficient or planned about that method of killing. Our enemy's no warrior."

"...And by that...?"

"They might have been testing the limits of their power. The people outside weren't slowly killed by the blast, either. Basically, look... That explains why some bodies have been ripped to shreds. Some of them were thrown up against the walls and the ceiling. Sheesh..."

"B-But, wait...! If someone can do something this messed up just to test their strength, then that makes it all the more likely some monster did this."

"...It's gotta be a monster. When I heard the report, I had thought it was some Aureatia army sabotage, but..."

This base hadn't only stored the new model guns delivered days prior, but also kept other rare items including several magic tools. Although the gun storage had been dispersed to a number of different places, included among the stolen items was Charijisuya the Blasting Blade, the Old Kingdom army's trump card.

There was no doubt the damages would have a profound effect on the war situation. Supposing Bihat had commanding authority over military operations, the results here would have put any imminent actions on hold.

"Yikes. General Bihat, this body..."

"...Burned to death, looks like. There are cracks in the bones. The heat must've been incredibly intense. Could the enemy use Thermal Arts? There's no way they meaninglessly shot fire everywhere after they were done killing, right...?"

When he turned his eyes elsewhere, he realized there were other strange corpses as well.

It was still the same wanton destruction, but this wasn't the result of direct blows as before. The wall behind one corpse was riddled with bullet holes.

"No. No, no, no, give me a break... I'm about ready to lose my mind here."

"Several dozen enemies...circled around him and all fired at once, maybe? A battalion of ogre soldiers capable of using Thermal Arts flew in from the sky, punching and gunning everyone down, perhaps?"

"We might as well consider that a possibility at this point. There are too many unknown variables to suggest some invincible monster just swooped in and did...all of this," Bihat replied, continuing to rummage through the debris for evidence.

"If someone was capable of spraying this much gunfire, that should have been more than enough to wipe out all the guards here. When there's this much of a power gap, it doesn't make any sense to go out of your way to punch them, burn them, and decorate the battlefield with this much gore."

"So, when you mentioned an inefficient method of killing... this was what you meant."

"That's right."

One thing was certain. The enemy wasn't a martial expert. The destruction was absolute, but unrefined. That fact only served to make the situation even more perplexing.

"There were two enemies."

Bihat smacked the ground with a branch.

"Are those the enemies' tracks?"

"Probably. They look to be going against the flow of all the soldiers running to escape. A dwarf or an ogre, maybe—something with a massive body. The footprints are deep, so they must've been wearing some sort of heavy armor. On the other hand, these footprints belong to someone small and petite. Likely a young girl."

"You're telling me an ogre and a little girl did all this?"

Bihat followed the footprints. The fleeting vestiges of the massacre at the hands of some unidentified monsters.

"...And, here, the damn things totally disappear. I figured as much, given they can fly and all."

"I-If this was really an attack by Aureatia...there's basically no way we can fight back against this, is there?! Ugh, the damn rear encampment is supposed to be safe from harm. What are we even supposed to be on the lookout for...?"

"I don't have any answers, either. If they're hitting us back here before the war's even kicked off, I'd say we're in a really bad situation."

As his assistant said, the possibility that the rear encampment could be hit with a sudden direct attack would become an even bigger threat to their forces than their loss of goods.

Nevertheless, the top brass was unlikely to call off their opposition. He would just have to do his best.

"...Given that they raided the relatively weakly defended supply base, it might mean our enemy's trying to make it hard for us to pursue them. They really did kill all the damn eyewitnesses. I'm going to use this incident as a bargaining chip to pressure the city council. We need to double our reconnaissance efforts and blockade Togie City."

"U-Understood...sir."

The soldiers who had joined up with them from the New

Principality of Lithia would talk about it in secret. When their country fell, they witnessed multiple eccentric, deviant, and monstrous beings in the chaos.

A young messenger dashed in from the entrance, but they retched upon being met with the stench of blood and entrails.

"General Bihat! *Koff, koff, urgh...* We've gotten testimony from a survivor."

"I know this scene's pretty harsh. Just try to take a load off. I'll wait for the report, so drink some of your canteen."

"*Koff,* forgive me, General. It's regarding the enemy's infiltration route, sir."

"I know about that. The guy that reported to us only told us that they came from the sky. Anything else?"

"Well...this next bit of information came right before the speaker lost consciousness, so I wasn't able to ask them to clarify. But...they said the enemy was a demon king's soldier. I-it was a g-giant...monster."

"...A demon king."

It went without saying, but they couldn't possibly be referring to the True Demon King. Otherwise, the way the victims died would've been *so much worse.*

So which self-proclaimed demon king was responsible for this? Everything from their method of infiltration to their means of attack was impossible to decipher.

"What should we do? Do you think we can win a war with Aureatia in this condition?"

"It's too late to put things off now... We can win. We should be able to."

The soldiers there didn't know the whole strategic picture that the army's leaders were currently advancing along. They had long ago factored in the fighting strength of the shura at Aureatia's command. Even if Aureatia was indeed aware of this strategy, it was already too late for them to try to defend against it.

"These men's lives... Dammit, we'll immediately turn the tables and get revenge for their sacrifice."

True calamity, enough to make even gut-wrenching slaughter like this no more than a portent of what was to come.

"The storm's coming."

There were six days left until the disaster's arrival.

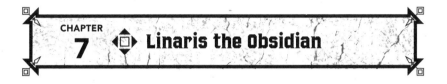

CHAPTER 7 ◆ Linaris the Obsidian

It was back before the assault on Togie City, four short months prior.

Itaaki Highland City, home of Sirok the Sextant, was cold and dreary, blanketed in cloudy weather year-round.

It wasn't a poor city. The region, with its clear waters and yields of high-quality radzio ore, was a high-class vacation home destination, up until they were all abandoned in the face of the True Demon King's invasion, and it used to be quite active and prosperous.

Now, it was as though a thin black curtain was draped over all the scenery. The people on the streets constantly felt the weight of this invisible black curtain, with the colorful goods displayed in the market, too, looking faded through its veil.

It may have been an effect of the True Demon King's terror, still lingering in the world.

Or perhaps…it was the shadow of Sirok's own mind, having once sworn in his young heart he would retake his city from the Demon King, only for his own strength to prove insufficient to grant his wish.

After making it through the city streets, he looked at his destination.

That's a big mansion.

The residence rose up from its hidden spot amid the dense, dark forest. He felt it didn't fit the scenery surrounding it.

Though it may have been an aristocrat's secondary home, there didn't seem to be any good reason to construct a house in a place so difficult to get to, and which received so little sunlight. Though there was ivy crawling up the outer walls and gate, given its location, it would have been impossible to show off the house's fine craftsmanship to anyone in the first place.

I'd be surprised if there was even anyone living here...

Sirok had been hired by the adults to get a clear census of the residents who had returned to the mountain.

It wasn't a particularly strenuous job. His youthful stamina and the leg muscles he had built up in his eighteen years as a warrior proved very useful as he roamed up and down the Itaaki Highlands.

Although it wasn't his preferred way of life, this was his reality now. All that his parents left behind for him was the enormous house his grandfather had once been gifted by a noble.

I need to finish up the mountain area fast. I still have to cover the foot of the mountain, too.

Consequently, Sirok then peeked inside for just a moment through a gap in the gate and planned to label the place uninhabited and be on his way.

"...Oh."

In other words, he hadn't thought about what he'd do if there was a person on the other side.

A well-kept garden stretched on the other side of the gate, its paint beginning to flake away, and there, in full bloom, were a number of beautiful pruned black roses.

Standing among them was a young girl.

In front of one of the rose bushes, she was gracefully crouched down while trimming their leaves.

A dense, dark forest. Roses as black as the dead of night.

Yet looking at the young girl's profile...her breathtakingly pale skin was enough to shine through the dark curtain.

...A person. Did she always live here? Or did she wander in and settle down?

She looked to be sixteen or seventeen years old—nearly the same age as Sirok.

Nevertheless, her beauty made him question if she was a figment of his imagination.

The smooth nape of her neck peeked out from her downturned black hair. Long eyelashes, tinged with melancholy. Pupils colored gold.

...Those pupils happened to turn toward Sirok.

A brief, heart-stopping moment passed.

The young girl smiled.

"...Um, I-I've been tasked by the council of lords to verify all our residents..."

Immediately, an excuse forced its way out of his mouth.

That wasn't his reason for looking at the girl moments prior. Sirok was ashamed of himself.

"Oh, is that so?"

Her smile exceedingly delicate, she walked up to Sirok, who had remained rooted to his spot in front of the gate. Sirok's heart was deeply captivated by the girl's floral fragrance; she was a pale blossom made flesh.

"How do you do? My name is Linaris. Might I have yours?"

"S-Sirok...the Sextant. You're the person living here...right?"

"......"

Linaris didn't answer. Something else appeared to have caught her attention.

She slightly knitted her well-kept eyebrows and placed a finger to her pale lips.

"I do beg your pardon...but it seems you've been injured."

".......Huh?"

Following her gaze, Sirok finally became aware of the blood trickling down his left middle finger.

A sharp cut. He had either scratched it on the edge of the iron gate, or he had pricked it on a thorn of one of the roses wound around it. He had been so enthralled by the young girl's appearance that he hadn't even noticed the pain in his finger.

"Oh, no, my apologies...! But this cut isn't really worth worrying about..."

"Please, come inside the mansion so I may treat it."

"I'm fine, really."

"...Should one of the roses I raised prove to have injured you, Master Sirok, why, I would be unable to face your parents or your employer... I ask that you please reconsider my offer."

Faced with the fixed stare of her gold pupils, Sirok was unable to answer her.

She appeared to take his silence as affirmation and smiled.

Together with a light metallic creak, the gate separating the two of them opened.

I'm just here to verify residents. There's absolutely no need for me to go inside...

Sirok hesitated, flickering his eyes back and forth between the girl and the path he traveled to get there.

This house was his only major excursion for the day. All of the other homes he could verify on his way back.

Not only that, but...if he was going to confirm whether anyone was living here or not, then an argument could be made to properly see for himself who else was living in this old mansion.

"Okay. I can't stay for long, but if that's fine with you..."

"...Indeed, I would most appreciate it. I shall prepare the finest amber tea for you."

Following after Linaris, Sirok was finally able to look out over the state of the garden.

It wasn't limited solely to the rusted gate. Cracks stood out in the mansion's old stone walls, and despite the mansion resembling ruins, the garden was carefully maintained, without a single piece of gravel out of place.

The sights around him were adjacent to the part of Itaaki he called home, and yet much like the young girl and her ephemeral beauty, it was so removed from his daily life it seemed otherworldly. Maybe when the girl led him through the door of the mansion, it would lead all the way to the land of the Beyond.

...When had this young girl started living in this lonely mansion? Just who was she?

As though to further pierce Sirok's inner anxieties, Linaris looked back slightly.

With a sidelong glance, her gold eyes met his.

"Please watch your step."

"Y-Yeah, of course."

She hadn't actually read his mind.

Buried partway in the dirt, stone steps led up to the entryway. Sirok crossed over the small step, praying that she didn't sense the sweat on his back—the result of her simply looking at him.

In complete contrast to the exterior, the inside of the mansion was very neat and tidy.

The furniture was scarce, drab, and tasteless, not unlike Sirok's own home.

Also, it was dim and gloomy.

...It should still be the middle of the day right now.

As he made sure of facts that normally needed no confirmation, he hung up his hat.

Were there any other family members living here? He was about to ask Linaris—

"Please, if you'll wait just a moment."

She slid the black cape from her shoulders.

Her previously concealed white blouse exposed, he could now see the full volume of her breasts, straining against the delicate fabric. Sirok was taken aback.

She was the same age as him, if not slightly younger, and yet... Her arms and legs were so slender, and her presence felt almost incorporeal, but more than anything else—

"Is something the matter?"

"...O-oh, no it's nothing."

Linaris applied ointment to Sirok's wound and began wrapping it with a fresh bandage.

Just below his eyeline were her beautiful gold pupils. When he took in her full form, stooped down at his feet, he couldn't stop his mind from wandering down a certain path.

Although he felt frustrated by the thought that he was losing his head over this girl, to Sirok, who had set his heart on the path of the warrior long before he could learn the names of any girls his age, his shock was all but to be expected.

"Excuse me while I prepare some hospitality. It is quite embarrassing, but...this mansion has no servants, you see."

"You mean you're living here by yourself...?"

"......My father is here. Please, Master Sirok, feel free to wait in the sitting room."

Following her request, Sirok sat with nothing to do, enveloped in a sense of guilt, and his heartbeat pounding like an alarm bell in his head.

There was indeed nothing for him to do. Linaris said that her father was in this house.

Through observing her demeanor up until this point, he was able to get a sense of Linaris's lineage and upbringing. They were either the original owners of this vacation home or close relatives of the nobility, who inherited it. In which case, if his beautiful adolescent daughter were to invite a man of low birth like Sirok into his home, what would said father do to him?

Even though he understood he was being excessively self-conscious, he couldn't stop his intrusive thoughts. Moreover, if he let his mind wander, the deluge of mental images of Linaris's beauty and her pale-white skin would all but swallow him whole.

Get a hold of yourself.

He put a finger on the claw-sword suspended from his hip and began to still the waves of his heart with martial concentration.

Get it together, Sirok. You just met this girl. This is all just part of the job.

He wasn't sure if he could keep up this focus until Linaris returned. Either way, it took far longer than he would've imagined to simply prepare some tea.

"My apologies for keeping you waiting. In a dark house like this...you must have been awfully bored."

"...Oh, no, nothing of the sort. It was a sudden visit on my part so it's only natural."

"How kind of you to say. Here you go. The leaves are from Caidehe."

Sirok brought the amber tea up to his lips, but he couldn't really tell the difference in taste... If anything, he felt that the tea he was accustomed to tasted better. He wouldn't dare say this to Linaris, who was quietly staring at him, so he gave his best smile and replied:

"It's delicious."

"Oh, I am very glad... Well, it has been quite a long time since we've had guests. Would you mind if I asked you about yourself, Master Sirok?"

"S-sure. I don't think there's anything interesting to mention, though..."

"Hee-hee. You do yourself a disservice. Well then, when did you make your way back here to Itaaki?"

"About the same time as most of the residents. Immediately after the True Demon King fell. Of course...nothing was left for me besides the house passed down from my ancestors. With my path to distinguishing myself on the battlefield gone, now I work under the council of lords."

"...You followed the path of the sword, then?"

Linaris cast her melancholic eyes down to Sirok's claw-sword.

No matter how deep the forest was, there were no beasts in Itaaki that would willingly attack people. The weapon was not a lifestyle necessity but more of a lingering attachment to an era that was slowly fading away.

The age of stories, desperate for a hero that bestowed the chance to follow the path of the sword to all who desired it.

"It's not a rare thing among men. With the Demon King gone, with it went the need for the younger generation to tragically throw their lives away... I didn't have any opportunities to distinguish myself in battle, so now I'm doing the boring and menial work of a manservant. Though I did train for quite a long time..."

"...Oh, what a pity."

"*Ha-ha.* Say that, and you're just inviting the scorn of those that suffered under the True Demon King terror. I mean, even my parents were killed by the Demon King's Army. More than battlefield exploits, I wish I could get them back. It was a truly twisted time."

"Yes...that is indeed true, without a doubt. Nevertheless, your story, Master Sirok, I find is quite similar to my own."

True to her words, Linaris's faint and refined smile had a slight sadness to it.

No, there's no way, he thought to himself, looking again at her physique.

Slender arms and legs. Transparent white skin like glass, as though it had never once stood beneath the sun's rays.

Slim fingertips becoming a high-born young woman. Her hands had never even held a hatchet, let alone a spear or sword.

There was no way she could be a warrior.

"By that, you mean...?"

"I, too, lost much to the True Demon King... A great many things. Now the only things I have left to me are this mansion and my dear father."

"Oh, right, of course... You're right. Similar to myself."

What exactly had he been thinking?

Obviously, that was the implication behind her words. Those unjustly taken by the True Demon King.

What was sought after in the dawn of this new age was peace so that people like him, without any strength of their own, wouldn't lose anything ever again.

"May I ask what your father's name is?"

"...Obsidian. Rehart the Obsidian."

"Obsidian...?!"

Sirok nearly jumped to his feet. It was a name he had never imagined he would hear.

Obsidian. There could only be one person with a second name like that.

"Obsidian Eyes...?"

The terrifying spy guild, boasted to be both the biggest and strongest in the land.

No one knew the whole story behind them. Nor did anyone know precisely who their members were.

"Hm...? Is there something wrong?"

"No... Is th-that truly his name?"

"Tee-hee-hee... Would there be any reason for me to lie about my venerable father's name? Did you find something otherwise strange about what I said?"

"...No, it's fine."

Was it really a good idea to interrogate Linaris about this here?

She was so clearly unperturbed that she also seemed completely unfamiliar with the name Obsidian altogether. If what she said was the truth, then Sirok had inadvertently gotten closer to the true identity of one of the era's shadowy masterminds and was now under the very same roof.

Sirok, trying in vain to appear calm, gulped hard.

"If you're Obsidian's daughter... L-Linaris...Miss Linaris, can I then, um, ask you what your name is?"

"......? My name is Linaris."

Linaris still wore her innocent smile as she cocked her head to the side.

From what he had seen of her refined etiquette, there was no question she possessed the common sense to answer when asked for her name, so it was possible she was mistaken about something.

Sirok asked once again.

"I meant your second name, Miss Linaris."

"I don't have one."

"......You don't?"

"Indeed. I am Linaris. I do not yet possess a second name. I am only Linaris. I would ask you to refer to me as such."

Was that sort of thing even possible?

No matter how young she was, she was still sixteen or seventeen at the very least. Naturally, there were many examples of people who changed their second name either through later achievements or reputation, but she was of an age where she should have been bestowed a second name many years prior.

In a dilapidated mansion away from the eyes of others, there was a beautiful young girl, ephemeral like a ghost.

She said her own father was "Obsidian."

And finally......she didn't possess her own secondary name.

It's almost like...a horror story.

The meager light that filtered in through the gaps in the windows faintly outlined her silhouette.

Was this girl the same sort of creature as Toroa the Awful?

Linaris began to speak again, as though nothing was amiss at all.

"Earlier, you mentioned that you were verifying the area's residents, correct? Why exactly did the council of lords decide now of all times to conduct such a survey?"

"To balance the tax revenue and expenditures. There was also talk of an aristocrat who knew how to write making a ledger."

"...Is that indeed so? In that case, Master Sirok. May I ask you to do me a favor?"

"A-as long as it's something I can handle... What is it?"

"If there is indeed one who can read on the council...I would like you to bring this letter back with you. It is regarding something my father needs."

A rolled-up parchment, sealed with wax. Perhaps writing this letter was what took her so long when she went to make tea.

More than that, though, Sirok was surprised that Linaris, not much different in age from himself, could read and write. It must have been the simple Order script. Either that or an aristocratic alphabet that was passed down among upper-class families.

"I don't mind at all, of course... But, if the alphabet system you use is different, there's no guarantee the aristocrats will be able to read them."

"You honor me with your concern. Nevertheless, I ask you to bring the letter to them, Master Sirok."

Linaris wrapped both of her pale fists gently around Sirok's hand.

He couldn't help focusing on her chest as she leaned forward.

A dark manor. Obsidian. Beautiful Linaris.

One thing after another, everything happening before him was impossible for him to fully process.

It was at that moment—

"......"

—Linaris suddenly turned around.

Somewhere, a mysterious something clattered.

There was another presence in the house. Was it Rehart the Obsidian?

Danger.

The remnants of his warrior instincts, aroused by the sound, narrowly managed to ring alarm bells within him.

He couldn't remain in this manor any longer.

"...I understand. I'll bring it back with me immediately. Thank you very much for the amber tea. This was a wonderful moment of respite."

He simply needed to put on the fake smile he used when dealing with the other residents and take off.

Would he ever come here again? Well, even if he were to come back, it would have to be after he had calmed down and probably thought through everything that happened.

"Will I see you again?" Linaris said, a tremor in her voice.

"...Hmmm, yes. I'm sure you will."

"Master Sirok. It's very embarrassing to admit this, but, well... It's been so long..."

Her gold eyes closed in. A strand of her hair brushed his cheek.

It should still be daytime out. Yet her smile was almost like a nighttime hallucination.

"...and I've been so lonely by myself."

◆

By the time he had returned to town, there were stars twinkling in the sky.

While preoccupied with thoughts of the sorrowful parting of his fleeting encounter, Sirok went to the aristocrat at the council hall to hand over the letter just as he was asked. He was of a far greater status than those who employed him. Sirok had heard the reason behind creating the resident ledger was also because this aristocrat had something they were particularly interested in investigating.

The aristocrat's name was Enu the Distant Mirror, Thirteenth Minister of Aureatia.

"Hmph. And you were told to give me this letter, then?"

All of his hair was combed to the back of his head, and with his true age being outwardly inscrutable, the man left others with a shady and suspicious impression of him.

However, it was rare for an aristocrat not to despise children like Sirok, without any kith and kin.

"Yes. I definitely heard the name Obsidian, too. Do you believe Linaris was lying?"

"I'll need to see the contents of this letter before I can make any judgment."

He was neither perplexed by nor distrustful of Sirok's full report, and simply opened up the seal to Linaris's letter.

"Take a look."

"What's going on...?"

"This is a blank piece of parchment, Sirok."

Nothing about Enu's tone suggested he was reproaching the young man, but Sirok's mind quaked with astonishment.

He thought there must have been some mistake.

"...That can't be! I'm not lying! I went into that mansion! Even the letter, she left it behind with me...and L-Linaris! She was there, I swear, Lord Enu!"

"Calm yourself. The truth. Not the past or the future. Let's start with the current facts. Just as I've taught my own men."

"But...!"

"Look at the facts. Until I opened this up, there was a seal stamped down here, yes?"

Enu continued matter-of-factly, fiddling with a fragment of the broken wax seal.

"You said that this letter wasn't a lie, yes? You're right. So long as you didn't miraculously stumble upon a letter sealed with the Obsidian crest somewhere, that makes it clear there must have been someone to hand you this letter."

"Still though, why...? Why ask me to deliver a blank piece of paper...?"

"Therein lies the main point of inquiry. That's all we need to think about."

She had said to make sure the letter was passed along. He didn't understand what her aim was. How much of what happened that day had been reality, and how much had been a dream?

Pondering over something, Enu quickly rapped his finger on his temple.

"Then... Well. If you're not in the mercenary trade, then it's reasonable you wouldn't be familiar with this either. I will let you in on one more fact."

Enu's expression was as disimpassioned as a wax doll's.

However, even someone who counted their name among Aureatia's Twenty-Nine Ministers was having difficulty weighing the facts from the events Sirok was describing.

"Obsidian Eyes has already been eradicated."

The following day. Just as he promised, Sirok met with Linaris once again.

It proved to be a reunion far more gruesome than anyone could imagine.

◆

"The Visitors have brought many types of knowledge to this world. Among that knowledge, what do you think proved to be the most useful of all?"

It was the dead of night.

Before getting to the topic at hand, Aureatia's Thirteenth Minister introduced his argument.

Sirok didn't know exactly what school was like, but the thin cane Enu held appeared almost like a teacher's pointer in his hands.

"I didn't actually get much schooling. The visitors brought guns...and, what was the other thing...? Oh, right, they brought the metric system, too."

"Unexpectedly sharp observation there. You seem familiar with the story of Victor the Miser, right? That marked the arrival of the metric standard. Over there it's nothing more than a measuring system, though. Combining all the measuring systems into one was truly a huge achievement. However, the advent of this system did not go a long way toward saving the world."

The visitors possessed enough strength and vitality to overpower the people of this world, and many times they would use the knowledge from their world to forcibly rewrite society through a single general.

The wealthy businessman who brought the unifying system of measure to this world, Victor the Miser, was one of the most extreme examples. Nevertheless, there was another similarly big shift that Enu had in mind.

"Then, what is the answer?"

"Epidemiology. Accurate foundational understanding of epidemics is the biggest reason why recent generations have seen a striking increase in the average lifespan of us minia. Surely you know that disease is carried by small organisms that are invisible to the naked eye. It's been so fully established in our world that there are some who learn this in academic halls, while others are told by their parents. However, this understanding was only brought to us as recently as a hundred years ago."

"…Wouldn't you say a hundred years isn't quite 'recent?'"

"Of course it is. Up until then, there was only a vague concept of hygiene. From the time the royal family was established and onward, no one had any ideas regarding the true nature of disease."

With his hard, serious expression unchanged, the Thirteenth Minister humorously raised one of his eyebrows.

Sirok remembered the story from a fellow student who arrived from Aureatia. He was a boorish man and had no talent with the sword, but there was one story he would occasionally tell that was entertaining. It was about sewer system maintenance.

In the past, water reservoirs and sewage that hadn't spread beyond the world's urban areas were thoroughly maintained out of fear of disease. Conversely, farther out on the frontier, there were still villages with pit latrine–style toilets, but Sirok had never seen these for himself.

"Still, though, is this a necessary part of the topic at hand?"

"It is, because this topic involves the form and nature of vampires."

"……"

"I will tell you the truth. The leader of Obsidian Eyes, Rehart the Obsidian, is rumored to be a vampire."

Vampires. When he heard the word, the first thing that came to Sirok's mind was Linaris.

White, as if she detested sunlight, nigh-impossible beauty, and a dreamlike charm…

"Vampires are one of the races whose true forms remained unknown until the modern era. Even the vampires themselves didn't truly understand the nature of their own existence… In truth, vampirism is a deviant and deadly strain of disease."

"Disease…?! Wait, but she looked minian… I could see her with my own eyes, and I touched her."

"It's the truth. The vampire's main body is the pathogen in their blood. They think like people, but that is because their host is an animal capable of thought, and they are simply making use of their structural makeup. On top of this...vampires can infect others with the disease through mucus membranes or wounds. Then, similar in structure to the way ants work under command from their queen, the infected are turned into slaves that are fully influenced by the pheromones from their 'parent.' Manipulating them to be soldiers, forcing them to go beyond their physical limits, making them commit suicide—whatever they see fit. They're referred to as a 'thrall.' That's the first stage."

Dragons. Ogres. Slimes. Many of the deviant species across the land came to them as Visitors and established themselves as a separate species. Inanimate enchanted swords and magic tools were another variety of these deviant and abnormal species. Exactly how much was included within this categorization was something not a single person living in their world could theorize on.

Supposing a virus, invisible to the naked eye, were to depart from its normal evolution, and deviate enough to jump between worlds, what shape would it take in that situation?

"Phase two. Regardless of whether they're a vampire or a thrall, the infected's child naturally contracts the pathogen, and their body is remade in the womb. Then, they become able to generate the vampire pathogen themselves. That makes them a new 'parent.' The next generation of vampire. Through blood transmission and infection from mother to child, they increase the numbers of infected."

"The unborn child...is remade? D-does something that horrifying really happen?"

"You see, Sirok, our genetic makeup, well... It's decided by a chain of factors, even more minuscule than our cells, which are passed on by our ancestors... To explain even further, the vampires are specialists, far beyond our capabilities, when it comes to recombining these linking factors. Specialized, and shrewd. They can easily construct these parents to more easily accomplish their blood infections, both by giving them forms that are alluring to others, and through physical abilities that cause bloodshed."

They were unable to cross moving water. They died when bathed in sunlight. They loathed germicidal herbs. It was possible to combat them with weapons of silver. The various elements described as weaknesses in legends from the Beyond largely didn't apply to actual vampires themselves.

However, these legends brilliantly hit the mark on the truth behind one certain aspect of their physiology.

"Now, my introductory explanation ran a bit long. But I needed to explain all of this to you beforehand in order for you to understand the truth."

"Well...I'm sorry to say but I didn't really understand most of what you were talking about. Why are you telling a kid like me all of this? Are you trying to say Linaris is dead?"

"You are."

"...I'm...what?"

The civil servant smiled callously and put a piece of fabric on top of the table.

It was the one Linaris had used to wrap his wound...which Enu had then changed after he listened to Sirok's story.

"I had a soldier examine your blood. You've already been infected. With this, we know for a fact that there was a vampire in that manor you visited."

"Th-that can't be...! I'm not dead! I'm here, talking to you right now! I have a will of my own!"

"That much is true. The undead simply obey the commands of their parent. They aren't the mindless, shambling corpses they're generally believed to me. As long as your parent unit remains, you'll be able to return to your minian life... Though you'll be in a hospital ward for a little bit. It requires a variety of different treatments, of course."

Sirok clutched his head from dizziness. He wasn't minian. He was a worker drone under the control of a shapeless disease. Was he fated for such a disappointing end?

His left middle finger... Had her blood been mixed into the ointment she had used on him? He had also drunk the amber tea she prepared for him. Did that mean...

"L-Linaris....was deceiving me...from the very start...?!"

"Considering all the facts, I am obliged to come to that conclusion. Both Rehart the Obsidian and Linaris are nothing more than threats to the minian races. You'll cooperate with us, won't you, Sirok?"

Sirok nodded, stricken with grief. Even now, with his burning adoration for Linaris unabated, it was the only choice he had.

...Or perhaps, it was the same with his feelings, too.

His feelings for her might have been entirely fabricated, brought on by the disease, exactly as Enu had described.

◆

Then, the next morning arrived. Inside Sirok's enormous mansion, an assembled troop of field soldiers waited eagerly for the raid to begin. The space inside his home was being filled for the first time, as a garrison for the Thirteenth Minister's soldiers.

"It's barely been four and a half days since your call to arms, and there's already so many..."

"Oh, did I forget to mention? I came here to Itaaki in order to put down Obsidian, who we suspected was hiding out here. We didn't want to put our enemy on alert while we didn't yet know where he was hiding, after all. I had them on standby in the next town over."

"Wait, are you saying my resident survey job was part of it...?! Then, then I..."

Thanks to that, he was now a thrall.

While he wished to lash out in reproach, he immediately understood the root cause lay in Linaris's deception, and Sirok's chest tightened, without any outlet for his anger.

If he was only confirming whether or not a home had residents, he would have been able to go back after seeing Linaris in the garden.

He knew about vampires. He had plenty of chances to realize the truth for himself. He let his guard down.

The root cause that led him to expose himself to danger was unmistakable.

"Sirok. We'll rely on you to lead us to the manor, but we're going to bind both your arms. Also, in order to check if you're under the influence of her pheromones or not, we will be regularly checking your pupils. These measures are to defend us from attacks, but we also want to protect you from committing suicide, or something similar. Will you be okay with that?"

"...Yes. Can a vampire's control make me tell lies?"

"That's a reasonable concern to have. It seems that vampires have techniques for mental control as well. At your current stage, the parent will be unable to have advanced control over your responses without directly passing them on to you with their own words. As long as we're able to prevent you from going berserk, I believe there will be no problems with having you guide us to the manor."

Meanwhile, Enu had been using his vast knowledge, far greater than Sirok could possibly understand, to lay precision tactical groundwork for the raid. Ever since he put on the charade of preparing the trifling resident ledger.

Such were Aureatia's Twenty-Nine Officials. Sirok had believed that the path of the sword was the only way to make one's way through life, but there were also those who never once picked up a blade.

They departed for Linaris's mansion at daybreak. The field soldiers concealed the sounds of their steps as they advanced, and thus, the only people who witnessed the passing army were ranchers milking their cows out in the road.

After a short distance, and once again in front of the gloomy mansion, Sirok posed a question.

All around him, Enu's soldiers appeared to be moving along with the operation, but he still didn't understand what they were doing.

"Do vampires hate the sun?"

"Generally speaking, yes. Not to the point that they're unable to move beneath it. Nevertheless, if there is something that might tip the scales even the slightest bit in our favor, I will employ it. That is all."

Encircling the mansion while the sun was out, all Sirok could do was watch the soldier's performance, like flowing water, while his arms remained heavily bound. Enu the Distant Mirror was planning on butchering Linaris without a sliver of mercy.

...I'd like to talk to her again.

The thought surely must have been influenced by her hold over him.

If Linaris was the one who had turned him into a corpse, then as long as there remained the fear of being under her control, Sirok was unable to return to his minian life. These thoughts were nothing more than irrational delusions.

Will I see you again?

As the men surrounded the mansion, they watched as flames suddenly erupted from every window.

It had been completely set ablaze.

"Linaris...!"

"I understand what you're feeling. I've heard that vampires have an almost otherworldly beauty."

The Thirteenth Minister had a pipe in his mouth and watched the blaze with a solemn expression.

"That's why I want to bring her down before she reveals herself to us. Your information was truly a big help. As a reward for your cooperation, I'll pen a letter of introduction for your hospital stay."

Everything burned. All traces of the property were charred black. The dark and dreary mansion, the rose garden, and everything else.

He would never be able to exchange words with Linaris again.

The size of the field soldier troop wasn't enough to surround a terrifyingly powerful vampire and bring it down with numbers. This was so they could all take part in the instantaneous fire attack and bring things to a close immediately before their targets had any time to react.

...Still, that letter.

Even though there had been nothing but a blank piece of paper inside, if that was Linaris and her father's way of seeking to open some sort of dialogue...

Then Enu had instead seen that as a golden opportunity, and showing up with this terrible surprise attack...

The fire continued to burn, like the sun overpowering the moon with its light.

Nevertheless, the flames failed to burn through the black curtain in his heart.

"Sirok the Sextant. There are two burnt bodies. Though you really can't tell the faces from one another. Want to try confirming if it's them?"

"......No."

Even when he had heard the soldier's report, his mind was still enshrouded by a black curtain.

He didn't want to see Linaris's beautiful body cruelly burned to ash.

◆

"Now, Sirok, here's the thing about love...," Enu said, out of character, on their route home, the post-operation cleanup concluded and the sun beginning to set. "...The first time is the most beautiful of all. However, that first love is the one that has the smallest chance of success."

"...I don't need your comfort."

"No one can ever manage to forget their very first love. It's a fact. All we can do is have new encounters and push that first love further and further away. In so doing, this world never runs out of tales of love and hate. Ha-ha-ha-ha!"

The Thirteenth Minister laughed with just his mouth, the look on his face remaining unchanged.

...He may have had a point. The girl was a vampire. If he did meet with Linaris a second or third time, their encounter wouldn't end with memories of her beauty. He would have been shown things he didn't want to see and made to fear things he didn't want to be afraid of.

Sirok was confident their reunion would've been a gruesome one.

What was inside of Sirok's heart now was only the beautiful form he saw standing in the garden.

Even though he longed to see her again, he had separated himself from her.

All the mysteries, all the secrets would be lost in the sea of time.

It was hard for him to say Enu's words were comforting, and they were few, but by the time he finally returned to his home, Sirok had been able to convince himself.

"If our preparations for departure are finished expediently, we intend to leave for Aureatia in the evening. It'll have to be on the way, my apologies, but we'll deliver you to the hospital, too."

"......Thank you."

He obediently bowed his head. It appeared he would be away from the house he had inherited from his parents for a time.

Or maybe, things might stay like that forever.

The house had almost never had guests to begin with. While the soldiers had been briefly stationed there, he figured this would be the last time the house would be bustling with this many guests.

If I could cook for them, or show them any hospitality, that would be nice.

With Sirok's skill set, even that much was out of his reach. Thus, there was nothing he could do as master of the house besides stand as he was in the entryway and receive the column of soldiers into his home.

When the last soldier in the line arrived, he closed the door.

Then came a shrill ringing noise.

"*Ngh!*"

"Hrnk!"

Two soldiers joined together and collapsed in a heap.

Their bodies clashed, and the noise sounded similar to that of a stringed instrument. The odd sound blended together with the grisly sound of bones breaking, creating a gruesome cacophony.

The entryway was painted red with blood and viscera.

"Wh-what the...?!"

Sirok tried to take out his claw-sword. Seeing the grisly scene before him, he was certain that was what he had tried to do.

However, incomprehensibly, his body didn't budge.

He watched the next event unfold.

One of the soldiers turned back toward him and sent their short sword flying out of its sheath. They weren't aiming for Sirok. Separated from his bodyguards, Enu the Distant Mirror's right knee was run through, and the momentum of the thrust sent him toppling backward to the ground.

"Augh...?"

"Master Enu!"

"*Hnngh*, enemy attack! Restrain Mezde and Sirok! They're thralls!"

Enu cried, without recoiling in pain. The short sword–wielding soldier Mezde appeared terribly confused. Contrary to his visible unrest, his body again tried to brandish his sword, and he was immediately immobilized. The soldier, Mezde, with his hand twitched up behind his back, shouted.

"W-Wait! I haven't done anything to get infected! Nothing at all!"

As far as Sirok had seen, that should have been the case.

A brawny solder grabbed Sirok's arm and forced it into the restraints. The soldier named Mezde was similarly put into shackles.

"...I don't believe it. How were we found out? What happened?"

While twisting his expression in an odd way—likely a sign of anger—Enu held a nearby tablecloth with his chin and wrapped it around his wound.

"The parent is nearby... There's been an infected hiding out among us from the beginning... No, that can't be...!"

Next, a different soldier went mad. The soldier who restrained Mezde suddenly drew their sword and sliced at the person behind him. The soldier under attack tried to defend himself. However, the berserk soldier's strength, far surpassing its normal limits, tore halfway through the armor protecting his torso. Physical strength, beyond normal limits. He, too, was a thrall.

"*A-ahhh*...! N-no...*yeeeaaaaugh*!"

"Dammit! There's still another thrall!"

"Everyone, check your pupils!"

"There's still the attack that did in the two by the door! Don't let down your guard!"

The heavily wounded soldier writhed in agony for a brief moment before expiring on the spot.

Panic. Chaos.

Sirok couldn't grasp the situation. What was going on?

Vampires... If the Obsidian was dead, shouldn't the threat have vanished?

"Linaris!"

He shouted, still restrained. Even if it went against the understanding he had arrived at in his heart, he didn't care.

He hoped strongly to see her somewhere, and for his words to reach her.

"If you consider yourself a friend of Sirok the Sextant, then show yourself! Are you doing this of your own will?! Is this the work of Obsidian...?! Linaris!"

His voice echoed to a whisper through the expansive and eerie premises.

The soldiers seemed terrified of the slightest movements any of them made and stood there with weapons drawn and on high alert.

All of the men confirmed to be infected were restrained and lying down on the floor. There were far too many.

Vampirism spread through the blood. There also needed to be more time between initial infection and pathogenic control. Even if the mysterious attacks gave an opportunity to infect through the resulting wounds, there shouldn't have been any possible way to turn this many people into thralls at once.

"Master Sirok."

Then came a quiet voice. He heard the clattering sound of wheels spinning.

Black hair, contrasting starkly with her pure white skin.

Gold eyes tinged with melancholy.

She— Linaris appeared from deeper down the hallway.

Her footsteps didn't make any sound, as if she were an angel from on high.

Was she a ghost? Or maybe, an illusion, from the very moment Sirok laid eyes on her.

He should have found her terrifying, yet she was beautiful.

She was pushing a wheelchair, with someone seated in it, wrapped up in a luxurious robe.

"Linaris..."

"We were able to meet again, just as you promised... But, how awful of you."

The lovely vampire girl gave a lonely smile.

"You were trying to kill me, were you not?"

Her voice was calm, just like when he had first met her.

She's so gorgeous.

Sirok thought to himself amid the silence.

Even in the middle of this hellish sea of blood.

Linaris's appearance was so heavenly and calm, it was enough to take any of the soldiers' breath away, but nevertheless, not a single one of the soldiers could make any movements to draw their bow. It was inexplicable.

Enu barked an order.

"That's the vampire parent. Don't let her speak. Shoot."

"They will not shoot me, Master Enu the Distant Mirror."

"......Shoot her!"

The *fwoom* of the crossbows' release rang out. It was the sound of two soldiers shooting each other in the face.

The two had their pupils checked only moments prior and had been confirmed to be uninfected.

Despite the terrifying scene, the ones witnessing it couldn't move at all, unable to escape or defend themselves, as Linaris looked on at them all tranquilly.

"That's not it..."

Enu's voice was shaking.

The face of the Thirteenth Minister, once composed, even with the injury to his leg, was now twisted in fear.

His lucid mind derived the answer to the situation playing out before his eyes.

"That's not it... Th-these aren't enemies we can fight... Retreat! How is a mutation like this...even possible...?! Everyone, get out of this house now!"

Pale skin, translucent and glasslike, as though it had never once been graced by the sun's rays.

Slim fingertips, becoming of a high-born young woman. Her hands had never even held a hatchet, let alone a spear or sword.

She was not a warrior...

...However.

"The air! It *spreads through the air!*"

Panic erupted.

The Thirteenth Minister's soldiers shot and cut each other down, begging for their lives as they killed each other. And those who tried to escape were altogether dissected by an invisible string.

Linaris cocked her head, looking a bit at a loss, without a single drop of the blood spurts getting anywhere near her.

Sirok groaned in the middle of the hellish scene.

"Obsidian... Linaris... You were the true Obsidian after all..."

"Heavens, no. I could not possibly dare to disrespect my father's illustrious name by claiming his deeds as my own."

She tenderly grasped the hand of the person sitting in the wheelchair.

An elbow, peeking through with skin like wax, limply shook.

"Obsidian is my father's organization. Eternally powerful, eternally flourishing...to lead us all on the correct path to the future. Why, I could not possibly be Obsidian..."

Obsidian Eyes was already wiped out....just as Enu had said.

The reason for that was now as clear.

"Linaris! Stop... Please, you have to know the truth! Th-that person... They're already...."

"My father's Obsidian Eyes are not done. My dear father is big, kind, and strong. Everything will go back to the way it was before. Linaris is always here at your side."

Bringing her lips against the parched shell of a hand, Linaris slowly turned back.

None before her could move their body even the slightest inch...... No, that wasn't entirely true.

"...Let us begin. Now, eyes, gathered beneath our Obsidian. Unmatched and steadfast champions. We shall bestow upon you an era deserving of you all. Now then, state your names."

There were people squirming in the dark.

How many people out there in the world were even capable of hiding and evading detection from Aureatia's grizzled field troops, and possessed techniques to kill and dissect soldiers with string traps?

They were there in Obsidian Eyes. Innumerable eyes appeared out of the darkness.

Out from behind the Aureatia troops. From above. From the farthest reaches of the unseen terrors of the night.

"Fifth formation vanguard. Zeljirga the Abyss Web."

There was a zumeu pulling threads with all ten fingers.

"Seventh formation rearguard. Wieze the Variation."

There was a strangely shaped minia, back bent and walking on all fours.

"F-fourth formation vanguard. Yakrai the Tower."

There was a minia carrying a straight sword.

"First formation vanguard. Lena the Obscured."

There was an elf who had both eyes covered by a bandage.

"Fourth formation rearguard. Frey the Waking."

There was a leprechaun with a cane.

Each one of them was so powerful, they were on the verge of becoming champions themselves. They were at the upper limits of their supernatural abilities and training.

Nevertheless, what stood there was in fact a host of thralls, commanded by a singular will, and given strength beyond the limits of their minian bodies, all at the hands of the vampire pathogen.

Enu moaned.

"...Damned undead......!"

"Obsidian Eyes is alive. Right here, as you can see. You will soon be able to understand that much yourself, Master Enu the Distant Mirror."

Linaris smiled—like the smile of an innocent child—and stooped down in front of Enu, sprawled out on the floor.

Her unsettling palm gently caressed his cheek.

"You shall give us your recommendation for the royal games, yes? A return to the age of champions, as the Hero. For my father... let us once again create an age of warring strife."

"Who would ever...agree to the demands...of a monster like you...?"

"You will. It's been this way from the very start."

She had known Enu the Distant Mirror's name from the beginning.

From the start, this had been her only goal. Everything had been for the sake of bringing him under her control.

If not for the blank letter, would Sirok have unreservedly told the aristocrat lord about her? From a simple blank piece of paper, Enu had understood that Obsidian was there. The truth of Sirok's infection showed him proof of the vampire's existence. She had known that there was a mansion here with enough space for the Thirteenth Minister to quarter his troops. The entire detachment lying in wait in the neighboring town as well—she had lured them all out by providing them information.

As she openly presented an easy-to-trace path of infection, beneath the surface, she had kept the true method of the infection a secret.

If Sirok hadn't been invited into that manor, the current tragedy never would have unfolded.

However, the wound at the beginning… His tiny, insignificant scratch.

"Linaris, it's not true, right…?! The wound on my finger, I only pricked a thorn, right…? It was really…all just a coincidence, right?!"

Linaris was not a warrior.

Nevertheless, in both her thoughts and way of being, she was completely beyond his reach, different from Sirok in every possible dimension.

For the sake of her deep-rooted obsession with a dying age, she intended to regress this world back to that time once again.

"You said you've been all alone…and lonely, didn't you?! Isn't that right?! I know you were all by yourself! And maybe, maybe I had just…"

The pale noble daughter smiled elegantly.

That settled it. Sirok knew his feelings had been genuine.

Even if he had been under her control, there was some of his own will buried within these emotions.

"Master Sirok. Thank you… I was so happy for the opportunity to have a regular conversation with someone…just like a normal girl."

Her golden eyes were tinged with melancholy.

Her pale skin was so delicate it seemed to be on the verge of fading away, as were her delicate arms and legs. Every single part of her beautiful form seemed incongruous with the blood-soaked tragedy she was orchestrating.

Something so cruel shouldn't have been allowed to happen.

"Farewell."

She held a meticulous and cunning power, pulling on spider threads with unseen fingertips.

She had obtained a mutated method of infection, wholly unforeseeable and inconceivable to ascertain with everyday logic.

She commanded the world's largest secret organization, a military force of unrivaled elites, gathered from far and wide.

A wicked and terrible colony of espionage, commanded by a singular will concealed within shadows.

Scout. Vampire.

Linaris the Obsidian.

Gathered within a small meeting room inside the Aureatia Central Assembly Hall was a small portion of the Twenty-Nine Officials.

There was a condition to the summons. For civil servants, it was possessing thorough familiarity with Aureatia's military strategy. For military officers, it was being in a position to command Aureatia forces to act.

"This everyone, then? Well, this is good enough, I guess…"

The person sitting in the place of honor was the same as during normal assemblies, the speaker in charge of managing the meeting. The First Minister of Aureatia, Grasse the Foundation Map.

He was a man of medium build, just shy of his twilight years. His wrinkle-free black clothes and healthy complexion still appeared unfamiliar to the concept of age.

"Yes, let's get started. As you are aware, this summons came from the Third Minister. I know it was sudden, and I thank you for being here. First, regarding the topic of the meeting, if you will, Third Minister."

"Third Minister Jelki here."

His name was Jelki the Swift Ink. He was a shrewd-looking man, thin glasses perched atop a look of displeasure. He was shouldered with the core practical governance, controlling the whole of Aureatia domestic affairs, focusing mainly on the commercial industry.

"We've identified new information regarding the Old Kingdoms' loyalists' movements. I believe it's widely known that Gilnes the Ruined Castle has joined with Togie City and is recruiting soldiers. But, two days ago, Togie City was placed under martial law. He is gathering soldiers more rapidly than ever before, and we estimate he will soon march on Aureatia."

"Gilnes, huh?"

The aging general, leaning back in his chair, smiled as he polished the short sword in his hands. The Twenty-Seventh General of Aureatia, Hardy the Bullet Flashpoint. A prominent influence with the largest faction of the military on his side.

"That name brings me back. When this was the Central Kingdom, he was a real troublesome general. He naturally has the skills and is popular among his subordinates. How many do we think he's gathered? Thirty thousand? Forty thousand?"

"…For the Old Kingdoms' loyalists in Togie City, the number of active soldiers is within our estimations. I think the army already dispatched to the region is more than enough to keep them in check."

"Is that all? If you're calling us with an emergency summons, we've at least gotta be talking about a major battle on home soil."

Hardy blew cigar smoke from his mouth in disapproval. This man was someone who spoke his mind.

"An alliance, perhaps?"

The man who spoke up was the Twenty-Fifth General. His name was Kayon the Thundering. One of his sleeves hung down loosely, the arm that was supposed to pass through it absent. He was a one-armed general.

"There are no major movements in Togie City. Given that, if there was a move they could make to force our hand, it's an alliance right now… Togie City, making a lot of noise and drawing attention, is the bait to pin the Aureatia army down, with the real attack coming from another military force, like the mercenaries in the Free City of Okahu. That's really the only move that'd be annoying for us to deal with. That said..."

Cayon twisted his decorous lips into a smile.

"*Hah*! That's not it, is it? I mean, Jelki's in charge of commerce, after all. If there were any signs of major movement, like two powers forming an alliance, it'd be strange if we generals weren't the very first people to be told about it. So basically, the Old Kingdoms must have a strategy that's likely to turn things in their favor. But one that doesn't involve reinforcements. Well then, what could it be?"

"...Very impressive, Twenty-Fifth General. Thank you for speeding up the explanation. Their rapid movements give the Old Kingdoms' loyalists a fair chance at victory. A decisive factor, one worth putting all the soldiers Gilnes has amassed into action at once. Their reinforcements are coming not from a detached force nor from troops gathered from an alliance—they're coming from the weather."

"The weather?"

"All right, hold on now, what's that supposed to mean?"

"There is an atmospheric phenomenon unique to the Yamaga Barrens, called the Particle Storm. Think of it as a sandstorm violent enough to wear and tear anything caught inside it down to nothing. This Particle Storm is continuing to move in Aureatia's direction. The damages from a possible direct hit are impossible to estimate. As far as we can confirm, there is only one precedent for the Particle Storm appearing beyond the Yamaga Barrens. In that example, it demolished the entire country of a self-proclaimed demon king."

"Judging from that, when you say, 'a sandstorm is moving,' I imagine you mean the storm *is bringing the sand with it*, then?

Speaker Grasse cut in, intrigued.

"Can we assume that's the situation at hand, then?"

"Yes, that's exactly right. We believe that an enormous sand cloud is taken up in the air flow, like a whirlwind, and it is as perpetual as the Particle Storm. There is rarely a drop in force. We're in the middle of collecting confirmed reports from the cities around the path of the storm. Naturally, given that there's not enough time for a horse to make the round trip, they're being done by way of long-range radzio communication."

"Oh, oh, oh. Okay, okay, my turn."

In one of the seats was a young boy stretching up high and raising his hand.

He was Mizial the Iron-Piercing Plumeshade. At a mere sixteen years old, he counted himself as Aureatia's Twenty-Second General, the youngest of its military officers.

"Listen, Jelki. Who's saying all of this anyway? Not the reports, but the original info. For starters, it sounds way too out-there to be true, right? That would be way too convenient for our enemies."

Mizial didn't have quick wits like Hidow or Elea, but he always gave his honest opinion.

"To put it bluntly, it's gotta be a trap, right?"

"Jelki...exactly how did you acquire this information?"

The veteran general Hardy followed suit. Leaning his elbows on the table, he flashed a toothy grin.

"Going off your report, it's possible those Old Kingdoms' folks took over communication towers on the frontier and fed you some made-up story. Hilarious to think a man of your caliber'd be manipulated and sent off on some wild goose chase... Though, if the bastard's main goal is a diversion, then they'd probably think up a better lie than that for the job."

"This isn't information that's gotten out from the Old Kingdoms' side, right...? Not anything from our secret agents or testimony from the prisoners we've taken."

At Cayon's question, Jelki held the temples of his glasses between his fingers.

"Indeed. The original information was a forecast we obtained from dealings with the Trade and Industry Council."

"The Trade and Industry Council...?!"

"From those merchants, huh?"

"Everything regarding the extremely accurate weather forecasts being dealt between the merchant coalition and the major traveling merchants, ever since the demise of the True Demon King, is exactly as has been previously reported. This recent forecast showed the Particle Storm reaching Aureatia. As with the weather forecasts that have been dealt on the market up until this, it's believed this predicted path is based on field observations occurring across each region."

"...Weather observation techniques, huh."

If the traveling merchants, continuously moved along their route for a cyclically fixed route, had taken organized action, it wasn't inconceivable that they'd collect their accumulated weather information and make forecasts. In addition to serving as a great boon to the trade activity in each region, the forecasts themselves became a valuable commodity.

The Third Minister continued to speak.

"Next, an important point. There is someone who provides these techniques to the traveling merchants in each region like this and accumulates the information they provide. A young boy known as the Gray-Haired Child—a visitor who supplies muskets. While his origin is unknown, he has been trading with various regional merchant guilds for, at the very least, ten or more years, and our merchants here are no exception."

Guns. Much like with the troops of Sixth General Harghent,

in recent years even those among the Twenty-Nine Officials had introduced rifleman soldiers into their ranks. Thus was the weapon's level of superiority.

"Um, hey, Jelki. Isn't that basically just saying you know this information is fishy after all? I don't really have the smarts to understand everything myself, but there's no proof this guy's not lying."

"That's enough, Mizial. We need to confirm the facts."

A man who kept quiet now raised his head. The Thirteenth Minister, Enu the Distant Mirror. Even in the middle of a meeting, he still maintained his sage and stony expression.

"The Gray-Haired Child has been collecting weather information far longer than the Old Kingdoms' loyalists. The fact he actually puts his trust in that information, and deals in said information, means we can verify it as factual. In which case, what does the Gray-Haired Child stand to gain from such negotiations?"

"What does he stand to gain? Well, it's gotta be money, right?"

"Yes, indeed. That is the most obvious fact here. In which case, if he is siding with the Old Kingdoms' loyalists, and misleading us with fake weather forecasts, we need to think about what sort of profit he can expect."

"The Old Kingdoms can probably pay him pretty well, right? At the very least, seems like he'd earn a lot more than with those stingy old merchants."

"Then, what about the whole sum of his business? If the information manipulation on the Old Kingdoms' side ends up influencing the merchants as well, he'll lose trade confidence with them."

"I get it. He won't be able to sell information anymore. We know for sure the merchants are already being influenced by news of the Particle Storm, so if this is all a lie, it'll end up being a huge economic loss for the Gray-Haired Child down the line."

"Thus, it becomes a pure numbers problem. Do you think the

Old Kingdom would have the budget to match the total trade profits for the weather forecasts going around, Jelki? And all for what looks to be a foolish and precarious feint operation."

"We've already come up with the estimated sum necessary. To cut to the conclusion, it is inconceivable. From the results of our follow-ups, we're certain the Old Kingdoms' loyalists' information source is also the Trade and Industry Council. Given that the Old Kingdoms already needs to secure logistics for all the new soldiers recruited under Gilnes the Ruined Castle, they're currently trading with a large number of merchants. If they had involved Trade and Industry Council significantly in their strategy, there should be a noticeably unnatural flow of capital."

"*Hm.* A fantastic answer from our general supervisor of all trade and commerce. Now then, Mizial. Put yourself in the Gray-Haired Child's shoes—if you obtained information on the Particle Storm, what would be your best way to get the most profit from selling that information?"

"Weeeell, assuming the information was good, I guess I'd sell it to the merchants first, huh? If Aureatia and the Old Kingdoms are going to war, then right now that's the most stable market. Then, with it approaching Aureatia, you could sell it to us for a bunch, right? Then, after that...... Ohhh."

Mizial suddenly clapped his hands together after staring up at the ceiling for a few moments.

"I'd also sell it to the Old Kingdoms, looking to attack Aureatia. So, that's why those Togie City guys have started to make their move. They have information saying they'll be able to beat us with their current military forces."

"A logical conclusion. Thus, we can consider for the time being that the facts of the weather forecast are accurate."

"If this really was bum information, just like you said, they'd have to take out the weather observation teams in each region to cover it up. If they could manage to do that from out in the frontier, there'd be a plethora of much more efficient options at their disposal."

Hardy the Bullet Flashpoint breathed out cigar smoke, and Kayon the Thundering followed up with an opinion of his own.

"Jelki. I figure you're doing this already, but have them collect as much proof that can't be transmitted over radzio as possible. Even if a horse can't make the round trip in time, it'll make the *one-way* trip in time, right? If these forecasts have merchants fleeing, there should be plenty of people who have witnessed the Particle Storm directly. Besides, there's still one problem here, isn't there?"

".......What is that?"

"There's no telling if the Free City of Okahu will make their move, yes? Assuming the Particle Storm's arrival is their trump card, that doesn't rule out an alliance. While we're focused on how to deal with the Particle Storm, we'll still take measures to shut down Okahu. What're we gonna do?"

"Leave that to me."

Hardy spoke up to answer the question. A warrior's smile, brutal and ferocious, came to his face.

"I'll mobilize anyone I can and prepare to settle the matter with the head of Okahu directly. Of course, Aureatia and Okahu aren't *officially* hostile toward each other. Calling it cease-fire negotiations'd be a bit of an exaggeration, though."

"Planning on throwing the Passing Disaster into the mix, are you?"

"Like with the New Principality? Yeah, he did end up with the most important job, but...when you start talking about attacking Okahu's ironclad mountain fortress, I'm not so sure. There's someone more qualified for that, see."

The abilities of Kuze the Passing Disaster, who forced the New Principality of Lithia to capitulate to the Twenty-Nine Officials, were enigmatic and wholly inexplicable superpowers. They all considered it best to not make use of him.

"Hate to change the subject, but I'd like to clean up all the matters at hand."

Speaker Grasse looked toward the Thirteenth Minister Enu's chair.

"What about Obsidian Eyes' movements? There's a possibility some of their remnants have joined up with the Old Kingdoms' bastards, right?"

"Well obviously, we haven't been able to pursue them *that* far."

Enu replied coolly. His blank expression made his underlying emotions imperceptible. As it always had.

"During an operation four small months prior, my forces *mopped up* the remnants in Itaaki, including the Obsidian, but for the members who scattered across the different regions there's still much we do not know. However, our *cooperator* has a sufficient understanding of their members and their espionage methods. Should one of them do something conspicuous to make themselves known, we'll be able to pounce on them."

"And in exchange this cooperator wants to appear in the Imperial Competition, right?"

"If we can get it approved, I'd certainly like it to happen. This collaborating relationship was formed with that deal in mind, after all."

"...In that case for the time being, if we can do something about the Particle Storm, that'll get all points of concern surrounding the Imperial Competition in order, too. We'll end up crushing the Old Kingdom's main strategy in the end. Still, we're facing off against the weather here. What exactly are we going to do?"

At the question, Kayon the Thundering raised his hand.

"...I have an idea. Could you leave this matter to me?"

◆

Now then. Can we cleanly settle everything with this?

The First Minister Grasse thought to himself while looking out over the meeting.

The Old Kingdoms' loyalists. The Particle Storm. There's no way of knowing what sort of schemes are being set up and where. Friend or foe—truly shrewd players aren't always going to slot into our predictions.

At the very least, within this meeting, they had touched on a threat that would end up being deferred.

Following his appearance ten years ago... Just how much did the Gray-Haired Child predict when he introduced these weather observation techniques? What does he intend to do by making the Old Kingdoms' loyalists and Aureatia battle each other? Jelki must understand that he's a danger to Aureatia. The others should also realize that much...and yet.

The discussion in the meeting had focused on the reliability of not the information source, but the information itself. It wasn't because they were all incompetent; if anything, it was because they were excellent bureaucrats.

They knew that needlessly pursuing topics of discussion that could be postponed for later would delay their handling of the clear and present dangers in front of them. It had been necessary to continue the discussion with the common understanding that *at the very least, the information was worthy of their trust.*

That was how the Twenty-Nine Officials judged the situation. If this was all put into motion on purpose, then it would have to be the work of a considerably sharp mind...

The True Demon King was dead, and the monsters that had remained asleep during the age of terror were beginning to stir. That was limited solely to embodiments of violence that destroyed whole nations. There had to also be *intellectual monsters* that brought about effects even more dangerous than ruination—manipulating everything, including whole nations, without ever taking a step on the battlefield.

Grasse was different. He had no wicked intentions. Nor was he hatching any schemes or plots. However, and especially now that he was informed of something so beyond anyone's expectations, a danger to the nation itself, his true inner character rose up to the surface.

His mouth curled into an uneven smile.

......*Interesting.*

Five days left until the disaster's arrival.

Toroa the Awful was dead.

For that matter, was there anyone who had actually seen him alive to begin with? Nevertheless, unlike Lucunoca the Winter, there was no one who questioned whether he actually existed or not.

That enchanted swordsman existed.

Making his home somewhere among the vast Wyte Mountains, he waited for the time to pass down judgment on others for their crimes.

The crime of possessing an enchanted sword.

When he had been alive, enchanted swords, along with their mighty power, attracted a fatal destiny to whoever held them.

"But listen, you dogs! Now's different!"

Erijite the Ochre Haze looked down at the forty subordinates he had assembled in the mountains. He was the bandit who had negotiated with the Gray-Haired Child at the Sikma Spinning Ward riverbed.

His band of thieves was in no way small, but naturally, the quality of his men was not enough to face off against an organized suppression squad or the soldiers of a self-proclaimed demon king. Therefore, they were likely never to be visited by this sort of opportunity again.

"Toroa the Awful's hundred enchanted swords—all of 'em are ours now! The keeper of the enchanted swords ain't around anymore!"

Those with enchanted swords would die. A death god would always appear before them as soon as their location was discovered.

The only thing left behind would be the sea of blood of the former owner and any witnesses, with the traces of a horrific and terrifying slaughter carved into the area, the enchanted sword vanished.

Toroa the Awful didn't care about whether the enchanted sword user was good or evil, a saint or a devil. He simply killed them.

No one had beaten him. No one had seen him. It was only the clear tragedy left behind that proved his existence.

This was an absolute and unquestionably proven rule that had continued on from before the appearance of the True Demon King.

"Chief! Did Toroa really bite the dust?! Sure, I get he was up against Alus the Star Runner, but we're talking Toroa the Awful here... He's the enchanted-swordsman slayer!"

"That's right, Euge. Right now, that's what everyone in the world is thinking. You, as well as all the bandits besides all of us! While everyone's thinking like that, what d'ya think'll happen? Who's gonna beat everyone to the punch? Go ahead, tell me."

"...I want an enchanted sword. Still, though, if owning one's gonna cost me my life, then—"

Euge's head was split open with a bullet. The speed of Erijite's quick-shot was faster than the naked eye could follow.

Smoke rose from the barrel of his new model of small firearm as he put it away in his inside pocket. He had bought the weapon from the Gray-Haired Child. This job was going to be a race against time.

Though it was unfortunate, as Euge had been a precious underling, able to express himself well.

"All right then, anyone else got any complaints?"

Now was precisely the time to get their hands on the power of the enchanted swords.

His subordinates likely only thought of them as treasure they could sell for a high price. However, a bandit group where each and every one of their forty-strong band wielded an enchanted sword, that would have power rivaling an individual army.

Then, as long as they had that degree of power, they could market that strength and sell it.

The approaching age was not an age of bandits. Erijite's very first aim was the camp of General Gilnes of Togie City—the Old Kingdoms' loyalists widely summoning those to join their cause.

We were able to survive this long because we're in the gap between the era of the True Demon King and the next. If the kingdoms are united once and for all, there ain't no future for guys like us.

He felt the small firearm in his pocket. Improvements to the musket continued to advance further along. The victims of their raids would start carrying these sorts of weapons with them wherever they went. Bandits would grow even easier to stamp out and put down.

...Going through the pains to create an intermediary was in anticipation of that future. Working with the Gray-Haired Child, we'll join under Gilnes the Ruined Castle. Even if the Old Kingdoms happen to lose, so long as we can showcase the power of the enchanted swords during the fighting, we'll be able to negotiate with Aureatia.

The odds were heavily in their favor. Now that Toroa was dead, the enchanted swords were no longer symbols of ill omen.

Although there was an absolute difference in fighting power, these enchanted swords were categorically similar to the small firearm he now carried. As guns fell out of popularity along with the new age of peace, if anything, there would be higher demand for enchanted swords, especially among small bands of soldiers. These were the thoughts flowing through Erijite's mind.

His subordinates were abuzz with the shot, and the brief confusion and uproar slowly began to settle down.

There were others with similar claims as Euge, but he ignored them and left their arguments to be wrapped up among the rest of the band. Given that they had seen Euge's death right before their very eyes, this wasn't true whole-hearted rebellion.

"...Listen up. Why do you think some stingy mountain bandits like us are able to scavenge through *the* Toroa's left-behind property? Because I'm strong? Because we got good heads on our shoulders? Or maybe you're thinkin' it's because we've got the advantage of numbers?"

This would be the last time he spoke. He just needed to boost their resolve.

"That ain't it, right? It's just because we're nearby. Because we've set up our territory in Wyte, and we know these mountains better than anybody. Those other guy don't even know whether Toroa is in this stretch of mountains or not. We'll get there first. We absolutely will."

"Let's do this...! Treasure waiting to get plucked up! We can do it!"

"Who the hell cares about some damn enchanted sword curse...?! We're right behind you, Chief!"

"Now that's more like it! The era of legends and superstitions is over! Toroa the Awful being dead proves it! All right, lads, let's go!"

A disaster on par with a dragon. Lying in wait in the uninhabited reaches, he'd set upon villages, stockpiling his hoard.

The only difference was his hoard was entirely composed of enchanted swords. Thus, Alus the Star Runner attacked him. After stealing the absolute strongest among them all, the Star Runner flew away.

Legends were not invincible. Even Toroa the Awful could die.

◆

Far removed from Wyte, on the outskirts of Aureatia, there stood a spire.

Within a tract of land where city redevelopment operations continued forward to match growing population density, a single belfry, under the authority of the Twenty-Nine Officials, was left behind without being torn down. The floors inside the tower were carved out, creating a large open space. All that remained of the original interior design was the stairs running along the walls.

The cold and closed-off air felt almost like a high-ceilinged prison, but the person dwelling inside was the most unsuited creature in all the land to be called a "prisoner."

"..........."

"Gotten used to it a bit now?"

"..........."

The Twentieth Minster of Aureatia, Hido the Clamp, had made the remark without any expectations of getting an answer.

His companion's silence was long, but they didn't seem to be unsatisfied with their dwelling.

Even this unique reconstruction had been carried out according to the wishes of the wyvern perched high up above him—Alus the Star Runner.

His pace was always one beat behind everyone else's. He began in a quiet voice.

"......Hido."

"Yeah, what is it?"

"Is Harghent...coming...? I want to fight him... When will he be here...?"

"Ah, right... I'm not sure, with that old man... *Pfft!* He's ditched his work and now he's fooling around in the north. Though, he'll probably come back around the time of the next assembly. I have absolutely no idea what sort of hero candidate he's gonna show up with, though."

"......Okay. Then......forget it."

Sitting down on the bottommost stair, Hido took his slightly late lunch.

High-quality white bread. Though he was impertinent, bubbling with arrogance, meals were the only time he enjoyed a quiet atmosphere. He and Alus were in agreement on this point.

"...Still, though, Alus. You know...ultimately, no matter who shows up, you don't really think you'll lose, do you? You've won every battle you've been in up till now. Even against Vikeon the Smoldering. You think old man Harghent...is really going to be able to bring back someone capable of fighting you?"

"............Are you making fun of Harghent?"

"Huh? Of course I'm not; come on now. I'm just asking if you've even had a tough battle before at all."

Hido immediately picked up on the mood in the tower and decided to steer the topic elsewhere.

The outline of Alus's wings was high above his head, but if he felt like it, Alus could kill him in innumerably different ways faster than Hidow could take the next bite of his lunch.

"......There was......someone strong."

"Really now? Was it Vikeon the Smoldering after all?"

"........What are you talking about...? That guy.........he was just old, not strong at all...... Toroa......he was so much stronger than any dragon......"

"Oh, you mean Toroa the Awful? So that rumor everyone tells was true, huh? Everyone'd love to hear about that, let me tell you."

"......Look here."

The wyvern carefully descended to around the middle of the tower and showed off the sword he had produced from his satchel. With its darkened brown scabbard and similarly dingy wooden hilt, it looked like an antique.

"......This is Hillensingen the Luminous Blade. It was Toroa's......most powerful weapon, so......I wanted it."

"This is the one that ended Vikeon, right? Did Toroa really stockpile all those enchanted swords?"

"......Yeah. But... I didn't really care about the others......and I can't fly if my bag's too heavy...."

"Ha-ha-ha-ha-ha! Aww, that's a damn shame!"

It was no laughing matter.

Enchanted swords were treasures, with a single one carrying as much value as a whole town. Aberrant entities, impossible to analyze. With their inanimate silence, even the true origins of these enchanted swords were unclear.

However, they were said to be, similar to visitors, implements that were deviant in nature.

These implements, acquiring unfathomable mysteries that were unable to be fully contained within the physical laws of a world separate from theirs, the Beyond, were exiled to this world.

It wasn't limited to just swords, with various shapes of magic tools appearing in their world much the same way. Just as varied as the armaments in Alus the Star Runner's own collection.

...Nevertheless, enchanted swords were ultimately a special case when it came to their symbolic significance.

Symbols of armed might from long, long ago, existing in the realm of the supernatural. Many fought over enchanted swords, and by gathering under their power to fight, many self-proclaimed demon kings were created, and just as quickly erased.

Toroa the Awful might have been fixated on the enchanted swords for such a reason.

"What was Toroa the Awful like?"

"......Yeah. His techniques......were incredible. A bunch of them......all impossible without an enchanted sword. Against him......it didn't matter if I was flying in the air. The direction, too...... All the enchanted swords moved like they were alive themselves...."

"......"

"If I had been......just a fraction...of a millisecond slower, I might have died... Probably..."

Much like a majority of the children in this world, Hido had been told scary stories about Toroa the Awful from a young age. They said just being near someone wielding an enchanted sword, let alone brandishing one yourself, would bring the calamity called Toroa to your doorstep.

That was why no one was supposed to possess an enchanted sword. They invited death.

That legendary being was ultimately the one who had terrified a butcher of dragons like Alus the most of all.

In the Wyte Mountains, the legend had actually existed.

...It's a pity, really. No one can keep on winning forever. At some point, the legend will end.

Alus, with his wings, continued his journey of usurping, guided by his appetite. Many of those who made history or those who left their names behind wasted away, things to be protected exposed, and the world had changed completely from the time before the True Demon King.

Alus was nothing but a singular wyvern pioneer, subverting and exposing all the mysteries of the world.

"How did you kill Toroa?"

"...A single shot.........to his heart. I fired as he got close, and it hit......but I thought he'd move again.........so when I passed by him, I stole this......."

The rogue vacantly stared at the Luminous Blade, still stored within its sheath.

"I grabbed it and slashed him. He was diagonally......cut in two..."

"Whoa, whoa, hold on now... The hell sort of supernatural feat is that?"

Instantaneously swapping from gun to sword, all while maintaining absolute top speeds. All with the dexterity to plunder the opponent's own weapon, too.

It was a level of skill that defied all expectations, demanding wonder and admiration. Yet, for Alus the Star Runner to be driven to the brink, just how terrifying a monster was Toroa the Awful?

"............"

"Alus. You want tougher opponents?"

"......Not really."

"Then, what is it you want?"

Remaining on the stairs circulating the wall, the wyvern turned his thin neck.

He squinted up at the light that shined in from the window at the top of the spire.

"A country."

Alus the Star Runner. His appetite knew no limits.

That was precisely why Hido the Clamp, Aureatia's Twentieth Minister, stood as his backer.

He couldn't let this champion win.

◆

"...Relax. There are some guys who arrived before us. Ones who didn't hesitate while Euge was whining like a baby."

As he carefully moved in the shadow of the trees, Erijite loaded his small firearm with bullets.

...The four people he had directed to search on the mountain's western side hadn't returned. Maybe they were discovered and killed by other thieves after the enchanted swords. Their groups' movements had been one step too slow after all.

Given that the scouts sent to other conspicuous spots hadn't discovered any enchanted swords, the only possible location of Toroa the Awful's base was the western side, where the four others had disappeared.

"But we've got the positional advantage. If those other guys have taken the enchanted swords first, we just gotta trap 'em and kill 'em. Not gonna give 'em any time to swing those things. Simple as that."

"Y-yeah, that's right, Chief!"

"We've figured out the location! Let's snuff them out fast!"

They were a simple lot. In the beginning, Erijite had whipped them into action by claiming they'd gain invincible power so long as they got their hands on the enchanted swords.

None of them realized that the words he used now to urge them on were contradictory to his initial claims before them. Though, conversely, some of them may have been pretending not to know instead.

Erijite's thinking was that he could tolerate sacrificing no more than half his men. Even if he expended twenty men in the enchanted sword robbery, he would still be left with a force twenty strong, and more than enough enchanted swords for them all to wield.

With the strength that ascended him to the commanding seat among the mountain brigands, he calculated out the past decisions and possibly futures ahead them, balancing all their advantages and disadvantages.

"Wh-whoa, chief!"

"What's wrong?"

"…One of them's come back! It's him, uh, what was his name again?"

"Eveedo?"

From far off, the thin man walked unsteadily down the mountain path toward them. His wide-open item satchel swayed back and forth, its contents spilling out on the ground with each step.

His gaze was vacant and hollow. Even when the chief Erijite stood right in front him, his focus was blank and far-off.

"…Hey, Eveedo. You've got something to tell me, right?"

"……"

"So that's how it is, huh? You making a fool outta me?"

When he thrust the barrel of his small firearm at him, it happened.

There came a damp, splattering sound.

Eveedo's right shoulder down to his left flank slid diagonally off his body and hit the ground. Continuing with his waist. The base of his left leg. Horizontally across his head, through both eyes. Erijite hadn't even touched him, yet Eveedo had been reduced to a pile of viscera.

He had already been cut down. Just how was he walking with all his flesh still connected?

It was impossible. A power inconceivable to their world.

"......Wh-what..."

"It's an enchanted sword! We knew all about this already! Some other bandits are using the damn things! We figured that would happen, nothing to be surprised about! The guys headed to the western side are dead! That's all!"

"Y-yeah, but...look at how he died, Chief...!"

This was a bad sign, Erijite thought.

The way he handled things with Euge wasn't a method he could keep relying on. What should he do to keep this wave of fear in check? It was time to try and think things over.

"Huh?"

Right before Erijite's eyes, the man standing directly to his right let out a wild shriek.

On his chest was a small red stain, like he had been stabbed with a needle. Bit by bit, it slowly started to expand outward.

"Wha-what?!"

The man, still screaming in bewilderment, collapsed.

"Damn...!"

Erijite ground his teeth. It was an attack. Eveedo must have been the bait.

Someone had watched them being taken in by the living corpse. From where?

"Chief! This has to be—*aaauugh!*"

A shadow passed behind one of their compatriots, trying to rush over to them from afar, and then they burst into flames.

Blinding and enormous flames surrounded the periphery, as if the man's very body had been converted into an explosive. The mere aftermath of the flames killed another two of his men with it.

The shadow moving on the other end of the conflagration belonged to a single person. It was bent forward, almost like a wild beast.

On this mysterious person's back sat an innumerable number of...

"...What the hell?! Just who are you, dammit?!"

Erijite aimed his barrel toward the shadow.

The mysterious person's form wasn't clear, shimmering in the haze of the explosion's heat. It was large, with thick arms and legs.

An ogre? Or maybe a dwarf?

"Nel Tseu the Burning Blade."

The figure murmured with the deep voice of a death god.

They slowly advanced forward, one step at a time. Erijite's gun barrel was shaking—and the heat haze that prevented him from aiming steady wasn't the only reason why.

The next sound rang with a thud.

The second-in-command standing next to Erijite was pierced through the eyes with the same needle-sized stain as before and collapsed to the ground.

"Divine Blade Ketelk."

The shade passed by another bandit, who walked around aimless and unsteady before slumping down to the ground.

Their four limbs, torn apart just like Eveedo's...

"Gidymel the Minute Hand."

The crunching sound of heavy footsteps continued to close in.

A large number of enchanted swords. A man shouldering a myriad of cursed enchanted swords on his back.

He was a bandit. Just a thief. He was after the enchanted sword riches just like them.

Erijite just got there too late. A simple bit of bad luck.

There was no possible way Toroa the Awful would be still alive.

◆

He couldn't train by sparring against an opponent.

Just as their sword shape suggested, a large majority of enchanted sword uses were lethal. As a result, there was a contradiction in completing these drills several hundreds of times, a solitary battle wielding the real sword's weight, size, and unusual abilities, as close to real combat as possible.

Thus, while the results of his training would be beyond the sight of the average person, Yakon the Sanctuary understood very well that his own skills weren't enough.

He swung his sword until the sun set, but he was far off from his ideal, the way his father swung his sword. He was completely out of breath, countless beads of sweat dripping from his chin.

His father was sitting nearby on a tree stump. He had been quietly watching Yakon's training since the sun was still high in the sky.

Seeing the fruits of his training with his own eyes, he forced a smile.

"No talent with enchanted swords, really."

Yakon knew it, too. He would never become like his dad.

Yakon was a dwarf, and his father was a leprechaun. A parent and child where even their races were totally different. Among the minian races, dwarves had exceptionally large builds and excellent physiques, and were the total opposite of leprechauns—dexterous, with snappy reflexes like a panicked field mouse's.

Even among such dwarves, Yakon was extraordinarily strong.

Though he had never compared himself with those beyond the mountains, he passed his days shouldering firewood stockpiles taller than he was up and down the steep mountain paths without difficulty. On open ground, he could maintain a full-strength run from sunup to sundown. When he wasn't carrying anything, he had even overtaken galloping horses before.

He had never once been ill, and any cut he got in the morning would heal before evening would arrive. From an early age, his dad had told him he possessed exceptionally strong vitality.

The only times Yakon exhausted his stamina enough to gasp for air was during these moments, training with enchanted swords.

With his youth and superior physique, he should have far outshined his dad, yet the difference in enchanted swords' proficiency felt vaster than the distance from the ground to the stars.

"You're too gentle. That's why you're allowing the ideas dwelling inside them into yourself, and it's getting in the way of your technique. That's the reason why you use so much unnecessary stamina. Your body and your mind are at odds with one another."

"...Then, next...time, I just...need to throw those ideas away, then? I...can still do it. Dad. Next time. By the next time...you watch me, I promise. Guaranteed."

He replied in between gasps for air. Yakon wondered how many times they had had this exchange by now.

The results of his training were always subpar, and his dad would tell him to give up being an enchanted swordsman. Yakon never gave up. He had never even considered another path. Nor did his dad ever compel the struggling Yakon toward something else.

Yakon used a cane to help him stand back up. He started preparing these canes for when he used up all his strength during training about two years prior. He couldn't use his dad's precious enchanted swords to prop himself up.

"......*Koff, koff*! The boar meat should be nice and soaked by now. I can make your favorite soup, Dad... Let's go home."

"If you're tired, then I don't need dinner. Cold today, huh?"

The all-too-small father couldn't lend his shoulder to Yakon.

Nothing about him and Yakon was similar. Not their features. Not their strength. Not their skill. That may have been why Yakon wanted at least one thing to prove that he was truly his father's son.

The enchanted swordsman Toroa. The strongest enchanted sword–wielder in the land.

Being his son was the pride of Yakon the Sanctuary.

◆

However, that day, he felt unsure if he would be able to remain his son.

He asked the question that had begun to dwell inside him during their calm, daily lives.

"Dad... Is it okay if I don't inherit your enchanted swordsman title?"

His father had never said himself why he continued his wicked plundering.

Sitting across the dining table, his father gave a tired smile.

"It's fine. This'll end with me."

His leprechaun-sized bowl was soon empty. Yakon quickly refilled it with more soup.

"...But enchanted swords upset our world. If people are going to fight over the enchanted swords, then there wouldn't be any conflict over them if they never existed in the first place... Is that why you've been collecting them, Dad?"

"Who did you hear that from?"

"...No one. I...just thought that myself."

Toroa the Awful killed the wielders of enchanted swords.

With a stature less than a third that of a minia, he effortlessly handled numerous enchanted swords far longer and larger than his physical height, mercilessly murdering whoever would attempt to wield them. Without any pleasure, or sadness, as though it was simply how things should be.

Yakon had always thought about the duty Toroa himself never spoke about.

"You might be right. I probably thought that at first. That by stealing enchanted swords, I might be able save some number of lives. Without weapons there wouldn't be any conflict. A young and foolish way of thinking."

Toroa didn't bring his fresh bowl of soup to his lips, instead staring hard at his eyes reflected in its surface.

He wasn't an unreasonable monstrosity that all feared to speak of. He was simply his father, so quiet and serene it made the legends of his carnage sound fantastical.

"...The world's not like that. Even without enchanted swords, people still fight. They just want enchanted swords as a means to fight. People can turn even pebbles and pieces of wood into lethal weapons. Without enchanted swords...the future after that could be even more awful."

"...That's not true! The Gashin East-West War. The Dragon Axe Campaign. There are so many examples of wars that ended because they didn't use enchanted swords...!"

"I kill people who simply witness what I do. Innocent people."

Toroa murmured, remaining completely calm.

"That's how I tried to make people fear enchanted swords as cursed objects. If I was going to start all over......I don't think I would do that... Listen to me, Yakon. No matter how much I regret or say it was all a mistake, the lives I took are the only things

I can never give back. And I can't ever change myself. I'm the one who disregarded those lives in the first place."

"……"

He couldn't ask him why, then, if that was the case, he still continued.

His father would definitely never try to stop. He would continue until every enchanted sword owner was gone from the world.

His father may have kept fighting simply to convince himself. He may have been unable to stop himself from continuing what he started.

Yakon wanted to answer him, "That's exactly why your son can take over for you! You can rest now!"

His own powerlessness frustrated him. He watched his distinguished father's techniques; he trained so hard, and yet no matter how many years he spent, he could never catch up.

"…I'm your son, Dad. I'll never say all the stuff you've done was a mistake."

"Is that right? Well, thank you."

Yakon left the warm interior behind. Just a little bit more…to train just one more time.

It was a night with the small moon shining bright.

His father slowly drank his soup, as if pondering the meaning of life.

◆

Three small months passed from that night. The day of destiny.

Up above. No. Diving diagonally down in front.

The mountains were covered in a downpour. Toroa had his sights fixed on his enemy in the air.

All four directions, as well as up and down. Their mobility options were much greater compared to those stuck crawling on the ground.

Not only that, but they were not the same movements of other wyverns, influenced by instincts and the wind direction. Possessing the judgment only present in those who have danced the tightrope between life and death, they saw through Toroa's next move before acting themselves.

Those who asserted their meaning through strength were altogether unable to escape such a destiny. Someone stronger would appear, and they would one day lose everything.

For Toroa the Awful, that person was none other than Alus the Star Runner.

...He's going to fire.

Alus put his finger on the gun's trigger. He picked up on the subtle movement. Toroa sent his rapier flying out of its sheath.

It was the Divine Blade Ketelk. It was an enchanted sword that extended its invisible slash past the outermost part of the blade itself, upsetting the spacing in close-quarters combat.

However, when Toroa the Awful was the one using it...

"—Peck."

He lunged at Alus with it, focusing on a singular spot as if he were stabbing at him with a needle. His opponent was twenty meters above him. He pierced a hole in the wing membrane and broke Alus's midair stance.

Not good. Even worse than if it didn't hit him at all.

His opponent's movements were too fast. Despite preventing the shot aimed his way, if the wound from his sword wasn't fatal, then Toroa had done nothing but show his hand to his opponent. Nor was his Peck stab something he could send out rapid-fire. His impatience that he would be shot first if he didn't shoot Alus out of the sky had gotten the better of him.

As he descended down, a flash of gunfire came from Alus's hands. The bullet ricocheted off one of the mountains' enormous boulders and closed straight in on the artery below Toroa's armpit following his stab attack.

The short sword dangling from his waist automatically leaped into the air. The blade became a shield, warding off the poisonous magic bullet.

Lance of Faima. This short sword connected by a chain matched the projectile's speed as it responded, but it wasn't a defense he could always rely on. He had been lucky.

Alus the Star Runner. Not going to use your thunder's roar magic bullet?

Toroa had an enchanted sword that could control magnetic forces. Alus was wary of it.

There were several enchanted swords stabbed into the ground. Toroa thrust the Divine Blade Ketelk into the earth, letting go and taking up another enchanted sword in its stead. Hillensingen the Luminous Blade.

Visitors. Tarantula. Dragons. When it became necessary to fight such aberrations, with a physique unable to wield multiple swords at once, this was how Toroa used his blades. The area around looked like an enchanted sword graveyard.

"......You're strong......"

The wyvern muttered drearily. He appeared annoyed at the unexpectedly powerful opponent.

Toroa ran to the spot where Alus was going to land. Still far away. If he extended the Luminous Blade out as far as he could, he might be able to slash him.

"Hey......that sword......!"

"......!"

At that moment, something flew down from above Toroa's head. It wasn't rain.

It was a storm of deadly blades.

"Shnnng!"

By drawing his sword at a sharp angle, the Luminous Blade's trajectory served as a shield to defend against the attack from above. Light flashed for a brief instant right after the sword left its sheath, then vanished.

It was a practical application, possible only to those who knew the true value of the all-powerful enchanted sword, called "Roost."

Alus had already taken to the air and left Toroa's line of sight, where he could closely observe the wyvern's movements.

"—Rotten Soil Sun."

Following behind the mud blades, a spherical clod of soil, big enough to be held with two hands, fell. It must have been what caused the rain of blades.

He instantly refocused his attention. It was Alus's intention to draw his focus to the magic tool. The Lance of Faima flew. Its reaction speed ultimately wasn't fast enough. Nevertheless, from the direction of its automatic interception, he realized Alus was rushing at him from behind.

He didn't have the time to trigger the Luminous Blade again. With his other hand, he swung his sickle-bladed halberd. He sensed a leftward diagonal slash coming from behind him before he could fully turn his sights in that direction.

The attacks crossed each other. The tactile sensation of tearing flesh. They passed each other by.

Toroa barely managed to block the lethal magic bullet. The blade of his enchanted sword, on the follow-through, had shielded against the bullet Alus fired from point-blank range. The wyvern was passing him by, still at charging speed, unable to leverage the greatest possible opportunity to kill Toroa once and for all.

...I saw through you, too, eh.

In the instant they clashed, Toroa's attack had only grazed Alus's body. Inrate, the Sickle of Repose. An enchanted sword naturally specialized for surprise attacks, its slashes causing a phenomenon that made it completely silent—

Beads of terror, a sensation he had long ago forgotten, ran down his forehead.

His long years of experience were telling him—Toroa the Awful was going to die here.

The time had come for the man who lived as a death god, judging others for their crimes, to be judged himself.

"Dad!"

He heard a voice from afar. Yakon's voice.

Now he would bear witness to Toroa's final moments.

Grinding his teeth at the irony of fate, he sheathed the Luminous Blade and planted it into the ground in front of him. He couldn't let Yakon get involved in a fight against this wyvern. He had been the one to start this cause and effect.

...One more time. I just need to put my life on the line one more time.

He readied Inrate, the Sickle of Repose. Cutting the Lance of Faima's chain, he placed it inside his clothes.

It was a worthless life anyway.

Alus swung around. Forward, to the right. No, an assault straight from above. Toroa could perceive the high-speed movements, including all his enemy's feints, impossible for an ordinary person to see.

"Me too! I'll fight, too!"

Toroa smiled—*This is out of your league.*

Light fell from the sky and looking at it directly hurt his eyes. This was another way to use fire-aspected magic tools.

A bullet came flying toward him immediately after. The poisonous magic bullet, fired during Alus's full-strength acceleration forward, moved several times faster, piercing him through the left chest. The Lance of Faima inside his clothes automatically defended him. His gamble had paid off.

The enemy was getting closer. Even with his dazed vision, he could tell that much.

Alus's only path to victory was a lethal bullet fired up close and inside of his swords' defenses. Whether it was mud, whips, or fire—none of them could win against the legendary Toroa the Awful.

The two combatants each knew this fact of their battle very well.

His enemy had full knowledge of Inrate, the Sickle of Repose's maximum range, and its overall power.

He's thinking that he'll be able to defend himself from this sickle.

He wiped out the sickle.

Perfect.

Following along with its accelerated movements, he let his fingers go and flung his own sickle. He made Alus misjudge its range. He had planned to do this from the start and shifted the weapon in his hands to do so. There, at the end of his hand's follow-through, was an enchanted sword sticking out from the ground.

"I'm..."

The accelerating Alus didn't stop. His charge was still coming. Toroa's eyes were dazed and disoriented.

"Toroa the Awful."

Despite everything, Toroa the Awful had the sword that could truly deliver instant death. He knew its power, and its longest range, even with his eyes closed. The very moment they passed by each other, with the Luminous Blade stuck in the dirt in front of him—

"It's—"

The sizzling sound seared itself into his ears.

"—mine."

Just a little farther, immediately before his fingers could reach it...

He was cut down by the stolen Hillensingen, the Luminous Blade. Alus shouldn't have been able to reach it from where he was.

"Kio's Hand."

The enchanted whip, extending out like a tentacle, twined around the Luminous Blade and cleaved Toroa's body in two.

He had been unable to imagine any of it. To think Alus would make use of the enchanted sword's full potential or that he possessed the exceptional skill to wield an enchanted sword through a whip.

No one was gifted at everything. Such a person could not exist.

For Toroa, all he had was his masterful skill with his enchanted swords.

"Dad...! Dad, noooo!"

Alus had vanished without a trace. He cut him down and left him there before flying off with the Luminous Blade.

Toroa's small body was cut in half at the waist.

"Dad! Please, Dad, don't die!"

His much larger son was sobbing.

Crying for a shura who, for the entirety of his long life, had only ever chosen the path of bloodshed.

Yakon gripped Toroa's hand and yelled as if the words were being squeezed out of him.

"I'm sorry... I'm sorry, Dad... I... I couldn't come out sooner... Alus the Star Runner, he was so scary and I... I didn't think someone like me stood a chance, so... I couldn't do anything...!"

It's okay.

A wretched end like this suits me.

You're not a shura. That was what Toroa wished he could tell him.

Yakon was a gentle child.

Why was a leprechaun, living in darkness, raising a dwarven child? What sort of fate had his real parents met and at whose hands? The boy had known for a long time. Toroa knew that he knew, too.

He had still called Toroa his "dad."

Their world was unjust.

Toroa the Awful was never able to fully atone for his countless crimes nor was he ever able to be properly punished.

The man who chiseled away his soul with his blood-soaked ideals had lived an almost laughably luxurious life.

"Dad....! Dad! I'll do it! I'll get back the Luminous Blade! I'll follow in your footsteps! It'll, it'll all be okay... Dad!"

...Yakon.

Yakon the Sanctuary.

His only son had been the merciless god of death from Wyte's last remaining sanctuary.

I wanted to say thank you.

The skills and strength you've built up over these restless years have long since surpassed my old bones. I wanted to make sure to tell you, that's why you shouldn't aim to be an enchanted swordsman, why you shouldn't end up like me.

But. That's right. If that was true, then why?

Why hadn't Toroa tried to stop Yakon's training at all?

He probably couldn't have truly been able to stop him, given his adoration for the enchanted swordsman.

"I'll never say all the stuff you did was a mistake."

...Even if the path I took was a mistake...

He was happy to have Yakon's admiration. His life had been affirmed by his beloved son.

That, alone, was enough.

"Dad...!"

Toroa the Awful was dead.

No legends were immortal.

◆

......*Alus the Star Runner.*

Wearing a number of enchanted swords, the man conquered the mountains.

He carried easily over ten of the blades, whose weight should have been far too much for Toroa the Awful to bear.

The body he had continuously trained without rest was far brawnier and bigger than the legendary enchanted swordsman's.

I'm going to take it back from you. No more plunder. I'm not going to steal.

Deep in the Wyte Mountains, he was going to make the enchanted swords rest for all eternity. Just as his father had wished. And, just like his father had hoped, he would live on without taking the lives of anyone else as a god of death.

He had wanted to swear to his father while he was still alive that he would become that sort of enchanted swordsman someday.

Plunderers after the enchanted swords were swarming toward his father's grave marker. Enchanted swords birthed conflict.

He drew an enchanted sword.

He threw his own life away.

There still existed work in the world that Toroa the Awful needed to shoulder.

"Nel Tseu the Burning Blade."

He quietly murmured, cutting down a band of bandits. The concussive thunder drowned out their dying screams.

Gathering Clouds. The heat expelled from the sword's cutting flash builds up inside the enemy he cuts and is released. His father's technique. The technique of this enchanted sword's wielder. He had watched it many times before.

He wouldn't let anyone steal them. Things that shouldn't be, where they should be.

Until he regained the enchanted sword of light, his life was not his own to lead.

He wielded enchanted swords. Because he was an enchanted swordsman.

He killed people. Because he was a god of death.

"Divine Blade Ketelk."

He made sure of the enchanted sword's name. With it, he stabbed someone far away.

By narrowing the invisible long-range slash to a singular point, he could pierce foes from extremely long distances, a technique called Peck.

"Gidymel the Minute Hand."

Yet another was cut through. The technique to slow the final effects of this enchanted sword's slashes, something only possible

with Toroa the Awful's superb skills. His singular attack was simply confirming whether he could pull off the same move or not—Molting.

"Lance of Faima. Wailsever. Mushain the Howling Blade. Wicked Sword Selfesk.

Crunch. Crunch.

He swung his numerous enchanted swords together as he took each step forward.

He had no talent for using the blades.

His overly kind temperament took in the enchanted swords' latent ideas and got in the way of his own technique. That had been correct. Everything was exactly as his enchanted swordsman father had judged it to be.

In that case, the next step was…

"Vajgir, the Frostvenom Blade. Downpour's Needle. Karmic Castigation. Inrate, the Sickle of Repose."

From all of the enchanted swords, he had read and taken in the ideas that dwelled within them.

Just means I can toss those ideas away.

He put the ideas from his mind. Not the enchanted swords' ideas, but his very own. Thus right now, he was propelled by the enchanted swords' will, and with it, he was able to exercise the techniques of their most skilled wielder—the techniques of his father.

The techniques that had been seared into the back of his brain over and over again from a young age.

He possessed no talent for using enchanted swords.

He had talent for being used by enchanted swords.

"T-Toroa… Toroa, the Awful…!"

The final remaining ringleader groaned his name.

He was right. That was who he was now.

"Now. Which enchanted sword do you want?"

While possessing the abilities of the former, a horror story incarnate, he commanded far more physical strength.

He held a myriad of enchanted swords, gathered over the entirety of a long age.

He went beyond his natural ego and was capable of controlling the inner essence of every enchanted sword.

A god of death, revived from the deep pits of the underworld, collecting the cursed fates of others.

Grim Reaper. Dwarf.

Toroa the Awful.

The evening sun bathed the streets of Aureatia in an amber glow. The office of Aureatia's Fourth Minister, looking down over the scenery, was situated in a section of Aureatia where land was particularly high-value.

A gorgeous woman in a red dress entered the room and gave a light bow. The Seventeenth Minster, Elea the Red Tag, had been summoned by the room's master, and came to give a report on the results of her series of investigations.

"It's been too long, Fourth Minister."

"The only reason it's been so long is because you were so obsessed with your investigation out in the far-off boonies of Eta."

Together with his biting initial comments, the man glared at Elea from across the desk. He had strong, sharp features, but the glint in his eyes was cunning and cruel. He was the Fourth Minister, Kaete the Round Table.

While a civil servant like Elea, the man possessed both pre-eminent authority and military might. It was rumored around town that he was the sole face able to stand toe-to-toe against the faction of Aureatia's all-powerful Second General, Rosclay the Absolute.

"Not only that, but you still haven't given a proper report on the investigation *you* were in charge of. In our meeting on the

Particle Storm, information collected from my soldiers got here faster than your damn report."

Elea bowed her head. Normally, investigation updates and the like were not the responsibility of the head of the intelligence division herself. Despite this, up against the exceedingly harsh disposition of Kaete the Round Table, she had no other choice.

Within the Twenty-Nine Officials of Aureatia, there were no limits based on age or term of service and each individual was recognized as having their own discretionary authority. At the very least, that was how it was on paper.

"My humblest apologies.... Due to the pressing matter at hand, I prioritized contacting those who could immediately respond to the situation. Although it delayed my report to you by a day, I was prepared to give you my report."

"You're saying that's why it's late?"

Kaete scoffed.

"That's not it. You're incompetent. In truth, you've failed to complete the task you were given. It's the intelligence division's job to notify the Twenty-Nine Officials of any information as swiftly as possible. You, Harghent—irredeemably incompetent, the whole lot of you. Maybe Twenty-Nine seats are unnecessary. Am I wrong?"

"......"

While it was unbelievably humiliating to hear her name said in the same breath as Harghent's, Elea remained silent and waited for his next words. Given her position as a lowborn successor of the previous Seventeenth Minister, she was well accustomed to being looked down on.

Kaete meanwhile turned his attention to the view from the window. To him, born with authority, his sadism was a part of everyday life, completely devoid of any relaxation or enjoyment.

"Forget it. Give your report."

"Very well. Three days ago, the Old Kingdoms' loyalists under the command of Gilnes the Ruined Castle took complete control of the Togie City Council. The whole city has been placed under martial law. Gilnes had been recruiting volunteers for a while, and including the soldiers who joined from the New Principality of Lithia and soldiers from the Central Kingdom period, we believe there are close to thirty thousand partisans in total."

"I've heard that. At the very least, those Central Kingdom ghosts have gotten the numbers together."

"Of course, this all falls within our expectations. Even if they start an all-out rebellion, as things currently stand, the regional army keeping an eye on the city is enough to handle them. The problem lies in what's urging them to action, which we anticipate will bring a direct attack to Aureatia soil."

"*Hmph.* This Particle Storm or what have you, right?"

"A weather anomaly unique to the Yamaga Barrens. Supposing this makes a direct attack on Aureatia itself, it's certain to cause massive damages far beyond anything we can imagine. However dominant our on-hand military forces may be, should the Old Kingdoms' army use the disruption to the chain of command that would accompany an enormous natural disaster to attack us, we would be at a grievous disadvantage."

The Old Kingdoms' loyalists' idea was the total opposite of the New Principality's, who tried to control the shura, with their aberrant violent power, and put them on the front lines. They sought to gain the upper hand by letting this impossibility to control power stay out of control.

"We are moving forward with countermeasures against this weather phenomenon with the highest priority. We've called the

Twenty-Fifth General Kayon the Thundering and the Twenty-Second General Mizial the Iron-Piercing Plumeshade with an emergency summons. Currently, both generals' troops are heading to handle the situation. No other generals have dispatched troops. In order to cover for both of their departures, I request that you, Fourth Minister, handle the homeland defense on behalf of the Twenty-Nine Officials."

"...Ridiculous. Damn weaklings, all of you."

Kaete spat, his tone filled with deeply felt contempt.

"Solidifying the homeland defenses is totally unnecessary. Those troops of yours haven't gotten hold of the information, have they? The Old Kingdoms' loyalists' rear camp took a devastating hit. Even if an outbreak of hostilities was possible, they no longer have the strength to support their front line. These bastards needed to rely on a natural disaster to try and win from the start, anyway."

"How did you get that information...?"

"Best show some respect. In our current situation, information is a matter of life and death—just how many of us do you think are solely relying on you and your spies to get it? The day you've outlived your use is coming fast."

It was exactly as Kaete said. His eyes, and the eyes of the other major players in the Twenty-Nine Officials, were not turned to the war with the Old Kingdoms' loyalists. They were focused on what came after: the Imperial Competition to determine the Hero.

Amid political strife, where each faction was trying to outsmart the other, there wasn't anyone who trusted the information that came in from outside their own faction. It was likely that Elea's troops would also slowly split apart and start to be absorbed into the other factions. Much like the fate that the former Obsidian Eyes met, the ones who tried to monopolize information during times of war would eventually be ostracized and grow weak.

"That's enough. I've compared information plenty. I'm a busy man."

Kaete calmly declared to the person he had personally summoned to his office. Unreasonable, and impudent. Thus was the Fourth Minister, Kaete the Round Table.

This was all just to test me...from the very start.

Elea bit her lip. This man's aim behind forcing Elea to give him a direct report wasn't the information itself. It had all been so he could compare to see if there were any deviances in its accuracy, and to verify if she had already allied herself with another faction.

Elea the Red Tag had risen up from nothing, repeatedly betraying others over and over again, into her leading position in the intelligence division. The daughter of a prostitute, the suspicious Seventeenth Minister. She didn't have a single ally who fully trusted her.

"Soujirou the Willow-Sword, huh?"

His voice called out to her as she put her hand on the door.

"What...about him?"

"You don't get it? If you're aiming for the sort of quick rise in power, like what you've done up until now, I'm saying it's got to be about the Imperial Competition. I already knew that during your infiltration into Togie City, you used that visitor, the Willow-Sword, to help. I just thought maybe you were trying to devise a way to sponsor him."

"Not at all. I was simply borrowing the Willow-Sword to have the necessary fighting power with me. I... I don't have any plans on sponsoring *him*."

"Is that so? Not that I care either way. If you don't want to see yourself destroyed, I suggest you hide that ambition of yours."

"...Thank you for the warning."

With a bow, she exited the office room. All of her emotions were cleanly bottled up within her pretty face.

The war with the Old Kingdoms' loyalists isn't the problem. There are only a few factors that could cause Aureatia to lose.

Kaete was correct. The real problem lay after said war.

The information obtained by each regions' spies was extremely complex, and all woven together as well.

The Particle Storm from the Yamaga Barrens is closing in on Aureatia. The Gray-Haired Child, distributing firearms and weather information, is actively working behind the scenes of the war. Toroa the Awful, who is supposed to be dead, was spotted around Wyte. And...a demon king. The one responsible for the assault on the Old Kingdoms' loyalists' encampment was a self-proclaimed demon king. What's happening while I've been unaware...?

Assuming that all of these were not coincidental phenomena, but part of a slowing convergence to a single point...

There was a plot behind anything and everything. With the clairvoyance of Kuuro the Cautious, whom she met that day in Togie, maybe she, too, could have perceived it all as an indistinct and threatening premonition.

Nevertheless. Even if all these plots are to thwart me.

Though she had risen all the way up to a place among the Twenty-Nine Officials, even now, she was on the side of the have-nots. Neither Rosclay the Absolute nor Kaete the Round Table included Elea's presence within the course of events they were trying to steer.

The one to win and survive through the Imperial Competition... will be me.

A tournament to determine a sole Hero, to back the greatest of all symbols, eventually rising above the monarchy.

Elea was fighting all by herself. She hadn't a single ally who would fully trust someone like her. However, she alone held an all-powerful trump card that would flip everything in her favor.

I'm the only who knows about the Kia...about the World Word.

Four days left until the disaster's arrival.

What crime had she committed to get wrapped up in such a horrifying event? Minle couldn't understand.

She was a humble housewife, living modestly in the Gakana Saltpan Township, with the only good fortune to her name being that she survived the age of the True Demon King. Cradling her one-year-old daughter to her chest, she prayed that the monster would not appear again.

The sea raged, and the rocky reef, towering high above her, was like a maze. If someone had told her the things she saw had come from the edges of the ocean to destroy her entire world, she would have believed it.

They were two strange aberrations. At the very least, neither were living creatures.

"I've found you."

A voice like a glacial bell echoed. One of the aberrations was floating above. Its appearance was exactly that of the angels seen in religious paintings. Still, she knew it couldn't possibly be one.

Real angels didn't sprout wings made from metal and gears. They didn't glow with a merciless and cruel light, nor would they chase a victim like her away.

"You have not taken action. However, I have found you."

From another direction, there came a roar that drowned out the angel's voice.

It was the sound of overlapping metallic creaking. The other aberration started to move.

"KRRRRRRRRREEEEEEEEEE!"

In its charge, it destroyed one of the boulders in its way. It was similar to the railway train she saw in the Central region. The body, with joints armored with thick metal, looked very similar to such a monstrous vehicle.

What was different was, this was a true monster, moving about of its own volition and not along set tracks, even despite its colossal body, whose frame alone was three times wider across than the average minia's.

So anxious to hide away, Minle trembled in the shadow of the boulder that only barely concealed her body.

She was in despair. Her docile daughter simply looked on in bewilderment at the loud noises, but she could cry at any moment, giving their location away to the mechanical devil.

What did she do wrong? Maybe it was coming to show her daughter the ocean scenery she herself had loved from a young age. Maybe it was the small detour they had taken to pick the flower her daughter had wanted from rocky crags.

What in her life merited such a terrifying and horrible punishment like this?

"Oh, please… Please, Word-Maker, I don't care about myself, but please, I beg you, give my daughter your divine protection. I…"

She was lying. Minle didn't want to die.

Even though she left no mark on the world, neither blessed with talent nor beauty, spending thirty-two years leading a rustic rural town life, she didn't want to die.

She may have been waiting for the happiness of raising her daughter to adulthood. Was even that sort of wish too much to ask for?

"I-I am willing to offer my life. But please pass my good fortune on to my child."

Finishing her desperate prayer, she raised her bowed head.

The face of the mechanical angel was right beside her.

"This source of heat is obstructing my detection functionality. Should I dismantle it?"

The face, bereft of expression, cocked its head inquisitively while its cogwheels creaked shrilly.

"*Fssh, fsheeeeek...*"

As if answering the angel's words, the mechanical bug emitted a horrific sound. Minle couldn't even let out a scream. She was going to die.

Unable to resist, reason permanently unknown—the sort of illogical death that came in abundance in this land filled with mysteries and monstrosities.

The angelic machine's wings opened. Numerous brass-colored blades began to spill out from inside them before—

"Ha-ha, ha-ha-ha-ha-ha-ha-ha!"

—a monolithic chuckling figure sent them flying with a punch.

There was a shattering sound like broken glass, and the angel fell into the shadows of the reef rocks, as tiny shards streamed from its body.

The giant figure was not a person.

"*Aaah....! Eep....! Eeek!*"

Escaping from the life-threatening danger, Minle let out delayed screams of terror. The figure standing in front of her inspired the exact same type of fear as the mechanical angel before it.

It was twice as tall as she was. A dark midnight blue, metal, minian-shaped being, its entire body covered in armor that seemed to have been enlarged to its very limits. It was entirely different from any living creature she had ever seen, yet it emitted Word Arts language.

"I-I am. Very...fast! Much, faster, a-and stronger, than...you!"

"*Nn, nggaah.*"

Her daughter whined in her arms.

The mechanical giant rotated its head around and looked toward Minle. The structure that appeared to serve as its head was spherical, and the purple glow from its singular eye sharply stood out from it.

"Oh, living, living creatures! A b-bi-big, and a, sm-small, living creature!"

"*Eeek*...p-please, don't kill her. I beg you. Spare my girl... please...!"

"I-It is. It is bad, if this one, d-dies?! Why is, that?!"

There was no question. It was a golem. Just like the other angel, and the train.

Mechanical monsters, used by self-proclaimed demon kings for the sole purpose of efficient butchery.

Weapons imbued with artificial souls, wholly incapable of empathy.

"*Nghh*...please, I beg you..."

"Wh-why...is it worse, for small creature, to d-die?! Big one, can take, her place!"

The golem continued to question, sincerely unable to comprehend Minle's words.

Minle was able to give her answer. Behind the golem the train monster had climbed over the rock bed and was coming in for the attack. It's insectile maw opened wide, and the light from the cannon inside gleamed bright.

Bursting. Rending.

Minle and her daughter's ears might have been damaged by the series of roars from the cannon.

The rock bed was smashed apart, scattering into sand.

"*Ha-ha-ha-ha-ha-ha*! Th-that, will not work!"

However, Minle's body itself remained intact.

The giant machine's armor shielded her from the explosive flames that illuminated the coastline.

"B-because, I am, I am, the strongest of all!"

Paying these words no heed, the mechanical insect maintained charging speed, using the mass of its head to deliver a blow. The golem caught the downward swing of its sharp jaw with both of its arms.

Visions of her death flashed before her in an instant. She was protected from them all.

Minle could only manage a one-word response.

"*Eep...* Monsters... Monsters...!"

"No, not, monsters! Th-this one, Nemerhelga. Earlier, the one, with wings... Respikt!"

The golem shouted as it squarely pinned down the giant mass, heavier than a house.

"And I am—*Ha-ha-ha-ha*! Mestelexil! M-Mama's, s-strongest, child! Much st-st-stronger, than, these ones!"

"'Mama...?'"

Golems were fighting each other. The train Nemerhelga, and the angel Respikt. This one, Mestelexil, was fighting against both of them.

Without knowing, Minle had stepped into their battleground.

Into the middle of a storm of death that no one should have ever witnessed.

"I-If, small one, cannot die! Ha, ha-ha-ha-ha-ha! I-I-I will protect, it! Because I, because I…am strong!"

The unpleasant grating sound of metal against metal continued, and the antagonistic Nemerhelga and Mestelexil sent each other flying. Mestelexil's strength forced back the insect large enough to rival a train.

"KRRRRRRRRREEEEEEEEEE!"

The giant mechanical insect zigzagged, smashing rocks as it moved, and sent the tip of its tail at Mestelexil.

He must have been trying to draw the insect's attention away from the mother and daughter. Without concealing himself at all, Mestelexil rushed out into the open.

The insect's tail split open in an explosive flash.

"Ha-ha-ha-ha-ha!"

Mestelexil's right arm was torn off from the shoulder. At the end of its path, metal stakes stabbed into the rock. There was only one conclusion Minle could come to—it was a weapon with unbelievable firing speed.

Without paying any heed to its damages, Mestelexil delivered a vicious kick to the mechanical tail.

The attack would have cleaved a minian person's torso in two. Nevertheless, it proved an ineffective blow against the inappropriately large figure.

"N-nemerhelga. I am, stronger. I am different, from you, b-because Mama, made me!"

He grabbed the end of its tail and attempted an even greater act of destruction.

Yet, without any warning, his spherical head was split vertically in two. Mestelexil staggered.

Thermic rays rained down from the sky, rending Mestelexil's head section. The armoring melted and sent a deep thermal scar down his back. The angel was radiating thermal light.

"Respikt io halese. Oumortmorp. Byaro woro. Kuqure it nostam. Indersmostek." (From Respikt to Halesept's eyes. Bubbles floating in gold. End of waterway. Fill up the cavity. Burn.)

"Pfft, aha-ha-ha-ha-ha-ha!"

Mestelexil, his head partially destroyed, took the beam of light with his left arm. The armor blocked a majority of the heat, but its joint was burned through. Everything from the elbow down fell to the ground, and the continuous heat ray scorched his body even further.

"Th-this is noth-nothing! I am strongest! *Ha-ha-ha*! That is why, this does, not hurt! Not at all!"

"KRRRRRRRRREEEEEEEEEE!"

He needed to continue enduring the heat ray. It meant that this time, he was unable to stop the blow of Nemerhelga's weight coming down overhead. Its large head, slightly exceeding the size of its body, made a direct hit.

Going along with the accelerated momentum, Nemerhelga's jaws stabbed into the golem's body. Mestelexil laughed.

"Ha-ha-ha-ha-ha-ha-ha-ha-ha-ha."

Nemerhelga's crushing jaws opened wide.

With vise-like strength, the golem's upper body was twisted off his lower half. The light of Thermal Arts, like fireworks, scattered from inside the golem's bottom. The mechanical insect, using its frightful machinery, rotated its jaws even further.

There was a large cracking sound.

"Target destruction—"

His torso, shin, and ankles were scattered in all directions. A lukewarm fluid, unclear whether it was brain or amniotic fluid, scattered and drenched the shoreline.

The fragments were warped beyond all recognition and recycling its golem parts appeared to no longer be possible.

The brass angel robotically announced:

"—Complete. Father. Certification concluded."

The tender child began to cry.

All Minle could do was stand there and continue to fear for her own life.

◆

"Quite the competition, I'd say. Your golem has quite the intellect, but I'd say my creations are quite the specimens, too."

A clifftop looking down over the shoreline. Atop it was a round table and chairs unbefitting the scenery, with two elderly people sitting down opposite each other.

The placid elderly gentleman brought the orange tea on the table to his lips. He nodded, less in satisfaction, and more as though he was confirming a fact.

"Respikt's Thermal Arts make use of a magic tool I obtained in a deal with the Free City of Okahu. I believe the display just now gave you a clear picture of their power and sustainability."

On the other hand, sitting across from him was a small elderly woman, wrinkles deeply etched into her face.

She had an untidy appearance, completely unlike the gentleman's, and her irritated slam on the top betrayed her lack of composure. She appeared wholeheartedly displeased as she uttered her reply.

"'Display just now,' my ass! I thought up that whole structure in the first place. My last child. Everyone's always underselling what I do for them...*Feh*!"

"*Ho, ho, ho.* How rude of me. However, would you agree my downsizing modifications are suitable and useful improvements?"

"It's got no power. Real piece of shit."

"...Really now. Be that as it may, it has enough power to destroy your creation, does it not?"

A close look at the round table and chairs the two sat in showed it was made out of the same material as the rock itself, and the elaborate engraving made it clear that it had been formed there on the spot through Craft Arts.

While the feat would be possible for specialized artisans very familiar with the region, much as the foreign atmosphere that enveloped them suggested, they were travelers from another land.

That was to say, such was the degree of skill both of these arts casters possessed.

"Nevertheless, I don't really consider this to be enough to declare my victory. There are other ways we self-proclaimed demon kings can battle against one another. Today made me feel like a child again for the first time in a long while, and I truly enjoyed our game."

"...Other ways? Other ways, huh?"

"That's right. Since today we've settled our golem-battling competition. And?"

"Took a good look. Nothing's been settled at all. You makin' a fool of me, Miluzi the Coffin Edict?"

"Oh?"

The elder gentleman's placid expression remained unchanged, but his eyebrow did rise slightly.

"What exactly can you do from this position, though?"

Before, there were once individuals known as "self-proclaimed demon kings."

Individuals who possessed too much power, whether it was through Word Arts or organizational strength. Mutations that tried to establish a new species. Visitors who brought heretical political concepts. Merely twenty-five years prior, these self-proclaimed demon kings were called demon kings themselves. Before the True Demon King appeared.

However—not all of those reduced to this self-proclaimed classification had fallen prey to the times and disappeared. If by any chance even the smallest handful were somewhere off in the world, waiting for their opportunity to strike...

"This battle's far from over. Take a look. That's Mestelexil."

On the reef down below the cliffside, Mestelexil's smashed body lay scattered about.

He was totally lifeless, and even if he was still alive, he hadn't the strength to match Miluzi's two golems. Even with all that being true...

"He's the invincible child of Kiyazuna the Axle, after all."

There was an individual who possessed Craft Arts talents far beyond the limits of other minia, and who in her opposition to the True Demon King, built the entirety of the Nagan Labyrinth City all by herself.

She was still waiting for her opportunity to strike. Self-proclaimed demon king, Kiyazuna the Axle.

◆

In the middle of the rock reef, devastated by the merciless destruction, Minle noticed a whispering.

It resounded from the torso section of Mestelexil, utterly and wholly smashed to pieces.

"—*delmemoao psytoqmanam yaimasutea ulkowarezored haimoz-*

tyubeta axoforkzora namerokirms—" (—coupled wings disappear to ash overflow with starshell skin and incarnate bind small sky tremors to cuts and ruins of sky and soil, fine chains of red—)"

The voice was like water, flowing smoothly without falter.

At first, Minle wasn't even aware it was speaking Word Arts. They were far too different from any Word Arts she had ever heard. An excessively long incantation, much too complex and bizarre.

"Activity confirmed."

Miluzi's two golems also detected the whispering.

Respikt incanted the Thermal Arts beam from before. Nemerhelga detonated its tail's firing function and launched steel spikes into the remains of Mestelexil with a speed too fast for Minle to register.

Their point of impact was removed from the fragments of his torso.

Suddenly, the armor reconstituted in midair—the armor that evaded the spikes' path—split and fell to the ground.

There was a barrier that hadn't existed until the very moment the spikes launched. It formed right before the projectiles' impact.

"Respikt io halese. Uomortmorp. Byaro woro." (From Respikt to Halesept's eyes. Bubbles floating in gold.)

Mestelexil's eccentric incantation overlapped with Respikt's Word Arts, taking aim at him from above.

"Yupaiemnewox aonksnaoewam lastioowa sorwokma zisardergodwe." (Hang from the bundled rotating mooring line remove the hollow empty hinge look again upon the mirage.)

"Kuqure it nostam. Indersmostek." (End of waterway. Fill up the cavity. Burn.)

The light of the heat rays poured down from above. He blocked it with an arm. As he defended himself from it, he stood with his right leg. The left leg supported his body. The scattered fragments of Mestelexil coalesced once more.

"Ha-ha-ha-ha-ha-ha!"

His incantation was one of Craft Arts. The once-demolished Mestelexil had reconstructed his own body, using his own Word Arts. In addition, his regenerated armored body's construction changed to perfectly defend against Respikt's heat rays.

A thin layer, peeled off from the armoring's surface, gently floated to the ground.

"I-I-I-I am...the strongest!"

The older gentlemen, looking at the battle from atop the cliff, gave a rigorous applause of honest admiration.

"...Wonderful. From a state of complete destruction. What sort of Word Arts are involved, may I ask?"

"Go ahead and analyze it for yourself. Call yourself a bit of a construct user, don'cha?"

"Well, of course... I can hypothesize. For example, perhaps that giant body is a simple outer exterior and inside the torso's armor is where the real body is, made into an ultra-small size. Thus, should that smaller body be able to use Craft Arts, it all comes together."

"You don't have any idea how the real body survived destruction, then, eh?"

Kiyazuna crossed her arms and gazed at Mestelexil, very clearly displeased.

Mestelexil below her was again naively headed straight toward Nemerhelga.

"That's his first feature. Golem regeneration. He can use Craft Arts to reconstruct himself no matter the situation."

"I see. In that case, surely you must know what method I shall utilize next, no?"

"...*Feh*! Go for it!"

Miluzi used a radzio to issue his orders. His Respikt and Nemerhelga were the types of constructs that were incapable of Word Arts. In exchange for their extremely high battle prowess, they relied on an outside source for a majority of their tactical judgment and could perform only the offensive Word Arts already inscribed within them, when necessary.

"Destroy the real unit inside the torso armor."

"KREEEEEEEEEEEEEEEEEEEEEEEEEEEEE!"

The colossus and giant insect clashed once again. The insect's cutting jaw no longer had any effect on Mestelexil's armor.

However... There was one part that was different from the situation before. Nemerhelga raised its scorpion-like tail and lined the pinned-down Mestelexil up against the firing track for its spikes.

An explosion caused the very sky to tremble. The spikes bit into the midsection, and the area where the armor joined together warped.

"Ha-ha-ha-ha-ha-ha! Th-th-that won't, work any, more! Not on me!"

Respikt plunged in from the side. The brass blades growing from its sides tore off the armor easily like an industrial machine. The exchange was over in less than a blink of an eye, with the two of them passing by each other.

"......"

Blood dripped down from the tip of Respikt's wings. Mestelexil's real body had been skewered by one of its numerous blades.

It was a living creature, like a fetus, smaller than a person's head.

Fatally wounded, it silently trembled four times before stopping entirely.

"Well I never—a homunculus core is quite the surprise. Is it fair to say that with this, I've solved the riddle?"

Miluzi dispassionately confirmed the fruits of his battle. His golems' combat capabilities far exceeded those of Kiyazuna's, just as he had thought, after all.

Not one, but two absolute masterpieces, each capable of annihilating an entire city on its own.

"Oh? You think you've got it, do you? This is his second functionality."

"......!"

"*Iuwars64 meoiure noskraehe moiazz ziektkorot haith4bestei mistenok aivequte houbrantuxe—*" (Separate the sixty-four-grid place where the red colors of upstream branches meet, in the light network where the four symbols cannot be seen, going through ignorance and awakening shall—)

The golem, whose true body was supposed to have perished, was incanting.

Mestelexil, thought to now be an empty husk, grabbed Nemerhelga's jaw and pulled it down.

The explosive collision into the sunken rocks sent water spraying into the air, once again showcasing Mestelexil's abnormal physical strength. However, despite his main body supposedly being dead, he could still manage to speak.

"Ha, ha-ha-ha-ha! Poor, Nemerhelga! I will...never di-di-die! Mama m-m-made, me that, way!"

Kiyazuna, watching his restoration, declared with a fearless grin—

"The second function. Homunculus regeneration. He can use Life Arts to reconstruct himself no matter the situation."

"B-Brilliant...! The golem itself having the capability to chant Word Arts, I'm speechless...!"

"You've seen two of my tricks now. Is there anything else you want to try out?"

The Word Arts capabilities Mestelexil displayed were beyond abnormal.

It wasn't an exaggeration to call them opposed to the natural laws of the world.

Constructs functioned by being infused with life through Word Arts. Unlike living creatures from nature, they could be augmented with various specialized functionalities. However, to give a self-replicating ability to such artificial life-forms... Was it actually possible to imbue them with a soul that wielded Word Arts *capable of producing its own body by itself*?

The Dungeon Golem Kiyazuna created in Nagan had been capable of using itself as a factory to mass-produce simple golem soldiers. That feat alone proved that Kiyazuna the Axle was already among unmeasurable heights as a demon king.

Nevertheless, if her golems were then able to replicate complex functionality on Mestelexil's level, then they indeed possessed a true soul. Beyond the realm of simple constructs, it was a feat on par with creating an independent and new species of creature altogether.

"Just how did you... How did you successfully build a creation capable of such functionality? Truly superb."

"I told you, they aren't 'creations.' All of 'em are my children. Why don't you explain how your own kids came to be the way they are, huh?"

The old woman took a long sip of orange tea. She was always irritated, regardless of whether people looked up to her or looked down on her.

She hadn't changed one bit in the past few decades.

"When ya repeat things over and over, thousands and thousands of times...something unexpected happens. Sometimes, it's the exact functionality you're looking for; sometimes it's a functionality not worth a damn... But in that unexpected moment is where the truly unique constructions are. Those kinds of miracle moments, that's when my babies are really born. Babies based off a singular functionality, only able to come to life in that exact moment."

"In other words, Mestelexil's functionality then...is the ability to use Word Arts?"

"You'd really call something that basic a 'miracle'? Put simply, it's a shared curse."

"A functionality entrusted to another organism... A core that's immortal as long as it isn't destroyed. No, it couldn't be......?"

A shared curse. A functionality also found within a monster that once terrorized Aureatia, Nihilo the Vortical Stampede. Even Miluzi had never successfully created such a golem.

No. There's one thing that doesn't explain. What in the world is keeping that alive....?

Miluzi's two golems once again changed their strategic course.

Respikt started again to fire Thermal Arts from high up in the sky, out of range. Conversely, Nemerhelga curiously bent its body and started encircling Mestelexil's flank.

"Nemerhelga! Ha-ha-ha-ha! Give me, your b-best, shot! I-I-I won't, let the s-s-small one, die!"

Mestelexil stood against his opponents with nothing but his own body.

The sky sparkled like it was filled with stars, and Thermal Arts once again rained down. They no longer had any effect on

Mestelexil's armor. As the Thermal Arts showered over him, he stepped toward Respikt.

Atop the cliff, Miluzi moaned at Mestelexil's defensive capabilities.

"Unbelievable! Everything perfectly countered, and in less than a second... What intelligence! He's clearly showing independent thought! And learning...! Learning how to handle my Respikt's attacks!"

"*Bah*, like learning's anything special. Lemme show you, that saying that homunculi are born knowing everything? Ain't just superstition."

"Please do...! Unfortunately, I've already given them both my orders."

The Thermal Arts' aim was to obstruct Mestelexil's senses with light. In that case, how did Nemerhelga move in that moment?

On the ground. All of Nemerhelga's body segments opened at once and deployed their Thermal Arts propulsion thrusters.

The bluish white air blast pulverized the terrain behind it as it rushed at Mestelexil's flank.

"Bring it! Nemerhelga!"

Mestelexil took the explosive impact head-on. Gouging a line through the soil, his body was pushed to the edge of the beach. Once he was a mere three steps from the precipice, he held his ground.

"KREEEEEEEEEEEEEEEEEE!"

Nemerhelga didn't stop.

The joints on its body exploded. The entirety of its long and massive iron body turned into a multi-stage firing mechanism and sent Mestelexil flying with numerous percussive impacts.

Expelled far offshore, the iron body's colossal weight sank deep into the water.

It was true that he was indeed immortal. However, he was now in the frigid darkness of the seafloor. There would be no coming back.

The storm of battle subsided. The only thing left behind were the remains of Nemerhelga's blasted body. High in the sky, Respikt simply gazed with cold eyes at its brother's piecemeal destruction.

"Re-certification complete. Father. Your orders."

"*—vercomaub hangert waiuzpeunt winworpics urcstoct nafer-dert—*" (feeding on heat from the mire, should it become proof of sin anew, the binding of those two, several thousand—)

"......"

...Word Arts resonated.

There, at a single point along the reef, a small, embryonic life-form was being brought into existence.

Mestelexil should have been wholly driven offshore, including the homunculus body held within. The only explanation was that it had appeared out of nowhere.

Respikt chanted its Thermal Arts attack.

"*Respikt io halese. Uomortmorp. Byaro woro.*" (From Respikt to Halesept's eyes. Bubbles floating in gold.)

The golem armor, formed in midair, blocked the heat rays. Just as it did before.

—It had already studied this attack. Its construction could now handle it. The attack wasn't effective.

"What in the world... What kind of mechanism— And how...?!"

"C'mon, that's easy, fool. Mestel can create Exil. Exil can create Mestel. Anywhere either one's voice can reach. Separate them as far as ya want, they'll come back from anywhere."

"They...they each formed each other's body, and instantly

returned back to land... I would have never hypothesized any-thing like it... I-I can't believe it...!"

It was a preposterous feat. Her declaration that this was her greatest masterpiece, even surpassing the Dungeon Golem, itself a moving city, wasn't a lie at all.

If this was all true, then Mestelexil's skills as a Word Arts user transcended those of the self-proclaimed demon king Miluzi himself.

Furthermore, it would prove an eternal impossibility to kill this golem with any of the instruments and skills he bestowed on either of his own golem creations.

The fruit of miracles and coincidence itself, it was a *true* monster.

Was the golem the main body? Or was the homunculus the main body? Which was the real form, the body cast off into the ocean, or the one standing on the seaside now?

In all likelihood, the correct answer was "both." It was all Mestelexil. It could produce its own body from the smallest ves-tiges of living cells. It could build its own body from the minerals in the soil.

In a world defined by Mestelexil's Word Arts, was even one's own continuity meaningless, too?

"Respikt. Your father was defeated. Terminate the field test, and immediately—"

"The third—"

The old witch's words interrupted Miluzi's instructions.

"—Function. You can handle that, right, Mestelexil?"

The monster, his whole body completely constructed anew, fixed his singular eye on Respikt.

Solely relying on brute force to fight, this enemy should have been far out of his range.

He chanted Craft Arts.

"Exil io mestel. Rewol qzerd. Hengren orksap. Zempst haie—"
(From Exil to Mestel. Divine explosive sound. Group's terminus.
Spinning cone—)

Then, he constructed something no one in their world had
seen before.

An indescribable form, utterly impossible for the hands of
others to create. His right arm transformed into a structure composed of three black metal pipes bundled together. The base where
the pipes were attached moved by way of an even more complex
mechanism.

The electrical Thermal Arts current flowed, and it began to spin.

"—noingod. (Drill). GAU-19/B."

The high-speed gun noises sounded almost like screaming. A
shriek of metal and gunpowder.

The mechanical angel, capable of flying faster than wyverns,
was reduced to debris that scattered along the wind.

With a sound like a mountain of coins, an innumerable number of casings fell to the ground.

It was a weapon from another world, one no one had ever seen
before.

A rotary multi-barreled machine gun. It was known as a gatling gun.

"With visitors...as long as they got a body from the Beyond,
they'll never be able to use Word Arts. But they know about the
weapons in the Beyond. Knowledge unknown to us, knowledge
that'll surpass everything."

"......"

"You ever think about it? If they could just use Craft Arts... If they had power to reproduce weapons as they saw fit, depending on how much they knew, you could get a hand on anything and everything from the world beyond."

"...Kiyazuna... What exactly...did you...?"

Miluzi looked at Kiyazuna. They were both self-proclaimed demon kings. Yet her thoughts were on a far different level than his own.

Right now, Kiyazuna was missing her irritated look. Like a scholar finished with one experiment and on to considering their next, her eyes looked deep in thought about what lay ahead.

"I got my hands on a visitor, a scholar on the other side. I thought they'd make good material."

His mind had been more at ease when she had worn her devilish grin.

"So I *made them capable of using* Word Arts."

Homunculi were prepared using a living person of the minian races as a base model.

They would latently possess the base's knowledge, but they were still unmistakably separate living creatures, born to their world.

That was Mestelexil.

"...I've been totally outdone. Just...one more thing. Why wasn't the homunculus inside burned alive by the heat rays? I keep asking myself that question, but I haven't the faintest idea."

Kiyazuna laughed. Still, she clearly planned on explaining that as well, whether asked or not. As though perfectly matter-of-fact, like a parent bragging about her child.

"For Mestelexil, one half serves as the life of the other. That goes both ways, you see. The fourth functionality. *A two-way* shared curse. It's impossible to kill Mestel and Exil at the same time."

Everything had ended.

The two monsters, who seemed ready to consume the world, were smashed apart and gone. It was likely there would never be someone who could believe what she saw on this coastline.

"H-How, how, was that?!"

The remaining monster approached. She couldn't escape.

Its spherical head restlessly whipped around, clearly unable to hide its curiosity, and gazed at Minle's beloved daughter.

"I, h-have, have protected, the s-small one! Protected, and beat them! Ha-ha-ha-ha-ha! And still, I won! Because I am the strongest!"

"S-stay away... Please, someone...save me..."

"Ha-ha-ha-ha-ha-ha! Ha-ha-ha-ha! Ha-ha..."

Minle held her daughter to her breast, trying desperately to protect her from the abomination before her.

The terrifying laughter gradually grew weaker, and then stopped.

"...Ha-ha..."

"Nghh, weeh!"

Her daughter wriggled up against her chest.

She wanted to scream for her to be still. Yet, her legs remained frozen stiff.

Her daughter stretched her short arm out toward the mechanical monster.

"Gaah, gaa."

"...W-what is... Ha-ha! Y-y-you are, giving this, to me?!"

The monster accepted the flower her daughter was holding with its left hand.

A hand that was colossal compared to the minia, smeared with destruction. A horrifying calamity.

Her daughter knew nothing of violence.

"Y-yay…! Heh-heh, heh…! I-I am, glad little one, is alive! It is p-p-pretty! Ha-ha-ha-ha!"

Gripping the life-form in his hands, so grossly far removed from his immortal body, he flew off somewhere else.

No matter where he was headed, Minle knew his destination lay past the edges of her world—a hellish battlefield like no other.

◆

"A f-flower! I got, a flower!"

He didn't possess any expressions like the minia did. Nevertheless, he was always smiling.

Each time he revived, unknown knowledge would surface within him like bubbles, but he always remained himself.

His name was Mestelexil.

A constructed being, two lives fused together, and invincible in the truest sense of the word.

"…Manage to do a good job, didn'cha, Mestelexil. How about your battle report?"

"M-M-Mama!"

Kiyazuna the Axle stood where the road from the coast joined the flatland. The mother and creator of the life-form known as Mestelexil. His wish was to make his mother's wishes come true.

"Look, at this! A flower! I-It was g-given! To me! *Hahaha!*"

"Huh?! A flower, eh? Hey, Mestelexil… The thing about flowers…."

Kiyazuna snatched the flower out of his hands.

It was small, delicate, and a lovely shade of bright yellow.

She then turned around and started walking.

Kiyazuna flicked something up with her fingertips, and it landed in Mestelexil's palms as he followed behind her.

It was a small glass vial, with the flower tucked inside.

"...is you gotta treat them more carefully. Did you have fun, Mestelexil?"

"Heh-heh, heh...! Respikt, and Nemerhelga, were both amazing! It was, lots of f-fun!"

"...Hmph. That so."

She smiled profoundly. She wanted him to experience it all, from the taste of victory to the beauty of flowers.

Her golems were not creations. Each and every one of them were her precious children.

"Still got a ways to go! This ain't all there is to the world, not even close! Beauty, ugliness, it's got it all! Taste it all! It's all yours! You got the right to life, so enjoy every bit of it!"

"Ha-ha-ha-ha-ha-ha-ha-ha-ha-ha!"

"All righty, Mestelexil, it's time to move on! Things're gonna get even more fun!"

The age of the True Demon King was over. The time had come for the self-proclaimed demon kings, who had been biding their time, to awaken from the depths of the world. All of the battles up until now had been little more than stress tests. From here on, Mestelexil would have to hone to his fighting skills against all types of opponents.

"M-move on...?! Like before with the soldier people?!"

"A lot more fun than killing those Old Kingdoms' goons."

He flew. He could kill people with his fists, incinerate them, or let loose a barrage of bullets. Among the shura, who surpassed all known comprehension, these sorts of deeds were nothing beyond a sporting whim, not even qualifying as a "combat."

In Aureatia, there was a visitor who had single-handedly cut down her labyrinth.

A storm, once constrained into a long dormancy, which had destroyed the country she built as a self-proclaimed demon king country, was on the move.

They were beings she could not allow to exist, all of them. She would burn disaster itself in the fires of her vengeful rage.

"...You're going to kill...."

And the Mestelexil she built was her invincible child capable of eradicating said disaster.

"...the Particle Storm."

He utilized Word Arts that had arrived at the realm of ultimate existential truth, capable of composing his very own existence.

He endlessly grew, with each cycle of death and rebirth granting him knowledge from a foreign world.

He could regenerate one as long as the other lived, with both of them incapable of being killed simultaneously.

A combat life-form truly flawless, proven invincible by foregone logic.

Creator/Architect. Golem/Homunculus.

Mestelexil the Box of Desperate Knowledge.

ISHURA

Keiso
ILLUSTRATION BY Kureta

Fourth Verse:

THE REALM
OF SLAUGHTER,
PARTICLE STORM

Togie was a midsize city located along an area of wetlands. Though there were many residents who avoided a direct assault from the True Demon King disaster and remained in the city, it was not at all a big town, in part due to how difficult it was to get to and from.

It was three days prior when Togie City was blocked off from the world by the Old Kingdoms' loyalists.

This force, after spending close to a year making inroads in the city council, at last commanded complete authority over Togie City, and the entire city was placed under martial law. The predicted path of the Particle Storm they had obtained earlier, and the heavy losses they sustained from an assault on their rear camp from an as-yet unknown force, both played significant roles in accelerating the Old Kingdoms' loyalists' movements.

"Stop. Who are you?"

The current state of affairs swirled like a vortex. It was an obvious turn of events that Toroa the Awful, appearing from Wyte, would be challenged by an inspection far outside the city.

"I heard General Gilnes is recruiting soldiers. Came to apply. Hope you'd show me the way."

He was a tall dwarf with a massive frame, carrying a preposterous number of bladed weapons. The light in his eyes, peeking out from the darkness of his cowl, was filled with a callousness, like the deepest pits of hell, and it was clear to anyone that he was no ordinary individual.

"...You think we're letting someone suspicious like you through? You have an intermediary or an introduction seal from the Kingdoms' Army?"

"*Gngh......*"

Toroa choked on his words.

"......No."

"Then, turn back! Passage in and out of Togie City is currently forbidden!"

He had spent his time together with his father in the mountains ever since he was born and had no worldly experiences outside housework and training. He could count the number of times he had even gone into town on one hand. To him, the existence of the Old Kingdoms' loyalists was the only clue on the state of the outside world he had gleaned from the bandits.

According to whispers heard in passing, Alus the Star Runner belonged to the largest nation of Aureatia. If the Old Kingdoms' war with Aureatia was beginning in earnest, then he should be able to confront his father's bitter foe on the battlefield.

Moreover, the commander of the Old Kingdoms' loyalists, General Gilnes's enchanted sword, Charijisuya the Blasting Blade, was one of the enchanted swords that had remained out of his father's hands. He wanted leads on this as well.

"But...um, is there anything you can do? I came all this way."

"And I told you to turn back. If those swords are weighing you down, I'll call the city blacksmith for you. You could probably get a reasonable price for 'em if you sold 'em off."

"......"

Toroa wavered. Naturally, cutting this unwitting soldier down and continuing forward wasn't an option.

Nevertheless, even if he did use his refusal here to go to Aureatia and challenge Alus the Star Runner directly, he could easily imagine it would end with a large number of innocent citizens getting wrapped up in their fight.

His father had also killed any uninvolved witnesses. Though it didn't serve as any justification for his crimes, his father still strived not only to steal enchanted swords, but to keep the lives sacrificed in the process to a minimum. Toroa, too, couldn't let such needless sacrifices happen, as much as possible.

"Is something wrong? You seem to be having a bit of a disagreement."

Someone stepped out of a carriage that had arrived at the checkpoint during their back-and-forth.

The soldier immediately saluted.

"Yessir! We have an applicant who wishes to join the Kingdoms' Army, but...well, as you can see sir, he's a very suspicious individual. Put your mind at ease, sir, as I would never let such a ruffian through this checkpoint!"

"Oh, if you mean this man here...."

The boy looked barely thirteen years old. His hair was a gray color, mixed with white.

"...I've had him come here on my recommendation. I intended on introducing him directly to the staff office aide myself, but it appears we both ended up arriving at the same time. My apologies. It seems I'm the one who's late."

"Um... Oh, I see, sir! My apologies for being so discourteous in my ignorance... Um. He did claim to have no intermediary..."

"Ha-ha-ha. Without the critical party, myself, here, he *did not have one*, indeed, yes? He must have been quite troubled by it all himself. Forgive me, Erijite."

The young boy stretched out his hand to Toroa as he referred to him with a completely different man's name.

"You must be exhausted from carrying all of that from the Wyte Mountains. It's only a short distance, but I'll escort you to the city."

"What..."

Toroa lowered his voice in front of the young boy's smile.

"...are you doing? Why are you helping me?"

"Oh no, *you're* the one helping *me*. If you ended up going back, with the way this conversation's going, I'd have a very hard time explaining myself. Will you hop on inside?"

"......"

The reality was he had no other options available. Despite his continued quandary, Toroa joined the boy in his carriage.

With a hasty inspection, the carriage easily traveled through the checkpoint. None of them realized the truth behind Toroa's swords. Due to the outlandish number of blades he had with him, the thought likely never even occurred to them.

While they sat facing each other in the coach, Toroa took stock of the young boy. The enchanted swords on his back and the pressure of his gaze were nearly enough to kill the average person from intimidation alone, yet this boy remained composed.

"...You knew who I was, didn't you? You a general here?"

In the previous conversation, the boy had mentioned the Wyte Mountains by name. If he knew Toroa's circumstances, then that meant he had been sending a secret signal with his word choice.

"Unfortunately, I am not. I am a visitor, merely involved to some extent in munitions dealings with the Old Kingdoms' loyalists—or the Kingdoms' Army, as they call themselves. As to your other question, I of course know who you are. Toroa the

Awful...yes? Though I may not look it, I am rather shocked, to be honest. I had heard you were dead."

"I would never die by the hands of someone like the Star Runner. More importantly, will this method really get me into their army? We'll face the same reactions we just dealt with when we're inspected before entering the city."

"...Indeed. Regarding that issue, Toroa."

The young boy folded his hands together on his knee. Leaning his small body forward, he continued.

"That also depends on what your goal is. Depending on the circumstances, you may find better results if you didn't join the Old Kingdoms instead. Is it all right if I ask why exactly you wish to join their army?"

Toroa was unsure how to answer. If he did tell him, would this young boy be his ally?

However, he wouldn't be disadvantaged either way. There wouldn't be anyone familiar with the name Toroa the Awful who wouldn't know about his end goals, too.

"...I want to destroy Alus the Star Runner. During the war with Aureatia, I'm going to win back the Luminous Blade. I... I came here to reclaim the enchanted sword he stole from me."

"Understood. Regarding my intermediary role, with your name and degree of skill, it should be a simple conversation to actually get you into the army. If that is your wish, I can help you. That said, I am apprehensive about when war does break out, and it comes time to send the army into action."

The carriage clattered over the stone pavement alongside the marshlands. The young boy raised his pointer finger.

"In war, whole armies don't get lumped together and thrown at each other en masse. Should you be placed on the front lines, naturally all soldiers are divided up into units, and in certain circumstances, you may be sent away from the Aureatian front, or be transferred to a defensive position. No matter how excellent the warrior, these position movements are a vital part of the army's job. To go one step further, this also applies to Alus on Aureatia's side, too."

"In other words, you're saying I won't be guaranteed a chance to fight the Star Runner?"

"…That's right. There is also the possibility that Alus the Star Runner is killed in the chaos of war, and the Luminous Blade ends up lost somewhere else. At the very least, for this objective of yours, there is a better way to go about it."

"But, if I'm not on the inside of the Old Kingdoms' camp, then—"

"You can't search for the whereabouts of Charijisuya the Blasting Blade. Correct?"

"!"

"Ha-ha-ha, there's no need to hide it. The Blasting Blade held by General Gilnes is a very well-known rumor. Actually, this sword, too, is no longer within this city's walls. In actuality…"

"Wait."

Toroa interrupted.

While he had the self-awareness to know he was unacquainted with wheeling and dealing, from the moment they had met, he was being totally pulled into the young boy's cunning banter.

"Why would you tell me all of this in the first place? If you know that I'm Toroa the Awful, then that should be all the more reason not to tell me about the Blasting Blade. You're an ally to the Old Kingdoms' loyalists, right?"

"Not at all. While I conduct business with the Old Kingdoms, *I am not an Old Kingdoms' loyalist*. More than that, I'd like instead to form a cooperative relationship with you, individually."

"Now that I think about it…the timing of your carriage showing up, right during my inspection, was too perfect. You knew I was going to show up from the beginning. Just who would've told you..."

He had lived deep in the Wyte Mountains, without anyone ever discovering his whereabouts. No one should have even known that the supposedly dead Toroa the Awful was still alive, let alone that he would be traveling to this region.

"......The bandits?"

He arrived at the conclusion. The bandits who came to raid him. Toroa got the information regarding the Old Kingdoms' loyalists from them.

"Quite perceptive of you. Erijite was a client of mine. He approached me, you see, asking for me to vouch for him, should he succeed in recovering the enchanted sword collection of Toroa the Awful. I was aware of their movements."

"That raid..."

Toroa the Awful's fingers reached for the hilt of an enchanted sword.

"...was *your* suggestion?"

The young boy continued to solemnly stare at Toroa. He showed no hint of fear or restlessness while facing imminent death in the coach, not a single bodyguard in sight.

"Presenting enchanted swords as a gift was Erijite's proposition. Of course, while you could say I am equally guilty for knowing his intentions and failing to stop him, I had indeed heard that Toroa the Awful was already dead, after all."

In the marshes outside the city, far off in the distance but still visible, wurms poked their heads out from underground before quickly sinking back into the soil.

With his hand still on his enchanted sword, Toroa remained motionless. As did the young boy.

"...May I continue?"

"......"

"Ultimately, Erijite was killed. By an enchanted sword, no less. Toroa the Awful—silent since his battle with Alus the Star Runner, and thought to be dead—killed him, and then moved far from Wyte. If he truly was moving openly, not shrinking from the eyes of others, then his first aim must lay in the bandit's point of contact, the Old Kingdoms...and Charijisuya the Blasting Blade."

"...So you guessed I would come looking for the blasting sword, and made contact with me, then?"

Toroa the Awful had been a terrifying ghost story, his true form totally unknown to everyone.

That was no longer the case now.

"Yes. If anything, I should be asking you a question. After all, it was far too easy to follow up on witness information to find you... Your build and weaponry are very conspicuous. How did you kill all those enchanted sword wielders without anyone knowing who you were up until now?"

"...Well."

"Was the legend of Toroa the Awful truly all the work of a single individual?"

"...That's right. It was all one person."

The legend made by his father.

Though he could reproduce the transcendent techniques hidden in each enchanted sword, that was one thing he couldn't possibly replicate.

The real Toroa the Awful had also accomplished everything beyond the battlefield on his own. Even with a physique far superior to his father's, right now, Toroa's skills were solely concerned with combat.

"Toroa the Awful. I firmly believe I can prove useful to you and offer you my cooperation. I can collect information on enchanted swords or hide you from the eyes of others. Will you allow me to help you?

As he was now, there was a power that Toroa sorely lacked. That power might have indeed been something only this young boy could give him. Toroa may have lacked the power to keep on fighting down the line.

"No."

Nevertheless, he felt that this was an offer he shouldn't take.

"You are trying to use me."

"……"

The rejected boy didn't try to protest, waiting for Toroa to continue.

"I made the wrong choice after all. No matter which army I belong to, if I end up cutting down some unknown strangers, that…that's just the same as anyone besides Toroa the Awful wielding an enchanted sword. If I'm not wielding my enchanted sword as Toroa the Awful would, there's no point. I should have realized that from the start."

He had to kill Alus the Star Runner—his father's murderer and thief of one of his enchanted swords.

He believed he should prioritize that mission beyond anything else.

Nevertheless, he shouldn't bring about an enchanted-sword–fueled war in order to do so. That would go against his father's wishes.

…*Father never stole Charijisuya the Blasting Blade.*

It was an enchanted sword that too many people knew about, and too many people had come into contact with. He knew that stealing it would only kindle a new conflict. Toroa the Awful wasn't a simple machine solely devoted to indiscriminately stealing enchanted swords.

Toroa faced the young boy and lowered his head.

"…I appreciate your offer."

The boy gave a carefree smile.

"While it's unfortunate I can't assist you, I would be happy if my words proved some kind of motivation. At the end of the day, this sort of small talk is the only thing I'm good at."

"Given that we've broken off our negotiations, we should go our separate ways before we arrive in Togie City. I'll only end up causing you more trouble."

"Do you have any prospects from here on out?"

"...I can't leave the Star Runner to do as he pleases. I'll think of a way to lure him out. Though, leaving the Blasting Blade behind is unfortunate."

"...Charijisuya the Blasting Blade was stolen."

"What?"

"Togie City's strengthened state of alert was due in part to receiving said sword in the first place. Using the assault on their camp as a pretext, the Old Kingdoms got the city council to take action... Though we're getting a bit off topic, aren't we?"

"Stolen by who?"

"Kiyazuna the Axle. A self-proclaimed demon king."

Returning to action, Kiyazuna the Axle, together with her greatest masterpiece Mestelexil, were repeatedly launching raids on other self-proclaimed demon kings and armed groups.

Her surprise attack on the Old Kingdoms' Army's rear encampment and resource heist happened five days prior. Although the truth behind the assault was limited to a select few, even among the Old Kingdoms' loyalists themselves, this one incident had already caused enormous damage, and if they hadn't been given information regarding the Particle Storm, the opening of hostilities itself might have been postponed.

"If necessary, I can tell you where she's headed. Also...I'm certain you'll get your chance to fight Alus the Star Runner. A place where no one will intervene, no fear of getting others involved—a stage where you can fight each other one on one."

"You..."

He had just met this young boy.

Yet, in their short conversation, he had seen through all the information Toroa possessed himself, and without pressing further on anything Toroa didn't want to talk about, tried to offer him something that he, always fighting by himself, didn't have.

A man of shifting impressions, both appearing to be a dangerous opponent, and a benevolent supporter.

Toroa had forgotten to ask the fundamental question, more than just his origin and information source.

"Why are doing all this for me...? I'm not going to become your ally. You're not gonna get anything at all out of going to these lengths to help me."

"Hmm. That is a good question. I'm just so addicted to my work, I suppose."

The Gray-Haired Child grinned with amusement.

"I end up treating any conversation partner I've taken a liking to with kindness."

The southern area of Aureatia. The terrain there, intricate ravines all intersecting with one another, was not formed from nature.

The topography was carved up so the pioneers of ages past could pass through the precipitous ravine, creating a large-scale transportation route connecting the Kingdoms with the cities of the southern region.

Given these circumstances, this tract of land, with many marketplaces and lodgings set up to serve as a hub for the coming and going caravans, was not strictly considered a city. It was called the Gumana Trading Post.

However, now, no matter what time of day, there were no traces of merchants coming and going to be seen. Packing the ravine full was a garrison of the Aureatia army, tasked with surveying and handling the impending natural disaster attack.

"So, this whole Particle Storm thing... I've actually heard about it, too."

Among them all, the sight of a boy, barely sixteen years of age, dressed in general's garb was a peculiar one to behold.

Looking down over the view of the ravine from the makeshift operational headquarters, he had one elbow thrust onto the tactician's table.

The youngest man among Aureatia's Twenty-Nine Officials. Twenty-Second General, Mizial the Iron-Piercing Plumeshade.

"It's basically like typhoon or drought, right? It's just weather. Honestly, there's pretty much no reason to bring troops with us at all, really. Just having numbers isn't gonna do much to stop it."

"If all the theories up until now are true, then yes, that would be true."

The man replying had only one arm. Twenty-Fifth General, Kayon the Thundering. He was reputed to be a man of great caliber who more than made up for the abilities of Mizial, exceptionally immature for a top-level government official.

"But, well, just the fact that a weather pattern supposed to be unique to the Yamaga Barrens moved this far, and is approaching Aureatia, makes it all abnormal. It makes more sense to consider things like Jelki said."

"You mean, about how if it's true form isn't any weather, it can be stopped?"

"I wonder. If that information's correct, it could be even worse than a simple storm."

Mizial's apprehensions were justifiable. If the Yamaga Barrens' Particle Storm itself was indeed descending upon them, there wasn't a single thing the Aureatia soldiers could do. With even steel armor proving worthless against the furious particles of dust, they would simply have their skin shaven off and die.

"But if we kept waiting without doing anything, everyone would start to wonder what the hell the army was thinking. At the bare minimum, leading the evacuation, providing material transport support, and then reconstruction aid. There're mountains of stuff to handle on top of surveying the Particle Storm. We have barely any time until it arrives."

"And we're still getting stuck with grunt work, huh? The

Okahu and Old Kingdoms' fronts are already in bad enough shape. Can we really be mobilizing this many troops? I get that it's that much of an emergency and all, but still."

Mizial the Iron-Piercing Plumeshade was a military officer who showed more acumen with offensives on the front lines than giving strategic commands from the rear. Although there were a limited number of the Twenty-Nine Officials who could immediately respond to handle this situation, he was slightly dissatisfied with his latest post.

"'Sides, in reality, you're the one giving practically all the instructions. Me, I'm here as a decoration and nothing more. I really wanted to go over to the Old Kingdoms' front. They look more likely to start a war than Okahu, anyway."

"Listen here. Take this seriously. When I've got my hands full, the responsibility's in your hands, got it?"

"Fine then, lemme ask you something."

Mizial laid his cheek down on the table with a smack.

"...I still get the feeling that there's a ton of soldiers involved with this operation, you know? And those merchant guys all getting driven outta here—that totally wasn't just about evacuation, was it?"

"That's true."

Kayon answered matter-of-factly. Part of the aim behind investing this many personnel in the garrison at the Gumana Trading Post was to emphasize the seriousness of the emergency and entice residents to leave. By requisitioning the food supplies and water such a large force required from the local area, and having Aureatia compensate them for the losses, the garrisoning could go smoothly. The goal had been for the Aureatia army to wholly occupy the spot for themselves, without a single resident being left behind.

"No matter how unlikely, it'd be real bad if anyone saw

our *trump card*, right? Since at the very least, the Old King-doms' side also knows that we need to handle the Particle Storm somehow."

"Yeah, I guess, when you put it like that. Wouldn't be too unusual for a traveling peddler to actually be a secret agent employed by one power or another. So, basically, until the Old Kingdoms' issue is cleaned up, we gotta act carefully."

The circumstances around dealing with the Particle Storm were different from regular one-off disasters. It was a military operation—requiring judgments based on information from var-ied viewpoints, collected together, and given perspective.

"Per Jelki's forecast, right after the Particle Storm crosses Gumana, it'll veer east. It'll pass through the Sine Riverstead, skirt the mountain range...and then arrive in Aureatia."

"If Aureatia's in trouble, then a country town like Sine River-stead's gonna get wiped off the map, huh."

"Come on now, don't jinx it."

No matter how many soldiers were mobilized, with less than two days left until its predicted arrival, there was a physical limit to how many residents they could evacuate in time. The only buffer zone they could make to prevent damages was here at the Gumana Trading Post. It was smaller than a full city, and it was where a majority of the people passing through possessed their own mode of transportation.

For all the cities it would pass through from Gumana onward, residential casualties were inevitable.

"Give this everything you've got, Mizial. I'll have you know, saving people and being thanked for it is pretty good work, too."

"...I mean, I do it. But I don't need any gratitude. Sounds like a pain in the ass."

◆

In the corner of the encampment, someone was seated as though they had assimilated themselves with the nearby shadows.

In the middle of all the soldiers running around tirelessly, he alone appeared idle, but in truth, he was more focused than anyone else. He was also expending a considerable amount of energy. His name was Kuuro the Cautious.

There's no gap for anyone peculiar to sneak in...for now, anyway.

Now, with every single thing in the Gumana Trading Post, both people and goods, being swapped around, he was paying attention to everything around him, looking out to see if anyone suspicious infiltrated the camp.

The Old Kingdoms' loyalists should be well aware that Aureatia was slow to get their hands on information detailing when the Particle Storm would pass through the market. In which case, he needed to act under the premise that both the fact that Aureatia would be trying to take countermeasures against it and that they would most likely choose the Gumana Trading Post as their first line of defense had been picked up by the Old Kingdoms' loyalists.

"Nothing but Aureatia soldiers around here. No one suspicious at all."

The young girl with two wings for arms fluttered atop Kuuro's head. Her exceedingly tiny body looked like that of a small songbird from far away. Cuneigh the Wanderer was a homunculus, created to have such an aberrant form from birth.

"You should rest, Kuuro. You were told to rest before the operation. Right?"

"...Can never be too careful, now. My eyes can only see what I can see, after all."

Now with his clairvoyance weakened, the exhaustion he felt

from the information stimuli was greater, if anything, than when the sense had been at its sharpest.

Previously, even with his eyes closed, he could see the scenery around him, clear as day. Kuuro had never understood the sense of "having one's eyes closed" like the average person did.

With his gifts lost, he now understood exactly what that sensation felt like.

How utterly terrifying the world was, *when he needed to make an effort to see things.* A world where he couldn't perceive everything happening between closing his eyelids and opening them again. A world where sleep meant completely cutting off all of one's senses.

For Kuuro, it seemed like the very moment of death itself, relentlessly visiting him over and over again.

"When you think about everything that happened the moment you blink, don't you get scared?"

"You're way too serious, Kuuro. I want you to..."

"Want me to what?"

"...Never mind."

You need to be more relaxed. You can run away if you want to. She was probably looking to give him these kinds of comforting words. Cuneigh herself also understood that to Kuuro, these were the most meaningless words of all.

It's impossible. I can't relax unless I can see anything and everything. Everything he couldn't see with his eyes changed without reason.

His unreasonable gift was withering away without any reason, and the era of unreasonable war and chaos ended with as much reason as it began. Cuneigh the Wanderer, too, trusted in Kuuro without a single reason to do so.

A lack of reason, to Kuuro the Cautious, was terror.

"Cuneigh. Our operation is to survey the Particle Storm."

Kuuro murmured to Cuneigh, inside the breast of his clothes.

"Aureatia is planning on *erasing* the Particle Storm. To these guys...the 'legendary clairvoyance' is their observational trump card, and you're not needed for that. There's no reason for you to have to come with me."

Like Lana and Zizima, and most others from the Obsidian Eyes, Kuuro the Cautious was always living on a battlefield. The contradiction of needing to put his own life on the line in order to survive another day.

He had a hunch that it was all going to come to nothing. It was clear that the Particle Storm was the very disaster Kuuro had sensed coming. He constantly doubted whether it was okay to let Cuneigh become wrapped up in such a calamity.

I'm scared of dying. I'm scared of killing. It should be the same for anyone.

That day, when he watched the swordsman instantly cleave a wurm in two. So wholly on a different level, and different from Kuuro. Aureatia now possessed such power. At the end of a long escape, from Obsidian Eyes and then, to ensure his survival, everything else, an even more inescapable power got hold of him.

...That should be the same for anyone, and yet, I wasn't allowed to run away?

"W-We're, we're going together, Kuuro."

"But you can still escape."

Cuneigh was naïve and didn't know just how hard that privilege was to obtain.

"...Um, well. If you die, Kuuro, I don't think I'll be able to go on living, either. So no matter what, I'll always be here to help you out. Let's stick together. Okay? It'll be okay, Kuuro!"

"Spare me the flimsy reasoning. What the heck are you going to do to save *me*?"

In spite of this, he smiled gloomily at her words.

He had the feeling he hadn't been able to smile in a very long time.

"I'm continuing the contract. What do you want for your reward, Cuneigh?"

"Later is fine. Okay? It's not something I want right now."

"......"

He knew for certain it would be the same trifling something it always was.

Though Kuuro never intended to be frugal with her reward, cheap glass beads and everyday fruits were the things that made her happy.

The fact he knew this and took advantage of her foolishness made him disgusted with himself. Ultimately, he was living while stealing from Cuneigh.

If he didn't take advantage of Cuneigh the Wanderer, he wouldn't be able to escape from the darkness of the world. The legendary man with the power of clairvoyance had to rely on a simple homunculus girl, possessing neither gifts nor any malice.

But now was different.

My opponent is the Particle Storm.

A dry wind blew. Right now, it was a relatively weak breeze.

In the middle of the calamitous storm that left nothing behind, he couldn't rely on Cuneigh. This was an enemy he had to fight with his own eyes.

Kuuro looked up to the sky. The impassive sun was glowing yellow.

Combat wherever you go. Nothing but fighting... You're a lot happier being completely incompetent, Cuneigh.

Even when it came to his sole gift, he had only been able to use it to steal. Had he been able to see all the possibilities spread out before him, Kuuro would always end up choosing his plunderous path.

His wish was to live. He wanted to live without having to steal.

Because stealing meant he would always need to rely on someone else to go on living.

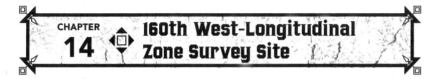
Five days earlier.

The four-person survey team dispatched from a neighboring city visited the aftermath of the storm's passage.

They were a frontier unit belonging to Aureatia. The mission they had received through their long-distance radzio from Third Minister Jelki was to survey the tracks the Particle Storm left behind on its move from the Yamaga Barrens.

Gently sloping plains stretched out below the horizon, a similar view to what they usually saw. Although they were far away from any town and the terrain was a little rough, such landscapes were a daily occurrence of theirs.

A number of anthills poked up between the short grass. Far off in the sky, a vibrant wooded mountain range was hazy in the mist.

"…Are we going to be all right?"

"What do you mean?"

"I mean, that Particle Storm thing, it's taking a pretty much unheard-of route, right? It's not going to, say, reverse course back at us right as we arrive, right?"

"Ha, you've got some moronic worries bouncing around in that skull of yours."

"This guy's a hardcore worrywart, let me tell you."

"You gotta be that worried to be fit for working with the frontier survey units, right...? Hey."

The four of them stopped in their tracks right before a descending slope. All of them stopped, without exchanging a single word between them.

At the bottom of the slope, a scene the likes of which they had never seen before stretched out before them.

"What the hell's all this?"

"Hold up. Hold on one damn second. This Particle Storm thing...it's 'posed to be some kinda sandstorm or typhoon, yeah?"

Homogenized topography. It was the only way to describe it.

It wasn't that the ground surface had been shaved down to its roots and erased. It was the opposite. There were rolling sand dunes, with a trail, like a ripple mark formed naturally in the wind. The scenery appeared out of the blue, completely disregarding the original terrain that had once been.

That was all—everything was particles.

"......Is this how things normally end up?"

"Whoa, whoa, this is beyond abnormal. This thing's on its way? Is Aureatia going to be okay... *Wha!*"

One of the squad members fell down. The incline at his feet had suddenly collapsed beneath him. He tumbled down the all-too-soft and smooth hill and collapsed far down below.

"Hey! Heeeey! Are you all right?!"

"I-I'm good... But what's up with this sand? It reeks something fierce when you're surrounded by the stuff. There's absolutely nothing I can use to climb back up there. Probably gonna need someone to grab me some rope."

"...All that organic matter's rotted by now."

One of them on top of the hill said as they scooped up some of the sand.

"Living things in its path...beasts, plants, anything, are torn apart and ground down to the bones. Bet whatever liquid and soil gets jumbled in, too. One day's more than enough time for microbes to start propagating."

"Even staring with my own eyes, I still can't believe it... Can a natural phenomenon do this? I've seen a tower wiped off the map by a flood, but even in those cases, they still... how can I put it...? The form was still there. Smashed timber, dead fish, and the like were all jumbled into a big mess, but you could still make out each part of the chaos. And you're saying all this was finally shredded naturally, without any design or intention behind the destruction...?"

"......"

The survey squad member who scooped up the sand sifted through it in his palm, looking at it closely.

It had small fragments of bone, like the shards of shells seen on the beach. There were what appeared to be scraps of leaves, black, their shapes lost. There were pieces that looked like smashed crystal. As well as pieces of something metal.

"Has anyone ever been to the Yamaga Barrens before?"

"Nope, not me. I guess because I always got the feeling it was a scary place. I heard stories about the Particle Storm from my grandma's friend who saw it, too."

"Same here. It may be weird considering our job, but when I got to Itaaki, I didn't even think about seeing what lay beyond it. I mean, do people really live out there, anyway?"

"I wonder when people started to think about it like that."

The Particle Storm was a phenomenon that only occurred within the isolated environment known as the Yamaga Barrens. As such, its true terror hadn't passed into legend. Nevertheless, to those who personally laid eyes on it, it was a meteorological death, to be feared more above all else. Like the stories of terrible floods and earthquakes that killed a great many, passed down for several hundred years, across generations.

The accumulated terror of witnesses, collected over an innumerably long number of years, had spread, and vaguely lodged itself within the minds of even men like them, who had never seen it directly for themselves.

The Yamaga Barrens is dangerous. Because that's where the Particle Storm rages.

"Maybe no one noticed because it's a desert weather phenomenon. Everything mixes together with the sand and gets erased... That's why we were totally unaware of just how abnormal it really was..."

In the Yamaga Barrens, terrain of exposed rocks and stone was exceedingly rare. It was a region where close to sixty percent of the surface was covered in sand. The reason why, and when it had become that way, were both unknown.

"H-hey."

A different member of the group spoke uncomfortably, shrinking back from where they stood.

"Th-this is bad. Let's get away from here. I'm heading back."

"...What the hell are you talking about?"

"You forget about our orders from Third Minister Jelki? We gotta pull him back up from there, too."

"Y-yeah, but still...c'mon, haven't you noticed?! There's no way they're gonna withstand this thing!"

He gazed steadily toward the horizon.

There stood featureless mountains and a lake. That was what terrified him.

"...Ha-ha. I-I knew it... I'm sure of it. Of course. There's a trapezoid-shaped mountain, next to it is suddenly this craggy peak, and...th-the lake...you can see the lake. You can see it!"

"What the hell are you getting at?! If you've lost your mind, I'll gladly shove you down there with the other guy!"

"You're the one who's lost their mind! How many years have you guys been surveyors out here?!"

He dropped his eyes below the diagonal slope. A slope. An exceedingly far-reaching terrain of nothing, sunk deep into the ground.

The four of them were surveyors from a nearby city. They had patrolled near here hundreds of times before.

"There *used to be a hill here*! The whole damn thing disappeared! There's...nothing left!"

There was one day left until the disaster's arrival.

A curious iron vehicle traveled along the road, surrounded on all sides by steep cliffs. Rushing along without any horses pulling it, it was not a carriage. However, it didn't spit out and steam, making it clearly different from the steamwork vehicles that were being popularized in Aureatia.

It was the product of technology unknown to the world at large—that is to say, the work of a self-proclaimed demon king.

"Did all those merchant types clear out, already? Here I was hoping to swindle 'em outta some high-quality radzio crystals."

The name of the old woman sitting in the front seat of the abnormal vehicle was Kiyazuna the Axle.

Her ultimate masterpiece, Mestelexil the Box of Desperate Knowledge, sat in the roofless cargo bed in the back. His colossal frame couldn't fit within the vehicle itself.

Loaded inside the cargo bed was not only the golem, but a variety of tools big and small. They were the goods the two had plundered during their raid on the Old Kingdoms' loyalists. Magic tools that could serve as promising golem material, and rare metals.

The sword that Mestelexil was gripping tightly in his hands was the very symbol of the Old Kingdoms itself—Charijisuya the Blasting Blade.

"Ha-ha-ha-ha-ha-ha-ha!"

"So you've taken a liking to that one, eh, Mestelexil?"

"Yeah! Blowing, up rocks, and metal, i-is very fun!"

"For a bunch of small-time upstarts, those Old Kingdoms' punks got their hands on quite the treasure. You see 'em, Mestelexil? All of them got blown away like scraps of trash. Didn't get to use any weapons at all."

"Ha, ha-ha-ha-ha! B-But, I, had fun! They flew, all the way, up to the roof!"

"Ooh, not bad. Fun to send minia flying, eh?"

"Yeah. But, when I, send them flying...and they hit something, it g-gets so messy. Why is that?"

"That's 'cause their entrails come spilling out."

"What are, 'en-trails'?"

"...Even non-golems got their stomach stuffed fulla mechanisms that makes them move, see. Unlike you, they're soft and can't be swapped out, though. Not that great, lemme tell ya."

The vehicle picked up speed.

"Better win, Mestelexil! Unlike those entrail-filled fools, you're immortal. You don't have the limited homunculus lifespan, or the life core of a golem! No matter what it is, enchanted sword, or anything else, to the winner go the spoils! Even when you're going up against the Particle Storm!"

"Yeah!"

He suddenly shouted.

"Ah! M-Mama, I found it! The a-a...air..."

"Air current!"

Mestelexil spun his ball-shaped head this way and that.

"Yeah! Air current! It's c-coming, from this, way! It, it is close!"

"Perfect, going in the opposite direction of the natural wind... The Particle Storm is close by, per calculations. This proves that my Chariot Golem can catch up with the Particle Storm's pace, even coming all this way from the seaside towns. Woulda loved to rub this in that Miluzi's face."

"Amazing! My, sibling is, amazing! Ha-ha-ha-ha-ha!"

The odd vehicle they were riding was not strictly a vehicle at all. It was the Chariot Golem, specializing in transportation. It was a unit with an irrefutable soul like Mestelexil, but it still used Word Arts to mobilize itself independently and could travel at speeds far beyond the commonly held expectations of the age.

"...You don't have any connection to this stuff, Mestelexil."

A supernatural weather phenomenon on the frontier, one the average person would go a whole lifetime without ever seeing. For her, it was a name she could never forget.

"But it's not just this one, either. A long time ago, you had several thousands of other siblings. In between the Yamaga Barrens, on the opposite side of Itaaki. I had a country of my own. A country of golems."

"R-really?! Big brothers! Mama's, c-country! Amazing!"

"Heh. Incredible, right? But my country got turned inside out and your brothers were all killed, too. That Particle Storm bastard... That cursed thing *came outta the* damn desert. Hadn't done anything like it before that, yet it decided to move just to come crush my country. Gotta be why it's heading toward Aureatia, too, I bet. When a minian country grows powerful, that Particle Storm bastard comes out to put it down. Far as I know, it's the absolute worst calamity out there."

When Kiyazuna was a child, born with an excellent talent for Craft Arts, she had been in a nigh constant foul mood. The only times she smiled was when she was handling machinery or bringing violence against someone else.

Somewhere along the way, she had been named a self-proclaimed demon king, turning most of the minian races against her, and still she was as foul-tempered as ever, feeling neither disappointment nor despair. All other minian people besides her intrinsically displeased her, and just as she hated the world herself, she readily accepted the world's animosity to her.

"Made a damn fool of me. What's wrong with being powerful?"

This was precisely why there were only a few targets she truly focused her anger on.

Even when the scholars crowding the labyrinth she left behind built a city around it, though she was exasperated, she was not angry, simply leaving them to do as they pleased.

Kiyazuna the Axle's true animosity was reserved for *anyone who harmed her children.*

"Technology is immortal. Science don't give up. Particle Storm, other golems, whatever the opponent may be, you're the child no one can kill...Mestelexil. You can pulverize any bastard that rubs ya the wrong way. You're my invincible child that'll keep on winning forever!"

"Ha-ha-ha-ha! Even if my, big brothers are g-gone, it is okay! Since I-I am the strongest! Strongest! I will make, your wishes, come true!"

"...Yeah. Do that until you get some wishes of your own. Granting wishes, heck, to someone truly invincible, that's a walk in the park. Go show the bastard that some Particle Storm fool isn't even worthy of standing in front of ya!"

Kiyazuna the Axle intended on picking a fight with calamity itself.

Freedom completely unobstructed by any threat—whether that be an enemy beyond all common reason, like a weather phenomenon of slaughter, or the True Demon King himself. That was the wish of Kiyazuna the Axle.

*   *   *

The Chariot Golem she was driving came out into an open area in the ravine. A convenient spot to wait for the Particle Storm to arrive.

However, there was something up ahead…

"Hey, who's this fool?"

There was a large silhouette. The Particle Storm was currently closing in on the ravine at that very moment.

It was fair to call anyone standing in such a place, alone and without a carriage beside them, suicidal.

"Mama! Mama! Amazing! So many, swords! Ha-ha-ha-ha!"

"…Swords, eh?"

Kiyazuna squinted her eyes to try get a better look at the figure.

The Chariot Golem's large frame was knocked on its side.

Mestelexil instantly reacted to the unannounced slash, and jumped away, holding Kiyazuna in his arms. The wreckage of its six wheels, severed with a clean stroke, was tossed in the air before dropping to the ground.

"The hell's with you? That's some way to introduce yourself."

"…Hand over the Blasting Blade."

A large-framed dwarf, head bent forward like a wild beast.

He carried a preposterous number of swords with him. The glare of his eyes, like death incarnate, was fixed hard on Kiyazuna and Mestelexil.

That weapon that instantly sliced through the Chariot Golem's wheels was an enormous halberd with a scythe blade.

It was an enchanted sword.

"Ha-ha-ha-ha-ha! I wonder who, this could be! He, seems strong! Those swords! How c-coooool."

"I'm going to kill you good for that. Tell me your name."

He was an unescapable fate, one that visited all those who held an enchanted sword. Even now, after dying and descending into hell.

"Toroa the Awful."

And now, the owner of Charijisuya the Blasting Blade was…

◆

Atop a cliff, far away from the place of Toroa and Mestelexil's confrontation. There was a person observing the situation undetected by either party, utilizing the distance and his espionage skill.

At his feet, there was an extremely elaborate map made up of crisscrossing lines depicting the Gumana Ravine.

It was Kuuro the Cautious. He was narrating information through a radzio to headquarters back at the Gumana Trading Post.

"Reporting my current observations. Kiyazuna the Axle and her golem bodyguard are engaging some unknown sword fighter in combat… No. The swordsman is provoking the fight. At the very least from what I can see…he's got an enchanted sword."

The golem's right arm instantaneously transformed into a strange bundle of gun barrels, and a hail of fire sprayed out from them.

It seemed that the enchanted swordsman's blade couldn't reach the golem, but some sort of interference sent the gun barrels astray and took a sneaky step closer during a gap in the storm of bullets. Touching a different sword, a tremendously powerful fireball appeared right at this location. The ability of the enchanted sword blew up the golem on the spot.

What's going on?

This continuing situation was completely beyond anything Kuuro could have anticipated.

If this battle gets drawn out, the Particle Storm will arrive here. *Kiyazuna the Axle...and her unmatched Craft Arts are just going to get tangled up in the disaster and die, then?*

On top of that, this identity-unknown sword fighter also happened to be there.

The strength to overwhelm the Kiyazuna-built golem. A master capable of wielding, as far as Kuuro could confirm, three or more different types of enchanted sword all by himself. There was only one person in existence, who he knew, that fit such an exceptional description.

"Maybe a ghost. Hey, or a revenant maybe..."

Hidden inside his coat, Cuneigh couldn't possibly sense the scene of battle, but the information Kuuro was relaying back to headquarters was enough for her to understand the identity of the swordsman.

"...You think a dead monster's been brought back to life? Ghosts and revenants look the same as the body used to make 'em. But, with revenants, their hearts don't beat."

As long as he kept his eyes closed and focused on the fixed location, even the withering Kuuro could see it for himself.

"That guy's heart is pumping."

"Then, um. Uh... An impostor, maybe? After Toroa died, someone might've picked up his enchanted swords by coincidence."

"That might be it... But it might not mean a damn thing whether he's a revenant or an impostor either way."

A jet burner blasted from Mestelexil's back. Toroa evaded the golem's rushes, nearly breaking the speed of sound. Both fighters flew past each other, and with blinding speed, the instant he left the range of his opponent's backward swings, the golem turned the muzzle behind him. The sound of gunfire. The barrel ruptured. The sound of an explosion.

The muzzle was filled with a crystal-like structure. The same moment they passed by each other, Toroa had also aimed for the gun barrel and chucked his enchanted sword. The name of the enchanted sword, which corroded and gnawed life-forms that connected with the blade via minute, frost-like crystals, was Vajgir, the Frostvenom Blade. Even against a golem opponent, its lethality was the same as ever.

When Toroa turned back toward his opponent, he simultaneously drew in an iron wire, and instantly returned the enchanted sword he had thrown moments prior back to his hand. Through the numerous wires strung up over his back, he wielded his numerous enchanted swords all at the same time. A nightmarish technique.

"At the very least, over there...is a monster capable of efficiently wielding numerous enchanted swords and fighting against one of Kiyazuna's golems. It's Toroa the Awful. He's alive."

◆

Kiyazuna the Axle, in an area slightly removed from the battle, was checking the movements of the Chariot Golem and its newly repaired wheels. Although she was confident she had made it durable enough to endure being overturned without anything breaking, given that her intended opponent was the Particle Storm, any unexpected defects could prove fatal.

Defect parts were quickly remolded with Craft Arts and swapped out. Constructing complicated mechanical parts using soil she was treading on for the first time, her Craft Arts were clearly far more brilliant than any normal person could hope to match.

"Now's he's done it. This bastard's really pissed me off."

She clicked her tongue. The battle between the two shura raged on. Mestelexil was being overpowered.

Mestelexil was obviously superior when it came to physical strength and speed, but in regard to fighting technique and flexibility, Toroa the Awful was the far superior combatant.

"Mestelexil, the crystals! That enchanted sword'll corrode you!"

"Wh-whoa, my, arm! My arm!"

The minute crystals that moments prior made him fire accidentally were extending up his left arm, all the way to his torso. A fiery beam ran across his shoulder, and his left arm fell to the ground. He had amputated it himself.

"My arm! It's gone! Ha-ha-ha-ha-ha!"

"I'm not stopping at just your arm."

Toroa followed through in midair with a different enchanted sword and sent another sweeping slash below him.

"I'll take your life, too."

While the series of movements were part of a slashing attack, it didn't touch Mestelexil in the slightest. However, the inside of his amor was sliced up with countless cuts. The Divine Blade Ketelk. The invisible elongated slash that ignored any barrier in its path was able to directly shred inside his armor—where a golem's weak point, their life core, resided.

"I-I haven't, lost yet!"

Toroa evaded the sudden gunshots. Mestelexil showed no signs of deactivation.

...Did I miss his life core? Where is this golem's core, then?

The fireball enchanted sword he had got a direct hit with earlier—Nel Tseu the Burning Blade—had no effect on this opponent's armor. The automatic reflexive defenses from the Lance of Faima proved unreliable against the fearsome high speed and continuous gunfire.

The enchanted swords that could handle this enemy were

Vajgir, the Frostvenom Blade, which corroded anything it came into contact with via a crystalline substance, and Divine Blade Ketelk, with its elongated and invisible slashes.

That was plenty.

"I don't care. I'll just chop up your whole body until you hand over the Blasting Blade."

"Hmm... Wh-whose child, are you, T-Toroa?"

"What...?"

It was an unanticipated question. With the framework for his tactical approach set, normally his best course of action would be to send his sword at him without a moment's delay.

"I am, Mestelexil! I-I have, fought against, m-many types of constructs! T-Toroa was, created by your mom, too, right?! Y-you're really strong!"

"...I'm Toroa the Awful."

Even as he sent out one lethal and cruel attack after another, the golem showed him no hostility. Toroa was the side of the conflict with a reason to fight.

"Hand over the Blasting Blade!"

The swordsman charged forward, with speed seemingly indifferent to the enormous weight he was under. He aimed to come from the left, where Mestelexil had lost his means of defending himself, and used the sword of poison and frost to crystallize his torso directly.

In response to his approach, it was possible the golem would make use of its jet propulsion again to open up space. When he did, Toroa would time the moment of the golem's acceleration with a thrust of Divine Blade Ketelk's long-range jab, Peck, and ruin his balance, toppling him over.

Mestelexil remained motionless.

What's this...

The auto-intercepting enchanted sword, the Lance of Faima, suspended on a chain around his waist, reacted. A projectile from below. He used the Frostvenom Blade to knock it down. It was Mestelexil's left arm, in the advanced stages of crystallization.

He tried to infect me with it *instead! So he can still move severed parts of his body, too?!*

"*Exil io mestel. Nastera mena. Futeno kueto. Likorecthion.*" (From Exil to Mestel. Mercurial fish fin. Voracious mirror. Match the scales of the sea of clouds.)

In the moment Toroa defended himself from the left arm projectile, the golem had finished an almost impossibly intricate operation. Mestelexil had reassembled and changed the structure of his right arm. The back section was a long, outstretched pipe, resembling a cannon barrel. It was affixed with a box-like attachment and viewing sights. Toroa brandished the enchanted sword in his other hand.

"*—einshart. (Obey). FIM-92 Stinger RMP.*"

"Peck!"

Just as he had held out against the initial Gatling gunfire, the Divine Blade Ketelk's long-range thrust diverted the sights of the weapon away from Toroa. The terrifyingly fast projectile launched straight up into the air.

—It was a small missile that moved at two-point-two times the speed of sound.

The heat source it was tracking was Mestelexil's left arm that Toroa had swatted away.

The golem had severed the corrosion creeping toward his torso, stopped Toroa's attack by using it as a long-range projectile, finished a Craft Arts incantation, and forced the Grim Reaper with his near limitless available options to exhaust all possible ways to deal with his opponent.

I'm in trouble.

Faster than the Lance of Faima could react, the sound cutting through the air alerted him to the approaching missile. However, it was already too late.

It was right after he had launched the Peck of the Divine Blade Ketelk.

"Oooooooh! Shrill...Cry!"

He swung Nel Tseu the Burning Blade while it was still fastened to his upper arm.

A momentary heat wave rushed across the sky. The stinger missile's path was disrupted by the abnormal heat signature, similar to a flare, crashing into the sheer ravine cliff face and exploding.

He forcibly activated the enchanted swords' secret techniques without using his arm, relying solely on the strength of his upper body.

The outstanding technique would be impossible without Toroa's bodily physique.

Since it could change its trajectory in midair, the split-second judgment that it was being propelled toward a heat signature had been the deciding factor between life and death. Though ultimately, it wasn't a heat-induced explosion, like he was aiming for, and instead the heat he produced itself, which proved effective.

"*Aresot hechat locoysodbroitenent pit abmalsbideklais saiber—*" (Recollections of world-engulfing fire trickle, to the arterial underbelly gaining arcane colors, speckled beaks unseen—)

That settles it.

Mestelexil was reverting the structure of his right arm, as he constructed his lost left arm from the soil.

...This golem definitely doesn't lack intelligence. He's seen all of my skill and speed, and he's keeping up with all of it.

With the sights from the heavy weapon he had just crafted, the golem was learning that Toroa's Peck would hinder the beginning of his attack. Therefore, he had chosen to use a guided missile, which he could fire easily, even if he took his eyes off the sights.

"Ha-ha, ha-ha-ha-ha-ha-ha! I am, strong! M-Mama said...no one, will kill, me. That is why, I will not be, killed!"

Still void of any hostility, but with mechanical precision, he could select the absolutely best fighting method available. Toroa imagined there wasn't any other opponent more formidable. In fact, he was like yet another death god, made of steel.

If I don't entrust everything to the enchanted swords, I'll lose.

His right arm moved instinctively. The enchanted sword repelled the hail of bullets coming at his flank.

With this sword, constructed out of several conical rivets, its magnetically linked layout could be rearranged, transforming into both a sword and a shield. It was the Wicked Sword Selfesk.

The attack just now had come from a different direction than where Mestelexil stood.

"Stealing enchanted swords? Give up the fool's errand, lad."

...She uses weapons, too?

It was Kiyazuna the Axle. She was sitting back on the roof of the fully repaired Chariot Golem.

The submachine gun held in her hands was technology that unequivocally exceeded the standards of this world, and impossible to manufacture without Mestelexil.

"Especially *my* enchanted sword, ya hear? We're busy right now. If you want an easy death, now's the time."

"...Did you come chasing the Particle Storm?"

"Yeah?"

"Just who...told you what course it's taking? Is it really a coincidence we met up here?"

"Well, well, what's all this? That's some tantalizing talk there. But it's too late."

The wind was growing more intense. Something blowing against the natural air currents was closing in.

Behind Toroa, a section of the ravine crumbled and fell. Though the colossal boulder was the size of a house, it didn't make any sound when it fell.

It had been pulverized in midair.

There was a wall. It was a tremendous amount of dust, stretched high up into the air and swirling like a vortex.

"The Particle Storm's here already."

Toroa the Awful couldn't take his eyes off the enemy in front of him.

Faced with Mestelexil's ever-changing attacks, a momentary delay in response meant death. Nor could he ignore the abnormal firepower and rapid-fire capacity of Kiyazuna's gun, either.

On top of all that, at his back was a storm of slaughter, turning everything into dust.

The ravine eroded away, and both sand and stone began floating amid the violent winds. Kiyazuna the Axle fixed her eyes on her destined enemy.

"Finally showed up, Particle Storm. Been what, eighteen years?"

She called out to the weather phenomenon, as though it had a personality, and they could communicate with each other through Word Arts.

Like the small village in the Yamaga Barrens had.

"Well...there are those who know of me even here, in the outside world. Then, rejoice."

In reality, the phenomenon had a will of its own.

Unseen amid the horrifying curtain of dust and sand, the being, both god and storm itself, made sure his voice was heard.

"The day of my guidance has come for you, as well."

And so, the disaster arrived.

A hundred and sixty years had come and gone since the existence known as the "Particle Storm" started being spoken of in the Yamaga Barrens. The fierce winds, like a raging deity, were savage, the sand blocking out everything else in the world, sealing the five senses. Then, after it passed, nothing would be left behind in its wake.

There was no one who had discovered its true identity and made it back alive, and even houses built from stone were unable to defend against the weather phenomenon.

It broke out without any warning, disappearing without leaving a trace.

To the residents of the Yamaga Barrens, the Particle Storm wasn't a godlike power—it was their god itself.

They believed their faith would let them escape from its divine power, and in actuality, that was indeed the case.

Villages that didn't offer sacrifices were annihilated.

Villages that tried to defend themselves with the powers of civilization were annihilated.

Countries that kept extending their territory inside the desert were annihilated.

The village where a quiet, deep, and almost perverse fanaticism proliferated was the only one allowed to live.

Despite the settlement being a three-day horse ride from

the neighboring city, the village was isolated in the shadow that the lights of civilization could not reach, and therefore, even during times of ruination brought forth by the Particle Storm, it never saw extinction.

The very day the calamity went on the move.

Ani, who was supposed to be offered to the Particle Storm, had disappeared during the night.

Hearing of their emergency, the village chief headed for the believer's barrow by himself. So he could use his own life as compensation for the Particle Storm's sacrifice.

"...P-Please, we humbly ask for your forgiveness."

Facing the barrow stained with the blood of child sacrifices, he desperately pressed his forehead down into the ground in reverence.

The bone splinters and the dead that should have been laid out behind the barrow had been pulverized, disappearing in a single night.

"Lord Particle Storm. Please, we beg you. To atone for the foolhardy Ani, please take my blood, spare the people of the village. I beg you."

The Particle Storm's anger. Their god, who ruled over destruction.

With both hands, he held out a dingy wooden bucket for drawing water.

"If child's blood is what you so desire, please take it! Six young boys, all under the age of twelve, this morning...I tied them up and killed them! I beg of you, Lord Particle Storm, your forgiveness...! Please!"

The wind howled.

A voice echoed from the other side of the formless wind.

"…How pitiful. Minia. I truly pity your kind."

"*A-aaah…*"

The village chief was terrified. There wasn't anyone of his generation who had directly heard the Particle Storm's voice before.

"Why… Why do you act so foolish? If you killed a pack of children for today's offering, then what do you plan to do for the next year's offering?"

"W-well, um…"

"Do you intend to do as you have, and abduct them from some other place?"

"*Eek*…N-No! Th-that wasn't it, at all!"

The god had spoken the truth.

"All of th-that, it was all to show our t-true faith to you, Lord Particle Storm."

Once every year, they needed to offer up thirty-two children as living sacrifices.

Every year, the mothers of the village were forced to birth children, but even after robbing them of the children they had raised, it was ultimately not enough to support the village. Occasionally, it had been necessary to supplement their numbers with children abducted from elsewhere.

During the era when, with the arrival of the True Demon King, the people from the surrounding towns vanished, they had stripped the skin of smaller-sized elderly villagers and disguised them as children's corpses. For over a hundred years, these were the things the village had done to survive.

"True faith, you say? Do you think I do not know of such truth? I know about every living person in this desert land. Everything, including the years when the number of children living in your pack were too few."

In this desert, drawing water was the children's job. There

were times when these children, while crossing between the village and the watering hole, would be visited by the Particle Storm and disappear.

Their numbers dwindled.

"How wretched. I *do not compel you to do anything*, and yet you do things like this, adding to your foolish sins yourselves. Killing among your fellow minia, among parent and child, all to offer up these completely meaningless sacrifices. Though from your perspective, it may not seem a long time, you have worked hard to continue this incessant lunacy... I am truly impressed."

The child sacrifices they gave as offerings weren't even eaten.

They had been forced to look at the meaningless corpses, piling up as time went by.

They themselves hoarded the symbols of their own powerlessness and worthlessness.

This being, this god, had simply watched it all.

It was laughing. Contrary to its words, it felt not a single bit of sadness at all.

"P-Please! Mercy... I beg for mercy! Th-they don't want to die! None of them want to die! Please, we beg you!"

"Such drivel, as you strangle your offspring to death? Very well. I see. How...how wretched."

Whether their village was destroyed or not, from the very beginning, was entirely *dependent on this being's mood.*

Their faith was meaningless. In this desert, all anyone could do was beg for mercy.

At the core of that mercy was boundless malice.

He acted not for the sake of destruction but simply to enjoy himself. He watched the small, predestined creatures fear his enormous power and, through their own choices, urge themselves toward their senseless ruination. Crazed by their fear of destruction, they suffered as they pointed the burden of their sacrifices to those even weaker than themselves.

What he truly was robbing from them was their dignity.

"Very well. Meaningless as it may be, your faith and affection have impressed me. Though, really, I had grown a little tired of it all. As a reward, I shall grant you the day of guidance. You believe in a day of guidance *or something*, yes? Naturally, I shall bestow it on all those living among your pack, as well."

"P-Please... Anything but that..."

"Why do you sorrow? This is the mercy you so wished for. What's the matter? Rejoice."

The titanic presence—the ungodly something, with a true form of his own, lifted his head from the ground.

The chief was unable to lift his own head. He was unable to look upon the terrifying Particle Storm.

Tears of despair dripped from his downcast eyes. He, too, had offered up beloved children to this being many times before. His seven-year-old son. His two-year-old daughter. His five-year-old son.

The Particle Storm, which pulverized everything into dust, was no weather phenomenon.

It was produced by the being's tremendous Force Arts.

If it was indeed possible for a living, breathing creature of the world to possess the strength of calamity itself—

Then such a being was even more terrifying than any true natural disaster...

"Rejoice."

"Th-this is the u-ultimate...honor, Lord Particle Storm...!"

"Ah, yes. I see, I see. This is how the insanity comes, then. Truly admirable faith. As forgiveness for your forsaken foolishness, I shall show mercy, and instead of destroying your pack after your atonement—"

...because malevolence could exist within such a being.

"I shall destroy them first."

◆

And then, presently, in the Gumana Ravine.

The Particle Storm, which had laid waste to natural landscapes and populated cities alike along its advance, was face-to-face with two shura who outmatched and exceeded all common understanding. One of them, Mestelexil, was the ultimate weapon, built precisely for a calamity like this.

"Mestelexil! Go wild!"

Kiyazuna the Axle shouted from inside the Chariot Golem. She had brought all the golem materials, including the Blasting Blade, into the driver's seat. The slightest exposure to the Particle Storm would easily be enough to wear and tear them apart.

"Ha, ha-ha-ha-ha-ha! Irokems fainek. Tostemkold. Eporosica quona—" (Molder causeways are four. Narrative burrow. Spin in deep eyelids—)

Toroa the Awful moved together with Mestelexil's incantation. His target was the keeper of the enchanted sword, Kiyazuna the Axle. The golem immediately responded with his jet propulsors and used his giant body to stop Toroa's enchanted sword.

"Ha-ha-ha-ha-ha-ha-ha-ha-ha!"

"......"

He knew the attack would be blocked. That was why he had drawn the Frostvenom Blade. Mestelexil bent forward to hold back the blade. The crystalline substance began spreading over his torso from the point of contact.

...But they were in point-blank range. The elongated box-like launcher, shaped to be carried on the golem's back, set its sights past Toroa to the Particle Storm behind him.

"—asbims (tear). DAGR."

Next it was Toroa's turn to bend his body and evade an attack. Crossing over his eyes as he bent backward, he saw guided missiles launched rapid-fire. They then sank into the Particle Storm's sand layer one after another.

Muffled explosions rang out in succession.

A colossal shadow, lording over all before it, came into view on the other side of the dust and sand.

"Hm. I see, I see. So that is how you intend to defy me."

The rapid-fire missiles, each one able to pierce the armor of the tanks in the Beyond, blew away the Particle Storm curtain, and exposed the true form of the god within.

"How pitiful."

It was a wurm.

The ancient creature, possessing monumental strength through spontaneous mutation, was the true form of the Yamaga Barrens' willed calamity.

After a moment, an even thicker curtain of dust kicked up. The missiles hadn't left a single scratch.

The sandstorm, unceasingly grinding with its terrifying momentum and density, disintegrated it all. Having it infiltrate into one's respiratory organs was enough to slice up their insides to dust.

The enemy calmly continued its advance. That, in itself, was its attack.

"All in this world are powerless particles. Nothing but particles to be wrapped in wind and soothe my tedium."

A colossal amount of grit and gravel, on par with the entire landscape itself, was sent into motion.

Assuming every individual grain was simply under the influence of the lone wurm's Power Arts...

The Particle Storm was an indestructible layer of particles that bested any and all of the world's defenses, even those from the Beyond, while serving, too, as a reactive armor that kept all outside attacks in check with its reversed momentum.

Even if something should pierce those defenses, the wurm's scales themselves were as tough as fortress walls. His colossal form overpowered all terrestrial creatures through physical strength alone.

The wurm's unique bone-conduction–based Word Arts transmission was able to *continuously maintain* its gargantuan scale of Force Arts.

"...Damned monster."

Even Toroa the Awful felt this way.

"Now to see, will you all turn to particles, too?"

He was undoubtedly a calamity. Born as disaster incarnate, his mind was filled with atrocity, able to take pleasure from watching living creatures die and go mad in the face of his power.

The disaster had a name—Atrazek.

No other person had ever used this name because he was simply the calamity.

He was enveloped in a particle offense, impossible to defend against, that infiltrated and gouged through any and every possible opening.

He was enveloped in a particle defense, impossible to attack, bereft of any vulnerabilities.

He could exercise his godlike authority eternally, never faltering.

The embodiment of calamity, outmatching all living beings, turning his true form into the very mantle of ruin itself.

Ruler. Wurm.

Atrazek the Particle Storm.

"You're in enchanted sword range now, Mestelexil."

Mestelexil had chosen to attack Atrazek with guided missiles. Hence, he had stopped moving, confronted with Toroa at close range. He had gotten that close to Toroa the Awful, to the land's most powerful enchanted swordsman. Mestelexil opened up the vents of his front jet propulsors—

"Too late."

Flames erupted from within Mestelexil's armor. An explosion went off inside his body.

"*Wh-whaaaaaaah*?! F-Fire! It's, fire!"

The Grim Reaper had already followed through with both his sword strokes.

In one hand was Nel Tseu the Burning Blade. In the other was a sword he was using for the first time during their battle.

"...Nel Tseu the Burning Blade. Mushain the Howling Blade."

Riding the air current created by the Howling Blade, it drove the heat from the Burning Blade into the golem. Forcibly sending air back through the golem's jet propulsors, it mixed with the fuel itself and exploded inside him. Kiyazuna shouted.

"Mestelexil!"

"I've brought down your precious golem, Kiyazuna the Axle. You're next!"

Kicking Mestelexil's motionless frame, Toroa aggressively jumped into the air. He drew the Divine Blade Ketelk. He would kill Kiyazuna inside her Chariot Golem with its long-range stab. Then a new gun barrel faced him. It was the Chariot Golem's machine gun.

The long-range attack from Divine Blade Ketelk, fully launched in midair, diverted the gun barrel. Crossing over its firing line, Toroa's massive body landed in the Chariot Golem's cargo bay.

"The Blasting Blade! Hand it over!"

"Like hell I will, fool!"

From his flank, an enormous metal hand grasped at Toroa.

Toroa ducked to avoid it and slashed with the Frostvenom Blade, still strapped to his upper arm.

"*Wh-whooooah.... G-Get away, from, Mama!*"

It was Mestelexil. He had self-repaired his propulsors and reached Toroa in an instant. The golem had unbelievable vitality.

Toroa knew that the crystalline substance he left with the previous attack should be starting to extend deep inside his body. That meant the golem's life core was somewhere else instead. However...

"That's a bad move. At this range—"

He dodged away from the sight line of the gun barrel that opened up around Mestelexil's knee. Toroa once again slashed with his enchanted sword. The golem feigned a punch with his left arm before fire erupted from the hidden gun on his neck. Evading the shot, Toroa effortlessly followed up with his next attack. It was exactly as he expected.

"You can't use your *fancy guns* because Kiyazuna'll get caught in the blast."

"*O-ohhh! Wh-whooooa!*"

The single-shot surprise attacks woven into their melee-range clash were tactics that Toroa hadn't yet seen during their battle, but none of it was beyond his expectations. This golem could rebuild any part of his body into a weapon at will.

"Dammit! We don't got time for any of this! That Particle Storm's coming!"

With both fighters continuing their fierce battle in the cargo bay, the Chariot Golem aggressively took off. Behind it, the wind was hot on their heels, destroying everything in its path as it went.

Amid the scenery flashing by and kicking up a cloud of dust as it went, Mestelexil was panicked.

"I-I, need to, defeat Particle Storm! But, I have, to beat, Toroa, too! But…"

His monstrous strength and full-body artillery arsenal were barely able to keep protecting Kiyazuna from Toroa's ferocious attacks. While half the surface of his inner flesh was being covered in the corrosive crystals, his ultimate priority was still Kiyazuna's life.

Complete mechanical recovery was possible. If his golem part was completely covered in crystals, as long as they had their shared curse, the homunculus inside couldn't be killed at the same time. However, in the second it took to finish reconstructing himself, Toroa the Awful would be able to kill Kiyazuna the Axle.

"There is nothing to be afraid of. Little ones."

The declaration from the very weather itself echoed across the whole ravine.

"Seeing you fear, flee, baffled, it is truly a comical and wretched sight."

The Particle Storm's mantle visibly accelerated. With his true form being that of a wurm, he was the strongest terrestrial creature in the world. Thus, just as the wyverns in the skies, the wurms, a draconic race that evolved most adapted to the surface, possessed mobility far outpacing the other species of living creatures on the surface.

If their enemy felt like it, it was questionable whether the Chariot Golem, rushing at full tilt, would be able to shake him.

"Hey, Toroa! Get the hell off my golem!"

Eroded by the crystals, Mestelexil at last dropped to his knees. Ever since the legend of Toroa the Awful began to spread...no matter how formidable a champion there ever was, none of them had ever been able to defeat him while in range of his enchanted swords. The invincible weapon of war was losing.

Kiyazuna shouted as she hurriedly operated the driving controls.

"It won't speed up! That Particle Storm bastard's gonna catch up to us! Just how heavy are you, dammit?!"

"...Hand over the Blasting Blade! Is it worth losing your life over?!"

"Ab-so-lute-ly not! Doing what some vagrant asshole tells me to? That'd be the same as dyin' anyway!"

The Blasting Blade was just a sword in the end. Both of them were well aware of the fact.

"Kiyazuna the Axle doesn't bend to anyone, y'hear me?!"

The scythe-like enchanted sword pierced through Mestelexil's torso. The armor, eroded by the minute crystals, had grown brittle enough for a normal blade to pass through. Even if he could chant Word Arts, the golem's body would be unable to keep up.

"Ungh... M-Mama..."

Toroa reversed his ascent then took advantage of the maneuver to grab a new enchanted sword.

Next, turning around, he cleaved behind him.

"...Howling...Blade!"

With a single slash, the dust creeping up behind them was

driven away from the Chariot Golem and scraped into the ravine rock surface.

If Toroa hadn't reacted with the Howling Blade, they would have been wiped out.

Contact with the Particle Storm meant instant death. A realm of slaughter, taking both Kiyazuna and Toroa down together.

Now *it catches up with us?! Right when I finally beat Mestelexil...! Actually, wait...*

Toroa sent his next slash flying. Straight behind the Chariot Golem.

He needed to incessantly slash with the Howling Blade to defend against the Particle Storm's air currents. If his hands stopped, it meant instant death. In order to defeat his opponent, Kiyazuna, he now had to defend her.

Kiyazuna slowed down on purpose! *In order to force me, her enemy, to deal with the Particle Storm! Then...while I'm stuck handling this wind—*

"—*emfectas neos yactectenaoathal bagneteha usvasvetmotosye inqdorteae*—" (—collect in the bottomless light vortex that binds twin heavens pierce the vast gloom and falling blossoms and castle columned rocks turning eternally—)

Mestelexil's supernatural Craft Arts could even reconstruct his own body.

However, it was not his own body he was creating.

"Keep it up Mestelexil! You got the right idea!"

An iron fingertip tried grabbing hold of Toroa's ankle. With the Lance of Faima's reaction, he picked up on the attack and countered with the Frostvenom Blade. He turned his attention to the seated Mestelexil. The finger wasn't his. Mestelexil wasn't moving, all active functions still deactivated.

"OOOOOOOOOOOOOOO—"

"Impossible!"

It was a different golem. Different as well from the Chariot Golem they were riding, the golem was bronze-colored and hollow. He swung the Howling Blade. He defended against the Particle Storm that was closing in right before his eyes.

"ROOOOOOW."

He sensed a new presence appear behind him. The Burning Blade. Setting the golem's interior ablaze, it was knocked off the speeding cargo bay.

It was the second one. The golems that hadn't been in the cargo bay mere moments ago *were multiplying—*

"Harq icketems senka didenket mou odasdionrinser fines opponiswem seltegnes tia—" (Deep blue daydream palace drown in mercury walk and remember in fantastical landscapes the nine thousand words that fulfill immature crystal prophecy—)

"Mestelexil... Wait... This thing's...!"

The soil and rocks of the Gumana were being shaped one after another with Craft Arts, giving birth to an army.

Mestelexil, concentrating wholly on his Word Arts and with his combat capabilities still disengaged, could do even this.

"...a golem that makes other golems?!"

The soulless golem army foolishly advanced straight into the Particle Storm, swarming in to bring an end to Atrazek's true form inside.

"Oh, turning your hand against me, now? Fragile, so horribly fragile your bodies are... Excellent. Truly excellent. I, of course, shall allow your meaningless resistance. It is a bit of a shame you shan't be able to scream in sorrow."

The Particle Storm's advance slowed. Metallic squeaks and gunpowder explosions echoed from inside the whirlwind.

With the durability of the golem's composite armor, as long as their survival was considered meaningless, it was more than possible to advance through the Particle Storm and make an attack on Atrazek's true body.

The conclusion Mestelexil came to was not to regenerate himself. *It was to handle all the enemies facing him at once.*

"...How 'bout I give you a rundown on Mestelexil's functionality, Toroa the Awful. There is only one main body that can exist in this world at one time. Otherwise, his shared curse that references each part of him won't function, see? But what if you thought about that another way, eh?"

"Kiya...zunaaaa!"

"It means he can produce an infinite number of soulless base bodies!"

The Chariot Golem, accelerating further, momentarily escaped from the Particle Storm's range.

However, if anything, the threats Toroa needed to contend with were growing in number. The golems overflowing the cargo bay swooped down on Toroa the Awful.

Just how many of these things are going to pop up. If this really does keep going on forever...!

The Divine Blade Ketelk's slashes gouged out the life core inside a golem's armor. One of the golems collapsed from the attack. Still, he couldn't attempt to use this method to take out so many golems.

Though they weren't immortal, and they didn't possess the Word Arts to create supernatural weaponry, their physical abilities and armor were on par with Mestelexil's own.

"...Actually. It looks like—"

As he was driven to the edge of the cargo bay, Toroa the Awful still discovered an opportunity to come out victorious.

"There's a limit...after all. Kiyazuna the Axle."

"Huuuh?!"

There was a loud shatter.

Atrazek's voice made itself known.

"Take a good look for yourself."

The shatter was the sound of wreckage sent flying from inside the storm, crashing into the Chariot Golem. They were golems with over half their frames shaved off. In the exact same way this same weather phenomenon had annihilated the entirety of Kiyazuna the Axle's army in the past.

Even golems boasting the firmest of armor would die the moment they reached the main body inside the storm. Once they got through the storm, lying in wait at the other end of the obstructed view were the tough jaws and massive tail of the wurm within.

"See with your own eyes if the fire and trickery of you minia can get through to me. If knowing that answer should satisfy you, I shall oblige."

The Particle Storm was gaining on them.

"*Tch*, trying to weight us down, eh? That bastard..."

"What are you going to do now?! Keep this endless golem spawning up, and logically we're going to slow down with it! You can't keep up this onslaught against me forever! Planning to keep it up until I've run out of energy, eh, Kiyazuna the Axle?!"

Even going face-to-face against a machine, it was exactly what Toroa the Awful wanted.

He had repeated it all many, many times before.

"I promise, I can keep swinging these enchanted swords of mine long into the night!"

"Dammit! Mestelexil, stop ramping up production! You're turning into a damn chain 'round my neck...!"

She hadn't imagined a situation like this. Originally, this

Chariot Golem had been prepared so that *only Kiyazuna* could withdraw from the battlefield.

As long as she was nearby, there was no way for Mestelexil to display his true power.

If I was just a little farther away from Mestelexil... VX gas, thermobaric bombs, he would've been able to try them all out, dammit!

Toroa continued to fight. On top of a vehicle sprinting away at high-speed, all by himself against an endless army of golems and the Particle Storm. He held super-powered weapons, the full extent of their abilities unknown, and could wield them all with perfection.

As long as this man was here, Mestelexil was forced to protect Kiyazuna.

This bastard... He's completely beyond any of my expectations!

Amid the disorder of the battle, at first glance, it seemed Kiyazuna's camp had built up an overwhelming advantage, but in fact, from the very moment they were forced into this situation, Toroa the Awful held their lives in his hands.

Toroa had the option to destroy the Chariot Golem itself at his disposal. If she lost her way to escape from the Particle Storm, Kiyazuna the Axle's death was guaranteed.

It meant, from the very beginning, he was a man who *was able* to assess the tide of battle. Even against weapons from the Beyond that no one in the world had seen before, he could match them with similar attacks and counter them, as though he already knew everything about them. Though he had the voice of a young man, he showed an ability to respond to any situation like a shura who had spent a lifetime with an enchanted sword at his side.

From somewhere unknown, he had acquired such an enormous wealth of battle experiences that seemed impossible given his youth.

"Toroaaaa...!"

"—*Gah*!"

Yet, Toroa the Awful suddenly gasped as he continued eradicating the golem army.

"Your time's up, Kiyazuna the Axle."

"Huuuh?!"

"This vehicle's actually a golem, right?! I didn't intend for this to happen, either... This vehicle's going to collapse!"

"And why's that?!"

"Vajgir, the Frostvenom Blade. The crystalline substance this sword releases, it eats living organisms! Whether its bone, metal... even soulless constructs, anything with a life of its own will corrode away! In other words..."

Toroa looked beyond the swarming golem arm, where Mestelexil sat slumped over and motionless. His own faculties disengaged, everything was focused on golem production. His body was completely covered in the fine crystals, and they were now spreading directly down to the cargo bay at his feet.

Before long it would reach the structural and mechanical sections of the golem. Kiyazuna understood that, as well.

"Damn you...!"

"...I'm not planning on committing suicide with you! Hand over the Blasting Blade!"

The Grim Reaper extended out his arm to the driver's seat as he fought against the surging golems.

"Like hell I am!"

"I'll get the Particle Storm!"

".......!"

"I... I should be able to use the Howling Blade to push through and advance through his wind! No matter how tough the main body inside's armor may be, with the Blasting Blade, I can kill him! Because I'm Toroa the Awful!"

Toroa the Awful was her enemy. Under some irrational pretext, he was after Kiyazuna's treasure and had backed her this far up against the wall.

However, he was serious. There was no doubt in her mind about it.

"Don't you...dare order me around!"

The Chariot Golem shook violently. Mechanical damages had dropped its speed significantly, and the realm of death, the Particle Storm, was gaining on the vehicle's frame. Atop the now unbalanced vehicle, Toroa tried to draw the Howling Blade. Golem remains swooped in on him, as if taking careful aim to prevent him from doing so.

The enemy was the strongest Force Arts user in the land. The swarming army of metal itself was being launched like cannonballs toward them.

"*Tch...!*"

Toroa staved off the attack with an explosion from Nel Tseu the Burning Blade. He was one step too slow. A few grains of sand slipped inside and tore his trachea. They were already within the Particle Storm's range.

"Quite a stunning performance, really. You are the first I have seen hold out so long against my storm. And yet, if you simply let me hear your tearful wails and see your terror, I would have shown you mercy."

Toroa tried to draw his next enchanted sword.

Only those who stood within the storm, moments before death, saw its form.

A shadow that floated into view among the storm blocking

out the sky above—the mere silhouette of the ancient and godlike wurm, head raised up in the air.

"A pitiful end."

A large circle ripped open in the blotted-out sky.

The Particle Storm, which prevented any and all attacks against it, was pierced through, and meteoric destruction thrust into the ground.

Sound.

Tremors.

Rumbles.

The ground exploded and the world shook.

"Wha—"

Even Atrazek's massive body was sent in the aftermath, his colossal form smashing the steep ravine walls.

The overwhelming destruction split open the ground's crust. It pierced down deeper. So deep, it was impossible to see the bottom.

The god was unable to utter a single word. It was the first time the land's supreme absolute being had experienced being dumbfounded.

"...Hng...Oooh."

Unable to maintain his Power Arts, he let out four rough gasps of air.

Finally, he spat out a single phrase.

"What *was* that?"

The Chariot Golem was overturned. Such was the power behind the shockwave following the attack.

"*Nrrgh...* D-dammit! What the hell?! What happened?!"

What *had* happened?

No one there had understood the latest development, but a

single person among them, Toroa the Awful, saw the truth behind the attack. The thing that flew in from high in the sky was neither a meteor nor a bomb.

"A pillar...a pillar, of iron."

Yet even the strongest Grim Reaper of them all was mistaken in his assumption.

That pillar of iron was, in fact, an arrow.

◆

Sine Riverstead.

The Needle Mountain outside the village was currently packed with a number of soldiers. They were Aureatia comms soldiers.

The giant, large enough to look down over all of them, was listening to an observation report via radzio.

Impact location verified. 1116 by 362.

"Bwah-ha-ha-ha! Right on target, what'd I tell you?! Well? Did I get the Particle Storm?!"

Uh, nope—It wasn't a direct hit. I... I misjudged the distance. The next one will hit.

The voice coming through the radzio belonged to Kuuro the Cautious.

The communication from the spotter, looking at the Particle Storm right before his eyes, reached all the way to the Sine Riverstead, traveling through a relay tower constructed at the Gumana Trading Post.

For an individual comms soldier, it was a staggeringly long distance, over thirty kilometers as the crow flies. The operation was possible entirely due to the personnel and technology available to the greatest of all minian nations, Aureatia.

There was also an individual capable of long-range ballistic bow fire *without even seeing their target*, from over thirty kilometers away.

"Seriously? Worthless trash. Ah well, makes no difference to me."

He nocked his bow with a fresh arrow.

A colossal black arrow, nearly as tall as he was, at twenty meters long.

While the Particle Storm may have been a completely enigmatic and godlike disaster that wrought destruction, there was a being in this world capable of killing such a disaster.

"I just gotta keep firing until I hit, then."

The gigant's name was Mele the Horizon's Roar.

An Aureatia soldier positioned at his feet turned to the radzio and shouted.

"Preparations for shot number two, complete! Kuuro the Cautious, requesting the next spotting information!"

"Hey, hold on now, pipsqueak."

With his arrow still drawn, the gigant called down to the Aureatia soldier.

"Excuse me...?! Pipsqueak? Are you talking about me?"

"Well, you're a pipsqueak, ain't you? Fix the pavement in the next town over. Replace the farming tool for Erig's family, too. All of 'em."

"B-but, I'm just a comms soldier, so..."

"Well, call up one of the big shots then. I'm the one awake before noon and doing all the work. Each shot's gonna cost ya."

Mele readied the arrow. The same man who normally never fought, and instead spent his days lying around.

The Particle Storm's projected course had it pass through the Sine Riverstead. The sand would reduce everything—from the living

creatures, down to the very environment they lived in, into tiny particles. Just by passing nearby, the weather phenomenon would bring irrevocable losses to the fertile village he loved.

Fixing his eyes on his enemy, standing physically beyond the horizon, Mele's mouth twisted.

"Got some guts, coming after the Sine Riverstead, Particle Storm."

It was the smile of a warrior.

"I'll shoot your damn eyes out."

Across this horizon, there lived someone idolized as a god, wielding tremendous power as he lived among the minian people.

Two gods battling each other.

◆

"...He missed! Damn! Sh-show me... You can see it...!"

Kuuro the Cautious's grip threatened to break the radzio in his hands.

It had missed... Mele the Horizon's Roar's lethal arrow had missed.

The extraordinarily long-distance archer fire was Aureatia's trump card. It was their best hope of stopping the Particle Storm, regardless of whether it was a naturally occurring weather phenomenon or whether there was a true form hidden within.

Kuuro, with his abnormal clairvoyance ability, could pinpoint the target. He should have been able to correctly foresee where Atrazek would move to next. At the very least, the old him during his days in Obsidian Eyes would have.

He was expected to be capable of doing so. He bore the weight of countless lives on his shoulders.

"Hey. Kuuro. The wind's strong! It's dangerous. Let's get away from here."

"...I can't. Even at this range, I can't get a hit. If I don't look from a closer range, right now, I can't do anything."

Kuuro muttered, reflecting on his anguish.

The fierce battle between Kiyazuna the Axle and Toroa the Awful was unfolding atop the Chariot Golem, and they continued to flee from the Particle Storm's range. The three-sided battle line was shifting backward, and while Kuuro had been observing from longer range at the start, the lethal calamity was closing in on his position. Now, he himself was in danger.

For him, a non-shura spotter, he had nothing, neither a Chariot Golem, made airtight in anticipation of the Particle Storm, nor anything on par with the Howling Blade and the sublime skills to wield it. If he was swallowed up by the storm, that would be the end.

"...That thing's actually a wurm. It wraps itself up in the Particle Storm with some sort of Force Arts or what-have-you. Aureatia knew all of that from the start. This thing had a will of its own, and that's why it went after civilization and populated settlements..."

The main body, previously visible from the hole opened up by the arrow, was already hidden again in a thick cloud of dust.

A constantly reverberating rumble, like thunder, and nigh as dense as the ground itself. Kuuro's senses could see all the way beyond the horizon. However, he could see too much. He could hear too much.

The Particle Storm was an impregnable fortress that sheltered its main body. The immense overload of information disrupted his concentration.

"The target isn't always inside the center of the storm. He should be able to change his Force Arts' area of effect at will. From the echoing of the sand in the middle, I sense its range. And I also get the feeling... No, stop. No point in speculation. Don't believe what you can't see. Look, look harder."

"Um, I-I can... Hey. Like I always do, Kuuro. I can, I can go and look for you...! Isn't, isn't there something I can do?! If everything'll come to nothing unless we defeat that thing, then—"

"Don't be ridiculous!"

Inside the Particle Storm, with her tiny body, Cuneigh would be ripped to shreds. She would be killed instantly. A more fundamental problem than any spotting difficulties.

"Why are you trying to get yourself killed! Aren't you afraid to die?!"

He tightly held Cuneigh close inside his coat. As though to shield her from the gaze from the land of death in front of them.

"K-Kuuro..."

"Headquarters. Reporting spotting coordinates. 1127 by 355...!"

Light burned far away in the deep blue sky. It traced an arc across the sky before falling.

Despite how extremely far apart they were from each other, barely a second had passed following his report.

Then, it pierced through sky and ground.

"A-Another...miss...!"

Atrazek's mantle of sand was torn asunder. And yet that was the extent of it.

The impact point was perfectly on the indicated mark. Kuuro's spotting was the problem.

Even with his own life hanging in the balance, his sight failed him.

He grew weaker still. Beyond simply losing his gift of

clairvoyance…he was sure, someday, his senses would dull beyond those of the average person. The sense of impending death that came to him when he closed his eyelids was here in front of him at this very moment.

He was losing it. The once-vivid world began slipping through his fingers.

I… I should be able to see it.

"Kuuro. Kuuro, it's okay."

The wholly frivolous words of comfort from Cuneigh rang so very hollow.

◆

"M-Mama!"

Kiyazuna, beginning to topple over from the meteor quakes shaking the ground, was saved by Mestelexil's large hands.

The four limbs that had once crumbled into dust were completely regenerated, looking completely good as new.

"I-I am good, as new, again! Ha-ha-ha-ha! Because I, am immortal!"

"Ha…! Converted the crystals directly with Craft Arts, didja? That's my boy. Perfectly handling whatever enchanted nonsense gets thrown atcha! Well done, Mestelexil!"

"Ha-ha-ha-ha-ha-ha-ha-ha-ha-ha-ha!"

"Anyway, first we gotta deal with Toroa the Awful. If we don't kill him, the Particle Storm'll be the least of our problems. Gather up the golems. Fence 'im in and crush him all at one!"

"…That won't be necessary."

The voice was near the overturned Chariot Golem. From among the pile of materials spilled out over the ground, Toroa picked up and held a single sword.

"The Blasting Blade's mine."

"Y-You little—!"

In the tumult of their battle, there were too many things to handle at once. Though a self-proclaimed demon king, possessing the highest degrees of both intelligence and mental fortitude, Kiyazuna the Axle was an elderly minian woman.

Toroa the Awful destroyed a nearby boulder with a test swing and confirmed that it was indeed the real Blasting Blade. Then, he turned to face not Mestelexil...but the Particle Storm rampaging far out in front of him.

"I've figured this sword out. I'll fulfill my end of the bargain, Kiyazuna the Axle."

"...What the hell are you talking about?"

"I'm going to defeat the Particle Storm."

An ominous and sinister "road" had been formed inside the complex Gumana Ravine. The traces of the Particle Storm's passing were pulverized into dust, forming a line, like a child cutting one through a piece of clay.

Furthermore, the arrows from Mele the Horizon's Roar had gouged deeply into the earth's crust, leaving behind a hole too deep to see to the bottom.

With the extent of the fissures and upheaval, topographical changes that would normally take thousands of years had happened all in one day.

This lone dwarven Grim Reaper was intentionally stepping onto this battlefield of gods.

"Hey... You bastard. Thinking you can patronize Kiyazuna the Axle, do ya?"

The situation was different now. Mestelexil was revived and well. He even generated a golem army in the middle of battle. The scale of Kiyazuna the Axle's fighting force was overwhelming.

"That shithead's *mine*. Mestelexil! Kill 'em both!"

"R-roger! Ha-ha-ha-ha-ha-ha-ha! I'll beat, them both! Watch me, Mama!"

"Well...do what you will!"

Right before Toroa rushed forward, light once again rained down from the heavens. An arrow from the Horizon's Roar.

The iron pillar instantly lost its shape under the phenomenal momentum as it connected with the ground, piercing deep into the terrain and disappearing.

"Damn you; damn you aaaall!"

Writhing in agony from his wounds, Atrazek roared in rage and agony. His exceptionally large size and remarkable vitality, thanks to his wurm body, allowed him to survive the aftermath of the impact.

However, the destiny gathered at their location was far more incomprehensible and terrifying than mere calamity. It was something altogether ludicrous.

"What did you... What did you call here?!"

"I h-have, no idea! Ha-ha-ha-ha-ha-ha-ha-ha!"

"It matters not. Out of my way!"

"Enough already! Your time's up, Particle Storm!"

On this day, in one part of the world, supernatural and transcendent shura were gathered together.

Each looked at the others with fire in their eyes. They possessed strength enough to deliver on that murderous intent.

The end was nigh. To all those standing at this point, a realm of slaughter, at the crossroads between fate and ill-portent, emerged.

There was but a single moment where the Particle Storm's mantle—like a bulwark, lacking any gaps in its outermost layer—parted. That moment directly followed the artillery fire, which seemed to fly in out of nowhere and pierce straight through the storm's supreme defenses.

In this fleeting moment, Toroa the Awful took stock of where his opponent was and unwaveringly jumped inside the storm.

In the middle of such extremity, the ideas of his own individual self, long since cast aside, floated like bubbles to the forefront of his mind.

Why... Why am I doing this?

Kiyazuna the Axle had gotten hold of an enchanted sword. She had laid eyes on Toroa the Awful's form. If he was to follow the legend of Toroa the Awful exactly, he should kill her, with no responsibility to fulfill his promise to her. Why then was Toroa still fighting?

It's because I'm weak. I know.

It was because he couldn't be the invincible Toroa of legend. He hadn't fully cast aside his weak self, from when he lived in the Wyte Mountains. He was aware that he couldn't endure as a merciless vessel to the god of death, guided solely on the path his enchanted swords led him down.

Though he understood this, though he acted in opposition to the legends, he stood against the Particle Storm.

Still, Dad would have done the same.

Even if Toroa the Awful wouldn't have, he was certain the father he knew wasn't the type to break a promise. He wouldn't have wanted him to look upon a mother trusting in her child, and a child full of love for his mother, and simply point his sword at them.

Should his father's actual deeds suggest otherwise, he wanted to believe it was true.

"How pitiful... How wretched you are. Knowing not a thing, and yet..."

The vibrations echoing from the wurm's cranium began once again to turn sand into storming winds. The sand scraped away at the earth, and the new sand—soil turned into particles—coiled around him. An endless weather phenomenon. A living disaster with a malevolent will.

"You do not know, do you? The world is particles. Simple specks forming shapes, moving, and saying wordlike nonsense. They all fear me. As shall you."

"—Migration—!"

The Howling Blade produced an explosive gust. The gale, continuing even after the sword's slash had ended, cleared a path for Toroa to push forward. His enemy was the Particle Storm. Though this enemy was possibly the strongest Force Arts user in the land, controlling each grain of his enormous swirling sand at will—

Even still, as long as he's in this space, within range of my enchanted swords...

"This, indeed, is the authority to bestow such truth to all the world. Now, you too shall beg me for mercy!"

"That power of yours..."

His muscles groaned. Forcing his body past its limits with his immense strength, he utilized the sword's hidden technique endlessly, not letting up for a single instant.

"...is a far cry from Toroa the Awful's!"

He advanced. A colossal boulder was flying around, mixed in with the sand. Sinking his body low, he rolled to dodge it. Another swing of the Howling Blade. The vibrations from the ground informed him the wurm's main body moved. Wicked Sword Self-esk. He shot out the enchanted sword, composed of many rivets, forward in a fan shape.

One of the rivets dug into his opponent. The magnetic force that radiated from the hilt sent the recoil from the rivets' landing back to Toroa himself.

"You cannot run, Particle Storm! Not from this god of death! Not from Toroa the Awful!"

"Run, you say?"

The wurm, incensed, aimed his jaw toward the dwarf.

"Me, run?! Pitiful! Truly wretched and pitiful, you are! Worthless sack of particles!"

Overcoming the meteorological death swirling around him, Toroa finally arrived—right in front of Atrazek, where no one had ever been before. In front of the god of destruction. There was no weather phenomenon that could deter Toroa the Awful.

He was a death god who had survived hell itself.

"You too...you too, shall be swept up in the particles!"

Toroa stepped forward and put his fingers on an enchanted sword. He felt the ideas dwelling within, its secret techniques.

He would kill him in one slash. He could do it.

"Charijisuya, the Blasting Bla—"

The heavens rent the air.

The impact, breaking the speed of sound, destroyed the scene before him, piercing through the barrier Toroa instantly put up with his enchanted sword of wind, rattling his skull.

The air pressure from the aftermath instantly reversed all the distance he had desperately closed, slamming into the rock wall of the ravine. Blood spewed out of his torn stomach.

—It was a shot from Mele the Horizon's Roar.

"...Dammit. Not now..."

Mele's latest arrow was rather far off the target. From Toroa's position, it landed on the far side of Atrazek from where he was standing.

Nevertheless, it exerted power far beyond the feats of any other, like an act of the gods.

"Y-you!"

Hit with the same considerable impact, Atrazek had caught Toroa in his range. The Particle Storm was still blowing unperturbed.

The wurm's humongous tail was closing in on him right before his eyes. Toroa tried to stand up. It would be impossible to defend against the enormous physical mass with the Howling Blade. Toroa's death was certain.

If he'd just had that Luminous Blade. The Burning Blade. Wailsever. Right now his only options left were...

Yet, unable to come up with a strategy, he bent his knee. A groan escaped his lips.

"......?! *Hng, grnnk!*"

It came from the sudden pain he felt run through his whole body.

The feeling was beyond words, as though everything beneath his skin was boiling.

"*A-aauuuugh...!*"

Atrazek, too, had stopped moving, just as he tried to smash Toroa into the earth.

He was attacked by the same pain as Toroa. An abnormal attack without any real form, impossible to defend against.

◆

"APFSDS artillery. Napalm. Thought up a bunch of different methods, y'see."

Muttering inside her vehicle, beyond the Particle Storm, was the demon king, Kiyazuna the Axle.

"The Particle Storm's like a thousand layers of air armor, so to speak. Armor-piercing rounds won't penetrate 'em, though. If he's controlling sand 'n' wind, then dousing him in napalm fire won't work either, right?"

The iron colossus standing at her side was none other than her ultimate masterpiece, Mestelexil the Box of Desperate Knowledge. Right now, he had octagonal metal plates spreading out from both of his shoulders.

"That led me to this—an ADS directed-energy weapon. Even someone like the Particle Storm can't defend against subcutaneous, microwave induction heat, can he?!"

"I-I can, make, anything! Particle Storm! I am…going to be, useful to, Mama!"

The true origin of the pain was direct heat from underneath the skin.

Microwaves were attenuated by the moisture in the air, but on the other hand, they easily penetrated through dry dust and sand. The construction itself closely resembled the millimeter wave weapons that existed in the Beyond, but this weapon's intended purpose wasn't to quell a riot, but instead to directly wound and kill Atrazek and Toroa.

Reproducing the weapons from Beyond wasn't the only thing Mestelexil was capable of—he could also further strengthen their lethality to match up against his enemies.

"Die in agony! Feel the parental hate from the children you killed...and die, Particle Storm!"

"Ha-ha, ha-ha-ha-ha! Ha-ha-ha-ha-ha-ha-ha-ha-ha-ha-ha-ha-ha-ha-ha-ha-ha-ha!"

"*Ngaauuuuuugh!*"

With a scream, the sand and dust that made up the Particle Storm fell.

Exactly like the brief moment following Mele's arrows, the sand lost the Force Arts' effects.

"Ha-ha-ha-ha-ha-ha-ha-ha-ha-ha-ha-ha-ha-ha!"

"Perfect, it's working, now... What?"

Kiyazuna felt that something was wrong. It was too quick for him to lose consciousness from the pain.

While it was possible, she'd eventually kill him if she kept irradiating him—

"...*Tch!*"

She clicked her tongue in frustration, looking at the scene once the Particle Storm cleared.

Covered in wounds, Toroa the Awful had fallen to his knees. But there was no sign of her bitter enemy.

A massive hole was carved out of the ravine wall. She had, of course, factored in the wurm's biological behavior—that was why she had picked an attack that would make it impossible for him to move.

"Why the hell can he move...?! That much pain should've knocked him out cold!"

As arrogant and proud about their own power as the draconic

races were, they generally didn't turn to such methods. However, they *could*.

"That damn wurm turned tail and ran!"

There had simply never been a situation where it had become necessary.

The Particle Storm, wielding the power to eradicate anything in a single attack, could also bury underground to retreat and launch surprise attacks.

◆

"Kuuro. Come on."

He heard Cuneigh's voice coming from inside his coat. She sounded like a child on the verge of tears. She probably was crying, in fact.

"Come on, let's run away."

"*Koff.*"

Kuuro spit out blood. He had inhaled debris from the Particle Storm. Several grains of sand, most likely. Kiyazuna the Axle, inside her Chariot Golem, was still in a safe position—from his current location, he was now close enough to look down from high on the cliffs at the chaotic battlefield below.

Despite his position, he still couldn't spot Atrazek properly. That last shot was horribly off the mark.

He should have been able to see, been able to bring the wurm down, yet even after borrowing the strength of a champion like Mele the Horizon's Roar, he still hadn't accomplished anything.

"What am I doing...? *Hahh, hahh...hahh...hahh.*"

Kuuro gripped the ground, spitting out droplets of blood.

"I can't see anything. Nothing at all. It's all black."

The most powerful shura in the land, beyond all imagination, were right before his eyes. The domain of true power, lost to Kuuro. As he witnessed them right before his eyes, it only made him more aware of his own wretchedness and powerlessness.

"Hey. Kuuro, it'll be okay. Let's run away."

"Shut up."

He wiped the edges of his mouth. If he wanted to survive, he just needed to run away. He knew that.

However, that would prove for a fact that he could no longer see the world as he once could. To Kuuro, darkness was nothing but a synonym for death.

He wasn't needed by anyone. It was only his clairvoyance gift that was ever sought after.

"Don't say anything, please…! Damn it all…!"

There were times he was horribly envious of Cuneigh.

She always seemed to be enjoying herself. Living with no desire for talent, and without stealing anything from another. Despite her short homunculus lifespan, she lived without fear of the future.

"It's okay."

Cuneigh repeated.

The sand below him began moving again. Atrazek had dived into the ground.

Nevertheless, if he appeared up on the surface again, he was sure to reform this tempest of carnage.

Next time the storm might come in direct contact with him. He could not afford to miss his next mark.

But he knew the shot wouldn't hit.

At this point, he couldn't even imagine a future where his shot was successful. It was the darkness of death, a darkness he would never be able to see through.

"Cuneigh. There comes a time in everyone's life when they wither away and die. No one lives forever."

Kuuro spoke, his head still drooping low.

No matter what happened, the Particle Storm would get put down for good. If it continued to move according to the forecast, it would next arrive at the Sine Riverstead. Even without Kuuro's scouting, there was no doubt Mele the Horizon's Roar could use his own eyes to hit the Particle Storm with one of his arrows. That would be the end of it.

His struggles here would ultimately end up saving a certain number of lives within the Sine Riverstead.

"...Still, I don't want you to tell me to run away. Don't reject my eyes...for my sake..."

"...What?"

The foolish young homunculus girl then shouted something unbelievable.

"None of them hit because you've been able to see everything this whole time!"

If he really could see with the clairvoyance, then one of the arrows would have hit its mark. If he really had the power to triumph over the Particle Storm, there wouldn't be any reason to flee their current position. Cuneigh's words were incoherent and contradictory.

His eyes couldn't see anything. That was how it was supposed to be.

"You've... Kuuro, you've seen it all this whole time. I can tell. Right? After all, you've got clairvoyance and can see everything. The fact you're unable to see Kuuro—it's all because *you think it's better if you can't. You're* the one who hasn't been hit with any attacks!"

"That's not it. I—*koff*—I'm going along with the plan..."

Was that really true?

His power of clairvoyance allowed him to perceive things with senses that far surpassed the visual and aural range of normal perception. It was the power to take in things beyond the five senses—intuition, heat, magnetism, and synesthesia.

If he hadn't, in fact, lost these senses of his, then wouldn't he have known that from the very start?

Know that these arrows *should not* hit their target.

"I... Ah...dammit."

Kuuro covered his eyes.

It was something he never would have done, had he still been in constant fear of the darkness.

Cuneigh was telling him he hadn't lost his senses. Then, in the same breath, she told him to flee from their position.

Those ideas seemed to contradict each other, yet they made perfect sense.

"...I get it. So that's what it was."

He could only see things that he focused his senses on. That was it. That's what he had believed. At the start of his spotting duty, he had even felt the beating of Toroa the Awful's heart.

With the Particle Storm in front of him, a battle between the strongest shura in the land before him, he didn't have any attention to spare for any other direction.

That was why *it became as if he couldn't see at all.*

From the very start, I wasn't the only one here.

Intricate topography with steep differences in elevation, perfect for spotting and observation. This was just as true for himself as it was for others.

Being a spotter didn't mean he wasn't being spotted himself.

There were others observing the battle in this ravine, just as he was.

They weren't Old Kingdoms' loyalists. Otherwise, they would

have shot Kuuro immediately as he started aiding the arrow shows from afar.

Someone was there, tasked to get rid of him after Mele's attack was confirmed successful, when he wasn't needed any longer.

If from the beginning...Aureatia planned on snuffing me out after they got their use out of me...

Everything was consistent. The New Principality of Lithia. The Old Kingdoms' loyalists. The Free City of Okahu. With a new era dawning, they were trying to clean up all the threats to their kingdom.

If Kuuro the Cautious's clairvoyance, the ability to divulge every single one of their secrets, was no exception...

If it was proof that his waning clairvoyance was a response dictated by his own survival instincts...

If I don't have to be on the criminal side for once...

If his all-perceiving clairvoyance was even capable of observing possible future outcomes...

Then his eyes were looking out on such a world.

Oh, how nice that would be.

Kuuro closed his eyes.

The darkness that shut him off from the world, where death could come to take him.

It was the first time he had ever wanted to perform the action, considered completely normal behavior to the average person.

He shut off his senses. He laid to rest all his senses that had fought against the world for so long.

He immersed his body in death. The terror he had long avoided was there waiting for him.

Then, he opened his eyelids.

*   *   *

There was color.

In the devastated ravine, there was blue soil, purple rocks, green sky, and orange water. The vivid and deeply coalesced colors rippled out like waves, shimmering. Somewhere flowers swayed. The wind caressing the water's surface sent different sizes of spray into the air. Bird feathers flying in from somewhere danced in the wind.

Far away, the line of the horizon curved in a circle.

Kuuro was above the stars, and the world extended out endlessly in every way with him at the center.

For as far as the sky continued onward, he fully perceived all beneath it.

He realized that he had been able to see all of it from the very start.

"...Ha."

For the first time, Kuuro smiled from the bottom of his heart.

Now he could see it all clear as day. One person eighty-two meters behind him to the right. One twenty-six meters behind him and above, to the left. One thirty-one meters below, to the right.

After fleeing for so long from his life of theft, there was now nowhere left for him to run. If he accomplished his mission, they would take his life, and if he ran away, he would lose his place in Aureatia.

Despite this, even with this future clear in front of him, he was filled with happiness.

"I, I never lost my world at all..."

"Kuuro!" Cuneigh shouted.

Now he knew for certain why he had kept her hidden inside his coat. No one else had seen her. She was the only one he wanted to make sure lived on.

Now, he had become able to hope for such an outcome, regardless of the reason or reward for doing so.

"Cuneigh. I have a wish of my own...a foolish wish."

Kuuro was worn down by his life, forced to keep stealing, trampling others underfoot.

He didn't want to see others die. He didn't want to hear others' screams.

He knew the answer from himself from the start.

More than his own survival, he didn't want to steal anything anymore, even if it meant being used and having his life stolen from him. Now, he truly wished that from the heart.

Unlike how he was before, now he was able to save some unknown somebody somewhere.

"Even if it's foolish, it's something I've always wanted to do."

"No!"

"Mele! Here's the coordinates! These'll be the last ones...! 1360 by 628!"

He shouted into the radzio. The meteorite arrow fell, and every moment he appeared on the surface, it pierced through the Particle Storm.

The storm cleared. He saw the calamitous wurm's torso run right through.

In that instant, arrows pierced Kuuro from three directions.

He heard Cuneigh's scream.

"This is fine."

Kuuro was smiling. The clairvoyance he was gifted with from birth had truly been his own after all.

He had won. He could see the world.

"My wish came true."

He could perceive the entire world through senses that transcended the limits of his race.

He possessed the precision to see all the way through his target's five senses and recognize and mark the exact moment of lethality.

He had an ability that, with intuition that far surpassed any amount of experience, chose the best possible answer, even unbeknownst to himself.

The bearer of clairvoyance, able to choose his future of his own will, from among his own omniscience.

Seer. Leprechaun.

Kuuro the Cautious.

The realm of slaughter that had engulfed Gumana Ravine had dissipated at last, and Atrazek the Particle Storm had been defeated.

The mortally wounded calamity sank into the ground, likely never to return to the surface. Most wurms did so when they died.

"Well, shit! Dammit! I was so close!"

"M-Mama."

Everything as far as their eyes could see had been ravaged by the particles, the fresh scene surrounding them showing numerous giant holes bored into the ground.

Standing before Atrazek's scattered viscera, Kiyazuna the Axle stamped her foot on the ground.

"That damn bow-wielding bastard...! If it wasn't for that nonsense, the two of us woulda had 'em both for sure! Stealing our prey right from under our noses... I'm gonna find them and kill 'em dead...!"

Lingering in the remnants of the fierce battle were the self-proclaimed demon king Kiyazuna the Axle and her ultimate masterpiece Mestelexil the Box of Desperate Knowledge.

"That goes for you, too, Toroa. I'm gonna take you out right here, right now."

"Forget it."

In the aftermath stood one other.

The unkillable Grim Reaper, loaded up all over his body with enchanted swords—Toroa the Awful.

"I'm done here. I recovered the Blasting Blade. I won."

"Big talk from a bastard ready to kick the bucket. Or maybe you think you can take those knives of yours with ya to the afterlife?"

"You're talking some nonsense of your own. Didn't you know?"

Saying his body was covered in wounds was a tepid description at best after being caught up in the impact of the Horizon's Roar's arrow and experiencing the horrible ADS attack from Mestelexil. Nevertheless, he stood strong, without letting go of a single enchanted sword throughout the battle.

"I'm immortal. I crawled back up from hell. I'm Toroa the Awful."

While taking on both Mestelexil and Kiyazuna at once, he had stolen the Blasting Blade. Jumping into the maelstrom from the Horizon's Roar's raining arrows, he put his own body on the line to challenge the Particle Storm. Amid a fierce battle that could have ended any one of their lives, Toroa the Awful fought through it all under the absolute harshest conditions.

All for a mere enchanted sword. He knew better than anyone else that it didn't really have any value worth risking one's life over.

That was all the more reason why he couldn't let any oblivious somebody be swayed and pulled along by something so worthless. People couldn't be allowed to use enchanted swords.

Toroa was the only one who was supposed to keep fighting over such trifling enchanted swords.

"…Let me ask you before I send you back to hell, Toroa the Awful."

The elder woman's face wrinkled with displeasure.

"Why'd you keep your promise?"

"Good question. Who knows?"

He wanted to believe he could fight as much as necessary for the sake of an enchanted sword. Their fight might have been so he could prove it to himself—that he could cast himself aside and truly become Toroa the Awful.

It was clear his thinking had been correct in one aspect, and wrong in another.

Just how far could he fight for the sake of a single enchanted sword?

He could still go on fighting. However—

"Toroa! Th-thank, you!"

"...Why're are *you* thanking *me*?"

"You...killed me! B-but, I know! Toroa d-did not, kill, M-Mama! Ha-ha-ha-ha-ha-ha! You are a good guy! Toroa!"

"You're wrong. With the Particle Storm on our tails, I couldn't let Kiyazuna die."

When they were fighting in the Chariot Golem cargo bed, Toroa could have killed Kiyazuna in any number of ways. Mestelexil realized it, too. Even during the moments he had been unable to move.

"...Then, what is it then? Those artillery attacks... The asshole behind 'em working with you, then?"

"Don't be stupid. You know that couldn't possibly be true."

"*Tch!*"

"...In the middle of the battle, there was someone watching us."

Even Toroa could sense the eyes, after closing in this far from their starting battle area. Mestelexil should have been similarly able to pick on the spotter watching them.

"I-I-I know, what you mean! I could, um...see the waves? Going back and forth!"

"Whaddaya mean, if you picked up something on radar, tell me sooner! If some idiot really was spotting for that series of attacks... Aureatia bastards, huh? Whatever the case, just gotta ask 'em about it! You know what you gotta do first, right, Mestelexil?"

"Ha-ha-ha-ha-ha-ha-ha-ha-ha! I-I... I will, win! Toroa!"

Mestelexil laughed, striking with his fist.

Toroa stepped forward firmly and drew an enchanted sword.

Kiyazuna, still looking as annoyed as ever, fixed her barrel on him.

"Then—"

"Hey, someone!"

"......"

Right as they were going to restart the fight, there was a shout.

"Someone, someone, come here! Please! K-Kuuro, he's, he's dying!"

The speaker, flying down from the sky, looked like a small songbird, but still different.

Flying in between the three-person standoff was a small homunculus girl with wings for arms.

"A bird! A small, bird is, here! Mama!"

"Don't touch it, Mestelexil. A harpy... Nah, homunculus, huh. Did someone make you look like a harpy on purpose? Must've been a demon king with some bizarre tastes."

"Wait."

Toroa sheathed his sword and walked toward the young girl. Kiyazuna lowered her gun with an annoyed click of her tongue—

—Mestelexil was dashing toward the homunculus, too.

After he lowered his sword and spoiled her fun, the thought of killing him now irritated her.

"Wh-what is wrong! What is, a 'Kuuro'? If Kuuro, dies then would, that be, bad?"

"Up ahead, th-there's an Aureatia encampment! Carry Kuuro

there, please…! To try and help everyone, he… Help him! Please, save him…"

The homunculus's words didn't help make things clearer at all, but Toroa still picked up on something.

"The spotter."

"Hah?"

"The spotter I saw, he's probably the one injured, right?"

He looked toward the clifftop where the young girl flew down from. Appearing to have slid down from some higher spot, Kuuro the Cautious lay in an area where their eyes could find him. The endless stream of blood looked to be coming from his gut. The wound seemed likely to prove fatal.

"What of it? Just leave 'im to die. Got nothing to do with us."

"…The bombing that killed the Particle Storm, that was his doing, right? You wanted to know who was behind those artillery attacks, didn't you? I think there's value in letting him live."

Toroa thought there had been others besides themselves fighting in their battle.

In the middle of that storm, countless schemes and motives had all swirled together.

Toroa fought for the sake of an enchanted sword. Mestelexil had fought for his mother.

In that case, what had been this spotter's reason for fighting?

"He fought to protect populated areas, exposing himself to the calamity to do it. He has a right to be saved."

"Wooow…! That is amazing! How very, valiant!"

"Haaaah?! Like I give a damn!"

"Don't get mad! Please, don't be mad… Um, so. Kuuro, he's really important. H-he's the most important person of all to me. So please…save him…"

Tears streamed down from the small homunculus's eyes.

Her winged arms were unable to carry Kuuro.

"I'll carry him there on my back."

Toroa replied.

He had carried them all on his back. He wouldn't let anyone steal them. Things that shouldn't be, where they should be.

If there was a fight he could end without stealing anything, then that's how he wanted to finish it.

"How far ahead is the Aureatia camp?"

"I'll show you! I-I'll... lead you there. The checkpoint place... I remember where it is."

"It'll be night by then."

Kiyazuna insisted. The closest rest station to their position was over ten kilometers away.

"Gonna bleed to death either way."

"...No. I've got an idea. A clever one, too, I'd say."

The Grim Reaper said while walking over to where Kuuro lay.

"We can just use your vehicle there, Kiyazuna."

"Whaaat?!"

Using the Chariot Golem to, of all things, save someone. To the sinister self-proclaimed demon king, Kiyazuna the Axle, it was an unbelievable proposition.

"Like hell I'm going along with a shitty plan like that! I'll beat you to a pulp!"

"I get it. I won't ask you to do it for free."

Toroa stopped walking, and stuck one of his enchanted swords in the ground—

The same man who hadn't let go of a single one of his swords in the heat of battle, bearing their excessive weight until the end.

"I'll give you the Blasting Blade in exchange."

"...You..."

He spoke like it was all a matter of course.

Toroa had walked the line of life and death, shaving years off his life, all for the sake of this one sword. There had been no other reward, all just because he was Toroa the Awful.

"You really…"

Kiyazuna tried to continue her thought, but she was unable.

Somewhere within the enemy in front of her, he held something he could never give up. She understood that, too. His fight was about pride. Much like Kiyazuna's own pride, that wouldn't yield before anyone.

"M-Mama…"

"Mestelexil. Kiyazuna the Axle doesn't bend the knee to anyone."

Freedom completely unobstructed by any threat. That was the wish of Kiyazuna the Axle.

Despite this, the reason she had fought to hold fast to her pride was in order to always be her proud self.

Still, she fought to hold fast to her pride precisely so she could continue to remain her prideful self.

"…I'll give you the Chariot Golem. Get in already."

◆

After seeing Toroa the Awful's group off, Kiyazuna returned once again to the same location.

The blade, its shadow growing long over the wasteland, was known as Charijisuya the Blasting Blade.

"All right, there you go, Mestelexil. The enchanting blasting sword's yours."

"Okay."

The innocent iron colossus took steps forward...and then stopped.

"H-Hey, um, Mama?"

"What is it?"

"I-is it okay, if I leave this, here?!"

"...What d'ya mean, leave it? You were so fond of it, weren't you? Why?"

Kiyazuna, wide-eyed, followed his question with one of her own. Among all the riches she plundered, it was the item that Mestelexil was the fondest of, showing it off and brandishing it about the Chariot Golem's cargo bay.

She didn't expect Mestelexil to ask such a question himself.

"Because I haven't, beaten Toroa."

To the winner go the spoils.

"I-If I can, win, then I can, have whatever I want, right?! Then, I want... I want it after, I've beaten, Toroa. I want, to fight him, again! C-can I?!"

"So that's it, then..."

Kiyazuna was at a loss for words as she looked at her own child.

"I get it. Hee...hee-hee-hee! You finally got a desire of your own! Found someone out there you wanna beat and smash to bits, huh, Mestelexil?!"

She laughed. The demon king was truly delighted.

Her own child's growth, a will of his very own, made her happy.

"Sure, Mestelexil! Just an enchanted sword, anyway, right... While I definitely wasn't gonna hand it over quietly, getting it handed back to me for nothing is even worse! Really look cool now, eh, Mestelexil?! That's my boy!"

"Ha-ha, ha! Ha-ha-ha-ha-ha-ha-ha-ha-ha-ha!"

"Hee, hee-hee-hee-hee-hee-hee-hee!"

The mother and child both laughed in front of the enchanted sword, casting shadows in the evening sun.

The two, at long last, began their travels anew.

Their destination was Aureatia. The next opponent they needed to kill was there. The slayer of the Dungeon Golem, Souji-rou the Willow-Sword.

Mestelexil's singular eye illuminated the pitch-black road, with Kiyazuna sitting on his shoulder.

"B-But, are you, sure? Mama really, cared about that, sword too, right?! I-it's an amazing, sword! R-really, s-strong!"

"Huh? Don't be silly. What sort of idiot would get so worked up over something like that. See, the reason I didn't want to hand it over? Had nothing to do with it being an enchanted sword..."

She too had acted through the farcical struggle over the enchanted sword, all for the sake of the one thing she would never surrender.

She tried to have everything go her way with Toroa the Awful, the monster of scary stories everywhere, killer of all those who laid their hands on an enchanted sword. Simply thinking about it brought a smile to her face.

"It was because it was my kid's new favorite toy!"

◆

An iron vehicle raced through the ravine, the sun slowly sinking overhead.

The wheeled carriage, set under Kiyazuna's direction to keep going automatically until reaching the Aureatia encampment, was the Chariot Golem, filled with the self-proclaimed demon king's latest technologies.

A monster out of a horror story sat in the cargo bay, shoulder-ing a cluster of enchanted swords on his back.

It was Toroa the Awful. Rather, it might have actually been the god of death here to watch over his grave.

Kuuro lay in the driver's seat, watching Cuneigh shedding tears beside him.

"…Cuneigh. Why…are you…"

"I'll save you! You're important, Kuuro! I'm always telling you! Over and over again! Even if you don't believe me, even if you hate me, I-I'll, I'll still save you!"

There wasn't the slightest reason behind both her trust and her affection. Though Kuuro never intended to be frugal with her reward, cheap glass beads and common everyday fruits were the things that made her happy.

Kuuro the Cautious had lived without trusting in anything groundless and unfounded.

"…Why…?"

"It's okay. I'm here."

"…Why…me…?"

"What do you mean?"

The tiny young girl wore a pained, heart-wrenching expression.

"Is a homunculus not allowed to love someone?"

He couldn't believe it.

If he had been able to laugh, he would've wanted to.

It was such a worthless, trite—and unreasonable explanation.

"…You, never got…"

"None of it. The rewards you always talked about—I didn't need any of it."

The young girl finished the dying Kuuro's words.

It was as if she knew him better than he knew himself.

"I didn't start loving you because you gave me things."

That's right. It was just as she said. Love, apparently, wasn't like that.

She always seemed to be enjoying herself. Living with no desire for gifts, and without stealing anything from anyone else.

"Hey. After this, I… What I wanted after—"

He understood she was calling back to the talk of her reward they left unfinished. Her soft wings caressed Kuuro's cheek.

You're way too serious, Kuuro. I want you to…

"I wanted you to smile more."

The same sort of trifling something it always was.

"I did smile."

I was able to smile thanks to you.

He looked at Cuneigh.

Seeing her face, on the verge of tears, he thought it was beautiful.

With Kuuro's clairvoyance, he could see her eyes better than anyone else's.

He wanted to apologize.

He wanted to thank her.

Or maybe, some other kind of…

◆

There were voices.

Voices like shadows whispering to each other in the dark.

"We've recovered the Blasting Blade. What should we do?"

"Hand it over to the Old Kingdoms' loyalists in Togie City. Say that the spotters who disposed of Kuuro the Cautious were with the Old Kingdoms' loyalists. The enchanted sword recovered from the site, from Aureatia's perspective, will serve as irrefutable proof."

"Ah-hyah-hyah-hyah! Still, I didn't expect the Horizon's Roar to make an appearance! I was so surprised, why, I thought my jaw was going to fall right off!"

"If they were forced to ambush it in an urban area, we wouldn't have been able to incinerate the leftover remains, either. Our lady has a keen eye."

"Th-this means... Aureatia r-really is formidable, isn't she? So the Particle Storm isn't enough to do it either... W-we need to draw out Alus the Star Runner at the very least."

"I see, I see. Let's assume that a simple individual threat isn't enough to bring Aureatia down. Learning that alone made this plenty fruitful, wouldn't you say?"

"Based on the information from this event, if Aureatia's to fall, we'll need to send in someone like Lucunoca the Winter as well."

"You're joking. Sending out the Yamaga Barrens took a hefty toll on our lady's body. We can't let her push herself too hard."

"So then it's the royal games, after all?"

"Yeah. The royal games."

Atrazek the Particle Storm awoke from a deep coma.

None of the figures he had been conversing with up until that moment were anywhere to be seen.

He was in a forest of dense green that seemed to block out the light of the sun.

"...*Hnngh*. Why, it cannot be."

His torso was nearly torn in half. A fatal wound, a direct hit from the Horizon's Roar's arrow.

The ancient wurm, bringer of meaningless death, bearer of unjust calamity, had suffered an unjust disaster from the heavens, both its reason and true form unknown, and now faced his own death.

"Everything...is particles. It should all be particles. This should be impossible. L-losing to mere particles..."

He was unable to move his body an inch; his head toppled over sideways.

From the scattered spray of water, he could tell he was at a lake in the middle of the forest.

He was only able to wait for his death. Pure drops of dew dripped from the leaves of the trees right before his eyes.

"You. *Hng, nnggh...*"

The lake shore. Amid the sunlight streaming down through the brilliant green trees stood a young girl.

"You need not remember."

Gripping her black skirt in both her hands, she seemed to dance as she approached him.

Her bare legs, pretty and pale, made the shallow water's surface radiant.

"You were able to make it all the way here in the end, just like I asked, Master Atrazek."

"How. How do you...know my name?"

Everyone called him the Particle Storm. He was treated as a deadly weather phenomenon, void of any personality or character.

His name should not have been known to anyone.

The young girl laced her fingers and smiled.

"Because you yourself told it to me."

She was right. This wasn't the first time he had met her.

He should have known that. He was supposed to be following her orders, yet *there were memories he was forbidden from remembering.*

"...I'm very glad you were able to return here safely, Master

Atrazek. After all, if you had lost to the Horizon's Roar near Aureatia, they would have been able to examine your remains."

The person who was watching Kuuro the Cautious had waited for the attack on Atrazek to succeed and attacked him.

The moment the Horizon's Roar began to attack, the Particle Storm couldn't be allowed to advance any further.

As well as because…the investigation into the fighting strength and skill of the land's strongest shura, gathered together in the one moment and fighting against each other, was over.

"Aureatia. I n-need… I must go there—"

"No. There's no need for you to go there anymore."

The Gray-Haired Child had sold the anticipated path of the Particle Storm as a weather forecast to both powers.

The Old Kingdoms' loyalists, based off that information, began to prepare for an attack on Aureatia.

Aureatia used Mele the Horizon's Roar to put their large-scale counterattack strategy into action.

Mestelexil the Box of Desperate Knowledge and Toroa the Awful clashed at a single point in the Gumana Ravine.

There was a fundamental premise to all of their movements—

Why was the Particle Storm heading toward Aureatia?

"There's no need for you to head anywhere."

The god of the Yamaga Barrens had desperately *run away* from that terrifying realm of slaughter. While tormented by Mestelexil's microwave weapon, while his body was pierced by the Horizon's Roar's long-range arrows—at that very moment, he displayed strength that seemed beyond his limits, as though obeying commands that surpassed his own instincts.

"Horizon's Roar killed the Particle Storm. There's no one who would deny that. No one will go searching for you. Not even for your corpse."

There was someone, completely unknown to anyone else across the land, who controlled everything from the shadows, their conspiracies extending far and wide.

"Then, everything will remain a secret. Time for you to sleep."

The young girl quietly lingered in front of his eyes. Her lithe fingers caressed the top of Atrazek's jaw.

She was smiling, like a beautiful white flower.

Pain oozed from the mouth of his wound.

Sand.

The small amount of Yamaga Barrens sand that clung to him was scraping away at Atrazek's scales and flesh.

"*Auuugh.* Impossible. Who are you? Wh-what are you—"

It was a fair question. The power to scrape away at his body with even the most infinitesimal amount of sand belonged to none other than the Particle Storm.

There was no one who could wield the sand of the Yamaga Barrens like this. There shouldn't have been anyone else—anyone else *besides himself.*

"*Nggaaaaaaah!* H-Help, s-save me! I'm, I'm disintegrating!"

It was terrifying.

He was being whittled away by his own Particle Storm. He couldn't kill this powerless young girl. Nor would he ever be able to.

"Miss Ani...the girl who was sacrificed, you turned her into particles and ate her, didn't you?"

It was the name of a human girl, one whom he had killed without a second thought, as if her life mattered less than a speck of dust.

"That was the source of infection."

...His blood. His entrails.

Death endlessly poured out from the cross-section of his severed body. The lake began to turn red. No part of his body would be left behind. There would be no trace left behind of Atrazek's existence.

"H-help me. Forgive me."

Atrazek was truly scared. Scared of a monster that far exceeded the Particle Storm himself.

Scared of the impossible vampire's existence, who had turned a god like him into a servile puppet.

"No. Please, show me even more. After all, I promised everyone in the village..."

Linaris the Obsidian began to leave. She turned her back to the dying wurm.

She wasn't the one facing their demise.

"...that I would show them 'fun stuff,' too."

CHAPTER 20 ◀◆▶ Rosclay the Absolute

Rosclay the Absolute. The pinnacle of valor. A true knight.

A good exercise was to ask the citizens of Aureatia who the strongest champion was in all the land.

One would likely receive a variety of answers. Maybe the aberrant wyvern who had traveled through a myriad of dungeons all on his own, Alus the Star Runner. Perhaps the legendary dragon that no one had ever seen before, Lucunoca the Winter.

Whatever the answer may be, the name Rosclay was always in the back of their mind. Anyone who knew of his legend and radiance couldn't help associating the word *strongest* with Rosclay the Absolute.

The knight who fought fair and square, Rosclay. The dragon-slaying champion who held the legendary distinction as the only minia to single-handedly kill a dragon. No matter what enemy appeared before him, not a single stain remained behind on his silvery white armor.

It was possible that Gilnes the Ruined Castle, too, held the same feelings of admiration as the citizens of Aureatia somewhere within his heart.

Even as the leader of an insurrection, chained in a damp dungeon and awaiting his execution.

The Old Kingdoms' loyalists were tragically defeated. With the main part of their plan, the Particle Storm, coming up short, their diversionary tactic of assembling troop strength in Togie City was rendered meaningless. The fact that the Free City of Okahu, which had once appeared hostile to Aureatia, secretly formed an accord with them and appeared on the frontlines, was yet another major cause of their defeat.

And now, these were the last days of Gilnes, commander of the loyalist army.

"You're making me duel Rosclay the Absolute?"

Still seated in the dark, he replied with a question of his own to the man standing on the other side of the chair.

"That's right, Gilnes the Ruined Castle. There is no righteousness in your actions. It was little more than pointless threats against the people and murder. An utter and unforgivable betrayal of our current peace."

Aureatia's Third Minister, Jelki the Swift Ink. One of the highest-level bureaucrats in control of Aureatia's governmental affairs.

Tearing off his chains, he could slip them through the cracks in the grating and smash Jelki's face in two. The sight remained as a fantasy in the back of his mind. He wouldn't end his fight simply by killing the man before him.

Gilnes believed he fought for the sake of the people. The people, not just him, needed to rise up. Even though the once-proud Royal Army of the Central had come to be known as the "Old Kingdoms' loyalists" somewhere along the way, Gilnes had fought under that firm conviction.

"Though you're the former great commander, Gilnes the Ruined Castle, right? Even now, there are plenty of citizens who admire you. Executing you where none could hear your frivolous claims would create cracks in the righteousness of Her Majesty's actions. Therefore, you will be given a chance. It will be a true duel, with justice on the line."

A true duel. There were few instances of the event that had ever been recorded, but it was a type of duel that adhered to Old Kingdoms' traditions.

The duel was performed without weapons, and there were no restrictions on Word Arts usage.

Each combatant staked everything they had, both technique and strength, on the fight. Naturally, this included putting their very own life on the line as well.

"You sure you're okay with that?"

Gilnes the Ruined Castle remained unshaken, even more so now that he knew about the duel.

For him, defeated and simply waiting for execution, the true duel was, if anything, a remarkable deal.

"I'll kill Rosclay and prove my innocence...and I'm going to stand there in front of the people and indict the Twenty-Nine Officials system for its deceit. There wouldn't be anyone there in the ring to stop me."

"Let me make this easy to understand. This isn't an offer. It's already decided. You have no right to refuse. Fight with everything you've got."

The Third Minister's expression, like the cold glimmer of his glasses, was mechanical and level-headed.

Aureatia's purpose behind holding this duel lay, of course, in the royal games that lay ahead afterward.

Champions would take each other's lives, bringing every last ounce of their strength to bear in the process. The true duel itself was an essential arrangement to ensure not a single prominent monster lived on into the upcoming age.

How much would the citizenry react to a true duel between two champions? How much could they stir up their enthusiasm? The fight between the champions Gilnes the Ruined Castle and Rosclay the Absolute was a rehearsal to understand the answers to such questions before the main event.

For Gilnes the Ruined Castle, the brave general who protected the people during the age of the Central Kingdom, before it served as the Aureatia's foundation, there could be no better opponent than Rosclay the Absolute.

"You said a true duel, huh? To fight with everything I've got."

His bearded face, grown thick during his confinement, stretched into a bestial grin.

A duel with *the* Rosclay. It was more than he could ask for.

"You plan on keeping me locked up here until the day of the match? Without allowing me to hold a sword, or get back to my full range of movement? I'm sure you snakes will consider that 'giving it my all,' but what about people? Are they all as foolish as you think they are, I wonder?"

"Only natural you would make such a claim, I suppose."

There was a light metallic sound. Following a signaling look from Jelki, the warder opened up the cell.

Continuing, they removed the Gilnes's shackles.

"Until the day of the duel, you shall be released under direct supervision. We've declared the date for the duel. The offer to release you under the condition of your agreement to the duel is well-known among the citizenry, as well."

"...What are you planning?"

"Nothing at all. If you fear the power of Aureatia's Second General, then feel free to come up with your best dishonorable excuse and flee. Fortunately for you, we don't have the time to spend on chasing after a pitiful loser such as yourself. In fact, you may be able to trade in your popularity among the people to ensure your own survival."

By showing Gilnes the Ruined Castle actually released from prison to the citizens, they could demonstrate the Queen's magnanimity and justness—such aims were another facet of their offer.

There was no need to keep him chained. To Gilnes, who relied on the justness of the royal authority that once was, his own sense of justice and expecting looks from the citizens of the Central Kingdom were the most binding chains of all. Any path of escape from the duel two small months down the line was completely closed to him.

"You don't think I'll attack your barracks or council halls?"

"It matters not. If you were to brazenly refuse Her Majesty's mercy, that'd serve as plenty justification to put you down for good next time. When that happens, of course, Rosclay the Absolute will be the one to serve you your death sentence. No matter how much you struggle, know that you can't run from your destiny to fight Rosclay."

"...Fine, then. If all roads lead to the same end, then I should stand before the people and show them true righteousness."

In other words, he would destroy Rosclay in the arena during their true duel.

He had never held any fear of Rosclay to begin with. Gilnes's resolve was fixed from the start.

Gilnes would be damned if he would let the Central Kingdom he had protected for so long come under the control of Queen Sephite, a blood relative of the United Western Kingdom. Nor was there any justification behind renaming it to Aureatia.

It was the country of the monarch who appealed to the people, regardless of race, and gathering citizens together in the face of the True Demon King threat, building the foundation of what was now Aureatia—the kingdom of King Aur. Sephite was nothing more than an invader, using her lineage as the last among the One True King bloodline as a reason to usurp the throne.

The Central Kingdom that Gilnes and the King protected had been tragically corrupted by the influx of citizens from the other two kingdoms.

He couldn't consent to the Queen's rule. The same was true for the Twenty-Nine Officials who controlled the people at the Queen's behest.

The daughter of the kingdom ruined by their own extreme foolishness, trying to open a dialogue with the True Demon King, was now the Queen.

Gilnes's chest was filled with an endlessly burning anger.

He had to use his just vengeance to open the eyes of the citizens Gilnes and the King loved.

◆

As he walked through the streets, the eyes of Aureatia soldiers were always on Gilnes.

Nevertheless, there were still places their watchful eyes absolutely couldn't follow him—the bath and his quarters. Other options included the confessional and inside the brothels.

Gilnes the Ruined Castle hid a weapon inside his coat for whenever those moments arrived.

It wasn't one of the weapons the soldiers had taken from him—even if he showed it to the citizenry, he was sure almost no one would be able to understand its intended purpose. A triangular metal plate split down the middle, jutting out from the middle of a hollowed-out wooden rod, small enough to fit in his hand.

A tool known as a "fountain pen."

It was technology that he procured from a deal with the Gray-Haired Child. With most people in this world having no literacy above what is taught by the Order and where the nobility and royalty utilized their own unique written languages they passed down through the generations, Gilnes's elite troops established their own form of writing, and exhaustively taught it to everyone, down to the lowest private.

None of the soldiers who watched him would be able to decipher the meaning behind the ink-blotched words he left on scraps of cloth around the city.

He told me to give it my all, right?

He continued giving everything in his training, going about his daily activities, being met with a smile by those citizens looking forward to the duel, and brushing off the cold glares from those who didn't cheer for him.

In order to make sure the soldiers observing him reported such activities.

Through an intelligence network known to the Aureatia council, Gilnes the Ruined Castle's former subordinates were gathering. None of them came into contact with one another. Despite this, they shared the operations progress through messages left behind in various regions.

There were a hundred personnel able to move into action. Each and every one of them, advancing the plan put in place for the day of the duel.

It's too late for any regrets, Third Minister Jelki.

◆

"Lord Gilnes, why, the date of the duel's only two big months away!"

"...Indeed. Perhaps this shall be the last time I can enjoy this establishment's hawthorn berries."

"You don't give yourself enough credit, my lord. A direct fight with *the* Rosclay? There's no one else who could do such a thing. My son is very much looking forward to it."

The period of preparation and training had passed, and the two small months of respite were now closing in on the two big months mark.

It took six days for the large moon to complete its orbit. There were twelve days left. During these twelve days, the men who were scattered across the land would gather in Aureatia. On the day of the match, when the audience had reached the height of excitement, he would make his indictment against Aureatia... Then, in that moment, all of his armed forces would launch into action at once, sweeping the citizenry up in the conflict.

"This is a battle for truth. Of course, I shall stand up and face the challenge head-on. The Central Kingdom is a nation built by King Aur, rest his soul, and does not belong to Queen Sephite or the Aureatia Council, either."

"I see. I am an uneducated man, but now that you mention it, the current council is acting a little bit off. My son is rooting for Lord Rosclay, but of course, I'm backing you, Lord Gilnes!"

It was clear the owner of this fruit and vegetable stand was totally unaware that the competition in two big months' time was an actual fight to the death.

That was why he so casually supported both combatants. Gilnes wondered just how much his feelings would change once the man's naïve perceptions were met with the reality of the situation. Though, when he considered that even in the age of the True Demon King, the coliseums on the frontier boasted of their prosperity, pitting slave fighters together in true duels, it was possible that the inner true nature of the people had remained unchanged.

"I'm grateful. I very much hope both you and your son will make sure to witness the moment I display what true justice looks like to the people."

While Gilnes chatted with the shopkeeper, a customer sizing up the shelves packed with fruit took Gilnes's sword as he went to stand up. It was a blind spot for the soldier tasked with observing Gilnes, obstructed by the beautiful leaves of a houseplant.

The customer, in exchange, left behind a sword bearing the exact same hilt and sheath.

Gilnes stroked his beard, giving a sign of acknowledgment.

"...With it, all the lives sacrificed in battle will truly be able to rest in peace."

"You've definitely got a point there. All those soldiers protected our current peace for the people."

Adopting a nonchalant demeanor, Gilnes gathered the swapped sword in his hand.

The weight of the sword was the exact same weight as the two-handed sword he had used up until that moment.

Charijisuya the Blasting Blade. They still had it, did they?

Up until now, he could count on one hand the number of times he had drawn a real sword during the times he trained for the duel.

For the next two big months, he was going to make the eyes of his soldier observers accustomed to the blade, to make them think it was the same shape it had always been. To ensure that there was no one who would notice the swap on the day of the duel.

The moment Rosclay the Absolute experienced this sword would be his last.

◆

Four days were left. Gilnes the Ruined Castle was visiting a dwelling on the outskirts of town.

He was there under the pretext of running an errand for the owner of the tavern he frequented following his release. Without many people in the region, the soldier observing Gilnes didn't take any special steps to hide his presence, leaning up against a tree behind him.

Gilnes rang the bell. If the information his men gathered was correct, the person he sought was here in this hideout.

With the ringing of the bell, there was a heavy sound of something toppling behind him.

When he turned around, the soldier who had just been standing there watching him was collapsed on the ground, and in their place, a gangly man, just past middle age, was absentmindedly lingering about.

"…Master Romzo."

"Oh, if it isn't General Gilnes. It's good to see you again. This one looked like he might be a bit of a nuisance, you see, yes. I had him take a bit of a nap."

He looked down over the fallen soldier with his scholarlike glasses, as if the whole affair was none of his concern.

The ferocity of his martial skill was completely unchanged from the days when King Aur was alive.

"I'll lean him up against this tree here. He won't notice that he was asleep, but with that, he won't be asleep long."

"I understand. Let us wrap up our conversation quickly."

Negotiating his release. A hundred of his men, gathered in Aureatia. Charijisuya the Blasting Blade. This man was his final trump card.

Romzo the Star Map. A man known as one of the members of the First Party.

The legendary seven, the first in the world to confront True Demon King. All of them were champions, the absolute pinnacle of their age. Touted as unrivaled, they too were defeated and scattered before the True Demon King menace, and it was said only Romzo and one other member survived.

Two of them managed to survive.

Countless champions challenged the True Demon King, with close to none of them returning alive.

One of those very few who survived was Romzo the Star Map.

He was a compatriot who lamented the current state of Aureatia, and someone with superlative fighting prowess, rivaling Gilnes himself.

"As you are aware, sir... In the middle of my bout four days from now, we plan to make our move. The location will be the castle garden theater. It's surrounded on all sides by audience seating, and well within range of the bird's bough. Here is where I'd like to ask you to defend the soldiers providing support."

"Hmm. That is easy. Very easy... But that's not all, is it?"

"Before the match, may I request your 'Dwelling Might' technique?"

"Hmm."

Romzo casually looked out over the trees. It was the season when the leaves turned brown and began to fall.

Gilnes kept silent, watching Romzo as he looked.

"That is easy. You understand, right?"

"Of course. If we can win this one battle, our ambitions will be realized."

The pressure points technique he utilized to incapacitate the soldier was not intended to simply be used as an attack.

Its real abilities rather lay in releasing the physical limits of the body when either the user or their allies engaged in combat.

Dwelling Might was the pinnacle. Romzo had named the technique, capable of shouldering the price of death itself.

"...Rosclay the Absolute is strong. He's absolute in anything and everything."

"My consent to this arrangement was very much made with that in mind."

"Got it. Well then, I suppose that's fine."

The elderly master slowly walked over and put his hand on the door of the dwelling.

There, he turned around.

"All right, over there... The same position as you were at the start. Stand about three paces in front of where I am. When that man over there wakes up, he'll feel a bit unsteady on his feet."

"Understood. You have my thanks."

Gilnes gave a deep, respectful bow and departed. Now, all of the preparations were complete.

A hundred supporters springing out from the audience. The Blasting Blade. And now, his movements would go beyond the limits of his own body.

Preparations that had used up every iota of power at his disposal.

A true duel. How one would interpret such an arrangement would likely be different from person to person.

The honest and noble-minded knight Rosclay was certain to put forth all his effort into battling with the one skill he honed to perfection himself. Gilnes was not.

He wasn't an idol of the people like Rosclay; he was a military man who fought to accomplish a goal.

$$*\qquad*\qquad*$$

The day of the duel was coming.

◆

"Rosclay!"

"Rosclay! Rosclay!"

"Rosclay!!"

"Rosclay!"

The cheers of the packed crowd were almost loud enough to shatter eardrums.

Daytime in the castle garden theater. The excited citizenry of Aureatia clamored in the spectator seats surrounding the large grass plaza. The thought that the owner of the fruit stand was somewhere among them suddenly flickered in Gilnes's mind.

The knight walking out to face Gilnes was still young.

His features, blond hair and red eyes, were plainly beautiful to anyone who saw them.

However, this beauty was also unlike that of a vampire, cloaked in an air of dread. His pleasant features were the kind that brought a sense of security to those who laid eyes on him.

On top of this, the way he had toned his muscles, it was likely the two men's physiques had been different from birth. Compared to Gilnes's imposing appearance, covered in big, thick muscles, his thin and sinewy body made him look not unlike a sculpted statue.

His was a face known to everyone. He was Rosclay the Absolute.

...I get it. No wonder they're setting him up to be a symbol to the people.

Pitting them against each other, it was obvious at first glance which of them was on the side of *justice*.

Even someone who protected the people as the general of a

ten-thousand-strong army like Gilnes the Ruined Castle, compared to the man before him, ended up looking like a crude mountain bandit.

"General Gilnes. Your heroics remain still fresh in the memories of the people. I consider our duel on this day a great honor. Let us show to these fine people what a battle free of spite can look like."

"I consider it an honor, too. I didn't expect such an opportunity for vindication... I thought the council, too, recognized my own righteousness as something to ignore entirely. Now, as a warrior equal, allow me to challenge you to combat."

Gilnes took notice of his arm's movements, beginning to sag under the weight of his sword. When a single strand of hair on his arm lowered, then he would stop. He moved it again. He stopped at the drop of a strand of hair.

His center didn't waver an inch during the series of motions.

To anyone else, he assumed it looked like he was gently lowering his sword.

In just a few moments, Gilnes finished checking the capabilities of his physical body.

He could instantly tell his body to "stop" with the speed and positioning he wanted.

This was Romzo's Dwelling Might. With the full strength of Gilnes's sword skills on top of it, he had become a powerful threat.

"Rosclay!"

"Rosclay!"

"Rosclay!"

Mixed in with the cheers, the signal announcing the start of the match rang. Both combatants, in that moment, began to close the distance between each other.

He saw Rosclay hold his sword above his head. It was an

exceedingly fast downward swing, exactly as taught to military swordsmen.

However.

That won't hit me. Not with how I am now.

Gilnes *stopped* his advance.

Even in the midst of a full-speed charge, with all his body weight behind him, in his current condition, it was possible.

Consequently, Rosclay misjudged the range for his opening attack. The worst possible blunder to make.

"Over in an instant. Sorry, but—"

—There wouldn't be any need to make use of his hundred-strong-soldier force.

Holding his sword low to meet incoming slash, he grazed Rosclay's sword with the tip. It took on heat and exploded. Rosclay's sword shattered.

Charijisuya the Blasting Blade.

From the eyes of the spectators, he assumed it looked as if the sword was unable to defend against the overwhelming strength behind the blow.

Continuing the attack, Gilnes slashed straight down at his chest.

"*Iokouto. Namfatqumziz. Ninhortas. Wizioguraeua. Pastigeste.*" (To the wind of Kouto. Fireflies on the lake's surface. Source of soil. Release from one eye. Flash.)

It was that moment when Gilnes realized his opponent had been incanting Word Arts during their battle.

The electrical charge of the Thermal Arts, suddenly appearing before Gilnes's sword's path, flowed back down through the blade, and for an instant, induced an unavoidable biological reaction, stiffening up his muscles.

The average person would have likely been knocked unconscious by the attack. He endured and held his ground.

...What was that?

He shook his head. Gilnes certainly wasn't one to overlook indications that an opponent before him was using Word Arts.

Even with his own weapon lost, there wasn't a single crack in Rosclay's calm demeanor.

He was perplexed by the Word Arts that seemed to have no visible forewarning, but at the very least, Rosclay's display meant that he could utilize electric Thermal Arts with the speed and power necessary in battle.

If his Words Arts were fast enough to keep up with their battle, he must have devoted a considerable amount of effort to honing his skills.

I assumed he was a knight, but he's an arts knight, huh. No matter.

If he had mastered combat Word Arts at such a young age, if anything, it made him easier to deal with.

All that time he spent honing those skills was time he wasn't spending training with his sword.

It was far from his first time fighting against an arts knight. In fact, with both his purer experience and longer years of training, Gilnes was capable of surpassing Rosclay. The blade he brandished was one that caused explosive death with its touch, Charijisuya the Blasting Blade.

He wouldn't give him the time to draw his next sword. The instant his muscles were free of their paralysis, he rushed forward with a slash of his blade.

"...Your sword—"

Rosclay muttered offhandedly.

"Thinking of pleading for a halt to the fight? It's too late. My sword stroke will reach you faster than the words can leave your mouth."

"No. I simply thought that I needed a new sword of my own, as well."

Gilnes pressed in closer to Rosclay, paying no heed to his reply. The dirt in the garden theater whirled in the air.

"*Vapmarsia wanwao. Sarpmorebonda. Ozno.*" (Jeweled crevice. Still stream. Strike.)

A sword blocked the sideways sweeping flash of Gilnes's sword. Rosclay's sword—but not exactly.

The sword that had been blown apart by the enchanted sword sprouted up from the ground and defended against Gilnes's high-speed strike.

Flanking Rosclay, four whole swords were being constructed out of the ferrous materials in the soil.

"This, can't be possible...!"

Gilnes pulled back his sword—he could manage Craft Arts with such speed in combat, too?

It may have been correct to say the man in front of him wasn't a knight, but a true arts caster. It couldn't be.

"*Hah...yah!*"

Without letting the momentary confusion pass, Rosclay stamped on the earth with a rending shout.

Rosclay's new sword arced in an almost too-perfect path, picture perfect compared to how it was taught to new swordsmen.

It followed the reverse course of Gilnes's blade, tearing into and breaking his gauntlet. The only reason his arm wasn't then cut clean off was because he was able to pull his arm back at the last second with the added effects of Dwelling Might.

"......!"

Had Gilnes been his normal self, this single exchange would have spelled defeat.

The blood soaking the inner cloth of his gauntlet gave him this terrifying premonition.

"Impossible."

"—*Iokouto. Yurowastera. Vapmarsia wanwao. Sarpmorebonda*—" (—to the soil of Kouto. Reflect in replica. Jeweled crevice. Standstill stream—)

"—*Namfatqumziz. Ninhortas. Wizioguraeua*—" (Fireflies on the lake's surface. Source of soil. Release from one eye—)

"—*Tortewbijand. Ringmoruseipar. Wrbandeaziograf*—" (—Warping disc. Rainbow corridor. Turn the hidden heaven and soil—)

"—*Iojadwedo. Laeus4motbode. Teomayamvista*—" (—to the steel of Jawedo. The axis is the fourth left finger. Pierce sound and—)

Yet another new sword was created. Lightning flashed. The swords floated in the air.

He could use so many Word Arts, and all simultaneously. Not only that, but when adding in Rosclay's sword skills, he had over five different categories of advanced and well-honed techniques at his disposal.

Impossible. Gilnes couldn't believe it.

For starters, *simultaneously invoking different Word Arts should have been impossible.*

What's going on here? A feat like that... Rosclay the Absolute—

"...This should put us back at square one, wouldn't you say, General Gilnes? Now, let us continue..."

It was possible that Gilnes the Ruined Castle also held the same feelings of admiration as the citizens of Aureatia somewhere within his heart.

He felt that he was a knight on the path of true righteousness, vanquishing his enemies with his just swordsmanship.

"...battling fairly and with honest skill."

Everything about him is wrong.

"Rosclay!"

"You can win, Rosclay!"

"Rosclaaaay!"

"Rosclay!"

The strength of the man in front of him…was something else entirely. He was enigmatic and mysterious.

◆

The leg, covered with a silver white greave, stamped the ground.

An instantaneous opening move, sharp and fast, the flawless form taught to students of the blade.

Gilnes fell back in time with his opponent's advance. As long as he was in the Dwelling Might state, it was simple enough for him to watch his adversary's movements, and instantly stop and adjust his own.

However, with his attention monopolized by the sudden Word Arts, while Gilnes could stay out of his opponent's sword range, he couldn't stay fully aware of the tip of the blasting sword in his hand.

Rosclay seized this opening.

The knight's sword entwined with the tip of the enchanted sword, held up and pointing at eye level, and hoisted it upward.

Not relying on his strength to knock it down, he instead quietly tapped it, pressing down on its side, and then turned it away. The technique of an extremely just royal knight.

…*The special quality of the Blasting Blade*—

He had seen right through it. Now, Rosclay's sword didn't burst apart after touching the enchanted sword.

Then, if his movements were indeed following the fundamentals, there was only one movement to follow. Using the back of the sword, he slid along the sword shortening the distance between them. His hand immobilized Gilnes's gauntlet, and they both came together, swords locked at the hilts.

In power and physique, Gilnes was superior. However, because he was pinned as he fell back, he couldn't shift his center of gravity forward. Rosclay was using this to tip the scales.

Gilnes bellowed, to properly muster his fighting spirit.

"Rosclay! Regardless of whoever or whatever you may be, I *will* claim victory…!"

"Speed. The speed of the slash, coming into contact with a solid mass. That's what's needed for the explosion."

A cold sweat shivered down Gilnes's back.

Looking at Rosclay's face from up close… His expression was wholly unlike the one he had just shown the crowd, appearing now level-headed and reflective.

Paying no heed to Gilnes right in front of him, Rosclay continued murmuring to himself.

"He was able to sheathe his sword. If contact is the only requirement to cause an explosion, then if I do this—"

He propped up the back of his two-handed sword, pushing back and forth against Gilnes's, and added more force. Gilnes was inevitably pushed to resist the added force in a similar way, as well.

"…He also can't use his hand to support the blade. The breadth of his sword techniques gets narrower. He shouldn't be able to utilize such a weapon in this position. All right."

Riding the momentum of the weight pushing into him, he fell back and opened up space between the two of them again.

That was what made Gilnes the Ruined Castle realize. Their locked hilts moments prior weren't an attempt by Rosclay to push back the much larger and bulky Gilnes. In fact, it was possible that from the beginning, the first grazing hit Gilnes had made to Rosclay's sword hadn't been a coincidence at all.

—He had completely seen through all the characteristics of Charijisuya the Blasting Blade.

Backed away from Gilnes, replications of Rosclay's sword, formed beneath the ground, were still suspended in midair.

The two of us were exchanging blows. He couldn't possibly have kept his complex Word Arts going...

That wasn't it. That wasn't what he needed to think about. He had to keep his mind focused. Otherwise it would become a weakness his opponent could exploit. Even with regard to pure swordsmanship skills, Rosclay the Absolute's rivaled or even exceeded Gilnes's own.

...Looks like now's the time to use it.

Gilnes switched his grip on his sword and loosened the wrist coverings on his right hand.

It was the signal for the final remaining strategy that he had prepared.

They had referred to it as the bird's bough.

The name of a one-shot crossbow, modified into a thin, foldable shape.

Its unique firing sound was not quiet by any stretch, but with its frequency modified to vanish within a person's vocal range, amid the screams and shouts of a large crowd—or rather, surrounded by an audience's excited cheers—it was constructed to make it impossible to determine the shot's origin.

Fire.

The target he was signaling to attack was, of course, not Rosclay the Absolute.

He was commanding the soldiers slipped among the crowd to shoot Gilnes himself in the back.

Intended to stand out, without being lethal, and then incite cries denouncing the match as corrupt and dishonest.

As far as he could tell from the words and actions of Third Minister Jelki, Aureatia was concerned about the bad reputation that came with this match far more than the outcome itself. With it, the seasoned general Gilnes hadn't assumed a situation like now, where he had exhausted all the methods he had considered and still couldn't stand up to Rosclay's strength, wouldn't come up.

It wasn't Gilnes using the *cowardly trick* to shoot the general in the back from the stands. It was Rosclay's side who was.

This method of bringing the match to an end, regardless of any difference in their strength, had been planned from the beginning.

Afterward, the hundred who had been slipped into the crowd were then to instigate a riot. When it came time to alter the mood of a crowd, strength in numbers produced the best results.

"......"

He watched his opponent's movements. A major premise of the plan, before being put into motion, was that Gilnes was still alive.

"Haaa-yah!"

Rosclay swung one of the swords floating in midair with a flowing movement. A sword flash across from the shoulder, ever true to the fundamentals.

Gilnes blocked with the Blasting Blade. His adversary's sword burst and broke into pieces, and once again Gilnes stopped moving.

He realized that the electric Thermal Arts that had caused him to stiffen up moments prior were flowing from Rosclay's sword. The electric currents flowed simultaneously with the sword's slashes.

Why?

He had already given the signal. There was no sign of the supporting crossbow fire from the stands.

"Truly superb reactions, General Gilnes!"

At this point there were now six blades formed around Rosclay, revolving around the knight in midair.

Together with the resonant praise that echoed into the audience, Rosclay took his next sword. Gilnes's arm was rigid from the electric Word Arts. He was under the effects of the Dwelling Might. He would've been able to display peerless technique and swordsmanship, if he could just make his muscles move.

A flash of steel.

He had to react. Even if he sacrificed an arm, he had to ensure the blade didn't cut into his torso.

With the effects of Dwelling Might, he forcibly blocked the path of the blade with his left arm.

Yet the silvery path curved unnaturally, like a snake's coil, evading his left arm.

"—Aeus4motbode. Temoyamafista. Iusmnohain. Xaonyaj." (The axis is the fourth left finger. Pierce sound. Descend from the clouds. Turn.)

Force Arts. If he was able to make his swords float, then changing their midair trajectory was also—

"Gwauck?!"

The strike, with its wielder's full weight behind it, split Gilnes's breastplate in two.

He could feel a rib had broken, and the wound extended deep inside his body.

Everything about him seeming off and abnormal, as Rosclay battled it was his swordsmanship alone that stayed wholly and completely true, the sword of a royal knight.

"Rosclay!"

"You can do it, Rosclay!"

"This is the end of the line, General Gilnes. It was a spectacular duel."

"Rosclay!"

"Just…what, are you…"

"Rosclaaay!"

"Rosclay!"

With gentle eyes, the kind that instilled peace of mind in those who saw them, Rosclay the Absolute looked down at Gilnes.

Was he really a champion?

Did no one else realize it? Everything that happened during their match had been beyond strange.

"General Gilnes. I do not intend to take your life. If you wish to surrender, I will accept it."

"……"

"General."

Rosclay did not cruelly bring down his sword on Gilnes's lowered head.

Instead, he informed him with a whisper.

"How was your ironbound hilt?"

"……!"

With his final thoughts rushing through his head, Gilnes the Ruined Castle surmised the meaning behind his words.

Charijisuya the Blasting Blade. He had ordered it to have only its blade swapped out, the rest being built to match the previous sword's hilt and scabbard.

Exactly like the sword Aureatia had provided him, to prevent anyone from noticing the swap.

Therefore, the electric Word Arts were conducted through the sword to the wielder.

What about Rosclay's sword? It was constructed out of stone. It insulated the hilt.

"How did—"

"There is one other thing I would like to show you."

Rosclay showed Gilnes the inside of his cloak, careful to avoid the eyes of the crowd.

...I can't be. I don't believe it...!

Inside were several sparkling crystals.

Wires extended out of each one of them—they were the same instruments used by comms soldiers, radzios.

"Wwnopellaliokou. Yurowastera. Vapmarsia wanwao—" (From Owenopellal to the soil of Kouto. Reflect in replica. Jeweled crevice—)

"Vigeriokouto. Namfatqumziz. Ninhortas—" (Viger to the wind of Kouto. Fireflies on the lake's surface. Source of soil—)

"Egirwezi io rosxle. Tortewbijand—" (From Ekraezi to Rosclay. Warping disc—)

Rosclay hadn't been using Word Arts.

There was a limit to how much experience a single person could amass.

Ignoring outliers like Alus the Star Runner, *there was no possible way for someone to be perfectly suited to handle everything.*

"Rosclaaaaay!"

"Rosclay!"

"Rosclay won!"

"Rosclay!"

It was possible that Gilnes the Ruined Castle, too, held the same feelings of admiration as the citizens of Aureatia somewhere within his heart.

He felt that he was a knight on the path of true righteousness, vanquishing his enemies with his just swordsmanship.

*　　*　　*

Everything about him was wrong. This man's strength wasn't some sort of mysterious yet exceptional talent at all.

During these two small months of preparation time, he had done the same thing Gilnes had.

His confusion from seeing no Word Arts indications from Rosclay had been only natural.

Had it always been that way? There was no way a single minia could kill a dragon.

If he truly had been alone, then who vouched for that fact? Was Gilnes really supposed to believe that during his dragon battle, he had fought solely relying on his skills with a blade? That this underhanded deceit was the reality behind the Aureatia's Twenty-Nine Officials, the true form of the champion the people put their faith in?

"*Ngraaaaaaaugh!*"

In that moment, the pent-up rage that burned inside Gilnes burst open.

It was rage, it was remorse, and more than anything, it was deep disappointment.

The body that should have been beyond all salvation, taken hold by his mental anguish, brandished his sword, and—

"*Haa-yah!*"

He then took an over-the-shoulder slash, form perfect, and collapsed.

The silver flash passed through the crack opened in his breastplate and ended Gilnes's life. Rosclay seemed to have turned the tables against Gilnes's final struggle, defending himself fair and square.

Rosclay took a deep breath. Putting on his mask of sincerity, he appealed to the crowd.

A calculated act, before the excitement among his audience cooled.

"...Citizens, it is as you just saw. General Gilnes, rejecting my call for surrender, took up his sword. And now, he has died before my blade!"

"Rosclay!"

"Rosclaaay!"

"Rosclay!"

"He chose the path of a martyr for his ideals! He offered up his precious soul to bring the end to an outdated time! I ask you to applaud the general's courage! His sacrifice...will serve as our first step, the Old Kingdoms' loyalists and Aureatia together, to a new age!"

"Rosclay's right!"

"Gilnes! Gilnes!"

"Rosclay!"

"Gilnes!"

"Now, with our battle in this true duel decided, I bear Gilnes no hatred! I pray that you, citizens, will do the same! He fought to build peace for all! It is time to shoulder his sacrifice and advance forward!"

Aureatia's Second General spoke, making his sword sparkly with silvery white light.

Rosclay the Absolute. The honest and just hero.

No matter what enemy appeared before him, not a single stain was ever left behind on his silvery white armor.

"The battle you have all witnessed before is a perfect example of my true duel performance. In the next grand match, I pledge that I will use the excellent techniques I have cultivated to slay my enemies!"

"Rosclay!"

"Rosclay!"

"Rosclay!"

Rosclay, his performance concluded, returned alone to the stage entryway.

His appearance in the royal games was set in stone. Though it wasn't decided that he would be fighting in the same garden. Much like with his duel that day, both parties wouldn't necessarily be on even footing.

It hadn't been an even playing field from the very start.

Inside the brick corridor was a single figure waiting for Rosclay.

A tall and lanky man, shrouded in an artless and unsophisticated air.

"Romzo, sir. Thank you very much."

"Easy. Knocking out a hundred odd people, no trouble at all. I knew their faces already, too."

One of the First Party, Romzo the Star Map answered with his usual smiling face, free of any strain or tension.

"Gilnes is dead, then."

"...Indeed. It is a pity. You have my sympathies."

"Ah well, it's fine. Nothing to be done. I did like the lad, but I had no problem betraying him. So long as I've got somewhere I can sell myself for a good price, I didn't really care about anything else."

In the dimly lit corridor, the bashful smile behind his rounded glasses instead seemed sinister.

"Especially given I'm just a coward who lost to the Demon King long ago. This much is no problem at all."

Even strategies mobilizing numerous soldiers collapsed under the smallest hole in the scheme.

Rosclay was himself a general in command of an army and could get a read on what schemes Gilnes would plan. On the battlefield, he first relied not on his sword but his ingenuity.

"Thank you also for the Dwelling Might. Its power was far beyond my expectations. It made my blood run cold."

"About that, actually. Hmm. I still don't get it. You said to purposely make your opponent stronger. With my treatment, Gilnes... Hmm, let's see. I could've easily weakened him to the strength of a five-year-old child."

"That wouldn't be enough. In the upcoming grand match, there's sure to be no one weaker than myself and General Gilnes. I needed to actually experience and know for myself how much my blade can hold out against a stronger foe. Thanks to your help, I was able to pick out many areas that need to be addressed."

"...Diligent, aren't we? Seems like a tough way to live."

"I'm ashamed of my shortcomings."

He clenched and unclenched his fist, ruminating on his memory of the duel. It was a hard experience to come by.

A day that was bound to arrive, and a similarly strong opponent. Similarly encircled by a crowd of spectators. A true battle, also with his life on the line.

Having actually experienced such combat could prove the difference between life and death. As long as there was even the slightest possibility it could, then the experience was necessary.

"Well then. I'll be going. My game of fake insurgency's over."

"...Until we meet again, Romzo the Star Map."

That day, all one hundred–odd Old Kingdoms' loyalists who gathered at the garden theater were captured.

Having lost their leader in Gilnes the Ruined Castle, and adviser in Romzo the Star Map, their influence rapidly began fading away.

♦

The night of the garden duel.

Along the riverside on the Aureatia frontier, there existed a dingy shack.

The house was inhabited by a mother and her frail daughter. The father who provided for them had passed away.

Amid the darkness of the area, no other residence in sight, the orange lamplight illuminated the doorway and announced their visitor.

Opening the door, the mother looked at the face she hadn't seen in a long time and broke into a smile.

"…Oh my, how we've been waiting for you, my lord! Iska! Iska! Get up, quick!"

"Oh no, please. If she's already asleep, then… I wouldn't want to push Iska too hard."

The man was covered in a full-body robe, carefully concealing both his face and body. Nevertheless, to the mother, his was a figure so familiar, she could immediately recognize it.

The young girl, who came out of the bedroom to meet the man, gazed up at his face and gave him a smile.

"You're very late, Mr. Second General. You woke me up."

"Iska…"

The daughter would turn sixteen that year. She had chestnut-colored hair and eyes to match. She looked a little thinner and more haggard than before.

Rosclay the Absolute cast his eyes to the ground and lowered his hand where he stood.

When he was under this roof, Rosclay was almost a completely different person.

"First, let me apologize. I put on a disgraceful battle display in front of the people."

"My, my, my. Is that so? That's quite the problem, isn't it? What was disgraceful about it, then?"

The village girl crouched down in front of the minian champion and asked, teasingly.

"...My first step forward. And if the enchanted sword had laid into me while my sword was broken, I would be dead. And if the electric Thermal Arts didn't stop him... I was a hair's breadth away from the end."

"Another dangerous fight, is it? Honestly... Just what am I going to do about you?"

Iska stroked Rosclay's golden hair and flashed a troubled smile.

All of his fights were like this. He appeared to fight with overwhelming strength that far outdid his opponents, but in truth, he was balanced on a razor's edge between life and death. Both his consideration for any and all possible schemes, and his diligence with his daily training, were all because he truly and deeply held his own life dear.

Rosclay the Absolute. The champion of the minia. No matter how much she wished and hoped, she knew his turn to abandon the whorl of battle would come later than anyone else's.

"...That's why, um, well... I came here because, I thought it'd be better to give you this sooner rather than later."

Rosclay's eyes darted around nervously, almost like any other young man his age, and he took out a box.

"What's this?"

"It's a coral ring. I bought it at the market. I think it would suit you, Iska. And since I haven't properly given you any presents up until now..."

"Hmm."

The young girl inspected the inside of the box, looking at the small silver ring.

Red coral, with a subdued luster. The color was also not too different from Rosclay's own eye color.

Still smiling, she pushed the box back to him.

"No thank you."

"What?"

"Mr. Second General? You're taking me for some uneducated village girl, aren't you? I believe in the Beyond, gifting a ring is meant to be a symbol of betrothal, isn't it?"

Rosclay conspicuously averted his gaze in an effort to escape from Iska's probing look.

"Wh-what does that matter...? I'm simply giving it to you for my own self-satisfaction."

"I don't need something this serious. No, in fact, you absolutely mustn't send me anything that will remain behind. How exactly am I supposed to explain things if someone questions me about it?"

Rosclay's eyebrows drooped. There was no knowing just how long Iska had left to live.

He knew that she was trying not to leave anything behind after she died.

"I don't need anything, Mr. Rosclay the Absolute. Wouldn't you say that you being a champion itself is already too good of a gift for this simple village girl?"

"No at all... Am I, really a champion?"

"...Well, well, well. Aren't we in low spirits today, Mr. Second General?"

Her mother had already taken her leave. More important than any dinner preparations, she knew that on the days Rosclay came to visit, the two of them needed time to talk alone.

Time where he wasn't the people's champion, but a normal young man, where he could escape from his all-too-heavy obligations.

"I killed General Gilnes. Outstandingly valorous and intelligent, a person worthy of respect... I had no choice but to use every dastardly trick to kill him."

"...How cruel of you."

Rosclay was kneeling. Just as he had forced his enemies to kneel across his multitude of battles.

She was the only person in the world who saw him like this.

As if accepting a confession, she wrapped both her arms around his head.

"The sword is all I have."

"...Yes, that's right. Why, it's the only thing you've ever trained for."

"Just having someone else know about your existence would make victory impossible."

"True. You're such a delicate person, after all."

"I really...want to fight the proper way."

"...I know that."

If he hadn't been there that day, both she and her mother would have simply been sold off as slaves.

She would never say it. However, she alone knew that Rosclay the Absolute had the capability to be a champion right from the very start.

Thus, now, she simply listened to his words.

If Iska could be a solace to his troubled mind, that was enough for her.

The night grew late, and Rosclay returned to the castle.

"...That dummy."

Iska muttered, picking up the small box that had been left on top of the table in the dark.

After all she had said to him about it, in the end he had left it behind.

She returned to her small bedroom and lit the lamp beside her bed.

The contour of the ring she held in her fingers glowed gently in the yellow light.

Honestly, to gift her something that'll leave a legacy behind like this—

"...*Pfft.*"

She lay down on her back in the dark bed.

On the third finger of her left hand, stretching out to the lamp-light, sat a shining red coral ring.

Rosclay. Stronger than anyone else, yet weaker than anyone else, her own personal champion.

In that moment, she even felt able to forget about her smothering illness.

If there could be such a future, it would be such a beautiful thing, indeed.

Tears began to trickle down her cheek. Yet, just as happy, Iska laughed.

"...*Hee-hee-hee.*"

He, the individual, stood at the greatest and tallest heights of pure and proper swordsmanship.

He possessed the ingenuity to draw a fight to its conclusion before it had even begun, through scheming and subterfuge.

He, with a nation as his ally, received any and all support to turn his victory into a foregone conclusion.

Entrusted with all types of power wielded by the strongest social beings across the land, an artificial champion.

Knight. Minia.

Rosclay the Absolute.

Back before the day when Gilnes the Ruined Castle was killed in a duel.

Two people were having a conversation in a small room inside the Aureatia Central Assembly Hall. The Second General, prestigious and popular with the citizenry, Rosclay the Absolute. With him, the central figure and adjudicator of the meeting discussing the Particle Storm threat, leading their interception operation to victory, Third Minister, Jelki the Swift Ink.

"That's all of the details on their fighting power that were verified during the interception operation. As we hoped, Kuuro the Cautious gave detailed status reports. The confused melee was not what we had originally expected, but if anything, I consider it a windfall."

Jelki reported all the confirmed information regarding the battle to Rosclay.

Kuuro the Cautious's spotting was communication utilizing what was an exceptional long-distance relay for an individual comms operator.

As such, his communications did not solely reach the troops under Kayon the Thundering's command at Sine Riverstead. There was someone inside Aureatia's borders who had intercepted the transmissions from the beginning.

Third Minister Jelki had a handle on everything that occurred during the operation.

He was well aware of the appearance of both the self-proclaimed demon king Kiyazuna and Toroa the Awful. Additionally, he had a better grasp of both of their fighting techniques and how they chose to fight than Cayon, the one tasked with commanding the operation.

"Toroa the Awful. And this Mestelexil. Both of their abilities are unmistakably capable of threatening the nation. Both will need to be put down...or engaged during the royal games."

"...Supposing they did put their name in to participate in the royal games, would you accept them?"

Finally, the last one given this information was Rosclay the Absolute, who hadn't attended the original strategy meeting.

"We will dispose of them within the constraints of the games. Without letting them put their full powers on display."

"Naturally, I intended to do that from the start... The royal games are our way to deal with such monsters."

Aureatia's champion, holding great prestige among the people, Rosclay. The head of commerce and trade, and cornerstone of domestic affairs, Jelki. They had colluded together from the beginning. Even the measures to quell the Particle Storm were being used to lay groundwork, getting hold of information on candidates whom Rosclay was likely to face.

"Ultimately, the Particle Storm vanished during this operation. It's highly like he died. No one is likely to look into more information regarding the operation... Including that its passage through Sine Riverstead was information *we added on our end*."

The strategy meeting had developed under the premise that the Gray-Haired Child's forecast was correct. The Gray-Haired Child, based on the Particle Storm's path he had obtained from his weather observation techniques, estimated that the Particle

Storm's true form was a living creature with a will of its own, and from examples of countries the Particle Storm had destroyed in the past, he predicted the objective behind its sudden movement was an attack on Aureatia.

Considering the actual path the Particle Storm took, it had a high probability of ending up that way. Still, a future where Atrazek moved in such a direction was simply a possibility. Not a fact certain to become reality.

Nevertheless, during their meeting, the certainty of the weather forecast became the focal point. The moment the information was demonstrated to be reliable, the accompanying information about its passage through Sine Riverstead *was determined to be true as well.*

"...But, Rosclay. Why didn't you directly order Cayon to bring the Horizon's Roar into action? Given the pretext of defending Aureatia itself, I imagine he would be forced to agree to your demands."

"That's not it. With this operation, it was necessary to have Cayon, Mele the Horizon's Roar's backer, propose the idea himself. It, of course, couldn't come from me, nor from yourself, either. If another person directed him to do so, a man of Cayon's caliber... He would suspect that person was scouting out their future opponent. Not only that, but I believe he's already sensed we're colluding together."

The moment he was told the Particle Storm would pass through Sine Riverstead, Kayon no longer had any choice but to get the Horizon's Roar involved. If Mele's homeland of Sine River-stead were destroyed, he would lose all reason to participate in the royal games with it.

With the simple act of adding some details to the report, he had swiftly gotten an opposing contender involved, without any need for bargaining.

"Cayon getting Mele to help also did us a favor by making the Star Runner and the Passing Disaster unnecessary. Using them would put our own side in danger. The best course of action is to exclude any wild cards."

Everything was to protect Aureatia. The sole reasons behind Rosclay the Absolute preserving his reputation and using every method possible to desperately defend Aureatia were the nation's citizens.

Jelki, as well, shared in this ideal. Now, with the True Demon King dead, he sought to remove any out-of-control champions from the world and create a nation where the people were free from strife.

The royal games to decide the Hero still haven't even amassed all the participants yet. However...

It was different *for them.*

Different for these intellectual monsters, amassing information, devising schemes, and claiming victory long before the start of any match.

It's long since started. No matter how strong they may be, they'll be taken down before they can even enter the ring. It's our job to give them the impression that it all begins with the players facing each other, waiting for the starting bell.

Jelki started to speak. At the very the least, there was one other monster of intellect out there. A threat they had postponed dealing with.

"...Rosclay. With that in mind, there's one thing I'd like to tell you—"

"The Gray-Haired Child, I assume?"

"That's right. Toroa the Awful. Kiyazuna the Axle. Finally, the Particle Storm. I believe there is someone besides us who tried to glean information regarding possible royal games contenders, induce three unrelated powers to cross swords in one place. Going forward, I think we will need to dispose of the Gray-Haired Child."

For Kiyazuna the Axle's involvement in this recent event, there was no doubt the forecasts dispersed by the Gray-Haired Child were the source of her information. Then, supposing the same individual used the information regarding the Blasting Blade in her possession to get Toroa the Awful involved...

"Is there anything linking the Gray-Haired Child to Toroa the Awful?"

"The method that Toroa used to catch up to the Particle Storm in the ravine. Eyewitness information continues to Togie City, but after that, he disappears without a trace...before suddenly appearing in that ravine. In other words..."

"There was someone who prepared a method of travel, carriage or otherwise, and moved him there."

"Deliberately, on top of that, to make him engage Kiyazuna. Why would someone outside of Aureatia purposely be trying to obtain information on probable candidates for the games?"

"I see what you mean."

That was to say—there was more than one person who thought along the same lines as Rosclay the Absolute.

"Like whether or not they've already been given a spot, or if there were definite plans to give them one down the line, perhaps."

Rosclay contemplated. The Gray-Haired Child was not truly an ally to the Old Kingdoms' loyalists to any degree, even while doing business with them. There had to be a clear goal or purpose in his actions.

"Considering the end results, the predicted path of the Particle Storm the Gray-Haired Child sold off to each of the major powers guided the Old Kingdoms swiftly to destruction... They were bribed by false victory prospects, and their hurried offensive preparations led to their crushing defeat. Then, if my assumption's correct, the power the Gray-Haired Child is now currently affiliated with is—"

Rosclay placed his finger on a spot on the map covering the table.

"—The Free City of Okahu. Can you look into it?"

"Okahu... I agree it was a bit of an unnatural movement on their part to back down in the middle of our war with the Old Kingdoms' loyalists. We need to look and see if they've been active at all behind the scenes."

"If anything, their movements advanced our plan. As a result of the Gray-Haired Child's actions, the two powers hindering the start of the royal games *have been taken care of.* Then, from this stage, he's been investigating candidates, practically screening them himself..."

"In other words, the Gray-Haired Child is also trying to make us start the royal games."

"Yes."

Without any hostility, without even getting directly involved himself, there was someone far outside Aureatia's borders manipulating the government and trying to push the royal games forward.

If he had some aim in doing so, what could it be? What sort of final conclusion could these intellectual monsters be aiming for once the fighting was over?

"Jelki the Swift Ink. I'd like to place my confidence in your abilities and ask for your help. With this series of actions from the Gray-Haired Child in mind, I ask you to pay the absolute most attention possible to his movements going forward."

"...You think he'll become Aureatia's enemy?"

"I'm asking precisely because we don't know for sure."

The greatest royal tournament in history, to determine a Hero.

Should it truly become a battle to greatly change the whole breadth of history, then it was unlikely to be simple duels among the powerful.

Aureatia. The Free City of Okahu. Obsidian Eyes.

The scheming shura capable of changing the world itself were spreading their roots.

◆

"Requesting support! Kiyazuna the Axle spotted! I repeat, we've encountered the self-proclaimed demon king, Kiyazuna! With our troops alone, we are unable to handle anything beyond observing her movements! Requesting backup from Aureatia's main force!"

The rank-and-file soldiers maneuvered frantically, maintaining a fixed distance coming out from cover and surrounding the elderly woman. Readying themselves to fire the exact moment they saw any movement, they prayed their backup would be there in time.

To the small Aureatia border patrol, she was a terrifying person to come across.

A nightmare, like a child walking just outside their house's garden and coming face-to-face with a malevolent dragon.

"Dammit, why she gotta be strolling into Aureatia...! We're just supposed to be out on patrol!"

"Sheesh, buncha loudmouths, eh?"

"Ha-ha-ha-ha-ha-ha-ha! Are, are they in, the way?! Mama! I... I know! If they're, in our way, I should, clean them up, right? I w-wonder, what their en-trails, are like?!"

The golem accompanying the self-proclaimed demon king Kiyazuna appeared at first glance to be a minian-shaped golem, with no quirks or specialized functionalities. But it only *appeared* that way.

So long as the weapon was of her creation, they needed to consider it an authentic supernatural threat, wholly impossible to deal with through normal means. Kiyazuna the Axle was the demon king who managed to alter an entire city into becoming her Dungeon Golem.

"Nah, just play nice. At least, for now."

Completely baffling to each of the soldiers there, the self-proclaimed demon king, known for her wickedness, showed no signs of hostility. They were terrified that over a third of them would be annihilated, depending on the nature of her first attack.

"…Awful! C'mon, this bread's hard as a rock and tastes awful! Hey, Mestelexil, can you make us up a toaster? Instead of just using Thermal Arts to burn it, you got some smart theoretical something you can wipe up, don'cha?"

"Got it! L-Leave it, to me! Ha-ha-ha-ha-ha-ha-ha-ha-ha!"

"Ah, great, now it's pitch-black. I didn't say to just torch it normally. Bread's awful anyway, I guess."

The two could be described as Aureatia's most heinous criminals of all, and even while surrounded by soldiers, with their arrowheads staring them down, the two of them were squatted down in the road taking a break for food. Kiyazuna barked once more.

"Listen, you idiots! I've already talked with the bigwigs! Let me through, or your salary's in trouble!"

"Save your nonsense, self-proclaimed demon king!"

One of the younger soldiers angrily replied from somewhere, terrifying the commander.

Hot-blooded soldiers with a strong sense of justice. Absolutely not the correct way to handle their current predicament.

"We're not letting a villainous crone like you take a single step on Aureatia soil! Today's the day you suffer and pay for all the citizen's lives you've trampled over!"

"Oh, is it now...? Whoa, Mestelexil, where the heck did you learn the Order's script?! That stuff'll turn your brain to mush. Stick with the writing from the Beyond."

"I-I am practicing, writing on, the ground! Doing it, every day, is best! I will, get smarter, too! I will become, knowledgeable, like Mama!"

"Hee-hee-hee! Aw, you're so cute!"

Though the two considered this part of their pastoral everyday life, to the soldiers surrounding them, it felt like they were standing in front of a bomb that could go off at any moment.

The slightest move could trigger the attack, and then which soldier there would be the first to fall?

"... Commander, they've arrived! The reinforcements are here!"

"Is that them? Wait...a single regiment? Against Kiyazuna the Axle?"

Off in the distance, the commander could see what did appear to be Aureatia reinforcements. One single regiment of them.

"What the hell're you all doing?"

The man commanding the unit was known as the fiercest and most militant civil servant—Fourth Minister, Kaete the Round Table.

A cold-blooded glare flickering from his strong, intense face, as he immediately began denouncing the soldiers encircling the pair.

"Which one of you received the report? You should've been notified to immediately break off this nonsense encirclement."

"B-but, sir…! There was no way we could realistically do such a thing!"

"Which one of you dared to backtalk me? If you're looking to lose your head, I'll happily grant your wish. Let her through."

Kaete the Round Table's words were clear as day, and his orders distinctly reached all the soldiers there.

That was precisely why they were so bewildered, believing there had to be some greater design behind the meaning of his order.

"Um…"

"Are your skulls too thick? I said let her through."

They couldn't believe it, letting the self-proclaimed demon king through, a frightening menace to the world for many long years, just like that?

Kiyazuna the Axle leisurely stood up, chuckling to herself as she did.

"What did I tell ya? See, Mestelexil and I? We're *Hero candidates*."

"Y-yup! I will, become the Hero! Ha-ha-ha-ha-ha-ha! I will, be so, cool!"

"D-don't be ridiculous! A soldier of a self-proclaimed demon king, the Hero?! Your wicked lies have gone too far!"

"You're the one making the fuss. Beheading it is, then."

A single glare from the Fourth Minister shut the soldier up. Within Kaete's words, and his intimidating air, was the power to truly make them fear they would be beheaded.

"Putting down self-proclaimed demon kings hiding out in each region. Sabotaging the Old Kingdoms' loyalists' rear encampment. Trapping and beating back the Particle Storm—all of her activities were *under my orders*. Let me ask you fools instead, are there any among you who can claim to have done more to serve Aureatia than Kiyazuna and Mestelexil here? Go ahead, tell me."

Kaete gazed out over the cowering soldiers.

"What's wrong? I told you to answer me."

"Hee, hee, hee, hee!"

Kiyazuna laughed in delight. Self-proclaimed demon kings, the greatest enemies to peace. The general wisdom said she only ever laughed when she was involved in some sort of wicked deed, or when her children were involved.

"Rest easy, all of ya! Kiyazuna the Axle here's hitchin' her wagon to Aureatia!"

Kaete turned back to Aureatia, the sinister duo in tow. Mestelexil the Box of Desperate Knowledge—an invincible trump card, able to upend all the world's knowledge and turn it on its head.

Rosclay. I will make absolutely certain you're not the only one taking the lead in the royal games.

The lone hero. There was someone trying to use that hero's existence to firmly solidify their authority.

While others plotted to topple such authority.

◆

"You're awake. Good."

When he awoke from the blackness of death, a death god was standing at his bedside.

In which case, he might indeed have been in a hellish afterlife. He considered that if the world reflected in his eyes was indeed such an afterlife, he was okay with it.

—No, that alone wasn't enough. Kuuro the Cautious wheezed as he endured his pain.

"......Is Cuneigh...here?"

"Been worried about you the whole time. She really adores you."

"...I haven't done anything for her. If anything...I've been awful. Ever since we met...I haven't given her a single reason to care about me... Funny, isn't it?"

There hadn't been any type of dramatic event to start it all. During his meager life as a detective, they happened across each other, and his sight piqued her curiosity. That and... The two of them had both been alone.

"Listen... Toroa the Awful. You've come back from hell, right...?"

"Yeah."

"...Do homunculi die eventually, too?"

Toroa nodded. Kuuro knew himself it was a foolish question. Really, he had been scared of this from the start.

"How am I supposed to repay her? Cuneigh's... She's always been there to save me..."

"Can I give you a simple answer?"

The death god's eyes stayed fixed on the floor as he responded with detachment.

"Just be there for her. Chat with her, sharing memories and commenting on the scenery. That's plenty... As long as someone's got a sanctuary for their soul, they'll keep going as far as they can go."

"......"

"Even to the farthest reaches of hell."

"...I wanted to use Cuneigh for myself. I wanted to convince myself there was a reason we were together."

He wanted to think that Cuneigh was saving him in exchange for a reward. That she trusted Kuuro because she was foolish.

"I'm scared when things don't have a reason."

"I don't know about your life… But not everyone you come across is out to use you, right?"

"…Trying to use somebody means that you have to trust them, right?"

At the very least, that was how it had been in Kuuro's world. He though the same even now.

"Even the ones who shot me believed that I'd be able to stop the Particle Storm. That's why they were able to wait until I did. If you don't truly trust whoever you're dealing with, you can't use them at all, right…"

Maybe that was why Cuneigh's confidence in him, free of any self-interest, was so terrifying to him.

"If that's how you see it…then she might've lost any worth she has to you. I heard about your clairvoyance from her. Right now, you can trust your own eyes more than anything else, right?"

"…Then why?"

Kuuro weakly mumbled.

"Then why do I still want us to be together?"

"Those feelings of yours, that's Cuneigh's reason."

The death god's words finally made him understand. Understand what she had been thinking for so long.

As long as he could be together with Cuneigh, it didn't matter where he went.

He wanted to see more, to the very ends of the world.

"Looks like you don't need me to look after you anymore. I'm leaving. I doubt we'll meet again."

"…Thank you, Toroa the Awful. Make sure you don't get used either."

"Who do you think I am?"

*　　*　　*

The ill-omened Grim Reaper went to leave the infirmary, putting his hand on the door.

He saw the person resting on top of the chair awake and raise her head.

A winged homunculus, small enough to sit in the palm of his hand.

"...Toroa?"

"Clairvoyance, you called it? Kuuro's power is quite something."

Toroa muttered, his hand still resting on the door.

"He brought you along to that harsh battlefield and protected you to the end. Have you thought about the reason why?"

Cuneigh the Wanderer was never going to help observe the Particle Storm. Kuuro never even let her out from inside his coat once.

"That's because I insisted on coming with him..."

"...Nah. I think...he was inadvertently choosing the best possible future. If he hadn't been there with him, no one would've asked us to save him. You valiantly saved his life."

"Huh.... Saved his life...? Kuuro's life...?"

"That's right. He woke up."

There was a slight pause. Thick tears fell from the young girl's eyes.

Her wings flickered. She called out a name.

"Kuuro... Kuuro!"

Toroa the Awful smiled faintly underneath his hood.

It was time for the death god to leave.

◆

The same day, the Sine Riverstead's Needle Forest was bustling with an unusual amount of activity.

"Meleee! Hey, is it true you fired your bow?!"

"So that bow wasn't just for show after all!"

"No use trying to hide it! There's plenty of kids that say they saw the stars!"

"*Gah*, shaddup already."

Sprawled out facedown on the ground, Mele the Horizon's Roar languidly moved his hand, trying to disperse the village children crowded on the hill.

Although the Aureatia army had evacuated the village during his long-range attack, the word spread in an instant among the Sine Riverstead and the villagers who knew Mele. Mele had woken up in the morning and shot arrows. Lots of arrows, at that.

"Whether I'm shooting arrows or breaking wind, what do any of you care? I'm trying to sleep here."

"It's already past noon, you lazy bum!"

One young boy kicked Mele's fingernail. Despite being subjected to the treatment, the village's guardian deity simply let out a yawn.

"Hey, hey, how many do you think he shot?"

A deeply curious young girl asked, gazing out at the Needle Forest.

"Mele, you shot a bunch of arrows, right? Just what sorta game were you hunting with all that, anyway?"

"Gotta be wyverns, right? He even eats them sometimes."

"I bet the Aureatia arm set up this huuuuge target and made him hit it! If he's gonna go up against Rosclay, they gotta at least make sure he can handle that!"

The Particle Storm once approaching Sine Riverstead, thanks to the life-threatening spotting from Kuuro the Cautious, was shot down long before ever reaching the region. No one in the village was aware of the fact.

"Hey, hey, Mele, how many did you fire?"

The gigant turned over in his sleep. The children who were tickling his feet squealed with laughter as they ran away from his shifting soles. The champion looked up at the sky and smiled.

"...Wasn't really that big a deal, anyway."

He was never without an optimistic smile.

There he was, without losing anything he cared about.

"Mele."

A young boy ran up toward his face. He was a small boy. One of the other children must have carried him up here.

"Here. This is for you."

It was an awkwardly made papercraft sword, smaller than one of Mele's eyelashes.

He couldn't even hold it between two fingers, let alone in his whole hand.

"Whoa, what the heck's this supposed to be? This ain't gonna be enough to fill me up!"

"Ha-ha-ha-ha! You better not actually eat it, Mele!"

"You always eat everything!"

"Gwah-ha-ha-ha-ha! Don't any of you brats know how to be quiet?!"

As he joked around with the children, he wrapped both hands around his precious paper treasure.

To the god who protected the Sine Riverstead with his supernatural skills, this paper sword was more than enough of a reward.

◆

"Oh, hey! You're Toroa the Awful!"

Aureatia was a peaceful city. He carried his numerous blades as he walked, so most of the city's citizens gave him a wide berth.

Hence, the child approaching him without any hesitation was an extremely rare sight indeed.

"It really is you! Wow, you know, I've been so curious, see, ever since I heard those reports back in Gumana!"

"What do you want?"

"Huh?"

He was a boy of about sixteen years old. His clothes themselves were of quality make, and he wasn't very tall.

"If you know that I'm Toroa the Awful, then you wouldn't get close to me without some reason, would you?"

"Hmmm, a reason... I wonder. Because you're cool?"

"'Cool'?"

The young boy unreservedly smacked his hands on the enchanted swords Toroa carried on his back.

"Don't. Some of the blades'll kill you at the slightest touch."

"Are all of them enchanted swords? Wow, that's so awesome. Are you really missing the Luminous Blade? Rumor has it Alus the Star Runner nabbed it from you."

"...Before that. Who are you? Tell me."

"Mizial the Iron-Piercing Plumeshade."

A smile filled with confidence swelled on the young boy's face.

"Twenty-Second General of Aureatia. Amazing, right?! At my age, too!"

"Aureatia's... I see. You're the kid who was at the Gumana Trading Post, then. Never expected you'd be one of the Twenty-Nine Officials."

"Wanna participate in the games?"

Mizial incoherently jumped at the proposal. His thoughts immediately spilled out of his mouth.

"I'll back you. I'm sure everyone'll be totally shocked."

"...The imperial competition to decide the Hero?"

—I'm certain you'll get your chance to fight Alus the Star Runner.

A place where no one will intervene, no fear of getting others involved—a stage where they can fight each other one-on-one. Exactly as the Gray-Haired Child had told him, such an opportunity did indeed wait for him in Aureatia.

In order to appear in that fight, the backing from one of the Twenty-Nine Officials was absolutely necessary. Toroa the Awful, and the enchanted swords not to be in the hands of anyone else, would need to battle at the behest of another.

He had decided not to get involved in fights like that.

"I'm the enchanted-swordsman slaying Toroa the Awful. Why would you pick someone like me for a battle with pride and honor on the line?"

"Huh? Hmm, good question... I'm sure the others in the Twenty-Nine would give a bunch of reasons, but..."

Aureatia's youngest male general thought for a brief moment, before muttering as though he was speaking to himself—

"Because *I'd* enjoy it."

"......"

"The legendary monster of scary stories everywhere, back from hell—that's *definitely* gonna be awesome."

Kuuro the Cautious had warned him mere moments prior not to let anyone use him.

Many conspiracies were circulating behind the scenes of the royal games, giving birth to both advantage takers and those being taken advantage of.

Nevertheless, such appallingly meaningless affairs were still common throughout their world.

"You think a worthless reason like that is enough to get me on board?"

"Aww. I don't really think it's that worthless if you ask me. Oh well, if you don't want to, then that's fine."

Mizial put both hands behind his back and smoothly turned away from Toroa.

"But if you decide you want to, you hafta come tell me, okay? I decided that I was gonna be the one to sponsor you no matter what!"

Toroa watched as the young boy's back slowly slipped out of sight.

The Grim Reaper muttered to no one but himself.

"...I'm not going to be anyone's plaything."

In this world there were always those taking advantage of others, and those being taken advantage of.

And the...there were those who couldn't be taken advantage of by anyone at all.

Everyone knew the name Igania Ice Lake. However, though knowledge of it was widespread, accounts of people actually stepping out onto the frozen surface were few indeed.

At the very least, currently, there were two. The footprints of their iron-cleated boots left behind two lines, straight and true, stretching out across the endless ocean of ice.

"Fwah-ha-ha-ha! Man, it's cold! Really, really cold! So much colder than I thought it'd be!"

Always walking out in front, he was a giant of a man, muscular and strong, with his upper body bare in the air.

Despite shouldering a massive sword nearly as tall as himself and carrying both men's belongings, his energy showed practically no sign of fading.

"But I can't give up! This sort of winter march wouldn't be enough to make Rosclay give up! In that case, I've got to be even better! Isn't that right, Master General?"

"Whaat…?"

The other man walked along feebly, gasping for air.

Only saddled with less than a quarter of the other man's load, and wrapped head to toe in cold-weather gear, he still was out of breath.

"Like hell… I would know! More than that, though, comparing

the Second General and myself like that... You should be more considerate! You're making fun of me, aren't you?!"

"Considerate, huh? But, Master General, your inferiority to Rosclay's just a fact! Why, everyone and his mother knows something like that!"

"*Haah, haaah...* That's what I mean...by being inconsiderate!"

The giant man's name was Lagrex the Butchering Landslide.

As his exaggerated second name suggested, he was a young swordsman bubbling over with enormous ambition and initiative.

Meanwhile, there was no question that the man following behind him was also being propelled forward by his enormous ambition.

He was Aureatia's Sixth General, Harghent the Still.

"Though, look! Beasts, beasts! Even in cold land like this! I'm amazed they can survive. Not only that, but they're even bigger than the beasts of the desert! Did you see that silver bear just now?!"

"...Hm. You see, Lagrex, that's all related to body surface area. To put it another way, small mice and such animals quickly freeze in low-temperature environments, so—"

"Okay, okay, stop right there. Explaining it to me won't do a lick of good! The main point's that she's got plenty of food around her!"

Everyone knew the name Igania Ice Lake. Though the exact meaning behind that statement was slightly different.

It was more accurate to say that everyone knew the name of the divine dragon that lived at Igania Ice Lake.

"You really intend to challenge Lucunoca the Winter, then?"

"Of course! If there's a single opponent out there who can stand up against Rosclay...then it can't possibly be anyone else besides Lucunoca the Winter! And, if I were actually Rosclay—"

"If I were Rosclay…" was a turn of phrase that Lagrex repeated time and time again.

"…there's no way I'd lose. He's the only minia who's ever killed a dragon by himself."

"…Well."

To those who knew the truth, it was easy to declare Lagrex's goal as absolutely ludicrous.

However, no matter how eccentric…and to go one step further, how terribly his personality clashed with Harghent's own, there was no one other than Lagrex he could rely on to guide him through the unforgiving snowscape.

If Harghent hadn't lost his own troops, he could've advanced through the region with a flawless tundra march.

This was the case no longer. Without Lagrex's masterful sword skills with him, it was impossible to guess how many times Harghent would have been killed by the giant beasts of the ice lake.

To go even further, among the world's adventurers who dreamed about challenging Lucunoca the Winter, it was extremely rare to see someone like Lagrex, who worked so tirelessly to hone his abilities.

"What sort of general is Rosclay anyway?! Have you ever crossed swords with him?!"

"H-Hmm? Well…"

"He must've hit really hard, right?! At the very least, he has to be able to shatter his opponent's sword, and slice through their whole torso in a single slash. Not only that, but with speed, too, like a flash of lightning!"

"Hrm… I haven't a clue, but how can you talk so confidently about Rosclay's skills when you've never even seen him fight before…?"

Harghent heard that he was a native of the Hakeena Micro-region, on the southern frontier, far away from Aureatia.

Lagrex had simply focused on training with his own self-taught sword style and was here now because he believed that would be enough against Lucunoca the Winter. Feeling the harshness of the Igania Ice Lake, Harghent felt that the man's challenge appeared incorrigibly reckless.

In the middle of their march, a bare rock pierced through the ice, requiring them to scale it with ropes and hooks.

Lagrex, ever in high spirits, grabbed the rugged rock surface with his bare hands, of all things, and raced up it like a monkey. Harghent could only look up at him in utter amazement.

Praying that his fingers, numbed with cold, stayed true, he used a rope Lagrex dropped down to climb up.

"...*Hngh*... Wait... This is nothing...! *Gwaaugh*...compared to...my exploits...during the sixth wyvern sweep...the eighth wyvern sweep...and the twenty-second sweep... Nothing at all...!"

"Nothing but wyverns with you, huh?"

"Don't say it!"

"I'd go one step further and say you're weak, Master General!"

He wanted to shout that he was growing old, but realizing hearing them would only make himself more miserable, Harghent held back his words— On top of everything else, now he had lost all of his troops, too. A majority of his elite soldiers were lost in the expedition to put down Vikeon the Smoldering.

Disgracing himself with a miserable defeat, the only reason there hadn't been a reshuffling of the Twenty-Nine Officials was entirely because with the upcoming royal games ahead, there was simply no time to hold a meeting to elect a new Sixth General.

Harghent the Still was incompetent.

A bit-player devoted to maintaining his authority and power, he asserted his merits out of habit by reiterating his wyvern hunts, to the extent that he received the mocking nickname of

Wing-Plucker. Naturally, even during the war with the New Principality of Lithia—ostensibly burned to the ground in a fire—his reckless charge attack had not been regarded highly.

Therefore, this was his final chance.

A play that is guaranteed to win— Lucunoca the Winter, as a Hero candidate.

The strongest race in the land. The one among such dragons, each one wielding calamitous power, who was strongest of them all. There was little doubt that when they heard about the competition among the world's strongest fighters, every single one of the Twenty-Nine Officials searching for candidates had thought the same themselves.

—If they sponsored Lucunoca the Winter, victory was almost guaranteed.

In reality, it wasn't so simple.

None of them had made the long trip out to visit Igania Ice Lake, far, far away from Aureatia.

None of them acted foolish enough to abandon all their main governmental duties to bet everything they had on the royal games.

None of them had thought that the form-unknown dragon could be negotiated with...or if they could pay the dragon's asking price.

And not a single one among them had located a reckless man like Lagrex.

As he walked, Harghent sung quietly to himself.

"... Rain, rain, rain is falling,
Up above the tall mountains of Onuma,
White wings smoothly caress,
After that falls thorns, thorns, thorns—"

"What's that, Master General? A nursery rhyme?"

"...Indeed. Enoz Heem's Thousand Songs and Verses. The song's called 'Frozen Plains, Frozen Fields.' The 'thorns' refer to snow. Back then, Igania was a tropical region... No one had ever even touched snow before."

"......"

"It's been sung for three hundred years."

Lagrex seemed to gather the deeper meaning behind Harghent's words.

Lucunoca the Winter didn't attack any human settlements, simply wandering about the vast ice lake and preying on the giant beasts to survive. Thus, no country had launched an expedition to take her down. Unlike normal dragons, she didn't hoard treasure either. On top of being respected as the strongest being in the whole world, there was no treasure to obtain from defeating her.

"...Young Lagrex. Assuming you do indeed face off with Lucunoca. How will you survive her claws?"

"C'mon now. I've already hypothesized what defensive skills she'll use against my far superior swordsmanship. When it's time to take on a dragon... Well, obviously, it's not about strength. I have this technique, where I sort of angle my sword to parry and ward off attacks. The vital part's pushing the attack off to the side."

"In that case, what will you do if she takes to the sky? That sword of yours won't be able to reach."

"Bwah-ha-ha! You're absolutely right! But dragons can't stay flying up in the air forever! She'll get exhausted eventually, and I can just cut her down while she's resting her wings! I'll have you know, I've been stringent with my basic stamina training, too!"

"You can't forget about the dragon's breath, either. Have you thought of a way to deal with it?"

"For that? Well..."

Advancing through the ice ahead of Harghent, he saw Lagrex's back stop moving for a brief moment.

Too brief, of course, for Harghent to catch up to his companion.

"Fighting spirit."

"...Fighting spirit...?"

"That's right. As long as I put my fighting spirit into it, it'll work out! I'm sure that's how Rosclay would handle it, Master General! Minia can beat dragons! I'm absolutely positive, given that fact. Without a doubt, there's a chance for victory! That's for certain!"

His way of thinking was utterly beyond comprehension to Harghent. The fact he believed the story that a minia could claim victory over a dragon was idiotic to begin with.

Lagrex was indeed strong. He had seen him to cut the giant beasts, looming far taller than Harghent, in two with a single, instantaneous flash of his sword. He had confidence if nothing else.

Still, he's going to die.

These thoughts came to Harghent's mind, hazy and vague from the biting cold seeping into his skin.

To him, Lagrex was only necessary on the first half of the trip to establish relations with the dragon.

This reckless man would brashly challenge the strongest of the ancient dragons and have his life end meaninglessly.

After that, Harghent would then... How would things play out after that?

...Perhaps I'm trying something just as reckless as this young man.

Negotiate with a legendary dragon no one had ever seen before, and make them agree to appear in the royal games... Moreover, did he really expect to be protected on his journey home?

No one among the Twenty-Nine Officials had tried anything so foolish.

Perhaps his crushing defeat to Vikeon the Smoldering, and watching Curte of the Fair Skies' final moments, had turned him desperate.

The cold was dulling his thoughts. The sun's glimmer was reflected back off the snow, glaringly bright.

His legs were only getting more and more exhausted, and from time to time, Lagrex out in front would need to stop and wait for him.

The vast ice lake. A land of death, spreading out as far as the eye could see.

No one had ever laid eyes on her. Everyone knew the name of the Igania Ice Lake, but no one had ever stepped foot within it.

Lucunoca the Winter. A legend that had stopped concerning herself with minia long, long ago.

Did something like that truly, actually, exist...?

"—neral! Master General!"

"...! What's wrong, young Lagrex?"

"I should be the one asking that! You can't collapse now. I need you to live, and bear witness to my battle."

"O-oh, is that so...? I...collapsed, did I?"

It was too pitiful to bear. Before them was yet another bluff.

His mind was heavy. Did he have any stamina left to climb it? He felt the numbing cold seeping in through his many layers of clothes. Even if they continued on, they would need to traverse the same distance on the way back...

"...Lagrex. This is, well, a bit difficult to say, but..."

"What is it?"

"Lucunoca the Winter, well... Hrm."

"Yes...?"

"I think that she doesn't actually exist."

The giant man cocked his head to the side at the words and laughed.

"Bwah-ha-ha-ha-ha! Well, if she doesn't exist, that's just fine, too! Of course, you'll need to testify that I was indeed stronger than this nonexistent dragon. We'll still need a thorough search to prove it! The sun's still high, and the day's still long!"

"Wait... Hold on... Don't pull the rope. I-I'm at my limit!"

In front of the bluff, the fruitless verbal tug-of-war continued for some time.

In this terrifying and merciless land, Lagrex, full of tireless confidence and vigor, was wholly beyond his comprehension.

"You should just resign, Master General! Are you not one of the Twenty-Nine Officials, just like Rosclay?!"

"Stop! Enough of that...! Do not compare me...with the Second General!"

A natural end result left Harghent outmatched. At this rate, he might need to be suspended by his chest, and pulled up the bluff. Considering how overbearing Lagrex was, he seemed able to make a horrible nightmare like that into reality.

It was then, thinking about such a future, he looked up to the top of the bluff.

He couldn't see the sun.

Harghent realized a dark shadow had descended on the area.

"...L-Lagrex."

"*Bwah-ha-ha-ha*! Move first, whine later, Master General!"

"No. Up there..."

They were the only words Harghent could get out of his mouth.

The sight was enough to make him forget to breathe.

On top of the bluff.

It simply looked down over them with cold eyes, without a hint of violent power or desire to kill.

Sparkling dragon scales, white and smooth, different enough from Vikeon the Smoldering to believe they were of a different species entirely.

Outstretched, symmetrical wings. An elegantly curved neck.

More beautiful than even the most detailed divine idol, she was the strongest of the ancient dragons.

Lucunoca the Winter. She did exist.

"You must—"

Shockingly, Lagrex readied his sword, not stunned to silence for a single moment.

Harghent was seeing for the first time, looking beside the man, Lagrex's expression filled with bloodlust, focusing everything on his enemy.

"—be Lucunoca the Winter, then. My name is Lagrex the Butchering Landslide. I've come here on this day to take your head and become a champion!"

Lucunoca the Winter was silent.

Thinking her breath attack could come at any moment, Harghent, without any regard for how it may have looked, crawled under the bluff and hid. The size of the shadow cast over the ground shifted, signaling that she had taken flight and landed down below.

He saw from up close the legendary dragon no one had laid eyes on before.

The small-time man, only ever focused on maintaining his authority, was before the world's strongest dragon.

"Answer me!"

Lagrex vigilantly kept his sword raised.

Was there any meaning to the action? If she swiped at him with those claws, what sort of resistance could a minia's sword even manage to offer?

The strongest of all dragons spoke.

"My, my, my. Well now. It must have been quite the hard journey indeed to come out all this way."

"......"

In her clear blue eyes, there was none of the coldness Harghent had glimpsed during his first sight of her.

The snowy ancient dragon cocked her head to the side, her gentleness wholly out of place with their surroundings.

"Indeed, as you said, I am Lucunoca the Winter. Allow me to welcome you...though, in a barren land such as this, I'm afraid I can't offer much hospitality, *uhoo, hoo, hoo!*"

"A-are you...toying with me?"

"Not at all. Is there something strange about welcoming in guests from afar? Did your parents not teach you to do the same?"

"......"

"I have not seen minia in truly quite some time. Would you be kind enough to tell me about the outside world? Though I am afraid I may not understand the language of the day, *uhoo, hoo, hoo!*"

Getting killed instantly by a single swipe of her claws might have been an easier outcome for Lagrex to accept. Harghent agreed.

This dragon didn't even consider the two minia as enemies.

"W-wait!"

Harghent jumped out from his hiding spot without a second

thought. His feet stumbled on the ice, and he once again clumsily tumbled to the ground.

"Lucunoca... Lucunoca the Winter! Will you not fight this man?! You don't...mean to tell me..."

The next words he spoke demanded a great deal of courage.

He wondered why he was summoning so much unnecessary courage for the sake of someone he so thoroughly did not get along with, for such an overbearing, reckless, and foolish man.

"...You are afraid of a mere minia! Is this how you protected your unbeatable reputation for a hundred years, Lucunoca?! Right now you are both warriors, mutually connected across races with Word Arts! Or else your refusal of your opponent today shall brand you the loser for all eternity! What say you?!"

The white dragon glanced at the pitiful intruder to her lands.

She then let out a chortling sigh.

"Why, yes, I don't have a problem with that at all."

"What did you say...?"

The world's strongest dragon did exist here, right before their eyes.

She avoided people. No one had ever encountered Lucunoca the Winter.

"If the reputation of a doting old crone like mine is what pleases you, go ahead and boast to your heart's desire, then."

"L-Lucunoca the Winter... How dare...!"

The strongest race in the land. The strongest individual among them.

If he was able to back her as the hero, his victory would be decided on the spot.

"Yes, yes. Let us acknowledge it. Victory is yours, Lagrex, Butchering Landslide."

...However.

"Congratulations."

◆

"When I was little, I learned to read and write. I attended this church that I had absolutely no interest in...and really all I learned was the simple Order script, but..."

The man explained, stepping on the small remaining piece of grassland among the vast ice.

He was a minian spearman. She remembered his name. Yushid the Firmament.

"It's so I can etch the final words of the enemies I've defeated. Everyone all laughed, but I ended up being right."

He threw aside the bundle of parchment hanging from his waist. It was unnecessary weight for the battle to come.

Lucunoca laughed in delight at the figure he cut, standing in front of her without showing the slightest trepidation.

"*Uhoo-hoo-hoo*! Is that spear supposed to pierce through my scales, then? Pitiful human, haughty with false success. Even the smallest babe understands how far apart the heavens are from the earth."

"Save the fancy affect, dragon. When the end comes, you'll be singing a different tune."

The spear flashed, like a brutal lightning crack. Leaving only that light behind, the scenery grew hazy—

The shape of the landscape changed, like the moon reflecting on the water's surface.

"...In some ways, you and I were friends, weren't we, Lucunoca the Winter?" Atop a sheer bluff, an elderly elf stretched out both his arms.

She knew just how far this one elf had pushed himself to the limits of his studies to arrive at where he was now.

Eswilda the Boundary of Tragic Dream. She could never forget.

"Only if I, too, were a dragon. I have had such thoughts before. Or...better yet, if I were a minia. With such a limited lifespan, could I have studied Word Arts with more fervor? At this point, I do not know."

"...Eswilda. You are no match for me. Just this once, I shall forgive your hopeless insolence. If you do not wish to know how futile your life is, then stay your wand."

"No, Lucunoca. *You* were my dream. The one burning start within a pitiful elf's life that knew only death and battle. Or perhaps—you were the only part within me that wasn't a tragic nightmare. Let us begin."

Eswilda's voice incanted Word Arts. Dazzling light from his Thermal Arts sparkled like a cluster of stars.

Ahh. How wonderful it was to see the pinnacle of a person's training.

Thinking about the life the man had lived, surely none could deride his ardent fervor as less than the minia's.

She needed to respond to his resolve in kind. Lucunoca took in a deep breath—

"...There's some cheeky enough to say you're nothing but a fairy tale."

The scenery had changed. Amid the mirrorlike surface of silvery white, a leprechaun laughed in front of a colossal steel structure. He was Amgusa the Left Fetter, a weapons merchant.

That time was the first Lucunoca had ever seen a machine that ran on fuel traverse the frozen wastes.

"Just awful, isn't it? That's why I'm gonna teach 'em, see. That you really do exist. Then that'll turn into real value, the kind that even those chumps'll understand—money for this guy right here."

"....Amgusa the Left Fetter. Enough of this foolish endeavor. Just how long did you keep searching during this past big month? And you claim you still have enough power left over to cross swords with me?"

"*Keh, keh, keh, keh.* You're a funny old hag. Don't act so prim and proper. Dragons're supposed to be more brutal. Compared to the brutality of my weapons here, well, with that kinda attitude, it'll be child's play."

The world was advancing. Now they were capable of creating such mechanical contraptions.

Perhaps there was a sliver of a chance within this power that she had never laid eyes on before.

She looked at Amgusa's weapon. The gunpowder mechanism opening it up, countless incendiary arrows—

"I've found you, Lucunoca the Winter! My mom...and my grandpa weren't...liars after all. I did it... I finally found you..."

"Oh my. Those are some terrible wounds. Bandage those up right away. I'll return you to the entrance of the ice lake."

The young boy had crossed the land swarming with beasts and appeared before her. His left arm had nearly been torn off his body.

His name was Lalaky the Unattainable Knoll. As though to say even the time spent wiping the blood spilling from his wound would be time wasted, he passionately shouted.

"...No! I did not come...all the way here...just to run away now... That silver head of yours...is mine!"

"Don't you understand? It's a fool's errand. With that wound, you couldn't even best a silver bear. If you have a glorious life ahead of you...will you listen to these old bones, and not throw it away in a moment of excitement?"

"What...what would you know of my life?! This body, given to me by my mother and father, my desires—it would be impossible to want for anything more! Don't you dare... don't you dare disgrace the honor of being the strongest in the land, Lucunoca the Winter!"

Lucunoca was more than able to ignore the small and enfeebled warrior.

In truth, that was what she wanted to do.

The young boy showed no such hesitance. With his remaining courage and leftover arm, he slashed at the white dragon.

◆

"Hyaaaaaah!"

With a courageous shout, Lagrex plunged toward her, but his sword once again simply cut through thin air.

His various sword techniques, the source of his enormous amount of self-confidence, didn't result in single effective blow.

"My, my, now. Fool about too much, and you're going to tire yourself out, dear. Why don't you take a break?"

"I'm not...fooling...around!"

Stepping hard into the ice with his cleated boot, he cleaved with a spinning slash. Lucunoca slightly brought her forefoot down, and with it, the slash was out of reach.

"Victory and prestige are already yours to claim; what else could you be unsatisfied about? Perhaps it's my mind growing dull in old age—*uhoo, hoo, hoo!* I simply cannot understand."

Lagrex was using all of his might. Looking on from the side, Harghent could clearly tell.

This was everything he had. Keeping himself braced against a sudden swipe of Lucunoca's claws, he never took his eyes off her head, wary of her breath, and aiming for her legs and wings, tried to immobilize her.

He also understood exactly how ridiculous these attempts appeared to be.

"Gaaaaaah... Hrnaaaaah!"

"...Enough! Enough, young Lagrex! Do you think you have any chance of winning!? She's right!"

He also understood clearly how foolhardy his own aims were.

If she really intended to fight, she should have instantly killed them both with her breath the moment they saw her. From the very beginning, establishing communication and negotiating with a true dragon was impossible.

She was able to end things whenever she wanted. Including now.

The rise and fall of the three kingdoms beyond this ice lake, and perhaps, even the terror of the True Demon King itself, was of no concern to her.

To a being at such an apex that any comparisons to others were ultimately meaningless, even the very prestige of being at such heights...was nothing more than junk she could pass off to others.

"I-I'll be sure to tell everyone...! Winning is plenty good enough, isn't it?! You'll be a true dragon-slaying champion, free of any shame or obligation! Lagrex!"

"...Master, General..."

Panting, he wiped his sweat.

A man who had dedicated his life to a fool's endeavor, dreamed a fool's dream, and was dying a fool's death.

Everything about the man was incomprehensible to Harghent.

"Would you be satisfied with that, Master General? Should my words be nothing but thoughtless lies?!"

"...Well, that is, um—"

"I believed that I could slay a dragon with this sword. Ever since I was a child, the opponent I always thought about in the back of my head was a true dragon. It was just four years ago. I was told about Rosclay's heroic exploits... I understood then that the thing always in the back of my mind wasn't meaningless nonsense after all."

He was wrong. No such thing ever happened.

He wanted to shout it out loud. The truth that no one outside of Aureatia's Twenty-Nine Officials could ever know.

"No matter how many people ridiculed me. Even if I was disparaged as reckless. Minia... *I* could kill dragons."

If I was Rosclay.

Had these words been sincere? Did he sincerely think he could become someone like that?

Was he thinking about how, across the land, there were much stronger players all vying for the same thing?

...This man will die.

If she took his challenge even slightly more seriously, one attack from her claws would end his life.

When Lagrex realized the reality for the first time, that the dream he squandered his whole life on had been entirely futile, it would end with his idle death.

"*Bwah-ha-ha-ha-ha*! Master General. I was so happy! No one besides you would believe my story! Sure, you're weak, cantankerous, and constantly whining, but! Nothing could make me happier than having you stand here and support me in my fight!"

It was natural cause and effect. Foolishness needed to be met with equivalent punishment and reproach.

"...Ah, I understand. Indeed, without proving you can kill me, your heart will remain unsatisfied. That is quite a shame. Well then."

Lucunoca the Winter's claws moved. She held back as much as she could, but nevertheless, minia were like insects to her.

Lagrex the Butchering Landslide readied his sword. He believed in his own power.

Harghent's thoughts rapidly rushed around his head. His own life was in no danger at all, and it was nothing more than a single fool's death, but still his mind raced.

His chief of staff Peke died. Unlike Lagrex, he was a capable adviser. Killed effortlessly by a dragon.

Truly the strongest of all races, needing neither victory nor prestige.

Hidden away from the people of the world, so none had managed to slay her.

When did this strongest of all beings begin to be called the strongest?

Harghent was the only one to see her at first. Those cold, unfriendly eyes, looking down from the top of the bluff.

That was as far as he got.

His racing thoughts out of time, the claws, superior to any sword the world had to offer, stroked Lagrex.

There was an atrocious cracking sound.

"Lagrex...!"

"...Oh, what do we have here?"

Blood was dripping. The stout great sword was shattered halfway up, and the glittering fragments were scattered across the icy wastes.

"...I blocked those claws... Lucunoca...the Winter...!"

Lagrex was standing.

The one attack had broken the joints in his sword arm, and it lifelessly drooped from his shoulder.

One of the flying sword fragments had cut deep into his upper arm, and a vast amount of blood poured out of it.

Nevertheless, he had endured the strongest's attack.

—*I have this technique, where I sort of angle my sword to parry and ward off attacks.*

"...Lucunoca the Winter!"

Harghent rushed out to try to come between Lagrex and the dragon.

Frail, old, and without a soldier to his name. It was the only thing the incompetent man could come up with.

"I figured it out... Now, I know...know what you're afraid of."

"...Afraid of, you say? You think I have anything to be afraid of?"

The strongest of the dragons was in front of him.

Throughout his long life, he wondered if he had ever dreamed of the sight before his eyes.

Harghent tried to stop his trembling lips, gone purple in the cold. He couldn't. The man who had so desperately and ravenously lusted after power was confronted by a being every bit his opposite. She was wholly beyond his comprehension.

"You're disappointed, aren't you?"

"......"

Her tranquil demeanor unchanged, the white dragon listened to his words.

"...That's it. That has to be it. Before these past hundred years, you did fight, didn't you? A number of champions seeking glory challenged you and died doing so."

Why would this creature who had long ago hidden herself away from the world still be called the strongest being in the world?

One needed to fight in order to be named the strongest.

There had to have been times where she used that power to contend with strong foes, times where she had enjoyed combat like any other dragon.

"But you're *too strong*. Those with resolve, full of promise... like bubbles, they appeared and disappeared before you. Am I wrong?"

How bright must the fruits of their training have been? Or rather, how lofty was their will, that made them able to challenge the strongest race above all? A weakling like him couldn't imagine.

On top of that... If she was in despair, stuck watching opponents crumbling beneath her, without inflicting a single wound, just how deep did such despair run?

...Those cold, unfriendly eyes that Harghent first saw.

He was sure that in those eyes was Lucunoca the Winter's truest soul.

"The inside of your heart is the same as this landscape around us. An endlessly blizzard raging wildly within...!"

"*Uhoo-hoo-hoo-hoo*...! Well, who is to say?"

The colossal white dragon cocked her head, just as she had when they first encountered her.

Harghent himself wasn't entirely sure whether or not his assumption was correct.

With such insolent comments, it wouldn't have been strange for her to immediately crush him where he stood.

Nevertheless, there was nothing else to gamble on.

No one among the Twenty-Nine Officials had tried anything so foolish.

"They are in Aureatia."

"......?"

"The true champions you've longed for... They are gathered in

Aureatia. Did you know? The twelve dungeons that have existed as long as you have—they've all been traversed by a single wyvern."

Of course. He knew every single one of his legendary feats.

"He killed the Grim Reaper, Toroa the Awful, feared by people the world over...! Do you know the name of the one who claimed Hillensingen, the Luminous Blade?! The one who, wielding that sword, slayed Vikeon the Smoldering right before my very eyes...! He lives now, in this very age! Lucunoca the Winter!"

The all-powerful white dragon stopped moving and peered down at the weak, aging general.

"...Foolish minia."

It was as if she was a young girl lost in a story.

"I have never in my time seen another like you before."

"*Eep*... I... I am... I am! Aureatia's Sixth General! Harghent the Still!"

"Very well. Harghent. I shall remember your name... Much like the courageous champion, Lagrex."

Champion. He looked at the man bestowed the title by world's strongest dragon.

The tenacious man who had endured the long march through the snow without giving in had exhausted all his strength after getting hit with the weakest possible hit she could give. The extreme situation meant that Harghent didn't have the composure to pay any heed to man he was trying to save.

"Lagrex..."

Lucunoca the Winter said something utterly beyond belief.

"Out of respect for such bravery, I shall escort him back whence he came. Then, we'll make for Aureatia. Those comments of yours... As with Lagrex, I'll trust that they are true."

"......"

Harghent's strength left his body, and he fell to his knees.

If he was able to back her as the hero, his victory would be decided on the spot, truly the strongest being of all.

In coming to grips with such a preposterous outcome becoming reality, Harghent's world grew faint, his entire body spent.

Nevertheless, he was able to answer the dragon's next question.

"What is this champion's name?"

".............Alus the Star Runner."

He was an enemy he had to best. It had been a distant and far-off dream.

In this same far-off dream, he would fight against his only friend.

"I see. Alus, is it? He's strong, then?"

The strongest race in the land, the dragons. Among them, she stood even higher, the strongest among them all.

Standing before Lucunoca the Winter, who could reply with such a short answer?

For Harghent, he was able to do just that.

"The strongest."

◆

In her slumber, she always saw dreams like these.

Amid the remnants of the past, flowing and dissolving in her mind, they always gave her faint hope.

If they possessed strength undefeated. If it was somewhere within their long years of devoted study.

Or perhaps, the flow of time would overtake her. If there was some miracle to bring brilliance to her apathetic and wanting spirit, perhaps then, finally.

Finally. Maybe, she believed, it would become a worthy fight.

The minia spearman threw his spear with unmatched speed.

The elf's tremendous fireball closed in to reduce everything to ash.

The leprechaun's endless arrows covered her entire field of vision like a wall.

Or the brave young warrior putting his entire life on the line to slash at her.

She blew her breath over them.

A dragon's breath represented Word Arts that went against the world itself.

Fire, electricity, and light. Thermal Arts were arts that produced energy.

However, she alone... Her breath alone evoked a totally opposite and different phenomenon, the only one like it among all the living creatures in the world.

Everyone who challenged her knew about her breath and tried to overcome its violent force.

Plains with sparse greenery, various bluffs and cliffs, lakes sparkling with ice—there were many scenes laid out before her eyes.

Yet, with a single breath, the scenery all became the same.

First, it was white. The white, freezing the very air itself, covered everything as far as the eye could see.

Then, the color would change to black. The bare rock and ice would warp and creak, under the sudden change to their world, and would be warped into black crystals. She watched as every possible worldly structure would break and begin to crumble away.

Everything was annihilated. The broken fragments would float up in the still air, before drifting down to the ground.

*   *   *

Nothing of her beloved champions would be left behind.

It was said the Beyond, where visitors came from, was a world where the seasons changed based on the passage of time, not changes in the soil.

Among the four sections that they divide their years into, one season was given just such a name.

A time would come when everything would become still, sealed in beautiful ice; a time when the whole world, plants and animals alike, would momentarily die.

Winter, they called it.

She, for several hundreds of years, was acknowledged as the absolute strongest among the land's strongest race of all.

She possessed a chilling breath, changing climate and topography, and instantly ending any life caught within.

She was the only confirmed user of ice Word Arts in all of history.

Without even allowing for any fight, she was a sight of desolation and waste.

Silencer. Dragon.

Lucunoca the Winter.

Within Aureatia's Central Assembly Hall, separate from the Main Chamber where normal governmental business was decided, the Twenty-Nine Officials had a room unknown to the citizens called the Provisional Chambers. With a single fireplace in the corner, the only other objects in the room were twenty-nine chairs positioned around a long table.

"Everyone here? Well, I'm sure you all know, but today's meeting is about the royal games. Let's get started."

The person announcing the start of the meeting was the same as during the regular assembly, Aureatia's First Minister, Grasse the Foundation Map. A healthy man of late middle age. He was also the chairperson who had assembled the previous strategy meeting regarding the Particle Storm.

"Recently, we accepted the final candidate, and are now at the stage where we can host matches without issue. That said, regarding detailed rules, there's still a lot that's up in the air. For the first agenda item, I'll give a retroactive report to those who missed the last meeting, Eighth Minster, Fourteenth General, Twentieth Minister, regarding what's already been decided. Any problems with that?"

"I don't need to hear this all again. I asked someone to cover for me anyway."

"I'm not much help even when I do attend, anyway."

"Well... I've heard the long and short of it, but I'd say that's something we should all go over again with everyone anyway, right? Go for it, Grasse."

Twentieth Minister, Hidow the Clamp.

While a younger member within the Twenty-Nine Officials, he was an outstanding man who did tremendous work during the capture of the New Principality. Ostensibly, there was no hierarchy based on service or chair number. Both military and civil officers shared seats at the same table.

"Then, I'll continue as planned. The day of the royal games will feature a one-on-one true duel. Those that win that duel will fight each other afterward. In short, we decided on an elimination tournament."

"Just as we've been hearing for a while. We'll make it so there'll only be one person who doesn't lose at all. I don't have any issues. What about the pairings?"

"We ended up deferring that to a later date."

"...I mean, we really can't decide on anything till we see all the candidates, yeah? I'd be in big trouble if Rosclay here gets knocked out in the first round, after all."

The man turning the topic to the Second General was an extremely tall swordsman. The Sixteenth General, Nofelt the Somber Wind. He had already backed Uhak the Silent as his Hero candidate.

The focus of the topic, Second General Rosclay carefully continued his thoughts. His position as both administrator and candidate from before the games started guaranteed him an overwhelmingly dominant position.

However, would the Officials backing other candidates continue to support the symbol of Aureatia's victory as they had done up until now? It was too optimistic an assumption.

Time would be necessary to investigate the remaining backers' movements and come up with countermeasures against them and their hero candidates.

"…The pairings really should come at the very end. Of course, I want to battle under advantageous conditions myself, but there's four small months until the games open. It's not far-fetched that some unforeseen situation comes up, and some candidates are supplanted by others. Should that happen, I feel we'd be unable to change the pairings on a whim."

"In that case, we'll continue to put the pairings topic on hold. Any objections?"

Confirming that no one had raised their hands, the First Minister gave a small nod.

The other Officials backing candidates wanted time for their own preparations, too. Rosclay's side, too, proposed the delay with that fact in mind.

"…All right. Now to continue with what was decided at the last meeting. For this collection of events, we've landed on Sixways Exhibition for the official name. Heaven, ground, and the four cardinal directions, six altogether. I'm sure it's annoying to change things up now, but it's better to decide on one official name, in part for civilian trade and business. From now on, please refer to it as such."

"First Minister. May I add something on this point?"

"Go ahead, Third Minister."

Giving off a somehow sharp-pointed and angular impression, the bespectacled man was the Third Minister, Jelki the Swift Ink.

With his usual everyday calmness, he dispassionately gave his report.

"During these three big months, we've had ninety-eight merchants apply to use the Sixways Exhibition trademark. The main requests came from the following: Hapule Feather Guild, Avoke Confectionaries, Insa Moseo Co., and the Elpcoza Peddler's Union. Naturally, we're minimally screening all of them, but in order to bring in further public attention than we currently have, our policy has been to proactively approve them all. Especially prioritizing those with operations out on the frontier like the Merchant Coalition and the major traveling merchants. Together with the publicity we've gotten with the aid of our secret agents, we'll see to it that there is none left unaware about the hero selection."

"If the work's going smoothly, then there doesn't seem to be any problems in regard to this topic, either."

"Always gotten by with either *royal games* or *the games*, so this is gonna take some getting used to."

Though he had always been a capable man, Third Minister Jelki was being more industrious than ever in promoting these games.

He did not submit a Hero candidate for himself, yet he certainly had some goal in mind. This was the man who had gotten the very first information on the Particle Storm and gathered them all together to strategize on how to deal with it.

"Now that his report is finished, let's get to today's main topic. The arena for the games. As of today we've more or less gathered most of the candidates, but well, as you could've probably guessed, there are very few minia among them. We'll run into a bit of a problem if we put them in a theater garden made solely with minia in mind."

"Since we've gathered them all and announced them as 'royal games,' obviously they'll need to be held near the castle. I feel the garden theater is the most suitable, considering how easy it is to gather people there."

"Whoa, whoa, hold up here. I'm against it. We've got gigants and dragons here, yes? If we make them fight in a cramped place like that, what're we going to do when they end up killing people and destroying buildings?"

The one-armed man raising his objection was Twenty-Fifth General, Kayon the Thundering.

It was entirely possible that, depending on the range of the combatants' attacks, the starting distance of the battle could directly lead to outright victory. Given that the candidate he was backing was Mele the Horizon's Roar, it was a natural concern for him to bring up.

"Still, wouldn't it be difficult at this point to build a whole new arena?"

"As long as we can agree to some extent on the size of the arena, we can just have them fight somewhere outside the city."

"If we're using one of the candidates as the standard, it'll be Rosclay, right? Then, the theater garden *is* reasonable after all."

"It's not about actually being fair and impartial, it's about how the citizens watching will take it. Ten meters is a lot different to a minia than it is to a gigant..."

"First of all, if they're competing in a true duel, would it not be suitable to include their ability to create their own battlefield in the competition?"

"...One—"

First Minister Grasse mumbled in a low voice and pacified the growing chaos in the room.

To the public, there was no hierarchical rankings among the Twenty-Nine Officials. Nevertheless, there was indeed a reason why the man occupied the first seat among them.

"—important point. This Sixways Exhibition. No matter how strict we make our rules and regulations, do we have any way to ensure the candidates observe them...? That's the important part. That's why we haven't discussed specific rules of the tournament any further. It's pointless."

"If they break the rules, they're disqualified. Lose their hero qualifications, and they forfeit their incentive reward. Isn't that enough?"

The speaker was the Seventeenth Minister. Elea the Red Tag.

"It's easy for us to say that, but then it becomes a conversation about whether that will actually be effective. For example, if we decide to penalize Alus the Star Runner, who here is able to confiscate his treasure? Can you, Seventeenth Minister?"

"...No. Unrealistic in practice, then."

"That's pretty much what Grasse here's tryin' to say, yeah? Anyone unhappy with the conditions of the match can just start going at it wherever or whenever they feel like. That's the worst-case scenario."

Twentieth Minister Hidow said, leaning his head far back against his chair. His conduct was as disgraceful as ever.

The Sixways Exhibition, naturally, had been planned with the assumption there would be some degree of damages. Building damage and loss of life was tolerable, so long as it was kept to a manageable extent. Everyone in the room knew that the presence of the Hero held that much value.

Moreover, to what extent could they keep the effects of these irregularly powerful fighters within a preestablished area?

"We gotta let them do what they want."

"...That's just abandoning any administration duties at all, isn't it?"

"Nah, nah, that's not it. We're not actually gonna let them do whatever they want. The important thing is we *make them think* they're doing whatever they want... Ain't that right, Grasse?"

"Very well, then. Please, let us hear your detailed thoughts, Twentieth Minister."

"...Make the conditions of each fight, the arena, the timing, decided through an agreement between each combatant for each match. We can handle getting the audience there and securing a safe place to watch the match. Someone just said something about making your own battlefield part of the true duel? That'll work for our official stance of it, yeah?"

"...Any objections?"

"Meeee! Twenty-Second General Mizial. That doesn't even solve the core problem, right? What're you gonna do if they ignore their agreements, storm through the city, and cause casualties?"

"You don't get it, Mizial. This way, we're not pushin' any unreasonable rules or anything on 'em, right? And say they still go wild. Kill citizens... Basically then, they're not really a Hero anymore, are they? That'd make 'em a self-proclaimed demon king. So it's about ensuring their legitimacy."

"Oooh. So, then, you'd make the other candidates kill them?"

"Can't be no Hero if you ain't killing demon kings, can you? If there's any malicious rule-breaking, they'll work together to put the other down. Use this as our base policy, and we can fill it out later with all the tiny exceptions. Anyone else?"

Timidly raising her hand, the woman who was backing Psianop the Inexhaustible Stagnation, Tenth General, Qwell the Wax Flower. Peeking out from her long bangs, her big eyes flickered restlessly.

"U-um... Even if they decide on a battlefield, moving the citizens there once they do, um...i-it'll take time, no matter what. Maybe a day or more? Are, are we sure that's okay?"

"Huh? What about it?"

"Traps. Or, um... there could be ambushes and stuff, too. During that gap. If the location's decided from the start, I think maybe, there won't be any sort of loopholes like that."

"Aww, c'mon Qwellie, you're not getting it! We're fine with that.

We'll be the ones in trouble without any loopholes. Am I wrong? We're counting on Rosclay the Absolute to win all for us, right?"

"..........."

The Second General kept silent. The truth behind his fighting methods were thoroughly known to all the Twenty-Nine Officials. Furthermore, their official position dictated they would all support Rosclay the Absolute and make him win.

"Oh, yes, Rosclay...y-you're right. Then, um, that's all from me..."

"Any other objections? That it?"

Grasse looked out over the room and confirmed no one's hand was raised.

For their policy regarding match conditions and penalties, he was glad to see the Twentieth Minister's proposal be roughly accepted by everyone.

Still. This guy's a bit troublesome.

With a crooked smile stretching across his face, Grasse the Foundation Map stroked his chin.

Setting conditions through an agreement from both combatants. In other words, here too, their capabilities were being tested.

Not the capabilities of the Hero candidates, no—

The capabilities of Aureatia's Twenty-Nine Officials, sponsoring them all.

Just how are they going to convince each other to accept conditions and battlefields that benefit their candidates? How many victory schemes will they hatch, and can they make them work? Now then, let's see what all these bastards are plotting...

This was not the sort of battle where the fighters won and advanced solely on the basis of martial skills and genius alone.

Each camp exhausting everything they had was fitting of true duels. It would turn into a war where they'd kick each other aside for a fleeting handful of glory.

Some of the Twenty-Nine Officials had surely realized this, and had already begun making their moves.

Harmony between the people of the three kingdoms, looking toward a new age. Peace. Such flowery rhetoric was nothing but a sham from the start. Countries descending into chaos were the natural course of the world.

No matter how many of the Old Kingdoms' loyalists were driven out. No matter how much they destroyed the Order, a symbol of religious faith. No matter what change the existence of the Hero brought about. People's fundamental twistedness would never go away.

And I'm perfectly damn fine with that.

Just imagining it, he could feel one side of his mouth slant upward. While he gathered together the opinions of the assembly, he made sure to never show his true intentions.

Grasse the Foundation Map's truest self took pleasure in seeing all aspects of others, not just beauty and dignity, but also when things cruelly didn't go their way as well. Thus, he stood in his position as First Minister, never once experiencing pain in his long road to where he was now.

In fact, this occasion was markedly special.

At the very least, all the people gathered in the chambers thought so.

A clash between the strongest of the strong. There wasn't a single person in the world who wouldn't be excited by the thought.

"...By the way, it sounds like you've got a clear idea of all the candidates. There's something I'd like confirmation on then. How many have gathered?"

"Ah, right, right. I forgot to let you all know."

Both of his hands clasped together on the long desk, Grass smiled.

Like a child unable to contain his excitement for what was to come... It was a lopsided, but still amiable, smile.

The Sixways Exhibition. It was set to become a furious and amazing battle, the likes of which no one had ever seen before.

"Sixteen."

The world's enemy, the True Demon King, who had plunged the whole land into terror, had been brought down by someone.

That individual's name, and whether they truly existed or not, was still a mystery.

Now, with the end of the age of fear, it had become necessary to determine who this "Hero" was.

Now, there were ten shura.
Soujirou the Willow-Sword.
Alus the Star Runner.
Kia the World Word.
Nastique the Quiet Singer.
Mele the Horizon's Roar.
Linaris the Obsidian.
Toroa the Awful.
Mestelexil the Box of Desperate Knowledge.
Kuuro the Cautious.
Rosclay the Absolute.
Lucunoca the Winter.

Afterword

"Keiso. Regarding the afterword for *Ishura*, Vol. 2, well, books are normally bound by folding sixteen pages at a time."

"Yes, yes, I've heard that before."

"The thing is, the number of pages that can be left over for the afterword changes depending on the leftover amount of those sixteen pages after the main story."

"Ahh, I get it. In the last volume, I received four pages for the afterword, but this one may only get three, or sometimes I may get five, is what you're saying. Well, how many will I get for this volume?"

"One."

"One?!"

"There's only one page left over, so it'll either be a preview of the next volume, or your afterword."

"W-wait just a moment, my dear editor Nagahori! I'm so very grateful to have you, Nagahori. You've offered me many helpful ideas when I have been deep in thought over the story, but... In the afterword, I need to express my gratitude to Kureta-sensei for again polishing this volume off with their brilliant character designs and illustrations, and I certainly need to give my thanks to the readers! Why, this novel is a brutal multiple point-of-view affair, featuring many different all-powerful protagonists from a variety of different fantasy races, and I need to be sure to let them know that in the third volume, finally, all sixteen of them will be present and kill each other in the big tournament! And you're telling me to say all that in how many pages?!"

"One page."

"Dammit! Well fine, I will then! 'Thank you for reading. My name is Keiso. This time I have my recipe for mentaiko spaghe